DAYWORLD
A Hole in Wednesday

DAYWORLD
A Hole in Wednesday

Philip José Farmer
and Danny Adams

Meteor House

Dayworld: A Hole in Wednesday
by Philip José Farmer and Danny Adams

Copyright © 2016 by the Philip J. Farmer Family Trust and Danny Adams.
All rights reserved.

Introduction © 2016 by Michael A. Burstein. All rights reserved.

Foreword © 2016 by Paul Spiteri. All rights reserved.

Cover art, design, and frontispiece copyright © 2016 by Keith Howell.
All rights reserved.

Meteor House
ISBN 978-1-9454270-1-5
First Paperback Trade Edition

Ever, to Bette.

And to Danny's generation of the family:
Andi, Kim, Stephanie, Tom, Torin, and never forgotten, Matt.

INTRODUCTION

Michael A. Burstein

Human beings are time-based creatures. We follow the cycles of the day, the week, the month, and the year. Some of us even think about the century, millennium, and eon, and plan our lives accordingly. And many of us embody religious traditions intimately tangled with the calendar, whether we observe Christmas in the winter, Passover in the spring, or Ramadan in whatever season the moon determines.

Imagine a world in which your birthday arrives roughly every two months. A world in which each season lasts about two weeks before suddenly slamming into the next. A world in which time itself seems disconnected from what our bodies have evolved to accept.

In 1971, Philip José Farmer published the story "The Sliced-Crosswise Only-On-Tuesday World" in which he first introduced the concept of the Dayworld. The overpopulation problem of the future has been solved by use of "stoners," capsules in which people can be suspended for six days of the week. As a result, our ravaged planet can now support seven times the number of people as it could before. But the consequences are bizarre. The United States now has seven presidents, one for each Day. The Catholic Church has seven popes. People's pop culture vocabulary is limited to what gets developed in their own Day. The most brilliant novel might already have been written, but if the creator lives in Monday and you live in Thursday, you would never, ever learn of it. Every

Day is absolutely walled off from all the other Days around it—or at least, as walled off as the powers that be can make them.

As Farmer's first short story of Dayworld proposes, if you were born on a Tuesday, the only day you would ever experience or know about is Tuesday. Fortunately for humanity, Farmer did not postulate a Dayworld in which only one-seventh of the human race ever gets a perpetual day off. Instead, within subjective time, people could still enjoy a seven-day schedule with an effective weekend, but in the back of your mind you would know that you were always living in a Tuesday even if you treated it as a Saturday or a Sunday.

Farmer was obviously fascinated by his creation of the Dayworld, as he didn't leave it to rest in one story. Instead, he revisited the concept in three novels: *Dayworld* (1985), *Dayworld Rebel* (1987), and *Dayworld Breakup* (1990). Although there are some inconsistencies between the novels and the original short story, the element of living only one Day per week is essentially the same.

When I first read Farmer's Dayworld novels, they captured my imagination. I kept thinking about how my own Jewish religious tradition would handle being forced into the Dayworld model. Farmer actually touches on this in one of the books; apparently, the Jewish people adapt by declaring the weekly Sabbath to be the seventh day you experience, no matter what Day you are in.

(On a side note, there's actually precedent for this in Jewish law; in Tractate Shabbat of the Babylonian Talmud, Rabbi Huna notes that if someone who has been travelling in a desert loses track of which day is the Sabbath, that person must count six days from that point and then observe the seventh day as the Sabbath. In other words, the principle of observing a seventh day is more important than observing the right seventh day.)

As I read the books, I tried to imagine how my own lifestyle would fit into Farmer's Dayworld. Let's take Passover, which I mentioned earlier, as an example. Passover is a holiday that is also known in Hebrew as Chag Ha'Aviv, the holiday of the spring, and when the rabbis of two millennia ago established the Hebrew

Introduction

calendar they knew that a lunar calendar would fall out of sync with the seasons. So they established a leap year cycle, in which seven out of every nineteen years has an extra month, so the Jewish holidays stay with the appropriate season. (Incidentally, that's why Ramadan can fall in any season; the Muslim calendar is also a lunar calendar but it doesn't include a leap month.)

Today, Passover generally falls in April on the Gregorian calendar, and the weather is usually close enough to spring-like for those of us in the northern hemisphere to appreciate the connection between the holiday and the season. But in Dayworld, the eight days of Passover would be spread over eight weeks. On the objective calendar, assuming the holiday started on (let's say) April 23, the last day of the holiday wouldn't be April 30 but June 11. Incidentally, on a normal Hebrew calendar schedule, that would be when the next major Jewish holiday of Shavuot starts, as there is a deliberate forty-nine-day gap between the start of the two holidays that we count. But I'm more concerned with the weather. Instead of a week of spring, those of us observing Passover would wake up every morning to feel the weather rushing from spring warmth to summer heat far too quickly.

If I were living in that world, I think I'd become a daybreaker.

What's a daybreaker? As the name implies, it's someone who chooses to break the absolute rules of living in only one Day per week and who instead tries to live across all the Days. And as it so happens, Farmer knew that it was among daybreakers that his novels would find their strongest impact. It's not just enough to imagine a Dayworld and set stories in such a world; the good stories come from the conflict that happens when people realize that the Dayworld isn't enough.

Farmer's novels focus on those who would rebel against the Dayworld, those who don't fit in and would see it crashing down around them—despite what that would mean for humanity. It's not that hard to extrapolate. Think about your own home, your job, your commute. Think about the coffee shop you patronize every morning, the supermarket where you do your shopping, the library where you check out books.

Could you share your home with six more people?

Could your current lifestyle accommodate six more people tapping the same resources?

For many of us, a Dayworld might be a nightmare scenario. On the other hand, an overpopulated world that leads to disaster and death would be just as nightmarish. What is the right answer?

The governments of Dayworld believe that answer lies in the stoners. But there are others who disagree . . . and we now will know why.

Danny Adams fulfills the legacy of his great-uncle, Philip José Farmer, in the novel you are about to read. *A Hole in Wednesday* takes place before Farmer's previous Dayworld novels but is informed by the developments of those books. Whether you are coming back to Farmer's Dayworld or visiting for the first time, you'll discover that the solutions to humanity's problems are never easy.

But the struggle is worth it.

Foreword

Paul Spiteri

I couldn't begin to count how many times the words "fertile imagination" and "mind-blowing ideas" have been used to describe Philip José Farmer's work. And yet how else can you portray Phil's envisioned solution to world overcrowding? It's certainly a gentler solution than the one utilized in "Seventy Years of Decpop" (1972), where a well-meaning maniac renders most of the population infertile, or the sanitizing of earth by the Hoonhors (*Venus on the Half-Shell*, 1974). Or even the chilling predictions in Phil's REAP speech (1968) where he spoke of some of the challenges facing our species from so many sources.

In Dayworld, developing technology heralds a New Era for our overcrowded planet, one in which the burgeoning population can enjoy the fruits of the world, and the world is able to support the population. People are "stoned"—in suspended animation—for six days out of seven. How's that for an inventive idea! We first encountered this world in Farmer's short story "The Sliced-Crosswise Only-On-Tuesday World" (1971), with the full panorama being revealed in the Dayworld trilogy (*Dayworld*, 1985; *Dayworld Rebel*, 1987; and *Dayworld Breakup*, 1990).

It's unclear exactly when Phil started *A Hole in Wednesday*, but that he didn't finish it does not at all mean he totally abandoned the novel. Rather, he moved on to something else, and, I would be confident in saying, fully intended to come back to this story. The generator in Phil's head never stopped working, sparks never stopped flying. And we now have Danny Adams to thank and laud for rekindling the spark that is *A Hole in Wednesday*, giving us a blazing novel worthy of both authors. Although set before the Dayworld trilogy, *A Hole in Wednesday* fits seamlessly into the Dayworld continuum, as if Farmer's hand had never loosened from the tiller. That is Danny's gift for us.

As an aside, I have occasionally wondered if the stoning technology used in Dayworld is an adaption of that experimented on by Ulysses Singing Bear in Farmer's *The Stone God Awakens* (1970), where our protagonist is stoned, and remains stoned, for untold millennia until a freak occurrence awakens him to a very different world than the one he remembers. I've conjectured that Singing Bear was using an early stoner prototype, one that rendered him (nearly permanently) stoned. But what a world we get to see through Singing Bear's eyes. Yes, all together now, another world from the "fertile imagination," another "mind blowing idea," to come from Phil. The generator was a perpetual motion machine.

Working inside another person's world is a challenging but rewarding experience. I suspect one reason I was asked to contribute this foreword is that I collaborated with Phil on the short story "Getting Ready to Write," (*Farmerphile: The Magazine of Philip José Farmer* no. 13, 2008). I was more fortunate than Danny was when he was writing *A Hole in Wednesday*, in that I was able to discuss my humble input with Phil while he was still with us. Not that Danny is a stranger to working collaboratively with Phil. Many of you will know Danny as the coauthor, with Phil, of the magnificent novella *The City Beyond Play* (PS Publishing, 2007). Another world from the "fertile imagination," another "mind blowing idea" to originate from Phil. The generator sparked into life again. But now, a second generation generator. A new talent. A worthy inheritor. Danny is Phil's great nephew; sometimes apples truly don't fall far from the tree—sometimes sparks land close to the generator.

That Phil had a profound effect on Danny's writing career (perhaps even helping to kick-start it) is obvious; it exudes from

Foreword

every paragraph, every sentence, every word. The homage paid across the generations is palpable.

Danny is an artful and erudite writer who epitomizes the gentle soul coupled with deep knowledge. I've had the pleasure of spending more than a little time with Danny: several times at Phil's house for FarmerCons and other gatherings; once meeting for a meal as my family passed through his home state of Virginia; and in London when he stayed with me for a few days in the summer of 2015. During that latter visit, we explored my capital's sites and wandered further afield to Oxford and Canterbury. Our time together was filled with long train journeys full of chatter, laughter, and earnest conversation.

We talked about a lot of things over those few days. Danny had started work on *A Hole in Wednesday* and I was eager to know how the story would develop. I'd read Phil's original partial manuscript and knew Danny's outline, but there was so much more to know! Of course, Danny only gave me gobbets to chew on. I had to wait till the novel was completed to sit down to the feast. And what a book it is! Full of action, thought provocation, inspiring characters, and ideas. Ideas: the beating pulse of any writer, pounding hard in this spectacular adventure. Danny has mastered the skill of describing ordinary people in extraordinary situations and showing us, with startling reality, how a simple incident, a chance happenstance, can drag someone along a path at breakneck speed to destinations they could never have envisioned. His style is to excite, to educate, to entertain (remind you of anyone?) and I could not think of anyone better suited to have completed *A Hole in Wednesday*.

Preface

There are two parents, or perhaps more accurately a parent and grandparent, of this novel.

The first ancestor was the short story "The Sliced-Crosswise Only-On-Tuesday World," which was set in A.D. 2214, 130 years after the New Era began, and yet, as you will see, only a little more than a single generation afterward. What followed was the Dayworld trilogy: *Dayworld*, *Dayworld Rebel*, and *Dayworld Breakup*. Those books began in A.D. 3414, seven generations after the beginning of the New Era. *A Hole in Wednesday* steps back from the trilogy to a middle place three generations after the foundation of the New Era, which is to say, A.D. 2440.

The New Era and its most visible manifestation, the Dayworld, are established upon two foundations: the Thirteen Principles and the vertical calendar.

By the late twenty-first century, much of the world was ravaged by overpopulation, pollution, and warfare. Nation after exhausted and poisoned nation succumbed to a world conqueror, whose son then broke completely away from the father and turned the world government into one ostensibly based on thirteen egalitarian principles: Unity, Variety, Joy, Hope, Comradeship, Love, Freedom, Plenty, Peace, Knowledge, Wisdom, Serenity, and Fulfillment.

While some people resisted, most were so weary and weakened and hungry they accepted this New Era at face value.

However, despite the worldwide hardships that killed so many people, the planet was still choking under a population of eight billion. The Thirteen Principles and the supposedly benevolent World Organic Council alone could not rescue what was ruined in time to save humanity.

It was decided that those who lived outside the world's cities would be moved into them, within the shelters of a hundred domes and cubes built to protect people from the otherwise insurmountable devastations. Only officially sanctioned farmers and rangers were allowed to venture far outside. The environment, with the help of a Nature Rehabilitation Corps, would be given a chance to recover.

But once in the cities, people would only be allowed to live one day out of seven.

If your assigned Day is Wednesday, then Thursday through Tuesday you will be "stoned," placed in a suspended animation chamber called a stoner that uses an electromagnetic field to halt all motion in your body down to the molecular level. But this process also halts aging. Though you can only live one day out of seven, you will only age one day out of seven. Someone born in A.D. 2300 would, by 2440, be one hundred and forty calendar years old, but only age twenty physiologically.

This arrangement of living from Wednesday straight down to the next Wednesday instead of across from Wednesday to Thursday and onward became known as the "vertical calendar." The time periods involved in the vertical calendar were referred to as "subjective"—subdays, subyears, subgenerations, and so on. The old horizontal calendar became "objective," with obdays, obyears, and obgenerations.

Precious resources would be preserved this way. Instead of consuming and leaving waste all seven days of the week, people cut these by six-sevenths. Only one-seventh of what the struggling world could provide would be needed compared to the old world's demands. In exchange, the residents of the New Era were promised lives of ease and becoming fully self-actualized human beings under the auspices of the Thirteen Principles.

Preface

The stoners are the foundation of the New Era. They are the basis of its survival.

But alongside murder, rape, theft, and the ubiquitous host of other human crimes that have existed for as long as humans have walked the Earth, a new cardinal crime has appeared in society: daybreaking. Daybreakers stay out of their stoners longer than their assigned Day—sometimes for all seven days per obweek.

More so than all those ancient sins, the New Era considers daybreaking to be the worst crime of all . . .

Not well conceived of God, who, though his power
Creation could repeat, yet would be loath
Us to abolish, least the Adversary
Triumph, and say; "Fickle their state whom God
Most Favors; who can please him long?"
— John Milton, *Paradise Lost*

Yet maybe the chivalry and the enchanting of these times of ours follow different paths from those of earlier days.
— Miguel de Cervantes, *Don Quixote*

One

Jerry Carson awoke entombed, as he did every Wednesday.

He opened his eyes. His knees bent slightly in the conditioned reflex to keep him from falling as his muscles suddenly lost their tension. However, he could not fall, since the cylinder was so narrow his knees and back would wedge him at once on his downward slide.

He pushed the door open and stepped off the thick disc mounted in the center of the cylinder floor. He always had to orient himself after the increasingly vivid, ensnaring dreams he would have after going from the stoner to sleeping in his bedroom—the dreams out of history, though not always the history he taught in classes and far more detailed than any of his lectures. Or sometimes his dreams would cast him into the middle of the wildlands beyond Manhattan, alone with only his wits and strength to survive. After such dreams he would awake both relieved and disappointed to be back in his bedroom, but for a moment feeling out of place.

He made himself look around, take in what was real. The room was thirty feet by thirty feet by twelve feet. It contained twenty-eight gray cylinders, each two and a half feet in diameter and eight feet high. The cylinders were arranged in five rows of five abreast with the final row of three at the rear of the room.

He lit a cig-stick, then remembered after a distracted moment to smoke it. The Washingtons, the other couple who shared the apartment on Wednesdays, left their cylinders and moved past him, muttering, "Good morning."

Jerry said, "Good morning," but without his usual smile. He was still waiting for the door to his wife's cylinder to open. Six months ago, the timing device of her stoner had malfunctioned, and it now operated five minutes behind the others. The delay should have been reported, but it wasn't annoying enough.

Jerry smoked and waited and then he became more than annoyed. The five minutes passed, and the face behind the window in the cylinder door had not moved.

In another five minutes, he was alarmed. The stoners were supposed to be perfect, but nothing in this world was, and so they did malfunction now and then. But if something was seriously wrong, if the technicians couldn't locate the trouble . . . No, that was nonsense. All they had to do was to remove the device inside the base and put in a new one. Its field would be generated, and the motion of the molecules in her body and clothes would be resumed. She would be flesh and bone and blood again. Her heart, interrupted at fifteen minutes before midnight of last Thursday, would continue its beat, unaware that it had been halted for a week.

He looked through the window. Linda's face was a statue's, though of a substance far harder than stone. It was harder than anything in the universe, unscratchable, unbreakable, impervious to the worst ravages of Time.

Linda Yahzi Carson's skin was gray, as human skin always was when locked in the stoner field. It would become deeply tanned again the instant the field released, framed by her long, straight raven hair. Her eyes, when they opened, would be an earth brown as deep as the desert canyons her ancestors called home before the New Era's mass migration to the cities over three obcenturies, or two subgenerations, ago.

He started to turn away, intending to call the maintenance department. But he saw her face soften, her color return, and then the eyes open. She looked startled, probably because she did not expect to see his face in the window. He stepped back, the door opened, and she came out.

He kissed her and said, "Good morning," and then, "your timer is ten minutes late now. I'll have to call the techs. But I can do it after we get up."

"I don't understand it," she said. "I don't mind losing five minutes a day, but ten is too much. And it makes me nervous. What if it doesn't come on at all next time?"

"Nothing to worry about there," he said, though as soon as he said it he wasn't so sure he believed it. He took her hand, and they walked along the wall, past the gray and silent cases. They were tomblike in the half-light, a face behind each window. Then they opened a door and stepped out into the hallway.

The two bedrooms were on the opposite side of the hall, and the recreation room was next to the stoner room. At the end of the hall was the big round room which combined living room, the cleaning units, and the kitchen.

They entered the main room, which was always lit. Jerry pressed a button under the chin of a gargoyle on the wall, and the paintings on the wall disappeared. Wednesday's replaced them. The walls were covered with seven layers of paintings, but only one appeared at a time, the others remaining transparent. Each layer had a particular chemical makeup, the colors of which would be manifested only when a certain microvoltage was applied to it.

The paintings were the result of a group effort by the Carsons and the Washingtons. Some of the scenes and figures were caricatures of the couples. Each couple had painted their idea of the other three in terms of hate or scorn felt at the moment. But, to balance them, there were scenes and figures representing their love. Each of the four could look at them and be reminded of how the others felt about him and conduct himself accordingly—if he or she felt like it. And, some day, the four would paint on a new level, detach the electrodes from the edges of the old painting, reattach them to the new, and have a painting which would demonstrate what progress—if any—had been made in their adjustments to the group.

Linda checked the cleanliness and neatness of the room, making sure Tuesday's occupants had done what was expected of them. Then, murmuring that she was going to the bathroom, she went back down the hall to her bedroom. Rex and Ada Washington had gone immediately into their bedroom. They might be out a little later for a cup of hot coffee with dormigen, or they might just go straight to bed and to sleep.

Jerry decided to have some coffee and watched the canned news. He had missed last week's.

But Linda appeared at the end of the hall, calling in a strained voice, "Jerry!"

"What's wrong?" he said, and ran down the hall. She was leaning against the side of the doorway, her face white. She went into his arms and began to cry softly. After a minute, he let her go from his arms and wiped her eyes and nose. He insisted that she tell him what had happened. But he had guessed, correctly, that she had lost the embryo.

She wasn't suffering physical pain. The embryo had been too tiny and too loosely anchored at this stage of conception. If she had not been aware she was pregnant and might miscarry, she might not have even noticed the loss.

"I can't understand it," she said. "Doc Bunter says there's nothing wrong with me; I'm perfectly healthy. And you're all right."

"Even if this is the twenty-fifth century," he said, "the doctors still don't know everything."

Something was scratching at the back door of his mind, but he couldn't find his way through the darkness to the door.

He took her into the big room, his arms around her shoulders, and sat down.

"We'll talk a while," he said. "It's not as bad as it looks. It's just that this is a dreary time of the morning."

He took two packages from the wall-door, swung out a wall-table, and put cups and saucers on the table. He broke the packages open with the required twist in the required direction. The jelly-like stuff which filled the two cups turned into hot brown coffee a few minutes after the air touched it.

A Hole in Wednesday

Jerry gave Linda a cup and sat down beside her. Her eyes were red, but the tears were drying.

"You lost the first one the first day your timer was late, and now you're an extra five minutes late, and you lose this one," he said.

"Do you think the field could be affecting me?"

"I don't see how. The field is off simultaneously with the resumption of molecular motion. Anyway, it's been proven that the field can't hurt living cells. It either starts up the molecules or stops them, and that's all. Go or no go."

Then why did I mention the stoners at all? Jerry wondered. Something nagged at the back of his mind but he put it aside for Linda's sake.

They talked for half an hour, and she became less depressed. By then the dormigen he had put in the coffee was taking effect. They went to bed, stuck the electrodes of the sleep-speeders on their foreheads, kissed each other good night without getting the wires entangled, and quickly went into the dream-filled darkness.

Two

The speeder woke them with gentle words at 5:30 A.M. Jerry's first thoughts were that he would have to call the stoner maintenance men. Also, Linda would have to see the doctor today, if she could get in. If she couldn't, then she'd have to wait until tomorrow (next Wednesday). His next thought was that something felt peculiar about the coincidence of the miscarriage and the timer lag.

He went through shaving and showering, took his karate class before breakfast to work up an appetite, then ate with the Washingtons while watching the news—though with a tendency to slide away into The Question, as he was calling it.

Linda said she would go to work. Physically, she felt fine. She had a three-hour job at the Folk Library for Floors Ten and Eleven. She viewed the new books and prepared an audiovisual summary to be shown on *The Book Review Hour* over Gramercy Tower's local channel.

Jerry, thinking of this, pictured some author who had been bum-rapped by Linda sneaking in and tampering with her timer and then with her. But he was reaching too far out if he had to dream up such a theory.

At eight-fifteen the Carsons and the Washingtons walked down a thirty-foot wide hall lined with the doors to the East 20th Street side of Gramercy Tower's apartments. The doors were arched on top and painted brightly, some garishly, with geometric designs, animals, birds, insects, fish, totem poles, and even scenes from the lives of the occupants. The paintings were in layers, too, and each layer was activated by the tenants of each respective day, unless, as sometimes happened, the painting of another day was preferred. The corridor floor was covered with a neutral brown carpet six inches thick over which street cleaners ran powerful vacuum cleaners twice a day.

After a hundred-yard walk, the four came to the end of the corridor. Linda and Rex went left, and Jerry and Ada right. The corridor opened onto a "street," a much larger hall with a simulated sky and drifting clouds but no sun. This opened after fifty yards into an enormous circular chamber, the Folk Center. The central part was occupied by a fountain with a bronze statue in the middle, of Wang Shen emptying a cornucopia. Around the rim of the Center were the broad and glowing entrances to the Theater, the play arenas, the tower shops, the government administration offices, the health clinics, and the Tenth and Eleventh Manhattan Central University offices and lecture rooms.

Jerry waved goodbye to Ada and turned into the open door of MCU. At the end of the broad hall, he turned into his office and called the Municipal Maintenance Department, Tenth, Eleventh, and Twelfth Floors. The receiver was a short busty woman who sipped coffee while Jerry reported on the timer.

"Okay, I'll send out a tech, *dolce*," she said. "But I don't know if he'll be able to get there today. Something's been happening lately. We've been getting reports of malfunctioning timers for six months now. Not just here, on these levels, I mean, but all over the city. And it ain't supposed to happen."

"How many cases in the past six months?" Jerry said. He always liked to get precise reports.

"Gee, I dunno. You'd have to ask my super, Mr. Majid, and he might tell you that's classified information."

Then why are you talking about it? Jerry thought.

A bell rang and a light flashed on his desk. He hung up and picked up his tablet, selecting the social books he would be referencing in class, and walked down to the lecture room. The students' chairs were arranged in twelve concentric rings with the teacher's podium in the center. Jerry sat on a chair while the podium revolved slowly. Beside him was a plastic shaft rising to a height of ten feet; at its top was an array of four TV sets, each directed so one quadrant of students could see its screen.

Jerry said, "Good morning," and the students nodded or waved at him.

Three students were absent; Jerry noted this for his own purposes, since no official attendance was taken.

He did not think about the time or Linda's distress while he was in the classroom. He gave his all to his art. And it was art, even if not always good art. He was a teacher because he loved teaching. It wasn't a job, since he did not have to work to get necessities or luxuries. All those came to him automatically. He taught only three classes, but he threw himself into them so thoroughly that he felt emptied by noon. But a half hour's nap with a sleep-speeder would restore him, and he would be ready to play, study, or attend the Folk Theater.

The lecture for today was on the decision of the Founding Fathers of the Second Republic, the brief post-World War Three North American government which existed immediately before joining the World Organic Council, to agree to use the stoners to solve the population crisis. A number of students argued vigorously how the government had no right to "seventh" the population. But Jerry pointed out that civilization would have collapsed if this had not been done.

Then some of the students protested against being confined to one day. Jerry said exceptions could not be made (other than government officials on very special missions) because diurnal segregation was the only way to make the setup operable. At one time, people had been allowed to move from one day to another at petition. But even this had been cancelled. If anybody who wished to do so could move from one day to another, it would be impossible to maintain order. Moreover, some people would just keep on moving, live every day, and grow older faster than the rest of the population. Laxity about temporal emigration would cause the system to break down, and terrible suffering would be the result. *Had* been the result, until the late twenty-first century. There would be only one-seventh as much food and goods as now, and no room for people to live in. They would be spread out across the planet as they once had been, leaving no space for themselves or to produce the food to feed them all. Starvation, mass murders, and many things as dreadful would come about.

Behavioral sink, Jerry remembered. A twentieth-century theory proven by the twenty-first, about how any animals—including humans—would end up deranged and act out violently when confined to too small a space with too many others for too long a time: weekly mass shootings in the United States, riots in Europe and South America, massacres in Africa and Asia, the twenty-first-century nuclear exchange starting with India and Pakistan, and the climates of every continent wrecked. Those who objected to the stoners took up the phrase *escape from freedom*, snarled it. But by the time every nation began moving people into domes and stoners during the sweltering summer of 2084, most people believed escaping from freedom meant never having to starve again, or have loved ones murdered in front of them, or be incinerated in radioactive fire—or all of those and more.

"Yeah, but why couldn't we at least have guided tours of the other days?" a student said. "I'd like to take a trip into Sunday, say, and see what's happening there."

"What would you see?" Jerry said. "You'll see the same apartments and streets and folk stores. Only the people would be different."

"I'd like to find out if they are different. Maybe Sunday has some exotic citizens."

"There are enough people in Wednesday for you to get acquainted with," Jerry said. "If you want to see something different, travel. Go to the Fiji islands or Samarkand."

"I've been there a million times on TV."

"There are twenty human beings in this room," Jerry said. "How well do you know them? How deeply have you traveled into their souls? How well do you know yourself, how deeply have you dived into yourself?"

"Too dark and spooky down there," the student said, smiling, and everybody laughed.

This may or may not have been true, but psychic voyages were available to all who cared for them. A man could get a PhD in Self-Knowledge if he dared; he could spend the rest of his life being analyzed by others and himself. Some had done so, and they were now great gurus or else in mental hospitals. Everything that offered a reward concealed a danger. The road to the Holy Grail was strewn with rusty armor and old bones.

Jerry had tried the Self-Knowledge degree once. But every time he went to enroll, especially into the ones purporting to use self-psychic voyages to probe ever deeper into the mind, something always came up to interfere with him being able to finish. A new job offer; apartment families having to leave; and so on. Finally he gave up and turned to his other great love, history, and everything opened up to him. It was as if the universe was agreeing that history was the right path and smoothed the way for him.

I even dream it now. The dreams over his past week had him fighting at the Battle of the Little Big Horn. On both sides, depending on which part of the dream he was in. Every time he was about to die under Custer—never Custer himself—he switched to being a Sioux warrior, though was never Sitting Bull himself.

After his two classes, Jerry shook the dreams away and wondered if he might have anything in his library about stoner history. He found *Early Objections to the Stoner*, by Richard R. Randolph, inserted it into his tablet, and he swiped through about ten pages. The reading session ended with videos of a mob scene outside the White House, the Pennsylvania Avenue fence being pulled down while snipers on the executive mansion's roof took out people one by one until soldiers from Camp Walker surrounded and forcibly removed the rioters.

Is that what they want to go back to? Jerry wondered about his students. *They criticize the world today because they don't know anything else. The benefits are invisible . . . but take them* away, and I wonder how many of them would trample over themselves to go back?

Of course, Jerry hadn't known anything else either. Aside from handpicked farmers and those who raised livestock, and the rangers, those allowed to live in the open spaces between the cities, the last holdouts outside the city domes entered the towers 356 years before. Three and a half centuries in objective years; in subjective years, divided by seven, it was in his grandparents' time. Only about half of a subcentury ago. His grandfather died not long after they moved to Gramercy Tower in the Manhattan Dome, but Jerry vaguely remembered his grandmother as a frail elderly shadow, one who would quit talking whenever anyone mentioned the days before the stoners.

They're probably just rebelling, Jerry thought, giving his students the benefit of the doubt. That's what kids do, even in the twenty-fifth century.

Except Jerry hadn't. Not really. He was too immersed in his interests, too bookish as a teen . . .

Too interested in the past, maybe, but only as a curiosity. He certainly wouldn't want to live there. Yet why did he keep dreaming about it? And why did he feel a sudden pull to the wildlands beyond the domes and farms, even though his time out on what remained of the Illinois prairie during his six submonths with the Nature Rehabilitation Corps, when he was seventeen, were the most frightening of his life?

Though the most exciting, he admitted. Six submonths outside. True, he had modern technology at his disposal, and his father, an experienced Park ranger, was never far away. But he had been *outside*, helping rebuild a landscape ravaged by war, pollution, and blight by the late twenty-first century.

His head, or at least the left temple of it, burst into a sudden sharp pain almost like a buzzing. Jerry immediately shot to his feet to grab an elixir. But having just remembered his grandmother he also recalled something she had told him. Though he was a small child when she died, he remembered it because it was so strange and she said it so often: "Don't take a pill every time you hurt.

A Hole in Wednesday

Make your body strong first. Then you will know what your body needs and what it doesn't."

She was withered in his memory. But then, she had had children late, and was over ninety subyears old by Jerry's earliest memories. Withered, but the more Jerry thought about her, the more he remembered her . . . *doing*. Cleaning on her own, ignoring the automation. Going to the Museums. Walking in Gramercy Park below the tower.

For some reason, this time, he obeyed her advice. He stayed where he stood, as if he could will the pain away. And yet it did fade, as if obeying his command.

I'll ask the doctor about it sometime, Jerry thought. But Linda needs to see the doctor first.

As much as he had left that aside during his two classes, now she was in the front of his mind again, and he called her at the Library. She had regained her color without the use of cosmetics, and she was able to smile at him.

"Dr. Faber said he'd see me tomorrow," Linda said, "she's too busy today."

"She couldn't squeeze you in?"

"Are you kidding? She's working five hours a day now, as it is. We have such a high proportion of doctors to the general population now, compared to the old days, but they're so much busier . . ."

For an instant Jerry felt as if the shadow of his grandmother was behind him, scowling. But when he turned there was nothing but a blank crystalline wall—the paintings on it were malfunctioning, apparently, like other parts of the city's computer network had been weirdly acting up lately—and the nagging of childhood daydreams.

Three

Jerry tried reading a history book, one about dogfights in the First World War that swirled the biplanes around the text as he scrolled through it, or sometimes straight at him if the sun happened to be behind the print. Hoping for utter distraction he set the violence filter on his tablet to allow the bullet-ridden planes to burn as they crashed, and the pilots to show blood. This also served as a reminder of how good the world was today, his instincts warning him that digging too deeply would undermine his comfortable life. World War One, civilization's first attempt to commit suicide as twentieth-century raconteur Kurt Vonnegut called it, was supposed to end all war but only ended up ushering in a century filled with destruction. That century led to a twenty-first that witnessed humanity plunging deeper into suffering, saving itself only at the last minute in spite of itself. He'd flown some dogfights in his dreams, too, sometimes as an American pilot, sometimes a German.

Do you want to bring that back? flashed in his thoughts like bullets through a propeller. Yet try as he might, he couldn't get the dreams any farther away than the back of his mind.

And why would he think he could bring that back, anyway, even if he wanted to? He was happy preserving the past's memory, teaching it, and visiting it in the Museum. He never wanted to meet an angry Fokker triplane face-to-gun barrel, or fight from a trench or hedgerow, and for that matter, even the air raid sirens and phone warning signals in the Museum's World War Two, Ocean Wars, and World War Three simulations unsettled him.

It was possible to recreate his dreams. There was a professional dream recreator right on his floor who did colorful work. Of course the trouble with the audiovisual recreations of his dreams was that some of the recreators' psyches rubbed off on them. But so it should be, the psychologists claimed. No man was an island and so forth. And Jerry really didn't want to share them, anyway—he hadn't even much with Linda. Silly as it felt, they were his, like his own private passage through a wormhole into other times and places. Dangerous places, but ones to which he could escape anytime.

He turned on the weather report, and though it was hotter than usual for this spring, even in a climate-controlled dome, Jerry decided to go outside and play tennis. He needed fresh air, even if it was true that there was no difference in the chemical makeup of outside or inside atmosphere. There was a psychic difference. An inquiry to the Parks and Playgrounds Department resulted in a court being reserved for him if he could come up with a partner inside ten minutes. He called Michel Crypta, who taught The History of Pulp Magazine Literature of the Twentieth Century. Michel said he'd meet him at the court. Jerry called the PPD back to tell it he had a partner. Then he took an express to the ground floor and a mobway out of the city.

The sky was clear, the wind was slight, and the warm May sun delighted him. He got a bicycle from the lot and rode it down the bikeway which ran down the bluff through the Park to the tennis courts. These were near the East River, which sparkled as cleanly as in the pre-Columbian days. Now and then, giant trout leaped up from the surface, resurrected products of the biolabs. Behind it was the Manhattan Dome, with a diameter of three miles and a height of six thousand feet. It was windowless but any citizen could get an outside view by selecting the proper TV channel. Trees covered most of the hillsides and the area around the city except for the PPD area. A few miles beyond the thick forest the farms began, but these were ringed and perforated by broad bands of trees. Beyond those . . .

Wildlands. They were forbidden except under special circumstances for rangers and a few others, and Jerry had no reason to travel that far out anyway. But thinking about them gave him a nagging under his ribs he couldn't explain.

You could apply to visit them, he remembered. The Manhattan Council might approve you, if you say you're a history teacher who wants to visit historical sites . . .

Or the Council would just point out that he could visit any of those sites in physical or holographic recreations any time he wanted. That any human interaction with the real sites by anyone who wasn't a ranger was equivalent to tampering. And if a hound saw his application, and noticed he was asking about the stoner timers . . . No, it was all just too much of a risk, for no reason beyond foolish daydreaming.

Another idea struck him: maybe he could bring up a 3D holo of a stoner in his quest to figure out the problem with Linda's timer. But that would certainly get somebody's attention, and he didn't have the technical knowledge to make it worthwhile anyway. He had always learned fast, though . . . but not faster than anyone who might be triggered to monitor his holo use.

Jerry played his tennis games hard, driving any thoughts of the primitive world beyond the domes and farms out of his head, and won four sets. His mind wasn't really even on the game but his body took over. Afterward he showered and biked back up the hills to the city. When he got back to his apartment, he found two techs working on Linda's cylinder. One directed the end of a frequency-modulated beam at the cylinder base, and the seemingly unbroken surface suddenly revealed hairlines.

The stoner device slid out of the base. The techs put it in a metal case and locked that. They unlocked another case, took out a new stoner, and slid its elongated form halfway into the cavity. The tech flicked a button on his FM, and the coded frequencies activated the machinery within. The block slid in, and the surface of the cylinder was smooth again. The tech spoke into his phone, and its screen went blank. The operation had to be checked by a monitor at the Maintenance Department. Everything connected with the operation of the stoners was subject to a close supervision.

"Seems like the whole city's falling apart," the tech grumbled. "Too hot outside, all the computers running slow . . . I'm even still trying to get my tools to connect to the city network so I can check your stoner, that's why things're so slow. Sorry. Bureau of Ecosystems is getting flooded with complaints."

"You getting many of these malfunctions lately?" Jerry said to the tech.

"Too many, Doc," the tech said quietly. "There ain't been nothing like it since the stoners were invented. Nobody can figure out what it is. Them things're supposed to be foolproof, unbreakable, unmalfunctionable, you know. No moving parts except for the timer lock. By the way, how come you didn't report the lag the first time it happened?"

"What's five minutes?" Jerry said.

"In fifty day-years that amounts to near sixty-three days. But it's her life."

Jerry turned away, embarrassed for not having thought of that himself. The other tech had opened the cylinder door, stepped into it, and closed the door. He signaled through the window that he had tried the door and it couldn't be opened. The lead tech directed the laser at the base, using a code that overrode the normal timing circuits. The face within the window became rigid. The lead tech glanced at a dial on an instrument box at his feet, nodded, and turned the control on the laser. The face behind the window became mobile flesh again. The door swung out, and the tech came out.

"The field's okay," he said.

The lead tech reset the laser control and directed its end at the base. The frequencies were apparently resetting the timer.

"Tell me," Jerry said, "has this increase of timer malfunctions been associated with miscarriages of women in the cylinders?"

"What?" Then the lead tech shrugged and said, "Hell, I dunno. How could it?"

A Hole in Wednesday

"Is it possible for anyone to get hold of your tools? I mean, so someone could get to the stoners and tamper with them?"

The techs looked astonished, and the lead tech said, "No way in the world, Doc. We guard them like money was guarded in the old days."

"Who guards them?"

The lead tech looked at him almost suspiciously, and Jerry wondered if he'd crossed some sort of hidden behavioral boundary. "Not me, Doc," the tech finally said. "Above my pay grade. Something important as all that, you get appointed by the deputies of the World Organic Council."

He leaned in with the avidness of someone who wanted to talk about his work but never found anyone else interested. "But really, you get the tools, they still wouldn't do you much good." He paused for effect.

Jerry allowed himself to be led. "Why not?"

"When something's wrong with the timer, or whatever else in the stoners, Doc, we get an instant alert. The tools fix the parts; you can't use 'em to break things. See, these things are just, you know, receptacles. Not just for people but energy. The stoning field, but also the electricity that runs the timers. Nah, you want to mess with the stoners, you'd have to go a lot higher. To the engines that run them. The computers, I mean. The ones that regulate and generate the power for the fields that get sent to the stoners. But that's *way* over my pay grade."

It was obvious to Jerry that he would have to put in a request to the Department of Medical Statistics. But if the department found out why he wanted the information, it would think he was a nut. It might request he go to the psych bureau for a check on his Mental Balance Quotient. Legally, he did not have to report to them at a verbal request by the bureau. But if he refused or ignored the request, the bureau would consider this as an indication that he was disturbed. The bureau would start a campaign; it would annoy him with phone calls and set the police to watching him—worse yet, maybe a hound if they really wanted to rattle him—and generally bug him until he would come in for a checkup just to be rid of the nuisance. And if the bureau got very concerned, it could issue a formal order for him to be brought in.

He paused that line of thought. If the tech was right, and the problem went a lot higher than broken timers, people in much higher positions of power might want to find out why he wanted the information too.

Jerry smiled slightly, thanked the techs, and they left, their day's work done. He went into the kitchen, pulled out a tray, ripped off the cover, and heat ascended suddenly from the roast beef and gravy with mashed potatoes. He stripped off the cover from a milk bottle and its contents chilled a few seconds later.

Linda called while he was eating to say that she was playing bridge at the Folk Center. The prize today was a painting by Central Illinois Cube's own genius, Raymonda Reichenbach. Linda hoped she would win; it would look so lovely on the wall or the ceiling of the living room (on Wednesdays only, of course). Jerry said that it would indeed, if the Washingtons didn't mind another painting in that room. Some of the new paintings emitted frequencies that hurt Ada's too-sensitive ears.

"Well, if it does, we'll hang it in our bedroom and bring it out when we have company," she said.

Jerry dropped the glass and tray into the waste chute and then sat down in the living room to correct his students' themes. He plugged them one by one into the TV and checked them off for errors, adding some audio or video comments to the themes. Ada came in while he was working and kissed him. Rex came in a few minutes later. He was happy. He had just won the hundred-meter dash in the track meet at the Park, for men in the age category of thirty-five to thirty-seven. He danced around, kissed Ada and Jerry, and showed his medal. Then, grinning, he slapped Ada on the rear and said, "Thirty-six or not, I still got what it takes, eh, lover?"

"I don't mind you slowing down a bit," she said. "You always were over the finish line before I was."

She turned to Jerry. "How's Linda?"

A Hole in Wednesday

"Feeling okay," he said. "In better spirits, anyway, unless she's pretending. And she seldom does that."

Ada leaned over Jerry, her face serious.

"Do you think that, just maybe, the psychic atmosphere isn't quite tuned here? I mean, well, we seem to be getting along just fine, as well as can be expected, I'd say, more than could be . . . But maybe there's some unconscious friction here, and that's causing Linda to . . ."

"Lose the embryos?" he said. He smiled and shook his head. "I don't see how. That's pretty far out, Ada."

"Well, I'm halfway through my PhD in Self-Knowledge, you know, and I don't think . . . The body is so finely tuned to the mind, and vice versa, that, well . . ."

"Ten years of psyching, and she still can't finish a sentence," Rex said.

Ada stood up and said, angrily, "You ought to be working for a degree yourself, instead of spending so much time on those middle-aged athletics of yours!"

"*Mens sana in corpore sano,*" Rex said.

A throbbing ache found its way into Jerry's temples and he requested they to go into the bedroom if they meant to quarrel. Inasmuch as he had entered the room first, he had the right to ask anybody who was too negatively emotional to leave.

"All right, Jerry," Ada said. "But what about it? Do you really think . . ."

"No, you two are the best we've ever lived with. We've gone through a dozen couples and even lived in a twelver once, you know, though briefly. No, you're fine."

The Washingtons seemed relieved and sat down to watch their favorite shows on their sets. Jerry was relieved that the throbbing faded. He finished reading his students' papers on the mid-twenty-first-century reactions to the invention of the stoners and uploaded them and his marks and corrections to the links of their respective apartments. Jerry phoned his sister in Brooklyn, his father in the Forest Ranger Station in Illinois, and his mother in New Baghdad, Mesopotamian District, where for once she wasn't busy overseeing some social gathering at the North American Consulate. His mother cluck-clucked about Linda and then told him, for what seemed the hundredth time, the history of his delivery.

"You weren't a mentally handicapped child, thank God," she said, "but you had a difficult birth. The pains started at thirty minutes before midnight, and you were halfway out when stoning time came. Next Wednesday came and that was the terrible day the power station blew up, you remember?"

"Hardly, mother," he said, hoping his boredom wasn't showing. She always took such pleasure in the story.

"And so we weren't destoned until late that evening, and then you were so obstreperous, gave me so much trouble. You'd think modern techniques would do away with all that, wouldn't you? And wouldn't you know it, midnight came, and you still didn't want to leave me, and there we went again, right into the hospital cylinder. It took three days to deliver you, and . . ."

And it's taking three days to get through a phone call with her, Jerry groused.

"Your grandmother was so upset with me."

That pulled back his attention. "Why?"

"Oh, who knows? She must have been suffering dementia by then, she said the strangest things. During your labor it was something about evolution, and survival, and gallows . . . what are gallows?"

"Platforms they used to hang people on. For executions."

"How horrible. With a rope? And she always said—I remember, that I wasn't strong. She told me that quite a lot."

Make your body strong first.

"But then again I was so drugged up when you were born," his mother said cheerfully, "I may have dreamed up half of what I thought she said then too."

The rest of the day he spent watching a new book, or a recreation of an old book, rather. Thurber's *The 13 Clocks*, about a mysterious prince who undertakes an impossible quest to rescue a maiden who happened to be the niece of an evil duke. Linda might not have an evil duke for an uncle, but the stoners were like father and mother, and ruled the land, when you got right down to it. And Jerry did seem to have set an impossible quest before himself. Too bad his couldn't figure out his way through this problem as cleverly as Thurber, or the prince, who disguised himself as a minstrel but loudly announced his intentions to rescue the fair maiden.

Linda came home, and they sat around after supper talking with the Washingtons. After a while, Ada and Rex went out to bowl at the Folk Center. Jerry and Linda took the elevator to the ground floor and the rapid transit to the riverside, where they took a long walk.

When they got home, they cleaned up their bedroom and helped the Washingtons with the common part of the house. This only took ten minutes and could not be put off. It would never do for Thursday's occupants to find the bed sheets dirty or the ash trays full or the dinner trays not sped down the waste chute. They had been conditioned to prepare for the next day's arrivals since early childhood, and they would have felt very uneasy, perhaps even panicky, if they had been prevented by circumstances from cleaning.

By twenty minutes to midnight, while the bells clanged and the lights flashed all over the apartment, they were walking past the cylinders and the pale rigid faces behind the windows and entered their own cases. Jerry shut his cylinder door, and waited, wondering what recreational time travel awaited him through this next obweek, for the minute to pass before the field would envelope him in a microsecond, to halt all molecular motion in his body and clothes, yet somehow not whatever part of body, psyche, soul, or the trinity thereof that generated his vivid-as-life journeys into the past.

Four

He opened his eyes a moment later, or so it seemed to him. But the clock on the wall at the other end of the room told him that it was Wednesday, ten minutes past midnight again. Spring was over, and summer would leap, like a kangaroo, coming down fourteen times, and then metamorphose into fall.

Jerry gritted his teeth and continued to investigate, but only with people he trusted, saying nothing to anybody else, not even to Linda. He did not know exactly what he was doing or that there was anything *to* do. But he had lunch with Reginald Deering, who had been his best friend when the two had served in the Nature Rehabilitation Corps. Reginald was an administrator in the Department of Vital Statistics. But he was thinking of returning to school full-time and getting a PhD in James Joyce. That would take him about eight years at least. Basic requirements were a thorough knowledge of at least fifteen languages, a thorough grounding in theory of music, and numerous courses in history, mythology, religion, and Joycean criticism: Benjamin, Blish, Robinson, et al. At the moment, he was taking an afternoon course in Advanced Analysis and Creation of Puns and Portmanteaus.

Jerry led the conversation gradually around to medical statistics. Casually, he asked if the percentage of early pregnancy miscarriages had risen.

Reginald looked surprised and said, "Yes. But how did you know? That hasn't been released to the public as yet."

"How much increase?"

"Well, whereas one woman in twenty had early pregnancy miscarriages ten years ago, five women in twenty do now. In NYC, that is. I don't know about other cities."

"That's scary," Jerry said. "Don't the doctors have any explanations for this?"

"The best received theory is that medical science has kept alive too many who would otherwise have died without progeny. In other words, science has interfered, and genes that should have died with their owners have, instead, spread through the population."

"I thought the law didn't allow that sort of thing anymore."

"You mean the Hinxton Decrees? A lot of people think that, but really, they only specifically banned life extension. Why wouldn't they, when the whole world was living shoulder to shoulder by the time the domes and cubes were built? But there are loopholes. Cancer caused by genetic problems, issues in the womb, the activation of compassion genes, that sort of thing. Even some direct genetic repair is allowed, within reason."

"But if a woman has genes which tend to cause miscarriages, how can she transmit these to her descendants?"

"Special care and medicines have enabled women to keep embryos they would otherwise have lost," Reginald said. "But there is doubt that this theory explains the rise. It's just the best received, as I said."

"Why haven't the statistics been released?" Jerry asked. "The people have a right to know."

"That's all I am authorized to reveal and perhaps I shouldn't have done that. But you took me by surprise. Now, what's your interest in this?"

Jerry told him about Linda and the malfunctioning timer, and added, "I'd like to find out if other women's timers have been lagging coincidentally with miscarriages."

"You think the field could be causing the trouble?"

Jerry hesitated, then wondered why. Why shouldn't he voice his suspicions?

A Hole in Wednesday

"I don't know, I'm just trying to find out things. For Linda's sake especially."

"If you've got the crazy idea that anybody could be tampering with the stoners, forget it," Reginald said. "Why, why . . ."

He was pale, as if the thought of it was sucking his blood from his jugular vein. And Jerry felt panicky, too, now that he had spoken it aloud. The stoner was the foundation of civilization. Its stability was undoubted, *had* to be undoubted.

"Has there been any increase of malfunctioning timers?" he said. There, it was out!

"I really wouldn't know," Reginald said. "That wouldn't be a part of vital statistics."

He stood up quickly. "I must be going now, Jerry." He held out his hand and then dropped it as if he had suddenly felt that touching Jerry might cause a discharge of . . . of what? Of what must not exist?

He watched Reginald. He was hightailing out of the Folk Center Café as if he planned to fly as soon as he got through the door. Jerry suspected this was the last time he would see Reginald again, at least for a long while.

Jerry waited. If Reginald was going to bring a hound down on him, Jerry might as well get it over with. An hour passed, then two. At one point Jerry spotted two green-uniformed police on horses, but a moment of tense watching proved they were just doing their normal patrol. If the hounds were coming they would come by now; they tended not to do subtle things like having conversations in the privacy of someone's apartment.

Jerry's next move was to call the Stoner Supervisory Bureau. He did so in his official capacity as a Professor of History at MCU. He told the Public Information Secretary that he was after statistics for a class in Effects of the Stoner in the Middle Decades. He was interested in finding out if there had been a decrease or increase in timer malfunctions over the past twenty years.

"That data is available in the Public Library," she said.

"Not for the past five years," Jerry said. "I want up-to-date information."

"Just a minute," the woman said. Her video went off, and exactly seventy seconds later, it returned. "The figures have not been released yet," she said, smiling. "But the Bureau expects to do so soon."

"Is there any reason why I can't get them ahead of public transmission?" he said. "I don't want a big breakdown of the figures. Just an overall incidence."

She hesitated. "I'm sorry. For some reason, which I'm not aware of, of course, since I don't help make Bureau policy, that information is classified."

"Why would they classify public information?" he said, catching himself again too late, feeling a little trace of the panic he'd felt earlier with Reginald at any questioning of . . . any doubt about . . . the stoners.

"Sorry, Professor, I don't know," she said quickly, and the phone went dead.

Jerry continued asking questions, making inquiries among his neighbors, his professional friends, and his students. Linda reported that four of her coworkers had had recent miscarriages, but only two of these had timers which had lagged. Ada said three of her coworkers had lost their embryos quite recently. But they did not know of any timer lag. Rex said he knew two women who had been pregnant for eight and six months respectively. They had had no trouble whatsoever.

Some of his dreams changed. A few looked like he was looking at them through the wrong end of a telescope. That everything was backward. The feeling never completely went away when he was awake, either.

The days went by. Winter bounced out. Then Ada became pregnant. She said that all this talk about babies had inspired her. She had decided that it was time to have a family. It would mean separation from the Carsons, leaving the apartment after the baby was born, and getting somewhat smaller one-family quarters. She and Rex would miss living with the Carsons. Despite the population issues, every couple who had a high PQ, or Parent Quotient, was allowed to have up to two children, on rare occasions three with a special permit, to come to the aid of future generations, and so . . .

Could the stoner issue be population control? Many measures, including genocide, were tried frequently in the twenty-first century. Riots had just been some of the results when it was learned, or suspected, that only the poor and middle classes were made to adhere to the rules. But if this was the case now, why kill embryos but turn around and encourage people to have children? But only people with a high PQ were so encouraged, those whose children would serve the world well.

Jerry thought of asking Ada not to report to the doctor until she was well into her fifth month, but he decided against it. She wouldn't be able to conceal her condition, and she would also want to have the best of care for the baby. Also, from childhood, everyone was taught that civilization depended upon the flow of data through the proper channels. Holding back even a bit of data was antisocial and bordering on psychotic conduct.

The insistence on feeding in data seemed to work one way, however. The government wanted all the data right now, but it took its time digesting it and returning it to the public in organized and significant form. And sometimes they classified it, Jerry thought with frustration.

Fourteen days after she knew for sure she was pregnant, Ada lost the embryo. The loss was easy and resulted in no damage except to Ada's feelings. Nor had the timer malfunctioned.

Jerry, meanwhile, had deliberately gotten friendly with a teacher, Scottie Scotts, whom he did not like very much. But the man lived in a twelver and Jerry knew that three of the wives were pregnant. One lost the embryo early when she fell off a bicycle in the park. The other two had children, one six and one four, and neither had ever had any trouble retaining theirs.

Jerry went through the huge twelver apartment during a party. He looked through the big room containing eighty-four cylinders. It was also used to store odds and ends and had a number of enormous cabinets and shelves. There were plenty of hiding places for a camera or even a man.

The following Wednesday, Jerry walked into the apartment and asked for the Scotts. He knew they were absent but pretended that he had an appointment with them. Nobody paid him much attention in the noisy crowd. He went into the stoner room and set up a video camera.

When he checked the video one subday later, it was ruined by stars and crosses of light. Likewise, the tracking information was garbled, though there was no way for Jerry to tell whether the information had been jammed or obliterated as the video was, or the people doing the interfering had the means to keep their identities hidden.

The next Wednesday, he asked the Scotts if anything of interest had happened at the twelver. Scott said that things weren't dull but nothing unusual had happened. Jerry kept after him, and the Scotts finally said that one of the women had changed her mind and was having an abortion. The other two, he said (after Jerry was forced to ask him), were doing fine, as far as he knew. He wasn't very interested in their pregnancies except where they would begin to interfere with the group ecology, as he called it.

Even while doing this, though, he wondered if he should not abandon the project. The more time that passed, the less reasonable even the mildest of his suspicions seemed. He wished, however, that he had thought of putting a camera in their own chamber when Ada had gotten pregnant.

Then it occurred to him that he still could. After all, there were six other days—six other worlds—to consider. Why not set a camera in the stoner room so that it operated throughout the week, instead of only during Wednesday? Besides, now that he thought of it, tampering with stoners and their occupants was probably being done on other days, too—if tampering was being done. He should have thought of that, but, like everybody else, he had a blind spot. He tended to think of the world as existing only on his native day. Beyond the walls of Wednesday was nothing.

This time Jerry installed his video camera in the upper corner of the odds-and-ends cabinet. The next subday (the following

A Hole in Wednesday

Wednesday), he inspected it, but just as before, the images were ruined and the tracking information was useless. Jerry reasoned that an electronic "noise-maker" had done the damage to both videos, overwhelming the images the way jamming used to stifle radio signals. If he was right, then whatever images would have been on the videos were unrecoverable, or were never recorded in the first place.

The camera's timing markers were operating, however, and these indicated the days and minutes of the interference.

The "noise" in his stoner room had occurred on Friday between fifteen and five minutes to midnight of Saturday. The "noise" in the twelver had occurred on Monday between twelve and six minutes to midnight of Tuesday.

There was nothing to do but leave messages for Friday and Tuesday. Traveling between days was forbidden, but communication was not.

The risk was coming to the attention of whomever was behind the tampering. But he could not just forget the affair or leave it alone. He had to take some action.

He made recordings and left them in the two stoner rooms. They were set to operate a few seconds after the people for Friday and Tuesday had stepped out of the cylinders.

The next Wednesday, the records were still on the little shelves where he had left them. But both had the same message, though one was a man's voice and the other's a woman.

We feel that cross-communication between days is not profitable.

No signatures. Just that one short sentence.

Jerry removed the camera. But he wasn't defeated yet. Perhaps an obsolete camera, one with chemical film that would be impervious to electronic jamming, could be used. As a history professor, he could legitimately obtain one from the Museum for use in the classroom.

He put in a request for an early twenty-first-century motion picture camera. In two Wednesdays, he got a reply. He could have the artifact, but a Museum official would bring the valuable object, would stand by during the lecture, and would take it back to the Museum afterward. This angered and frustrated Jerry, yet he could not object. The procedure was logical because of the artifact's rarity.

By then, summer was over, and the twelve days of fall had started. And Linda announced, joyfully, that she had conceived again. She had been giving herself the Algeyn Test on rising every morning. This consisted of wiping a piece of plastic across her skin after exercising. If the pink changed to green, she contained the united spermatozoon and ovum. The pill she had been taking determined that only a YY wriggler would get to the egg.

"I'm very happy," he said. "And I'd like to stay that way. Linda, don't tell the doctor or anybody else, will you? Not for a while, anyway."

"Why not? I want to tell the world!"

"Let's say I'm superstitious. The last two times, we told everybody, and look what happened. This time, let's keep quiet. Let's not make the gods jealous."

"You, superstitious?"

"About this, yes."

Five

The Carsons and the Washingtons decided to visit one of the Museums the next day. This was a complex of huge buildings with transparent walls and roofs covering a total of five square miles across several buildings in and out of the NYC domes that rose over Manhattan and each of the city's boroughs. The one they chose for today was in Brooklyn and, for those who wanted to avoid the heavily trafficked bridges or ferries, it could be reached by a dozen underground tunnels or several enclosed bikepath/walkways or three open path/walkways on the surface. Once the foursome reached the South Street Seaport they chose the Museum access under the East River, strolling leisurely along the moving track to the Museum while chatting and listening to the soothing music of Bocuma Xax that mixed ancient instruments with urban sounds. Upon arrival at the surface of Pacific Park they entered an open doorway into the building, which, in turn, contained many smaller buildings.

Jerry liked this branch of the Museum best. It had been built over the old Pacific Park, with the history wing taking over the site of the decrepit Barclays Center, when he was a child. His parents took him there often, indulging the love of history he had at that age, especially since he asked for trips to the Museum far more than toys.

It was the Washingtons' turn to pick the first exhibits they visited, and they enjoyed the science halls. Jerry masked his impatience to get to history, particularly the Twentieth Century Hall. It wasn't that he didn't like science—he enjoyed it quite a lot, even if he didn't always understand what he was looking at—but he had a specific target in mind for today.

They gravitated toward a brand new exhibit, one on the evolutionarily isolated Galapagos Islands that straddled the Equator west of South America, and its Darwinian-divergent creatures. Along with robotic giant tortoises and albatrosses, there was a holo-exhibit of the islands' unique forms of bacteriophages. These were bizarre viruses that inhabited bacteria, microscopic creatures with five or six legs, a long neck with a central torus inside, and polygon-shaped heads. Bacteriophages got their name by "eating" bacteria, but despite how horrible that sounded, they had evolved with humans and many were beneficial. Even before modern science of the New Era, several had been used in medical treatments.

The Roots of Modern Science started with a basic exhibit of S-Wave Novas, the first personal quantum computers and ancestors of the Scout tablets that were so ubiquitous now, and concluded with the first stoners. These fifty on display were lined vertically along the wall, those that weren't meant to be horizontal (but those had reminded too many people of coffins early on), and were fashioned into various shapes and sizes rather than the cylinders of modern times. There was a warning sign on the wall written in twenty-four languages that these stoners were to be used in emergencies only.

Linda laughed cheerfully at that with a mischievous look at Jerry. She said to a nearby attendant, "I imagine you wouldn't want people jumping into these artifacts any more than you would the ancient Egyptian sarcophagi."

The attendant, an older, thin man in a green Museum uniform whose demeanor would have fit any New York City doorman since the eighteenth century, smiled indulgently. "That's true sure enough, ma'am. But also, these guys don't have the safety mechanisms ours do now. There's even the possibility that some might let their stoner fields activate while the doors are still open."

A Hole in Wednesday

"Oh my! What would happen then?"

The attendant jerked a thumb back the way they came. "I just make sure the kids don't climb all over the old stoners, ma'am. You'd need to ask the docs back in the science wing that one!"

At last they let the mobile walkways lead them to History. The nearest area was dedicated to houses which were replicas of those used in the old days. The old days were anything that existed before 2084—specifically June of that year, when the last over-populating populations of the old world, except the specially licensed agriculturalists, went into the city domes. The houses were everything from the skin tent of a Pleistocene Cro-Magnon through the mansion of a Victorian factory owner to the luxurious motor-homes of the middle-late-twentieth century. There were also complete villages, starting with mud houses and walls of ancient Jericho and continuing through the mid-twentieth-century suburbia, with even an eighteenth century American frontier trade post-fort.

Jerry did not want the others to know what his goal was, but when they went into a late-twentieth-century drugstore, he lingered before the camera display.

Cameras were everywhere, of course. But almost all were connected to the city or worldwide network, and every personal camera, including Jerry's, would come with a digital stamp identifying its owner. But there were a few exceptions, including isolated security cameras, which operated off the grid to prevent outside tampering. Their AI chips would also do a multitude of tasks that included identifying faces they recorded.

One of the "historical" cameras, Jerry figured out some time ago after repeated visits to the exhibit and noticing discrepancies between the artifact and others he had seen, was actually an isolated security cam constructed to look antique and blend in with the rest. It was made to look like an old Brownie, the kind where you looked through a mirrored square on top of the camera to take the picture, but one day someone had left the top cover open and Jerry spotted the video feed where an upside-down image should have been. So that camera was now his target.

The downside for security was that in order to keep these cameras isolated, their videos were only recorded at the end of every obday. But this was an upside for Jerry, who could replace the AI chip with a dumb one easily enough.

But he doubted that he could just pick up the camera and stuff it under his jacket or stick it into the lunch basket they were carrying. The exhibit might also be under the surveillance of a closed-circuit TV camera as a backup or diversion. He would have to come up with something less obvious.

Jerry, Linda, and the Washingtons wandered around until they came to a simulated set of a Hollywood stage. They watched the actors—pseudo-protein-electronic—go through their programmed actions, enhanced by AI brains that let them interact with visitors. At that moment, he saw the thin face of the lead maintenance tech who had worked on Linda's stoner. He walked through the people, muttering apologies, and they gave way with, "Not at all."

"Do you remember me?" he said.

"Sure, you're the professor fellow whose wife's timer was off ten minutes," he said. "How's the teaching game?"

"Fine, thank you," Jerry said. "I wanted to ask you if you are still getting calls about complaints on the timers?"

"That's funny you should ask, Doc. All of a sudden, we ain't getting no complaints. Not to mention that is. We always did get maybe ten a year. Then, all of a sudden, four or five a day. In my own group, that is. The department was getting ten times what it used to get. But, since five days ago, nada. Can't figure it out. Just one of them things, I guess. Even electronic devices get liverish, you know. Affected by changes in weather or sunspots."

"There are no weather changes inside NYC," Jerry said. "And how could sunspots . . ."

"Just a way of talking, Doc," the tech said. "Actually I just don't know. But I hate to see the trouble disappearing, you know. It gave me something to do. Why, for a while I was on a two-hour day and then we had four to five hours to put in and that cheered us up. All play and no work makes Jack a dull boy, y'know?"

"Thanks," Jerry said, and returned to his group.

A Hole in Wednesday

He tried to get into the holiday mood of the others, but he couldn't keep from thinking about the camera. Well guarded or not, he also needed to summon his nerve, which he had not yet managed to do. Something that seemed so feasible when he thought of it now appeared impossible in practice.

They visited only a small number of the villages. They had been many times to the Museum. Now, instead of studying everything at a run, they made an intent scrutiny of only a few. But exhibits were always being added, and the old ones torn down and rebuilt with many additions and changes.

"Did you notice something about the last exhibit?" Rex said as they left the early twenty-first-century supermarket.

"What?" Jerry said absently.

"The exhibits after the time the stoner was adopted are more often than not nonexistent. In fact, the end of the current history wing in this branch of the Museum is a display of fifty of the first stoners. Why? I'll tell you why. Because we haven't had many changes since the stoner came in. Things've been about the same for the last one hundred and fifty subyears."

"Naturally," Jerry said, multiplying his own subage into obyears. "Time's been slowed down. In effect, anyway. It takes 245 years for a man to become 35 years old."

"I wonder if that's really it," Rex said. "It seems to me the stoner petrifies more than the individual."

"Hell, I'm going to give it up," Jerry muttered.

"Give what up, dear?" Linda said.

"What? Oh, nothing. I was just thinking about trying a new slant on teaching, but it wouldn't work."

He was thinking that he would forget about the camera, forget the whole absurd business of the timers. As long as Linda kept her baby, what did he care? What could he do? What was there *to* do? And against whom? And it's not like he could jump days, become a daybreaker, to put the pieces of every day of the week together . . .

Why not? The thought came unbidden and clenched his heart. He tried shoving it away but it wouldn't quite let go.

They moved to the mobile walkways which were slowly sliding up and down the hill in a complex network. They passed large fields on which were being reenacted the great events of the past: the discovery of fire, the invention of the bow, of the wheel, the building of the Pyramids, the battles of Salamis, Agincourt, Gettysburg, Ypres, Shrinaga, and Kaliningrad, the signing of the Magna Carta, and some events not so great except in their size in men's minds. Thus, they came to Custer's Last Stand, saw the electronic pseudo-protein Indians on their electronic pseudo-protein ponies charging Custer and the 7th Cavalry, heard the war whoops and the gunshots, saw the men fall, their bodies torn open by bullets and arrows, blood gushing, scalps being ripped off, and Custer slashing away with his saber until the final blow from a coup stick.

It doesn't look right, Jerry caught himself thinking. But he was just remembering his dreams.

As they walked through the sections covering the wars fought before the New Era, Rex Washington would have appeared to be increasingly discomfited to anyone who didn't know him. He was actually growing increasingly unsettled, but everyone who shared an apartment with him knew that he liked to do this every now and then as a reminder for how good they had it in the peaceful New Era.

Most people living in the domes and cubes wouldn't comprehend why anyone would need such a reminder. The evidence was all around them, after all, with all of humanity striving toward the Thirteen Principles, the underpinnings of the New Era, every day, and the economy of plenty they had enjoyed for three sub-generations. But Jerry was self-aware enough of his own psyche to know that he too had an inexplicable restlessness. Whether it came from his history dreams, or his strange yens for the wildlands, or something else entirely, he wasn't sure. But he understood the need for a reminder.

As it was, Rex didn't even finish the war displays. Normally they would go all the way to the late twenty-first century between the starts of World War Three and the New Era. There they would see enhanced views of flingers, swarms of electromagnetic microscopic robots that targeted electronic equipment more specifically than a massive EM pulse bomb, or the stoner-shaped sliders, weapons that destroyed by "sliding" matter aside at the quantum level, and were considered so horrific that all civilized nations banned them even in the desperate middle years of WWIII. But by the time they reached The First Kings of the Skies, the combat pilots of World War One, and had watched the Red Baron in his robotic red Fokker Dr.1 triplane "shoot down" a French Nieuport biplane while they swirled around a stoner-shaped zeppelin, Rex was ready to call it a day.

They were all getting tired then anyway, but Linda wanted to see the Mad Tea Party and then the Los Angeles Freeway. The others indulged her because she was pregnant and also because they took joy from her joy. She loved the reenactment of Carroll's story in the Literary Museum section and she found something satisfying in the Freeway reproduction. Jerry thought she had a little monster in her, no pun intended, which made her resonate to the madness of the Freeway. This madness reminded him in some ungraspable way of Alice in Wonderland—and the Freeway was grim, too, though in a somewhat different sense from the grimness of Alice's world. Whatever it was in her, it enthralled her. She was gripped by the roar of the motors and the weaving in and out, the tailgating, the brakes screeching and then the crash through the safety fence and the smash of metal bodies and the flesh flying and the severing of heads in broken windshields.

All symptoms of the behavioral sink of the old world before the stoners and the domes, Jerry's internal history teacher told him. By then he was sick, not only from the too-realistic gore and screams but from the smog. Authentic to the last detail, the Freeway was shrouded in a substance which reproduced the toxic mix of pollutants and the remnants of warfare that California had suffered from both domestic sources and those blown in across the Pacific from Asia and India.

They finally got her away and boarded one of the electrically powered trains that cruised up and down along the walkways.

"I think," Linda said in reply to Jerry, "that I like to watch the Mad Tea Party and the Freeway because they have no sense and my own life is so ordered and sensible. And it pleases me to know that we don't have any bloody and utterly senseless wars anymore. I guess I like to watch such things because they give me a sense of superiority and of security."

They went by Cemetery Hill. The battlefield was still now, the black gunpowder was drifting away, and the techs were moving out onto the field to put the dead and wounded of Pickett's Charge together again and clean up the mess for the show tomorrow.

For Thursday's show, he thought. Like Tuesday cleans up for us.

Winter came, and on the morning of the sixth day, halfway through the season, Linda lost her third embryo. It happened just as it had before, while she was in the bathroom, a few minutes after leaving the cylinder.

This time, the destoning field was on schedule.

Or so it seemed. But some instinct urged Jerry to check just a little deeper. While he couldn't tamper with the timer, he could check its record by linking to it with his computer, which happened to be equipped with an atomic clock—the same one the city used to determine exactly when to open the stoners. Linking to the timer was an old feature, one installed in stoners right from the very beginning to keep people from being nervous about losing tiny increments of their lives. Practically no one checked them anymore, but Jerry still could.

The network connection was unusually slow again. But once Jerry linked to the city clock, he discovered the stoner was late. Only by a few microseconds. But Jerry's was absolutely punctual to six decimal places, and Linda's had been too, up until then.

Without saying a word to Linda or anyone, Jerry put together his latest figures. It was true that he did not have much of a sample, but he believed his narrow sample was representative.

Then another thought struck him, one that never would have occurred to him if he hadn't found the nearly infinitesimal discrepancy: what if he had it backward? What if the problem wasn't the timer, but something else, and the timer was a symptom? Or . . . a message? Some alert? A loss of five or ten minutes was noticeable, but who would think to look if the time was only five or ten one hundred-thousandths of a second off, or less?

The implications were even more dire. The timer issue would have been a simple malfunction, albeit with emotional issues attached. A problem with the field—the kind that scared Reginald . . . and Jerry . . . so much—was almost unimaginable. More so if there was anything intentional going on, as the sudden lack of reports might indicate.

But now Jerry's thoughts were swinging him into a dark place no public records bureau would or could touch. Where being a history professor was no help. The places that spawned both hounds and reverberating fears of the old violent world before the stoners.

The next step was not lightly taken. "Daybreaking" was a crime, and the criminal did not get off easily, though there was no more penal or capital punishment. But the lawbreaker was regarded as being a sick man, and he would not be released until he was healthy. This could be the rest of his life or a good part of it. Moreover, if the criminal was thought to be incurable by modern therapy, he could be stoned. He would then be classified as an abeyant, filed away in a warehouse, and left there until techniques for curing him became available.

Jerry thought of all this. But the mere idea of being a "daybreaker" was the strongest force holding him back.

I just can't do it!

A few minutes later, he said, "But I must! Something horrific is going on, and I want to find out what it is. Somebody is interfering with the freedom of people, the freedom to have babies, and I don't like it. It's not like it was in the old days when unrestricted breeding was ruining the world. Any couple can have two children now and not upset the balance. But somebody is tampering with the stoners and with human beings."

It was obvious that it wasn't just a somebody. It had to be a large organization, one with illegal access to the stoner maintenance stores.

And in tampering with the stoners, they weren't just tampering with only the cylinders, but the world itself, and the society built as a salvation from the brink of destroying civilization and probably humanity itself. Whoever was doing the tampering was a terrorist, and . . .

And why not, then, report the tampering to the authorities? Why take it on himself to find out what was going on?

Because the government already knows, something told him. And they haven't done anything. Or worse, the terrorists themselves were part of the government.

He would have had trouble sleeping if the speeder hadn't made insomnia impossible. But he had some strange dreams—stranger than usual. Alone in dark woods, nothing but his own wits to survive whatever threats waited just out of sight. They didn't feel like his history dreams, but more sinister. A trap. Nothing more than his own fears, he would tell himself upon waking. His fears made real by his own actions, the dreams whispered when he slept.

It took him all the rest of the winter and into the opening of the spring to put his plan into action. In the meantime, an official of the Department of Vital Statistics admitted, during a special show, that an unusually high number of miscarriages had occurred in four North American enclaves. These were the NYC domes, the Central Illinois Cube—which included Chicago—Los Angeles State, and the Toronto Dome. Elsewhere, a non-normal amount of miscarriages had taken place. Perhaps Old Mother Nature was taking a hand in reducing the population, they said, reminding us of why we left the old world in the first place. In any event, there was nothing to worry about. An economy of abundance did not depend on a great population to keep it going. In fact, this change indicated something good for humanity. Then, again, it might just be a temporary fluctuation in fertility.

Nothing was said about stoner timers.

Evidently, the government planned on doing nothing. Or it was keeping quiet about its actions. This only reinforced Jerry's idea about it being terrorism. But it seemed to him that federal men would have questioned him by now. Certainly his inquiries, however discreetly made, would come to the attention of Uncle Sam's sensitive sleuth-hounds. Perhaps they were aware of him but were keeping in the background so well he couldn't detect them. But why would they? Were they just waiting to see what he found out?

Or maybe *how* he found it out, so they could close those doors to anyone else trying to answer the same question.

He went ahead with his preparations nevertheless. His first theft was not of the isolated security cam he had eyed in the Museum, but a maintenance outfit from the Museum that he donned before brazenly walking up to the camera, making motions as if examining it, and then walking away with it plainly in hand. One other thing he remembered from his Grandmother Dora was a piece of advice he had never truly appreciated until now: "You can get away with almost anything when you look like you're supposed to be there and know exactly what you're doing."

That night, a few moments with a laser tracer and silicon printer made a lifelike mask of Jerry, and he set this on an inflatable dummy from the children's section of Macy's Tower. He had stored food in two places. One was in the cabinet of the twelver's stoner room, where he would also quickly store the dummy when the stoners opened on his morning, if he was able to successfully daybreak for so long. The other cache was in the Park near the Museum.

The evening of the "voyage into strange days," as he thought of it—a historical reference he couldn't quite place—he was especially tender to Linda. When the time came for them to enter the cylinders, he gave her a long kiss. She seemed to know something was troubling him because she did not let him go at once.

"What have you been thinking about all evening?" she finally asked him.

"Our future."

"We'll have a baby yet or know the reason why," she said, and kissed him again.

"Very true." He managed to smile at her. He opened the door of the cylinder for her, but she stopped, again. "You haven't done that for me for a long time. Are you sure you're all right?"

The Washingtons had already closed their doors, and their faces were like wax dummies, if wax could be made harder than stone. He said, "I'm fine, sure. We don't have time to talk, dear. I'll see you in the morning."

She went in slowly and turned around. He blew her a kiss and closed the door. The bells were still ringing and the lights along the walls and the top of the ceiling were flashing green, yellow, and red. He had to suppress a feeling of panic. All his life, those bells and lights had triggered a circuit grown by conditioning in his nervous system at an early age. It wasn't easy to ignore the strong urge to get into the cylinder, close the door, shut out the noise, and be suddenly turned into peaceful stone.

First he changed into a lime green kilt and a tunic that would continually alter color to match the color of the dome's artificial sky, both plain enough to avoid notice. He ran out to the cabinet, opened a big door, and took out the sagging dummy. He set the inflator attached to its feet, waited until it was half rigid, and set it inside the cylinder. Once the stoner closed only someone with a frequency-coder could open it before the timer released it.

The dummy continued to swell, and when it was almost full, Jerry shut the door.

Six

Jerry ran out of the apartment and down the great hall, passing only one person, a woman who was running desperately. She looked at him as if surprised to see another in her situation, and then she was past him. He turned and saw her enter an apartment three doors from his.

If she could not have made it to her apartment, she could have used an emergency stoner station. The cylinders stood everywhere throughout the city and in the Park and the Museum. Their timers were set to operate every day, ready for anyone to enter. If someone did open and close the door, and the mass sensors detected a body occupying the interior, then the timers were automatically set to reactivate the field at a minute after midnight on the occupant's following Day, six obdays later.

Jerry passed at least thirty emergency station cylinders on the way to the twelver apartment, and each time he had to resist the desire to get into one and shut its door and so be safe.

But he ran on. Before midnight, he was on the third shelf up of the giant cabinet in the great room containing eighty-four cylinders. He closed the cabinet door and looked through the peephole he had prepared, and five minutes later twelve cylinder doors began to open.

He was both thrilled and scared. He was seeing a new world. It was almost like going to Mars, except he had seen Mars so many times on TV and in books that if Jerry had gone there, he would have experienced little new. But this was breaking through the Hole in Wednesday into the fabulous and forbidden world of Thursday. And every second until he got back to Wednesday was a danger.

His forehead and armpits were wet, but his mouth was dry. He wanted a drink of water, but he refrained from reaching for a cup and the spigot of the twenty-gallon can he had put in the cabinet. He would wait until all twelve had left the room.

They went out quickly, while he kept his eye at the hole. He knew their faces because he had seen them while visiting the twelver, and he tried to memorize as best he could the names on the plates at the bases of the cylinders. He ate his breakfast, but the food insisted on sticking in his throat. He could not stop trembling, and he had a strong feeling of unreality. The walls of the cabinet were drifting away from him.

He told himself to straighten out. He was launched, no return, and he might as well carry it out with style and even with enjoyment, if he could manage it.

The worst part, he realized, was that he could spend an entire week here and still see nothing. There were three women pregnant in Wednesday's twelver, and there surely must be others for the remaining days. But that did not mean any tampering would be done even if his suspicions were correct. The organization causing the miscarriages would have to be very large to get around to every pregnant woman—even larger if they had any control of the stoners at all, no matter what the tech said. Of course, it probably was only tampering with certain women, but what criteria the saboteurs used, he had no idea. However, he knew women of the twelver had miscarried before. It was probable that they would again, unless the organization had been scared off for some reason.

But one that large won't be easily scared off, Jerry thought.

After an hour, he climbed down out of the cabinet. He stretched his muscles and wandered around, looking into the still faces behind the windows. Then he walked out into the hall. He almost walked into a woman who was striding along with her head bent down. She jumped on seeing him, and he murmured, "Pardon me." She did not ask him what he was doing there; twelver life was very open on Wednesdays, and apparently this held true for Thursdays too. Numerous people were always coming in and going out, even at this time of the morning.

He turned before she had disappeared into a bedroom door and said, "Citizen! Please! How is Miranda Coldwell?"

He knew Coldwell was one of Thursday's group, and he was gambling she wouldn't be within hearing distance. Most of the day's twelvers seemed to have gone to their bedrooms.

The woman stopped, surprised, and said, "Why don't you ask her?"

"I got here early," Jerry said. "I'm Dr. Car . . . Clark. I was supposed to see her . . ."

"She went to bed," the woman said. "I wouldn't want to get her up; you know what a headache you get if you don't let the speeder run its course. Or is it important?"

"She reported a miscarriage," Jerry said, then his heart clenched. A real doctor would not have broken confidentiality.

"I didn't know she was pregnant," the woman said. "But there's been a rash of women miscarrying lately. It's been all over the news. Do you know anything about that?"

"I'm . . . researching it," Jerry said. "That's why I'm here. I'm investigating every woman who has reported suffering a miscarriage in the past year. Do you know of any others? Or how many? Or where they live?"

Jerry realized once the words were out of his mouth that he said the wrong thing, and her eyes narrowed. "Can I see your medbadge? We've had a lot of hounds coming around lately, prying into our business, and I just want to make sure you are who you say—"

Jerry froze. Sweat had broken out on his forehead, and under his arms, and was trickling down his ribs. He'd hit the limit of his experience at improvising, and the feeling of unreality was inhibiting his quickness of thought.

The woman strode toward him. "Where's your medbadge, *doc*? Who are you, anyway? Where's your office?"

The first person I run into knows I don't belong here, or is paranoid, Jerry thought. He turned away, sputtering, "The Eighty-Sixth Floor of the Empire State Building. I'll go get my badge."

A man entered the hall at the other end. He was several inches taller than Jerry, broader-shouldered, and younger. He looked sleepy.

The woman called, "Don! Stop that guy! He's an undercover!"

Don halted and spread his arms out. "What do you people want with us?"

Jerry started to turn as if to go back down the hall. The man took a step forward, dropping his arms. Jerry wheeled, ducked, and was past the man as he spun around, bellowing. His fist described a horizontal arc but missed Jerry's back by a few inches. Jerry quit looking behind him and ran down the hall into the enormous living-room-kitchen of the twelver. A couple was sitting on a couch drinking coffee and a man was opening a breakfast package. Jerry went on by them and out the front door and down the hall. He was glad he had always kept in shape, but even so he was panting and his legs began to feel heavy before he had gone two blocks. Then he was out on a main thoroughfare, took a look behind him, saw the big man after him, and ran down another corridor. At its end, he turned the corner and entered the second door he came to. He had no idea what was on the other side, but he had to get out of sight.

The living room was empty. He went down the hall until he came to the stoner room, the door of which was marked, as every stoner door, with a circled cross.

Listening, he waited behind the door. Would they report him? Maybe not, if they thought he was an undercover hound . . . but then, a hound would not have run, either.

After fifteen minutes he walked out of the apartment. The corridors and streets were empty except for two policemen, each on an electric-powered trike, though only the trikes and the NYC badges identified them. Thursday's police wore bright-yellow, onion-shaped helmets with snap-up transparent visors. A silvery cord around each of their necks held a large green whistle, shaped like an owl. Their vests were electric blue with a large silver star on the left breast. Their broad sequined belts supported cream-yellow holsters for shock sticks, gas cans, and first-aid kits. Their shorts were white with black stars over the thighs, and they wore yellow tennis shoes. Their cheeks were rouged, and the eyelids were silver and the eyelashes were green. One wore lipstick not quite the regulation crimson.

Policemen, not hounds, who worked for the NYC domes instead of being directed straight from the World Organic Council. The hounds usually wore silver iopaint that protected their faces from any video recognition programs—though undercovers, which Don thought he was, would avoid using it to hide their true natures.

Either way, the hounds, like the dogs they were named for, seemed to have noses for anything the slightest bit off and would follow the scent trail relentlessly. But policemen he might be able to get past.

Jerry walked boldly toward them, though he had to shove down a panicky desire to duck back into the corridor. They only glanced at him and rode on, while low voices issued from the transceivers between the trike bars. He continued until he got to the giant bustling oval of Folk Square. He went into the Folk Café and sat down at a hexagonal table. He pressed a button on the upright panel before him, and the dome behind it opened. He took out the hot cup of coffee and drank slowly. There were only five people in the vast room. A couple were getting ready to bowl; the others were talking in a low voice, their heads bent together over the table as they watched a tablet between them, their foreheads almost touching.

A TV on the ceiling ran off the canned news. He tilted the chair back until he was almost lying down to watch it, using chair and droning newscaster alike to force calm on himself. But he was fascinated too. The newsman's face was strange, and the names and issues he spouted were unknown. The president of the North American Federal Union Province—Wednesday, Jerry's world, was still the U.S.A. of Western Terra—was attending a conference in New Baghdad. She'd be flying back tomorrow. A week from today, Jerry amended.

The reason for the increase in miscarriages had not, so far, been discovered. The medical authorities doubted a new type of bacteria was responsible. Actually, there was no cause for alarm. The increase was only one percent, and the rumors about the human species being threatened with extinction if the epidemic kept up were groundless.

The report cut to a live service at the Vatican, where Thursday's Pope, Benedict XVIII, was granting a benediction to all the women who suffered the loss of an unborn child.

Thursday's reaction was certainly different than Wednesday's, Jerry thought. They were digging overtly here, and asking for people to come to doctors, medical teachers, or any research professional with their personal information. At the same time, he felt pleased that he had not been wrong. There was something unexplained, perhaps even sinister, happening.

That knowledge alone made him feel somewhat better about breaking the cardinal rule of his society, though it made him feel even less safe than before. If they caught him daybreaking, and connected it with all the questions he'd been asking, and the saboteurs were as powerful as he thought... and only now Jerry realized they must be, to stretch across days... then he would likely be in for a lot worse than therapy or long-term stoning.

But what was done was done, and he focused back on the here and now. The news broadcasting now was old, the wrap up of last Thursday's events. In the evening, he might get a better idea of how this world differed from his.

The size and texture of Wednesday's small paper money was the same as Thursday's, so with a little discretion he could get coffee and such small goods without presenting his Day Identification card. But if he wanted to eat a good meal, he would have to put his card into the slot of the Folk Center restaurant. The detector would recognize at once that his card was a chronological trespasser, and then he would be in trouble. He only now wondered if he had cached enough food to last him through the week. If not he could take a chance, maybe subtly snatch up half a sandwich here and there some restaurant patron left behind. Or walk into an apartment chosen at random, and, if it weren't occupied, take food from the preserver. He might even get away with it in a twelver, since each person would think he was somebody else's guest.

But, at fifteen to midnight, he must be out of the streets and public places. If he was in a private place, he would have to hide there, because anyone seeing him would wonder why he wasn't going to his stoner.

Meanwhile, he had all day, and he meant to use it exploring. Layered shop signs flipped to their Thursday business names, but of the important things there was little to see that he had not seen—except people. Most were sleeping at this time and he should be sleeping, too. He did not want to be dull when others would be lively. He dropped the cup and plate of meat crullers in the waste chute and went outside. The lighting was sourceless except for in the simulated sky of the arched ceiling. Up there, the half-moon was a few degrees above the artificial horizon, and the artificial stars shone in a cloudless night sky.

Jerry stood for a few minutes at the entrance to the corridor from which he had first fled. Perhaps he should return to his own apartment and at least look inside. If no one was in the front room, he could presume the occupants were in bed. He would sneak in and lie down inside the big cabinet in the stoner room. The sleep wouldn't be nearly as refreshing as under a speeder, but it would help.

He decided to take the chance. He walked down the corridor and paused before the door to his apartment. He started to push on the door when he saw something out of the corner of his eye. He looked up and to his left. Coming down the corridor from the nearest street were four men. They walked abreast, two near the walls and the other two spaced out. They were silent and walked with a grim purposefulness. In that first second, he knew they were coming after him; their whole attitude revealed their intentions. They didn't have the sheened faces of hounds but that didn't mean they couldn't be undercovers.

He did not have time to wonder who they were or how they had found out about him. He just had time to be thankful they had not caught him inside the apartment. But running at top speed, he still managed to look behind him when he rounded the corner at the other end. The four were running silently after him.

He wondered why they hadn't sent men down both ends of the corridor and realized they would have if they had had time. So they must have been told about him and been sent off hastily. His feet pounded and his arms pumped, and his brain seemed to be turning over and over. The people are strange but the city is not, he told himself. I know the city as well as whoever's pursuing me.

There was a row of passenger elevators at the end of a corridor off the far end of the square. Jerry ran toward it, past the parking lot with its rows of minicars and trikes, past the Folk Theater, Café, and Recreation Center, the G.I. stores on one side and the big fountain in the center of the square. Several stopped to stare as he ran past them. Just before he got to the corridor, he saw a policeman on a trike coming into the square from a corridor on the left. His whistle shrilled.

The four men were still after Jerry. Behind them was the whistle-blowing officer. He wasn't likely to tackle all four men at once; he would call HQ on his radio. This transmitted to receivers along the wall made up as decorations: gargoyles, animal heads, heads of historical characters or fictional characters, heraldic monsters. HQ was only a block away on the other side of the square. Jerry slowed down as he came to the elevator entrance. Of the twenty, only three had closed doors. He shot into the round cage of one, hit its back wall with his spread-out hands, bounced back, turned, and punched the DOWN-EXPRESS button. The doors slid toward each other. The lead pursuer, tall, brassy-haired, with a long, green-dyed moustache, leaped forward and grabbed the edges of both doors. A slight pressure would keep them apart and so prevent the elevator from moving. Jerry removed the pressure by removing the man. He kicked the man in the belly, and the man, whoofing, fell away.

The doors touched and the cage dropped. It went down so

fast Jerry felt as if he were about to float. But its velocity was suddenly checked near the fourth level; his huntsmen must have pushed the emergency button.

What good it would do his pursuers to stop him here, he did not know. They had not had time to communicate with anybody on the Fourth Floor.

A glance at the indicator panel above the doors showed him that all elevators of this bank were on EMERGENCY STOP.

They would stay in that condition until the Maintenance Department sent men to locate the trouble. Fortunately, the doors to elevators that had properly stopped were not closed for the emergency.

The four men had, in their panicky thoughtlessness, prevented themselves from following in this bank. They could, however, run down the corridor to the next bank, only five hundred feet away. In the meantime, Jerry could do what he liked within the constrictions of circumstances and the city.

The policeman, if he were not being interfered with by the four, would see the elevators were stopped. He would send a message down to the police of this level, and they would come running. And Jerry, also running, would be gone.

There was no one in sight either in the corridor running along the elevator doors as far as he could see or down the corridor directly in front of him. Then a door opened halfway down the latter, and two couples, laughing, walked out. They turned away and walked on. He went slowly down the corridor. As soon as he saw them round the corner, he entered the door they had just shut. He hoped it would lead into a four-person apartment, not a twelver.

It did, but it was not the adults-only place he had expected. Two children were sleeping with speeder electrodes on their heads in one room. Apparently, the parents had been entertaining another couple, perhaps the one they had lived with before becoming parents. They must be heading toward the Folk Center for a coffee klatch or a bowling match.

Jerry did not go past the doorway of the children's room. His body's mass would set off an alarm at Police HQ and activate a TV connected to HQ. And an anesthetic gas might be released. No matter how causal adults were with their quarters or possessions, they took care to guard the children.

He went down the hall, looked into the stoner room, and decided he'd stay there for a while. He opened the cabinet door, moved around much junk—mostly toys—onto another shelf, and crawled in.

SEVEN

It took him a long time to get to sleep, and it seemed he was awakened by his wristwatch almost at once.

His watch said it was half-past twelve, and his mouth said it was long-past a drink of water. He got down off the shelf and staggered past the tall silent cylinders and opened the door to the hall. He could hear nothing. The children, who seemed to be about eight and ten, were probably in school, and the parents were either sleeping, at work, or still out having fun. He drank two cups of water, snatched a package labeled LUNCH D-2 from the preserver, and walked out of the apartment. The corridor was crowded, and the elevators were jammed. He saw no police or obvious hounds there. He traveled down to the first floor, which was mainly a tremendous plaza, and sat down on a stone bench.

While he ate his pilfered lunch, some sort of grainy dry beef as if punishing him for the theft with tastelessness, two cops strolled by. They did not seem to be looking for anyone in particular. He waited until they were gone before he went outside. He took a bike from the lot and sped toward the Brooklyn branch of the Museum. He'd spend the daylight hours there. At night, he'd return to Manhattan. He would find a place in some stoner room and sleep there.

Then he could return to the original twelver, since the woman and man had run him out would be in their cylinders. But now he had given up the idea of witnessing any crimes in the stoners.

He would be too busy surviving and keeping his own criminal career from being nipped to watch out for other criminals. All he wanted to do was to get back to the security of Wednesday, maybe forget he had ever broken days . . . though he doubt he could forget it, and he certainly could never forget what he had learned. Either way, to make it back to Wednesday he would use the storage cabinet as his hiding place.

After parking the bike, he went to the Museum, the one place in Manhattan beside his apartment building he knew better than anywhere. He went straight to the history exhibits and wandered around for a while, stopping suddenly, looking behind him, not too obviously, he hoped, going around corners, and waiting. But nobody seemed to be shadowing him. This, he knew, meant nothing. He was too inexperienced to detect an expert shadower.

He drank a fizz and felt better. The strain was dehydrating him.

He watched the burning of a witch at the Salem Village. The woman screamed as the flames ate the wood beneath her and tested the air just below the hem of her skirt. She lunged, and strove to break the ropes binding her; her face was bloodless, her eyes wild with knowledge of sure death. Then the screams were cut off as smoke made her choke and cough. Suddenly the flames gripped her skirt and ran up it. She tried to scream again, but the dense smoke filled her throat, and she slumped, her head fallen forward. The fire burned her clothes and turned her skin black, and the stench of burning flesh and hair filled the square. But she was dead before she felt the fire; the smoke had overcome her.

Jerry did not wait for the men to come and take away the charred body to the crossroads for burial. A few years ago, he had seen some of the circuits and wires when the fire had burned away too much of the pseudo-protein skin and muscles. The techs had been censured on some TV shows, but Jerry had been glad it had happened. It reminded him that the woman was not a real witch burning but, after all, only an historical and educational exhibit.

He had seen burnings in his dreams, and those were bad enough.

He left, a little shaken in spite of himself, and went into the Ant Hill, an inverted cone at least three hundred feet in height that replicated an ant hill in giant size, where the ants were as long as Jerry was tall. The tops of the ants' heads were level with his waist as they rushed by him, their antennae quivering and occasionally touching him. The huge black, many-faceted eyes stared at him, unsettling him even though—like the woman in Salem—they were robots. As long as he followed the wavy white line on the dirt floor, he was safe. The ants were programmed to veer away from it, and even if he did step off the path, they would freeze. But their doing so would send a signal to the techs, and he would be led away and forbidden to visit the Museum again for a month. And his picture and name would be shown on TV.

The usual result of a Museum censure was nothing more than shame. If it happened to him now, though, he would be exposed as a daybreaker. But he had no intention of straying from the assigned path. He would follow the line through the sloping tunnels of the ant hill, deeper and deeper, until he came to the great chamber where the queen laid her eggs. After watching her at her work, the storage of eggs by the workers, the hatching, and then the raid on the colony by another colony, he would go back to the surface. Meanwhile, any shadows would have a hard time staying unobserved. If the shadow waited outside to catch him, he would have to be lucky or have some accomplices. There were a number of side entrances. These would not exist, of course, in an exact replica of an ant hill, but were for the convenience of the visitor.

He left the six people with whom he had been watching the queen, and he went up a smaller tunnel. He knew the hill, having visited it at least fifty times. There was a final corner to round just before coming to the exit; beyond that there were no ants in the tunnel itself. He looked back as he reached the corner, and he saw a man duck behind the corner at the far end.

He was shaken. They had found him after all, and this time he knew it wasn't just Don and his paranoid friend; he was being tracked across days. And if they had planned better this time, they would be covering all the exits.

He stooped over and picked up an ant which was rebuilding the side of the tunnel. It had been repeating this task ever since the first day he entered here when he was six years old. It froze, the giant plastic simulated sand grain in its mandibles. The signal that the ant was malfunctioning or had been interfered with would be bringing the techs down from the maintenance department. They would enter this tunnel from the outside, and when they did, Jerry would point out his shadower as having caused the trouble. While the techs interviewed him, or tried to catch him, since the man would probably run away, Jerry could walk out.

He could not afford to be leisurely, of course, because the police might also come. And even if they were not looking for Jerry Carson, daybreaker, in particular, they would want to give his Day ID card a scopecheck as a matter of routine.

He set the ant down on its back and walked out of the tunnel. He was ready to jump back if anybody tried to detain him, but the only man nearby was walking slowly away. Perhaps the three techs striding toward them with tools hanging from their belts had scared his shadow off. About a dozen people were following the techs, and one was asking them if anything was wrong.

Jerry angled away from the man who had been near the exit. He walked up a grassy slope to the steps which led up to the walkway about twenty feet above. A man appeared by its top and leaned on the railing while he blew violet smoke from a cig-stick. He was a large man and looked as if he would enjoy a fight. He was not one of the four Jerry had seen yesterday, the objective yesterday.

Jerry turned away, snapping his fingers as if he had suddenly remembered something, and walked toward the Ant Hill. He cut across its western edge, following the white line, and went on by the main entrance. Two men came out of it and their expressions made it evident they were after him. Jerry stepped up his pace, looking back behind him once. The big rough man had come down the steps and was only forty paces or so behind him. The two men would reach Jerry's white line about ten paces behind him. If they took a short-cut, they could intercept him, but they would be freezing the ants in their path. And they were under the eyes of a hundred people on the walkway above.

A Hole in Wednesday

Again, Jerry stepped up his pace. When he was past the area of the white lines, he ran. Of the two stairways on this side, two were moving. He passed the one going downward, which was filled with visitors. He went up a stationary flight. Ten people were on it and several shouted, "This is a one-way!"

Jerry ignored them and forced a path through them. At the top of the stairway, he looked behind him. Three men were running toward the stepway moving upward. The walkway where Jerry stood was crowded, but if any of the people there were after him, they were successfully concealing their intention.

Jerry strode across the walkway and stepped off it onto the stationary part next to the railing. Most of the little valley below was filled with trees, but about twenty yards away was a little house. It had two chimneys shaped like rabbit ears and a roof thatched with fur. Near it, under some trees, was a long table set with silverware, dishes of bread, butter and crumpets, cups, saucers, a cream pitcher, a sugar bowl, and a kettle. Two strange figures sat at the table, one squat man in a tall hat, the other a little blonde girl.

A fence on top of which was a thick round railing enclosed this side of the valley. Beyond the woods was a hill, and on the other side, he knew, was a larger valley at the bottom of which was a small river, then further still a number of hills. Gunshots and clouds of white gunpowder were rising from the other side of the hill. He could see the clouds, but the explosions, and the screams of the wounded men and horses, the warwhoops, were cut off. A transparent wall sliced off one world from another, just as the roof, though invisible except when it was raining or snowing outside, separated the real sky from the false. Electronic screens were mounted along the railing so the spectators could bring the scene closer if they wished. Audio was automatically available; the voices of the two at the table below were loud. The spectators could also hear the voice of the little girl in the woods, visible through the branches of the trees near the ear-chimneyed house. She was talking to a monstrously large domestic cat crouching on a branch above her.

Jerry took the course to the right and walked as closely to the railing as he could. The little girl's voice came from the speakers as he passed them.

"Suppose it should be raving mad after all! I almost wish I'd . . ."

He didn't hear the rest. He saw a man coming up from the steps from the Ant Hill. His face belonged to one of the four who had chased him this morning.

He turned, and saw the three coming up from the steps behind him.

He could try to get by the man ahead and through the three behind. Then he could drop off one side thirty feet into the ant hill grounds or twenty feet into the nearest exhibit.

He took the shortest drop, let himself over, hung by his hands, and let go. He hit a soft lawn, rolled, was up, and running toward the woods. People shouted after him, but they would only be bystanders. The men after him wouldn't be attracting attention by shouting.

When he was into the woods far enough, feeling somewhat better for the cover, he dropped to the ground behind a tree. He could see one man falling on almost the same spot he had. If there were others, they weren't visible, but he supposed there would be.

He half-rose, and, crouching, ran through the woods. Seeing a trench, he got down and crawled into it. He wished it could be a rabbit-hole down which he could drop to the center of the earth and away from this mess. But he remembered the last one who had gone down a rabbit hole had gotten into a mess by doing so. This was not a rabbit hole, however. It was only a concrete-lined ditch, dug for power wires and service men. The trench could not be seen from the walkway above, and it was this that led Jerry to use it. If it went far enough, he might be able to pop out far from his hunters and maybe get away after all.

But the trench ended in the area under the long table. Pipe-enclosed wires led up a plastic shaft and entered the table itself and into several devices mounted on the underside of the table. At the bottom of the shaft were electrician's tools in a plastic box. A knife, used for cutting and scraping insulation, was sharp on the curved edge but too blunt for sticking through flesh. Jerry picked it up, anyway, and put it in the back pocket of his kilt.

He did not know whether to crawl out and make a run for it or wait and hope the hunters would overlook him and be forced to move on. He had noticed the narrow trench only because he had almost fallen into it. If the visitors saw the hunters and called the police, and the hunters fled, he might be able to hide in the trench until dark. On the other hand, the police might make a thorough search of the area.

Unable to make up his mind, he crouched by the shaft. Above him were furry crooked legs with big bunny feet. Suddenly, two adult male voices cried out, "No room! No room!"

A little girl's voice said, indignantly, "There's *plenty* of room!"

The voice was followed by the withdrawal of the chair legs and the appearance of little black shoes with yellow stockings and the bottoms of several petticoats and a red skirt and a short beige apron.

"Have some wine," a male voice said.

There was a pause, and the girl said, "I don't see any wine."

The same voice said, "There isn't any."

The little girl said, angrily, "Then it wasn't very civil of you to offer it!"

"It wasn't very civil of you to sit down without being invited," the voice said.

Another male voice, after a few seconds of silence, said, "Your hair wants cutting."

Jerry didn't hear the answer, because he saw, at the end of the ditch, two big feet in sandals. He cowered down behind the shaft and tried to make himself thinner than the shaft. The table and the tablecloth made it dark where he was. If the hunter just stooped down and looked along the trench, he might not see his quarry. But Jerry couldn't stay behind the shaft too long. He had to know if the man was coming after him before the man got too close.

A second male voice above said, "Two days wrong!" A sigh followed. "I told you butter wouldn't suit the works!"

The original male voice said, meekly, "It was the *best* butter."

Jerry scrooched down even further, though it was more important not to move than to reduce the bulk. Then he listened for sounds of the man coming down into the trench, but the conversation above was quite loud. If the hunter was bold enough, he could walk out of the woods and approach the trench from the other end and surprise him. Jerry stiffened at the thought, trying to remember those long-ago lessons his father and other rangers taught him during his time with the Nature Rehabilitation Corps. Lessons in tracking and not being tracked.

The first lesson was situational awareness, always being present and constantly knowing what was around you, along with potential dangers. A head could suddenly stick out over the edge of the trench, brushing aside the tablecloth, for one thing. And what would he do then?

"Have you guessed the riddle yet?" the first male voice said.

The little girl's voice said, "No, I give it up. What is the answer?"

"I haven't the slightest idea."

"Nor I," the second male voice said.

Nor I, Jerry thought. But there certainly is a riddle. I thought for a while maybe I was being paranoiac, seeing evil plots where none existed. But these men are not the police, and so . . .

He quivered, because he thought he'd heard something behind and above him. Unable to resist looking, but still careful to be silent, he turned to his right and looked past the shaft. The feet at the end of the trench were gone, and the bottom of the trench was empty.

He looked up but still could see, under the tablecloth, only three pairs of feet.

The second speaker was whispering, "I only wish it was."

Jerry stood up and looked out past the cloth. There were feet, sandaled feet, and bare legs with blond hair moving along toward the table. The man had come out of the woods and was circling to get at the table from the other end. And there were other feet now at the end of the trench.

A Hole in Wednesday

Jerry did not waste any time. He went up the trench on the other side, pulling himself up and then sliding out on the grass and under the tablecloth edge just as the Mad Hatter started to sing,

"Twinkle, twinkle, little bat!"

"How I wonder what you're at!"

It was unfortunate, because of the delay and because it gave the hunters some warning, that Jerry knocked the Hatter over. The android tipped over with a thud on its back, its tall hat fallen to one side. It said, "You know the song, perhaps?"

The sound from the crowd along the walkway had been loud before, but now men roared and women shrieked as Jerry slid out from under the table like a monstrous Dormouse. The roar and shrieks continued as he raced toward the hill, and then the shrills of police whistles cut through the crowd's noises.

By the time Jerry got to the top of the hill, the mob cry was a tremendous roar. Five men were running after him. No, eight, because three policemen were coming down a service stepway which had been let down. Jerry turned and then stopped, just in time to keep from ramming nose-on into the wall. He had seen it only because a butterfly had landed on it a few feet above him.

He turned and ran along it, tracing it with his right-hand fingers, and then he saw a white bar set horizontally in the grass. He stopped before it, pushed on the wall, and the door swung on its transparent hinges.

He looked back, saw the first man was halfway up the hill and began running. The river at the bottom of the hill was a quarter-mile away. There were copses of woods beyond it, then the hill where the battle was raging, a battle Jerry had watched many times and knew every second of, every charge, every thrown lance. There were hundreds of tepees on this side of the river with some bodies lying on the ground before them. More bodies lay in the ford by the village. Beyond, on the hill, all was motion, confusion, and uproar. The crack of rifles, the shrilling of eagle bone whistles, screaming of the wounded men and horses, the frenzied plunging gallop of wounded horses bolting the battle, the white skins of dead soldiers whose clothing had been removed by the looters, the sparkle of the sun on a saber swinging down on a brown shoulder, all this came to Jerry as if carried down by the centuries-old winds. It seemed too unreal at this distance. But when he got closer, it would seem real enough. And maybe real enough to his pursuers to unnerve them a little, and make them hesitate just enough . . .

By the time he reached the shallow river, Jerry was breathing as if all the air had been used up by the battle on the hill. He waded through the river but stopped before he was out and splashed water on his face, and drank, not knowing when he might get more. It was cool enough to give him new strength, and, if he was slowing down, so were his hunters. The police had not yet come over the top of the hill. But they did not necessarily have to be in a hurry. They would be transmitting a call for help, and police would be moving in from the other way to trap them. He cursed the hunters for having brought them into the situation.

Having wasted breath on that, he resumed wading. Back on land he walked directly toward the heart of the fight. This was raging by now on the highest part of the hill. In the center of the melee was a tall golden-haired man in buckskin with a pistol in one hand and a saber in the other. He was the only one of the 7th Cavalry still standing, though not the only one still fighting. A few badly wounded were shooting point-blank at the leather-wearing warriors who were trying to club, tomahawk, spear, or knife them. A few others were yet alive but too weak to resist being scalped. It would all be over within a few minutes. Even the white man whirling and shooting and sabering so desperately could not avoid the fatal bullet or blade very long. And, as if the soldiers were not outnumbered enough, up the hill, at about fifty yards opposite Jerry, a band of Sioux were urging their horses to run up the hill.

This reenactment was a very dramatic one but it had been criticized, some years ago, for being faithful only to myth. In reality, Custer had not been the last one to go down. He was wounded while crossing a ford and probably shot himself sometime later, leaving the survivors to fight on. Nor was his hair long; he had had it cut before the battle of Little Big Horn.

But wish was stronger than history, and Custer's Last Stand was as it had been presented in dime novels and movies in the old days. Now almost everybody admitted it was best to show Custer as the last and greatest of the heroes who fell that day. Just as it was best, and mythically appropriate, to show Sitting Bull as the aboriginal who would ride up and drive his lance through Custer's valiant heart. Since the real Sitting Bull had been murdered by whites on his reservation, let him have his posthumous moment of glory.

However, the moment had not yet arrived, and Jerry was hoping to use it when it did. So, instead of running on, he waited. He stood at the edge of the raging hell and regained his wind while the men below lost theirs coming up the hill after him. He wondered why they were still on his trail. They must know the police were following and other police would be closing in. They should be fleeing, too.

This discrepancy made him even more nervous. If they were coming so boldly, they must have something to rely upon—either hounds, or some shadow group with official-looking documents or cards which would fool the police long enough to get him away and out of their sight.

He looked at the walkway and saw no police. If they did not get there in time to block the stepways, he might get away yet. And then it occurred to him that he had no means of getting to the walkway unless a stepway was let down. He could not escape until the police came, and then he would have to dodge them and get up the stepway. But with a crowd there, and the strong possibility of police being left to guard the stepways, he did not have a chance.

Then he saw a stepway unfolding from the cavity in the upper part of the wall. It came down and pressed firmly on the earth. Two men came down it. Either they were plain clothes policemen, undercover hounds, or belonged to the organization that had been chasing him. In either event, if the stepway was left unguarded, he had a chance.

By then the first of the pursuers was a few yards away. He was a thin man, which probably accounted for his getting up the hill faster than the others, who were heavily muscled. The skinny one was outweighed by Jerry, but he did not seem impressed by this. He pulled a small gray tube from a pocket and, holding it in his palm, with the sharp end pointing at Jerry, approached. His knees were bent, and he was leaning forward with the free hand held to one side like a fencer's.

Jerry had been taking courses all his life in judo, karate, jukado, Greco-Roman wrestling, and sabot fighting. But the skinny man must have been doing the same, and he had a weapon which might be fatal, though Jerry doubted it. But it was undoubtedly designed, at the very least, to make an opponent unconscious. Also, that the man was not waiting for the others indicated much confidence in himself.

Jerry turned and ran, looking back over his shoulder, saw the man entering the fray after him, and then Jerry tripped over an Indian scalping a trooper. He went headlong into the back of the legs of another Indian who was aiming an arrow at Custer. The Indian fell forward just as the arrow was released, causing the arrow to plunge into Custer instead of missing him, as it had done in the many thousands of previous performances.

The Indian tried to go through its programmed actions while lying face down, and this resulted in some strange contortions.

Jerry was up and starting to run again, then he stopped and picked up an arrow and turned. The skinny man tried to stop, could not, and ducked. The arrow hit him in the top of the head and drove into this head, though not deeply, being stopped by the skull. Jerry had the advantage then, and he took it by kicking the man in the jaw as, on his knees and screaming, he clutched at the arrow.

Jerry was horrified at what he had done. He had never seen so much blood before nor so much pain. All the gory movies and books and the battles of the Museum had not prepared him for this. It was not that the man's blood looked any different from what spurted out from the androids around him. But he *knew* this was real blood, and the man's pain was real.

A Hole in Wednesday

An Indian whooped in his ear and swung a tomahawk. Its sharp edge cut at Jerry, but only because Jerry happened to be blocking its way. The tomahawk was intended for the trooper who had struggled up for one last resistance. The trooper pointed the gun, and Jerry had to duck to avoid being burned by the powder flash. He stepped back and fell again, and the second of the pursuers leaping over the still jerking Indian and the now-unconscious skinny man, was only an inch from the muzzle of the gun when it exploded. There were no bullets in the pistol, of course, but the flame burned the man's ribs. He screamed and danced away, then fell as a lance went through his thigh instead of into the throat of a soldier.

Jerry scrambled up and ran toward Custer, who had just half-severed an Indian's arm with his saber. The other three hunters came in after Jerry. And at that moment, Sitting Bull on his pony charged at Custer. The pony leaped over bodies and swerved past two Indians struggling with an officer, then its left shoulder struck the third pursuer. He fell down and Jerry bent down to run past Custer. His foot slipped in a pool of fake blood and he went down. The hoof of the pony struck him somewhere in the midriff, and he blacked out.

Eight

When he awoke, the yelling, screaming, and explosions were gone as if the battle of the Little Big Horn were actually six hundred years in the past. He was on a soft bed, not grass, and he was looking upward at a light green ceiling, not a blue pseudo-Montana sky.

He got to his elbow, wincing as he felt pain in his belly. He was bandaged around the middle; on his left wrist was a disc about a quarter inch thick and one and a quarter inches in diameter. A metal band, solid and inflexible, secured the disc to his wrist.

The room was narrow; the light coming only from a gentle glow within the yellow walls. The room was windowless and had one door. A football-shaped camera was on a rack in the upper corner of a wall and the ceiling near the door. He lay back down with a sigh and cursed the pain in his belly and his weakness. A moment later, the door opened, and two men entered. He did not recognize them.

The taller was about fifty; the shorter, about thirty. Both wore sandals and kilts and were painted conventionally. But the older man had an axe-like face and blue eyes like the flicker of swiftly wielded axes.

"I'm Northpath Marks," he said. "This is my secretary, Buster Donnelly."

Jerry did not say anything. That they were telling him their names meant they thought he would never be in a position to use them against them. He felt cold but not cold enough to freeze out the pain in his belly.

"You gave us quite a chase," Marks said. "And if Sitting Bull's horse hadn't stepped on you, you might have gotten away. You were very clever to use the battle for your own advantage. One should always use their environment to their own advantage whenever possible."

"Thanks," Jerry said. "But here I am, nevertheless. So who are you and what do you do and what's going to happen to me?"

His voice was steady, but he was afraid it was going to crack. He was scared.

Marks pulled a cig-stick out of the biometric pouch hanging from his belt. Donnelly produced a lighter and flicked the wire for him.

"First, you can tell me how you got me away from the cops," Jerry said. "Unless you are the cops?"

"We're members of the Psychic Rehabilitation Department," Marks said. "I am the Director for the NYC Domes. So we had no trouble getting rid of the police. They even helped us carry you to the ambulance. Of course, we would have liked it better if we could have taken you without the knowledge of the police force. But we carried it off, and the police think you are a citizen who escaped our hospital. We gave them the name of a prisoner who exists, of course. They didn't check your ID; they took our word without any need to remind them that their compliance is mandatory. We then needed to get you out of the hospital without nonmembers knowing about it."

Jerry closed his eyes for a moment. Opening them, feeling the strange boldness of someone who knows he cannot escape anyway, he said, "You belong to an organization of which some members actually hold positions in the PRD. The organization cuts across the days; it has to do so. Unless you're illegally in Thursday, too."

"It cuts across," Marks said. "By the way, though, today is Friday."

A Hole in Wednesday

Of course it was Friday. Jerry had run so much he'd forgotten he slept one night—the once-natural sleep of no stoners and no speeders. "Just where are we?"

"In a safe place," Marks said. "For us, that is."

"But not for me?" Jerry said quickly.

"That depends."

"On what?"

"On your decision. But, first, you have to know what's going on, don't you?"

He handed Donnelly the cig-stick, and the younger man simply stuck it into a vacuum tray that stoned the stick, and even the smoke in mid-curl.

"Three subgenerations ago the world was on the verge of destroying itself in a dozen different ways. Overpopulation, destruction of resources, wrecking the climate, nuclear exchanges. Any one of which we could have survived, but the combination more than likely would have done us in. As you know, since you are a history professor."

Jerry only nodded, not wondering how Marks would have known his profession. There could have been a dozen different ways for that, too.

Marks continued, "Left on such a course, perhaps we would have obliterated ourselves. But instead, with overpopulation and giving the planet breathing room to heal from our depredations as an excuse, the World Organic Council was formed by Sin Tzu the Compassionate, and it built our . . . Dayworld. And while we survive across the face of this planet, the extreme we had wrought by the late twenty-first century swung the pendulum to the other extreme of the New Era. Whatever we could have become at our best, whatever we might have evolved into, has been stopped. Stultified."

"Evolved into? What do you mean?"

The look Marks gave Jerry was strangely determined, as if he could make Jerry understand with sheer will instead of words.

"Before our Dayworld existed, those in power in every government had only one ultimate goal: to control the masses.

One side would complain that their opponents wanted cradle-to-grave control of the people through government; the other side would charge *their* opponents with wanting cradle-to-grave control through religion. Both were right, of course. Others used outright fear. Others used dangling carrots, the promise of phantom wealth, if you just work hard enough and do this thing and this-and-such, you too will become wealthy and powerful, like us. A carrot almost always out of reach.

"Whatever the means of control, the control was always there. And Dayworld did not eliminate authoritarian control or the controllers. It merely moved them into new sides of the chessboard. But it was still the same chessboard, with the entire world as their board. So then what is there to do? You either find a way to stop playing, or you find a way off the board. Or better yet, both at the same time."

Jerry still had little idea where Marks was going with this, but he did detect the increasing note of resolve in Marks' voice. One might say a fanatical resolve, of the sort he had picked up in so many speeches from history. Not that he thought Marks was another Hitler. But then again, Adolf Hitler had started out his political career as a failed young artist who never rose above the rank of corporal during World War One. Marks already had the ability to daybreak with impunity, which meant he was well ahead of Adolf Hitler by the time Hitler's first attempt to take over the German government, his Beerhall Putsch, got him thrown in prison.

Now Marks donned an almost fatherly smile, though nothing like what Jerry remembered from his own father. "We—my companions and I—do both, Jerry. The organization we have built is called Galapagos."

"Like the islands?"

"Exactly like the islands. A place where evolution developed on its own through isolation and a challenging, unforgiving environment, likewise forcing the intellect to develop to ensure continued survival. This is what we are doing. Even when in the middle of society we isolate ourselves, though sometimes we do so literally beyond the domes and cubes, and we evolve. We learn.

A Hole in Wednesday

We strengthen our bodies. We sharpen our minds. And we are laying large and far-reaching plans.

"Humanity before the New Era was the culmination of four billion years of ferociously competitive evolution, particularly of the intellect. Our so-called society of abundance has forced our development to a halt. So those of us in Galapagos will make ourselves better while all around us the world is stultified, including those in power who have caused this to be. When the time comes, we will be in control. No one will be able to challenge us, because we will have trained ourselves to be far beyond and above them."

Evolution. *Forced* evolution. Were these, then, the people who were killing embryos? The fact that Jerry was here now seemed too much of a coincidence to be one. But why were they doing it? And how did they choose when to trigger miscarriages, and in who? Yet Jerry's instincts warned him now was not the time to ask those questions.

After a moment, Jerry realized Marks had paused, waiting with an air of finality.

"You wouldn't be telling me all this unless you hoped I'd join you," Jerry said. "You couldn't let me return to my Day where I'd be sure to tell the authorities. The only way I'll get out of here alive is to join Galapagos, right?"

"This is the sum of your situation," Marks said. "Of course, you could tell us you were willing to join and then could turn us in after we'd released you. But we have ways of determining whether or not you're sincere. You know them."

"Narcohypnosis and Truth Mist." Techniques developed by the hounds. "I know I couldn't fool you. I hesitate to say this, but I must. Wouldn't it be easier for you just to kill me? Stone me, anyway, and lose me in some warehouse?"

"Easier, yes," Marks said. "But we believe unnecessary violence or killing is wasteful, when the material is promising. We are always seeking to recruit those with promise. You have proved to us that you are intelligent and courageous. Otherwise, you never would have thought of someone tampering with the timers and the women and then broken the day to find out who was doing it."

"I did everything wrong."

"Due to lack of experience, mainly. Plus the criminality of what you were doing may have inhibited your full intelligence, or from following your instincts."

"What will you do if I say no to your offer? Would that lead to my . . . necessary killing?"

"As you said, we will stone you and bury you. You'll be found some day, maybe a thousand years from now. You'll be brought back to life then, but we hope to have our objectives attained long before then."

Jerry closed his eyes again. Linda would grieve for him, and there'd be a big hullabaloo about his mysterious disappearance. Then Linda would get over her tragedy and fall in love with someone else. And she'd get older and eventually die. When he was destoned—if he ever was—he'd find her dead and stoned and stood up inside a cemetery vault with an identification plate on the pedestal. If some curious visitor pressed the button on the pedestal, he would hear the story of her life and see recordings of her from babyhood on. The most important events of her life would be shown briefly on the nameplate, and then the biomovie would end. If she had children, they could review their life with their mother and the grandchildren could see grandma when she was as young as they. If they cared about her.

It was possible Linda might have herself stoned while still young and wait for him. But this was asking too much of anyone. It would be more likely that she would use up her youth and middle age and then be stoned. Many did this, hoping the rejuvenation techniques would someday be available to restore them to youth.

He stopped thinking about her except as someone to get back to in the present.

"How long have I got to make up my mind?" he said.

"Until Tuesday night. You'll be sedated so you can sleep well tonight. Tomorrow, you'll be operated on before you wake. The broken blood vessels in your belly will be reconstituted, and you'll be as good as new there, better, in fact. Saturday, Sunday, and

A Hole in Wednesday

Monday you can think on this. Tuesday, you can tell us what you've decided. If you say yes, you go back into your case and wake up Wednesday with nobody the wiser. Except you and us, of course."

"And Linda and I can have a baby then?"

Marks gave Jerry a questioning look. But instead of answering, he gestured to Donnelly. The younger man approached Jerry with the gray tube with the narrow end. He held it close to Jerry's bare arm, and said, "This won't hurt at all."

"Wait!" Jerry said, but too late. The cold tip touched his skin, and he was gone.

NINE

Saturday, if it was Saturday, he awoke with all pain in his belly gone. The bandages were gone too. He ate well and after breakfast was taken out of the room by the women who had brought in the breakfast package. They wore nurses' insignia, a big golden H, on metal neck chains and white bikinis. One followed him; the other, carrying a gun, led him down a corridor of pale green walls and yellow doors, all shut. They passed several men with caduceuses hanging from chains around their necks and wearing white kilts and sandals. They came to an oval room which looked like the waiting room of a hospital. But the only exit led to another hall like the one they had just left.

He was shown to a couch and asked to sit down. The nurse with the gun sat behind him. After a few minutes, Marks and three men came in.

Jerry was not surprised to see Marks. By now it was obvious these people would pass back and forth through the walls of days as they pleased. They had no shame or social conscience whatsoever. They were filthy creatures.

He reminded himself that he had broken days, too. It was true he had done it to go after criminals, but he had no right to do it. He should have gone to the police. No, he could not have done that because they would have laughed at him, and the few who knew he was right—including Galapagos, Jerry was sure—

would be the very people he did not want to know he suspected anything. The organization would likely have their people among the police.

The difference between them and him, though, was that he had become a criminal for the good of humanity. Whereas they . . .

He stopped. They said they were devoted to the good of humanity, also.

They were undoubtedly sincere. They believe in their blueprint of the future. What they were doing was the best thing for mankind.

Marks introduced his companions, Mbala and Wang, along with reintroducing Buster Donnelly.

"My guests are from Wednesday," Marks said. "Wang heads the PRD in Los Angeles State, and Mbala heads the PRD in CIC." Jerry assumed at first Marks meant in the Psychic Rehabilitation Department, then wondered if that was the case or not. For all Jerry knew, either could be an undercover hound taking orders from Marks—or whatever he was called on Saturday—as much as the World Organic Council.

Three such important figures in one place? Surely they couldn't all be here for his sake. Maybe they were evaluating all of the prospects, the potential Galapagos recruits. But it was also clear the two newcomers deferred to Marks, even though officially, according to what Jerry knew of the Organic bureaucratic system, they were professional equals. Maybe something important had happened—something that would allow Marks to start implementing his plans.

"You're here to argue your case," Jerry said. "And tell me more about Galapagos?"

"Of course," Marks said. "We would not want you to ever come to believe you joined us out of ignorance. And I suspect"—by suspect, Jerry was sure, Marks meant in his capacity as someone whose profession was reading people—"that showing the aptitudes and skills you have demonstrated thus far, you at least have an innate leaning toward our goals of independence and human development, whether or not you agree with our means."

A Hole in Wednesday

"Means such as hunting me down? If you wanted me to join you, why not just approach me?"

"Where, Jerry? Your apartment? A Museum? Over a set of tennis, perhaps? Ask you outright to daybreak?" Then Marks smiled, one Jerry thought was his first genuine smile. "And of course, what a man does when he knows or suspects he is being hunted by a superior force is always telling. You gave us a great deal of trouble, but we learned much, and you proved yourself resourceful, as I said. So here we are."

"Daybreaking," Jerry said. "Doesn't it bother you? I don't mean for moral reasons. Physical. You're getting older faster than other people."

Wang laughed and said, "It doesn't bother us. You'll find out why."

They were served coffee, fruit salad, and cake, and then the brainwashing began. It was gentle enough, reasonable-sounding, and none of the five argued. They appealed to Jerry's deep knowledge of history; they appealed to his lesser but still broad knowledge of pre-2084 environmental conditions and what he had learned while serving with the Nature Rehabilitation Corps in Illinois. They reminded him of the lessons his ranger father taught him. What they did not do was go into any more substantive detail about Galapagos.

"You keep telling me the New Era has stopped human evolution and stunted our intellectual development," Jerry broke in at one point, "but then you continually remind me that our unchecked evolution nearly destroyed us and the planet. What makes you think we'll do any better this time?"

"No change in the world has ever come from nowhere," Marks said. "Take government regulation. Many people complained about it in the twentieth and twenty-first centuries, and yet those regulations, the seeds of our world today, were planted by people who had complained about the conditions of unregulated life. Food that was harmful. Drugs that were harmful or ineffective. Mines and bridges collapsing. Widespread financial collapses and panics every generation. Poisoned air, poisoned water supplies. It was easy to complain about regulations because the benefits were invisible, but those who complained would yell the loudest once they suffered from having those benefits taken away."

"But we have those invisible benefits, as you call them, now," Jerry argued. "We have opportunities to do the jobs we please. To pursue creative endeavors. To learn. Crime is almost nonexistent . . ."

"So far as you know," Donnelly chimed in, his tone quiet but more full of purpose than his companions. The perpetual true believer. "It exists, but much of it is invisible, because it is built into the system."

"Some regulation is helpful and necessary," Mbala said in a voice so rich as to almost be operatic. "As I have seen often in the CIC, helping those whose psychic and mental lives have gone out of attunement. But as the old unregulated world went too far, now ours has gone far beyond the pale as well. It is that the harm is now invisible, and so more insidious."

Realization hit Jerry. "You weren't just tampering with the stoners. You were the ones who were altering the climate control in the dome, and slowing down the network connections."

"Very good," Marks said.

"But why bother? Besides the stoners, those were small things."

"Small things can mean great tests to those who have never been challenged. Alter the temperature only five degrees, add only a few seconds to someone's Scout connecting with the city network, and yet the bureaus responsible for maintaining those amenities were flooded with complaints."

Mbala continued, "We were testing to see how much discomfort people would put up with, and discovered their thresholds to be very low."

"Yours is somewhat higher, Mr. Carson," Wang said. "We found no record of you making any such complaints. One who can learn in this day and age to deal with small discomforts may have the capability to raise their resourcefulness to much higher levels."

"You spoke of opportunities, Jerry," Marks pressed. "What opportunities? You must have noted how the Museum has no exhibits that postdate the creation of the Dayworld. Because there has been no true achievement. Art, books, music, dance... all soulless. No passion. No inventiveness. Exterior appearances have taken precedence over all. Standing out not with what you do but how you look."

"No war," Jerry interjected. "No nuclear attacks. No pandemics. No starvation."

"What does it profit a man to gain the world if he loses his soul?"

That startled Jerry. "Are you a religious man, Marks?"

"I am an observer, Jerry. I see with wide open eyes. We are all still being murdered, just more slowly and in greater comfort."

Wang knifed into the conversation. "We will do what we must to alter this path, and survive." Marks gave him a sidelong look as if this was more than he meant to reveal just yet.

Jerry understood perfectly. "*We* meaning those who follow you."

"In the beginning, perhaps," Marks admitted. "This is a war of sorts as well, but for the preservation of the human race. But those who survive will have the benefit of the work we have done. Work you can be a part of. And Linda as well, if she chooses to join us. And your children will inherit the strength we have rebuilt."

Jerry's vision reddened in a fit of anger and he leaped to his feet, knocking over his chair, even as he was surprised in the back of his mind at his own violent reaction. "You want to destroy the world to remake it! Destroy it to save it, as they used to say! You're nothing but criminals... insane fanatics. You have no right to do what you're doing!"

"We are doing it anyway," Wang answered.

Marks let out a long breath. "If you want to get violent, Jerry—verbally violent, anyway—we expect it. And we understand it at this stage. But there is a part of you that knows we are correct."

Jerry turned his back on them. The door was locked and no doubt guarded but he faced it anyway, as much of a rebellion as he could muster.

"A part of you understands," Marks continued. "Why else would you play tennis, take martial arts classes, and all the other physical activities you enjoy, while also building your mind alongside it? You make your body strong first, and then you know what you will need."

Jerry swung around, wondering wildly for a half second if he might see his grandmother standing behind Marks, mouthing those words in his ear.

But it was only Marks and his three companions, and the director's eyes were twinkling. "I think," he said, "now would be a good time for us to take a break. Catch our breaths, and let Jerry absorb what we have discussed so far."

Ten

Jerry's high-ranking captors left except for Marks, who, with two barrel- and bare-chested orderlies in orange kilts, conducted Jerry to a large combination restaurant-cafeteria-recreation room. Fifty others milled around there dressed, as Jerry was, in blue kilts and sandals. They ate and then played pool or bowled or watched TV or books. Most of them were eager to talk, however—"Talk to whomever you like about whatever you wish," Marks allowed—and Jerry soon found out that all were prisoners. Nearly all were NYC citizens but from different days.

Some, like him, had suspected someone was tampering with the timers and their embryos, or their wives' embryos, and had investigated. Others noticed other patterns which Jerry was starting to piece together: the overly warm days despite the climate controls, the slowed-down computer network connections, occasional drops in power to the apartments, and a dozen other piddling things Jerry had only considered inconveniences but now were signs of someone tampering with the domes' technology.

None had given Galapagos the trouble Jerry had. Most of them had been taken quietly and privately and awakened in this place. And they had been told the same story Jerry had heard and had been given the same choice.

Fifty in just the last few obdays? Jerry thought. He also wondered if maybe any here were fake prisoners, gauging the reactions of the true prisoners to report back to Marks or to gather other information.

Jerry wondered how many people at a time were processed here. Each person was given less than a week to make up his mind, so the place should be empty of prisoners in a few days. But he suspected that as fast as one went out—in whatever form—another came in. Which meant the organization was big, though relatively small compared to the population. But if it was growing, it would soon be big enough. He also reasoned that similar facilities would be in other domes and cubes, perhaps many of them. Then both here and elsewhere, Galapagos undoubtedly had a respectable number in high places. Otherwise, it couldn't have access to the stoner maintenance tools or have kept from being found out by the police, or worse, the hounds.

Or the World Organic Council, perhaps? Or had they infiltrated it as well?

There were five attendants, one for each ten men. It would be an easy thing for the fifty to overpower the five, since the attendants were unarmed. But Jerry had been informed of the security setup, and he could see the uselessness of an attempt at a violent escape. Each of the six rooms was monitored by a closed TV system; the only area not always observed was a five-foot square of the shower, and this could be seen if the camera turned that way. The cameras were installed inside the wall behind one-way, unbreakable windows. The monitor was in a room walled off from the others and could only be reached through a door the location of which was not revealed to the prisoners.

The single exit was wide enough for six men abreast to pass through but it was entered through two sets of doors. The locks to these were activated by the unreachable TV monitors or by frequency keys carried by Marks or other doctors.

The prisoners could seize the attendants and try to use them as hostages. But, if they did, they would be unconscious six seconds later. The discs secured to the prisoners' wrists contained radio receivers and devices for plunging needles one-sixteenth of an inch long into the skin of the wearers. Through the needle an anesthetic

A Hole in Wednesday

was squirted, knocking the wearer out. The device was activated when radio waves were transmitted to the receiver from sets placed along the junction of wall and ceiling about fourteen feet above the floor. The monitor had only to press a button, and all fifty would fall down, asleep, and would not regain consciousness until a half hour later.

"The set is clamped around your wrist and welded so that it must be cut off by a laser," Marks had told Jerry on the walk to the cafeteria. "It isn't tight enough to cause gangrene. But if you try to slip something between the skin and the underside of the disc to prevent the needle from coming out, an alarm will be set off. The disc also contains a transmitter and monitoring device. The device detects any foreign substance between it and your flesh and transmits notice of such to the monitor.

"So now you have nothing to occupy your mind except your decision, because you know you can't escape. The sooner you make up your mind, the better. It isn't easy to sneak you back into your stoner, you know. The time for doing it is limited."

That conversation should have prevented Jerry from wasting his time planning escape. But it didn't. It seemed to him that, tight as the setup was, it must have a weak point some place. That nobody had gotten free so far only meant the previous prisoners had lacked imagination or the courage to use their imagination, or both.

Nevertheless, as a fair-minded and unbiased man in spite of his present circumstances, Jerry had to study Marks' ideology and purposes, no matter how wrong Marks certainly was.

Think of it as history, Jerry told himself. Just history happening now.

There couldn't be any doubt Marks was wrong. He was more than just wrong, he was sick. And Marks should be in the hospital as a patient, not director of the psychic rehabilitation program. And yet Marks had a prescription for making all of society healthy and a plan for administering the prescriptions. He would carry it through whether it killed the patient and took five hundred years. Which it was likely to do.

Jerry did not know whether or how to classify Marks, but he had to put him in a frame which could be worked with. Science had to label entities and fields and distinguish them from similar entities before it could use them. This was not entirely true of course, since science had used entities and fields without knowing exactly, or even inexactly, what they were. Science had used electricity without knowing its basic nature for a century or more, even when the theories of electricity were not entirely valid.

So Jerry had to put Marks' ideology in a niche among the many millions in the universe, provide a handle for the pot, even though he was aware he knew little about Marks and his organization. But like electricity, Jerry didn't have to know everything. He knew Marks and his associates were already in powerful positions. Powerful enough, perhaps, to hold their positions against the World Organic Council. If they already had fifty citizens just from the last few obdays, they were likely gathering a great deal of support.

Jerry knew they had something to do with the stoner tampering, which meant they had infiltrated the most fundamental part of modern civilization. Marks wanted to make humanity evolve in isolation, starting with a chosen few (or not so few) disciples, but the only place you could do that nowadays was outside the domes and cubes. So he most likely held the idea that getting back to Nature was the ideal, with humans as Nature's creatures and inextricably tied to it—an idea reinforced by Marks' statement about the world being too reliant on technology.

Jerry longed for simplicity, but Marks' ideology defied a simple name. Part *Herrenmoral* and will to power of Nietzsche—he certainly thought Marks' beliefs were an assault on all things moral—part sinister Back to the Land, part amoral evolution made as moralistic as the most extreme fundamental religion. He didn't like using the term Galapagos, thought using it would corrupt the name of a harmless, fascinating group of islands the way the Nazis forever corrupted the swastika. But another short name . . .

. . . Or an abbreviated version of Galapagos. *Gallows.*

Jerry liked that the instant it came to mind. A symbol of

supposedly strengthening society by weeding out the corrupt and criminal, but in the end still brutal and a bringer of death.

Marks was as mad as the March Hare in the Museum. But this made him no less dangerous.

And one of the most disturbing things about him was that he had found so many to agree with him. Marks' organization was growing. If he were to be believed, he was getting many of his recruits from his prisoners.

Marks was apparently one of the many who was deeply disaffected with their lives. Unlike most of them, however, he had isolated and analyzed what was troubling him—to his satisfaction, anyway. The others were occasionally aware they were not content with their life, something was missing, or something extra and unwanted was present. They were not sure what it was, but they knew an ectoplasmic malaise drifted through the corridors of their minds at nights and sometimes before their eyes in the light of day.

Linda and Rex Washington were both examples of this unease and desire for something beyond the walls of the city. Or beyond themselves. But, though they expressed dissatisfaction, they had sublimated it in their various social and athletic activities.

As Jerry often had, truth be told. He hadn't delved too deeply into his dissatisfaction, especially after never quite being able to start work on a PhD in Self-Knowledge. Now he was forced to take the first steps, and was beginning to see how rootless he really did feel. On that count, Marks was unfortunately right.

When the time came to return to Marks' office, Jerry mustered the courage to try poking and prodding a little, to see how close his guesses came to the truth, or what Marks would reveal or claim to be the truth. This time Marks was alone; Jerry suspected the director's companions were likely interviewing other candidates now. He wondered if they had already made any kind of judgment or decision about him, or were waiting until he reached his own decision.

Jerry shot first. "How do you evolve in isolation in this day and age?"

Marks smiled broadly, though Jerry couldn't tell if the response was genuine or if Marks was prodding and poking as well. "By leaving the domes and cubes behind us. We are creatures of Nature, Jerry, and aside from our fellow humans, Nature itself provides us our greatest challenges. Our greatest adversaries. Bring those elements together, pit them against each other, until one masters the other."

"Oneness with Nature. Civilized man has been talking about this missing element in his life ever since the first city was built."

"Oneness, yes, but not in the sentimental way people used to talk about it. Oneness in the respect of mutual domination. Nature controls evolution, and so in that fashion controls us. But we can also have the means to control nature, and thus direct our own evolution. By separating ourselves from Nature we have been missing something, but what is missing is our own advancement."

"Symbiotes," Jerry said. "But until the early twenty-first century, people were able to escape the city and get some share of wilderness or rural country. Then the age of the enclosed cities came, and the only contact mankind has with Nature is through the Nature Rehabilitation Corps or the Parks. But farmers are close to Nature."

"Not close enough," Marks said. "They do most of their farming by means of automatic machines directed by computers. And, instead of roaming the stretches of forest around the farms, they spend their time watching the TV shows or traveling into the city to go to school, anything to get away from the country."

Jerry laughed then quit laughing when he caught Marks' dark expression.

"Perhaps I am mistaken," Marks said. "Perhaps you aren't as intelligent as I thought. Intelligent men don't make conclusions until they hear all the data, the evidence."

"I apologize," Jerry said. "But you must remember I am not myself."

He wondered if he would ever be again.

Marks' smiled faintly and said, "Accepted. As you see, it's not just a matter of getting the people back into the wilderness and living on a savage scale."

A Hole in Wednesday

"And how could you? There isn't any wilderness. The whole of North America outside the cities and the farms where Nature survives is a park. A well-cleared and tended Park."

"Most of it. There are places, again, that have been allowed to become wild. They are as classified and well secured as the machines which generate the stoner fields. Even most rangers are unaware of them. And the rangers, by the way, are the best adjusted and the healthiest people, physically and psychically. There's no argument about that, right?"

Jerry nodded. That could certainly be said about his father.

"Doesn't this mean anything to you?"

"It means only the best of the population, psychosomatically speaking, are chosen to be forest rangers."

Marks reddened.

He pulled back his lips to expose clenched teeth, and then said, "You're intelligent, anyway, though I don't know how intelligent. You're in a position where dissimulation would be your best policy, I'd think. But I like your honesty, and maybe you've figured out you'll be subject to a truth session and might as well say what you think."

Jerry didn't reply. Marks said, "You're right in your statement in one respect. The best are chosen for rangers, but the best are chosen also for other professions. And the members of the other professions don't reach the high levels of the rangers. There is a perceptible and easily explainable improvement over the already high P.I. levels. It comes from their contact with Nature, slight as it is compared with what it could be. And should be."

Jerry listened intently as Marks continued. He did not believe the man was right, but he was sincere. And there was just enough verified data and logical conclusions derived from the data to give Jerry some doubts about Marks' wrongness.

Marks said, "The plan is long range, of course. As for what set you on your path to discovering Galapagos, our original intention was to cause miscarriages by personal means . . ."

"But why?"

"We direct our own destinies, Jerry. For now, we test our

candidates in the wilderness. But this generation we begin to create our superior human beings from the beginning, from conception itself. Your genetic profile is excellent overall, and Linda's, as I have just looked into personally, is not nearly as good as yours. But you have the potential to create a superior child. For now, we have used the stoners to induce miscarriages if the fetus' genetic profile falls below a certain standard."

"Eugenics," Jerry growled, feeling his fury from earlier deepening. The movement had started in the United States in the early twentieth century to weed out "undesirables," the definition of undesirable being made by society or, more often, a small group of politicians and other power brokers. Within a few years it had mutated into the Aryan movement of the Nazis and the Holocaust.

Marks clearly noticed Jerry's anger. "Not in the way you understand, Jerry. We are not trying to eliminate anybody. As I said, we do not believe in unnecessary violence or killing. If I could wave a wand and bring about this evolution to everyone on Earth, I would do so. But Nature does not use wands, and neither can we. We are being no crueler than Nature itself." He leaned forward. "In fact, we are far kinder. If you agree, we can do non-invasive modifications on Linda that will guarantee a satisfactory fetus. And she will never have another miscarriage again."

Jerry felt his anger choke in his throat. "How?"

"The details are unimportant. Just know we have been working on this for an extended period of time."

"You really could . . . offer us a child?" Jerry wanted to sound as if he was wavering, stumbling over his convictions. But this wasn't difficult, because it was partly sincere.

"Yes, and I can offer more," Marks said. "In time, not too far in the future, we, those of Galapagos, will be able to live the natural way, seven days a week. And we won't be getting older faster than the rest of the population. Of course, until we attain The End, a man will have to live in each day with a different identity. But that can be arranged, because we have our programmers and policy makers implanted in the various bureaus. You,

A Hole in Wednesday

for instance, can continue to live as Jerry Carson on Wednesday. But you can also live as Robert Brown or Jesse James or whatever name we can get for you from the LifeLogs. And then . . ."

"What about Linda?" Jerry said. "Will she be able to live with me each day, under a different name and identity, or will she be confined to Wednesday?"

"Some men have a different wife for each day, and some women have a different husband. But some couples voyage through the days side by side. However, there is a danger in telling your wife what's going on, you know. If she refuses to do so, then she will be put away. There's no other way to do it. She'll be brought to the women's station and given the same choice you have. The question is, of course, whether or not you want to take a chance with her. Be satisfied with her as your Wednesday wife or else risk . . . well, you understand."

Jerry nodded. He understood too well.

"What about children?" he said. "Adults can keep their mouths shut. But if we have the children you're promising us and they accompanied me through the days, they would soon catch on to what was happening . . ."

"Children must be kept to one day," Marks said. "There's no other way out. If you and Linda were to have a child, you'd have to see him on Wednesday only. But I will be forthright, Jerry. Even if you and Linda both join us, a child for you must wait a long while—perhaps until we achieve our goals."

"Why?" Jerry said. He felt as if he couldn't control his urge to hit Marks. But he did.

"For the same reason we've aborted her zygotes," Marks said. "Her chromosome chart indicates she shouldn't have children without genetic assistance. She carries recessive genes for a tendency to have respiratory diseases. You know this."

"So what?" Jerry said, and then he paused. He was speaking too loudly and he did not want Marks to know how close he was to exploding. "And you just told me you could—"

"You also carry genes for an easily provoked temper. Although this we could overcome with our training."

Jerry didn't argue with him on this. It had been established by the end of the twentieth century that many such character traits were of genetic origin.

"Again, so what?" Jerry said. "Modern medicine overcomes the effects of the respiratory-gene complex, and my conditioning has enabled me to conduct myself as a reasonable and peaceable citizen. If I've lost my temper now and then, I haven't indulged in harmful behavior. Nor am I expected to repress my temper. Doing so is unhealthy and you know it. When the occasion demands, I let loose—within reasonable boundaries of social behavior. There's nothing wrong with exhibiting appropriate anger."

"Would your child, inheriting a weak resistance to respiratory ailments, and a hot temper, be able to resist such diseases, and conduct himself pro-socially, if he had no access to medicines, and if he were in a society where he is expected to repress his temper at all times, except on certain ritual occasions?"

"What do you mean by that?"

"First, you must know modern science has kept billions from dying who would have otherwise. The weak genes have proliferated until they're widespread today. Even modern medicine can't keep up with combating their effects. The ratio of sick people has been rising and rising. The hospitals are crowded. And despite being a society where help is available, where people don't have to work themselves into the grave, and where we are educated to offer our services, we can't get enough nurses and nurses' aides. Nor enough doctors. There is little private property to cause crimes and there is no poverty, so crime should be nil or almost nil. But crimes of violence are increasing, and compulsive theft, kleptomania, is increasing. Yet the objects stolen are valueless, and the murders, which are mostly crimes of passion, could have been avoided with a little reasonableness and restraint."

What Marks was saying was, in part, true. But Marks, like so many, was convinced he spoke the whole truth; that he had a pair of magic eyes enabling him to see what others could not.

And Jerry's eyes opened as well.

Marks intended to change the structure of society radically.

A Hole in Wednesday

His organization, though relatively small, could affect large results. If the members could get away with living seven days a week, then they would increase their effectiveness sevenfold. While others were locked in their molecular inanimation six days a week, Galapagos would be working every day.

They meant to create a Natural Man with generations of corporate backing and their machinations carried out by agents who might be capable of living for extra generations. The organization's small size was no longer a handicap if its recruits lived seven different lives.

"So when you are able to seize power," Jerry said slowly, "perhaps without the populace knowing it has been seized, then you will start the neo-Rousseauism? The cities will be deserted, in fact, torn down, and man will become a dweller in tents, in log cabins, and depend upon the soil and husbandry, or perhaps on hunting, to survive? And if he is sick, he will survive through his own toughness, or die?"

Marks nodded. "To an extent. We will keep some modern medicine—that which is capable of genetic repair and improvement. But first, you and Linda would need to show you have the resources necessary to survive in this society. *Then* you will have your children, because we will know they can survive and prosper as well."

Now for the first time Jerry truly understood Marks' madness, representing a sickness mankind seemed unable to throw off. There were always, and apparently always would be, people who thought a Return to Nature would cure what ailed mankind, though Marks' was far and away the most horrific version Jerry had ever encountered. Marks knew such a life would be fatal to many. But too bad for them. They needed to be weeded out for the benefit of the others.

Marks rose, indicating this session was over. "Join us, Jerry. As I have said already, make your body strong, and then it will know what it needs. And you will see I am correct."

This time only the orderlies accompanied Jerry to the recreation hall, but Jerry's mind was whirling too much to contemplate giving them any trouble just yet. Not just over all of what Marks said, but the last words again, the ones mimicking his grandmother.

Jerry thought about his last conversation with his mother, who considered herself Grandmother Dora's long-suffering daughter-in-law, especially in the older woman's last years. She was delusional, his mother would say. Saying all kinds of weird things. About evolution. And . . .

G*allows.*

And more of Marks' words: *We have been working on this for an extended period of time.*

An even darker thought spread over Jerry's psyche. Could they have been at this so long they had involved his grandmother in it too? Was that connection the real reason they took an interest in Jerry?

Wang's words when Jerry asked if they were worried about aging faster than everyone else: *It doesn't bother us. You'll find out why.*

Jerry remembered how genetics wasn't just used for eugenics. Scientists had been working frantically for over a century by 2084 to extend life through genetic repair. Some even believed that if one could constantly repair DNA, you could, barring accidents or murder, effectively become immortal.

Such research in a grindingly overpopulated world was banned with the coming of the enclosed cities. But what if Galapagos had been around then, or it was a descendant of those geneticists? Jerry could hardly imagine it, but what if its members didn't care about seeming to age faster than everyone in the stoners because they *didn't age?*

If his grandmother had been one of them . . . but no, she aged. And besides, Jerry vaguely remembered her speaking of such things negatively. So in other words, if Galapagos had tried to trap her, she found a way to wriggle out of the trap's jaws.

So Jerry would find a way too.

Eleven

As Jerry circulated through the three large rooms he absorbed all he could about the security setup and the physical location of the rooms. These interested him far more than what Marks was going to do for, or against, humanity.

Two were bedrooms at night. Each had pillows filled with cerefluid, a nano-saturated smart substance which hospitals used as special cushions to place under injured parts of patients' bodies to promote healing. They were also said to promote psychic healing and soothing, and could even block much of the "noise" from outside so one could concentrate on and commune with his own thoughts. Each pillow was emptied in the mornings and hung up to dry and for cleaning. There was the so-called hospital, the room in which Jerry had awakened. There was the operating room, but this was locked and could be opened only with the frequency keys the attendants carried.

Jerry asked the prisoners about the latter but no one knew what was kept in that room. They guessed the tools and supplies needed for the operations would also be stored there.

At noon, two men entered through the only entrance, pushing a cart. This was high with racks containing large sacks to carry items such as clothing in and out securely. The men who distributed the sacks to various rooms based on doctor's orders were guarded by two attendants. Jerry did not know why the guards were stationed there. At the first sign of trouble, the TV monitor would transmit the radio frequency, and all the prisoners would keel over.

He walked up to the cart and said to a guard, "Can I have one of those sacks?"

"What for?" the guard said.

"I need an extra pillow," he said. "They're longer than my pillows. I do a lot of rolling in my sleep, and often just roll right off the pillow. This is long enough to stretch across the top of my bed."

"I don't know," the guard said. He motioned to Dr. Simmons, the man who had accompanied Marks. Simmons looked hard at Jerry. Jerry looked as if he were at ease, or he tried to do so. Simmons said, "I'll get you another pillow."

"All right," Jerry said. "Thanks." He turned away. It would invite suspicion to protest or insist. He may have done enough damage to his suddenly conceived plan as it was. Simmons might tell the monitor to keep an eye on him.

Jerry grabbed a meal from a buffet machine and sat down at one of the long tables, in the middle of a group to avoid the suspicion people on their own always got, though he mostly ignored the conversations around him. Instead he reviewed the layout of the rooms, positions of the attendants and orderlies, and other small details over and over in his memory. He opened his package and ate the surprisingly tasty—best foot forward for the prospects, Jerry guessed—hot roast beef sandwich, mashed potatoes and gravy, cool lettuce salad, and hot bread and butter, with a cherry-flavored fizz. Then he dumped the remains down the waste chute. He abandoned the wild idea of sending a message down the chute. In the first place, he didn't have anything to write such a message. In the second place, nobody would ever see it. The waste went down various tunnels until it was spewed into the magnetohydrodynamic disintegrator. But the impulse to send a message was difficult to resist. It would help him emotionally to send out a cry for help.

The two dormitories were operated strictly and formally to prevent disturbing those who wanted to sleep without speeders. The bunks were in tiers three high and each was curtained. There were lights in each bunk for reading, but these would only come on if the curtains were pulled shut.

Jerry climbed into his, drew the curtains, and looked closely at his pillow. It, like the sacks and his mattress, was filled with cerefluid, which in the context of his pillow could adjust itself to the user's shape, sleeping patterns, and body temperature to promote a fully holistic sleep experience. Like the idea about psychic healing, some people claimed it blocked bad vibrations in order for the sleeper to enjoy happier dreams. Jerry wasn't certain about that, but one thing he did know from reading about old submarines trying to send and received radio signals was that fluid would impede those signals. The standard pillows weren't long enough to reach the part of his arm he needed to cover, and apparently getting a sack was out of the question. But if he could get a longer pillow, he could slit a hole along the upper edge, insert his arm, and then instead of flowing out, the cerefluid would encircle his arm as if the pillow was still intact.

Jerry had the privacy and the materials he needed with two exceptions. He didn't have a knife to cut open the strong plastic material of the pillow case, nor tape to reseal the cut.

He lay for a long time thinking before finally deciding to attach the speeder electrodes. When he got up for breakfast, he was told by Simmons he had not put on the speeder until 3:13 A.M. Simmons had no further comment. He had made this one just to let Jerry know he was being monitored even when the curtains were shut. Once the speeder was activated, a light or other signal notified the man in the monitor room. And it was possible the uprights in the bunk supports concealed tiny TV cameras which operated by black light.

Simmons was also probably telling him by the remark that he didn't have long to make up his mind and staying awake at nights wasn't going to help him.

Several prisoners were missing. These, Jerry supposed, were taken out at night when everyone slept. Whether they had been stoned or had joined the Gallows, or led to some other fate, he had no way of knowing.

At lunch time the two attendants pushed in the meal cart. Jerry spoke to Simmons. "I've got a crick in my neck from sleeping on a pillow that's too short. Even with the speeder, I toss and turn a lot, and I need a longer pillow."

"What about the extra one you got?" Simmons said.

"It doesn't help any. My head falls between the pillows, or else I shove them to one side. I never had this problem with just one long pillow."

Simmons stared as if he were trying to read Jerry's mind. Then he smiled, briefly, and said, "Very well. We wouldn't want anything to interfere with your ability to think clearly. You don't have much time, you know."

He spoke to the attendant standing behind the cart. "Give Carson a sack and foam. But make a record of it. We'll have to account for both next Tuesday."

Jerry felt chilled. By then he wouldn't be needing the sack, one way or another. And they weren't going to let anything float around unrecorded.

Getting a sack after all was a stroke of luck, though. That night, Jerry sealed the end of the sack. He merely had to pinch one end between his fingers and keep pressure while running his fingers along the edge. The sack closed as if it were sewed tightly shut. To unseal it, he just had to twist a little tab at the end, and an opening large enough to admit a finger would come into existence. Then he could run the inserted finger from one end to the other to open it completely.

Hoping he wasn't being observed, Jerry emptied his two pillows' cerefluid into the sack, then lay for a long time while thinking until finally putting on the speeder. If he was being watched, his actions should satisfy the monitor that he wanted the pillow only for the reasons he'd given. But he doubted he was under nocturnal visual surveillance. Otherwise, the watcher would have seen Jerry had had no trouble with his small single pillow. However, they might be letting him go on with whatever plan he had for the sack just to see what developed.

Maybe they were still judging his resourcefulness. Or they could have been up to what was a common tactic through history: let a prisoner try to escape to see how he would do it—then stop the prisoner, and stop other prisoners from using the same trick in the future.

His plan was a wild one and probably had little chance to succeed. But it was the only one he could think of. And if it failed, he wouldn't get another opportunity to try an escape. They would undoubtedly interpret his attempt as a negative answer to their offer, and he would disappear.

Dr. Marks' first words after greeting him in the morning upset Jerry. But he merely smiled.

"Did you sleep well with your sack?"

"Very well," Jerry said, wondering if there was anything behind the remark other than a polite interest.

"You were up late again," Marks said. "Have you made up your mind yet?"

"Not yet," Jerry said. "I must confess much of what you've said, and much of what you plan to do, appeals to me."

This was a lie, of course, and would be found out under narco-hypnotic questioning. But it would do to lull him for now—if Marks could be lulled.

"And which parts do you find less appealing?"

Jerry made himself look thoughtful and sought a truth to mix into the lie. "I can't quite believe any one man, or even a group, a small group, can really know what's best for mankind. Or, if they did know, that they'd be able to bring about what's best according to plan. I'm a history teacher, you know, and I've never forgotten a certain statement by Hegel:

"What experience and history teach us is this—that people and governments never have learned anything from history, or acted on principles deduced from it."

"Apparently, despite being a history professor, you have not read anything about the U.S. Constitution," Marks said. "Or much about twentieth century history. They made a great many efforts to advance. Some worked well. But in the end, of course, they fell short, usually victims to those who would destroy for greed and self-gain."

"Hegel should have said, instead of *never have learned anything, never have learned much*," Jerry amended.

Marks paused and then said, "And this is your main objection?"

Jerry nodded. He did not think it would do any good at all to tell Marks his main objection was that Marks and his followers were mad. Or, if not insane, grievously misguided.

"But people's failure to learn much from the past does not mean they never will," Marks said. "Often this requires an external force. Sometimes, a breaking point, or an outright crash. Do you agree?"

"Yes," Jerry said reluctantly. "Many of history's greatest positive movements came about this way."

"I understand you find our methods, both those we use now and those we plan to use, extreme. But the extremity is by necessity. This world will not be altered, and thus not be saved, except through an external force putting it *in extremis*. As the artist suffers to produce great art, as nations and the environment were saved only when we reached the point of total societal and environmental collapse, so must our world be pushed against the wall to shock its system back into survival."

Marks smiled the charming smile of the sociopath, and not for the first time did Jerry wonder how someone so obviously unbalanced could weave his way through a world of careful psychiatric and psychic testing to not only thrive, but rise to the head of the psych departments of North America's largest domes. "Think about that. And tie it in with what I've told you."

Marks left him and passed through the other prisoners. Many of them spoke more than briefly to him, and by the time he was ready to leave, he was beaming. He stopped in front of Jerry, who was standing near the exit.

"Thirty of the forty-five have made up their minds," he said. "All say they will join."

"But you have to put each through a vera test first to make sure of this sincerity?" Jerry said.

"Oh, there'll be a few who'll think we can't catch them out," Marks said. "But the rest mean it. That's the way it's always been so far."

A Hole in Wednesday

A few minutes later, two burly men entered with a man who looked like a medical doctor. He carried a black bag chained to a band around his wrist. He was taking no chances some prisoner might grab it from his hand, open it, and use whatever weapons there were in it, even if the prisoner couldn't possibly stay conscious long enough to get the bag open.

The doctor spoke to Simmons. Simmons, looking at a list in his hand, called out a name. A tall thin man with yellow hair answered, and he went with the doctor and the two burly men to the door of the operating-supply room. Jerry walked along the wall across the room from the door. He turned his head as the door opened, and he glimpsed an operating table, a rack of surgical instruments, shelves with tall wide bottles, and a centrifuge. He also saw a chair, like a dentist's chair, with straps on the side. The man who was being interrogated would sit there.

Then the four men entered, and the door swung shut.

Jerry sat down on a chair from which he could see into the door when it opened. Men kept crossing in front of him and several times groups formed which blocked his view of the door. Jerry looked at the book he'd picked up from its rack by the chair. He wasn't actually reading it, though he swiped the screen every minute or so. Scenes kept jumping, and the tiny voices issuing from them said things he did not hear.

The door of the operating-interrogating room was shut about ten minutes, if Jerry's time perception was functioning correctly. Then the prisoner, a middle aged man who still looked toned with exercise, emerged smiling, and walked straight toward the entrance. The doctor nodded at Simmons, who raised his right hand with the thumb and first finger forming an O. The prisoner—no longer a prisoner, Jerry thought enviously—walked through the doors, which opened at a signal from the monitor, and then closed. Jerry supposed the man would be taken into some sort of custody. If he belonged to another day than Sunday, he would have to be taken back to his cylinder and put in without others noticing. And that would be done only in the interim period between days.

No longer a prisoner, but what had become of him in the meantime? Brainwashing? Genetic repair? Or maybe just a series of medical tests to prove his fitness for the Gallows' savage new world? There was no way to tell, until Jerry walked through those doors himself.

The doctor called another name, and a squat, pudgy man looking grave went into the operating room.

This time Jerry wondered if the first man had been a genuine prisoner or a shill. He may have been planted solely to induce an imitative desire to join. A sort of Judas goat, except he would be leading the sheep to happiness and salvation—from Marks' viewpoint.

It did not matter whether the first man was a fake or not. Jerry's decision wouldn't be changed. He would sit here and watch them go in and out, and, if Marks had not lied, the room would be almost empty at the end of the interrogation. Then there would be ten attendants and Simmons to watch over only five prisoners. And the odds would be increased enormously against him.

While he sat frozen with his ignored book, four new prisoners were brought in. They were inside a big long cart, which was covered over to conceal the fact that four men were laid out on racks on it. Jerry got up and followed the cart to the ward room, where he saw the cover pulled off, and the four lying unconscious therein.

He returned to his chair. So his suspicion about this area being part of a general hospital was correct. The rooms had been requisitioned by Marks and his accomplices in other days so no one would suspect what was going on in them. The records had been faked, of course. The other hospital personnel must believe the area was used for the rehabilitation of extraordinarily psychotic prisoners.

The door to the ward was shut and, doubtless, locked. The two new attendants and two of the old ones, plus Simmons, were inside it. This left eight attendants with the prisoners, but these relaxed after the pudgy man, smiling, emerged from the interrogation room and then out through the big doors.

A Hole in Wednesday

A third prisoner went in with Simmons and the two attendants. Jerry rose and put aside the book. He might never get another chance to have so many prisoners in one room and only eight attendants to watch them. The odds were better than normal, but still were far too high against. It was now or never.

The trouble was that all the other prisoners were in the biggest room. If he walked out, he would be conspicuous, and he would have to carry out his plans under surveillance concentrated on him. But it was possible the monitor knew his case, knew he had resisted Marks' arguments, and had not yet made up his mind. It was possible the monitor did not think it so strange that Jerry should become depressed by seeing other men walk out free just by saying Yes. Perhaps he would not call someone to investigate when Jerry crawled into his bunk and pulled the curtains shut.

Too many possibilities, unknowns. Jerry knew this would not change. There was only one way to find out.

He walked out, his head down as if he was discouraged, and went into the bunkroom, which was at the extreme end of the area. From there he went to the bathroom for a few minutes, hoping the monitor would think this was the only reason he had left the general room and so would forget about him for a few minutes. Then he went to his bunk and closed the curtains.

His heart was beating so hard he could hear nothing but it, and his hands were shaking so badly he could hardly manage to unseal the sack which he used for a pillow. He had difficulty holding the open end up with one hand so some water spilled out. And when he plunged his left arm in the sack almost up to his shoulder, more water ran out over the foot of the bunk and it was only partially retained within the bunk by the curtains. The rest, he imagined, could be clearly seen by the monitor as it trickled out.

He sealed the end of the sack around his arm with the fingers of his right hand and then pulled the curtain back. He climbed out of the bunk and strode out of the dormitory and into the corridor. The wardroom was on his left; the small office of Dr. Marks on his right. Beyond was the first large room, empty, and then, beyond a wide doorway the outer general room. So far, nobody in the outer room had looked down the corridor toward him. And the monitor must not have noticed him as yet. But he would see Jerry in a few more seconds. Jerry would know as soon as the prisoners collapsed or a voice from the loudspeaker system warned the attendants. Or both at once. He was halfway through the inner general room when a voice blared from the speakers, "Dr. Simmons! Jerry Carson has a sack full of cerefluid on his arm! Come immediately!"

Jerry ran. As he came through the doorway from the inner into the outer general room, several things happened at once.

The door to the operating room swung open, and Dr. Simmons stepped out. And the prisoners began collapsing.

Jerry had hoped they would be knocked out at once. In the first place, even if none tried to stop him, they were crowding the room, and he would have a hard time getting around them. Moreover, it was likely that many would try to stop him if they had made up their minds to join the Gallows. They might grab at him before they collapsed, and tear off the sack. Once the water shield was removed, the weak radio waves emitting from the broadcasters would be able to activate machinery which would plunge the drug-coated needle into his flesh. The three inches of water prevented the feeble waves from reaching the receiver now. But it was a fragile protection, and he wouldn't keep it long unless time and circumstances worked for him.

Jerry had been so sure his plan would be obvious the moment he asked for a sack as a long pillow. But his idea was too obvious; it was another purloined letter. The Gallows had taken precautions to make sure nothing was available which could be wrapped around the device as an obstacle for the waves. But they had not thought of the possibility of using fluid. Perhaps they had not known submarines, when operating underwater, could not use radio to communicate to the outside unless an antenna was sent up to the surface. Even water, far less dense than cerefluid, stopped powerful transmitters from sending the electromagnetic waves more than a few feet.

A Hole in Wednesday

Jerry had not been sure just how strong the transmitters here were. He had had to take a chance on them being feeble. The other attendants were caught flatfooted. They were alert but had expected all the prisoners to fall down, and the sight of one dashing on by them unnerved them. The mob of men slumped, and each one fell in place, forming piles in several places. Jerry had to jump over bodies and, once, he stepped on a man who was lying on his back. The air went *whoomp!* out of the man.

Simmons shouted at the two attendants in the room behind him. Other shouts were probably from the ward. Simmons then ran to cut him off. His face was pale and contorted, and one hand was inside his white coat. Jerry hoped it wasn't a weapon which shot a missile of some kind. Then Simmons was before him, and Jerry whirled and came around, the sack and water-enclosed arm stiff, rotating like a horizontal wind mill arm. Simmons ducked, and it was lucky for Jerry he did. An impact with Simmons might have knocked Simmons down, but it would have unsealed the sack, and water would have spurted out.

But Jerry came around and raised his right leg while still spinning on his left, and he kicked. Simmons, rising from the floor, was caught under the chin. He went backward. Shock ran through Jerry's foot, but he was too excited to feel any pain as yet. He bent down and picked up the cylinder which Simmons had dropped. It wasn't the frequency key the warders used. It was some sort of weapon, Jerry was sure.

He was elated. It was strictly against orders for any of the warders to bring in weapons. But Simmons had disobeyed; he had felt too insecure even with all the measures taken for his protection.

Jerry flipped the cylinder over with one hand as the attendants came at him. One end was closed; the other had a narrow opening. And there was a little stud on the side.

Jerry pointed it at the attendants and yelled, "I'll shoot you if you don't stop!"

The attendants halted as if they were on strings manipulated by a single puppeteer. Simmons, groaning, got up onto all fours and shook his head. But he did not seem to know what was going on, or, if he did, to care.

Jerry sidled over to Simmons. He said, "Give me the frequency key."

Simmons looked up with dull eyes at him. "What?" he said.

"The key."

He couldn't use the other hand, and he couldn't drop the weapon to go through Simmons' pockets himself. Simmons looked down at the floor, his arms gave way, and he crumpled on his face.

Jerry shouted at the attendants, "Give me the key! Or I'll blast all of you right now, do you hear?"

Time was falling through a trapdoor. The monitor must have notified Marks and others on the outside, and they would be running toward him.

One of the attendants reached into his pocket and withdrew a silvery star, a shaped key that would press into an indentation by the door. He tossed it at Jerry, and it fell at Jerry's feet.

Jerry cursed. If he put the weapon down to pick up the key, he would be open to attack. But he had to attempt it. And so he stooped quickly, dropped the weapon, and picked up the key, stuck it between his teeth, and picked up the weapon again. The attendants did not move; they saw they didn't have time to rush him, or else just didn't know how to react fast enough to such a situation.

He removed the key from his mouth with the first finger and the thumb while still holding on to the weapon with the other side of the first finger and the second finger. He turned the key inward, pushed it against his chest to slide it further into his fingers, and then his thumb was on the stud. He turned it outward to the door and pushed on the stud with the thumb. The door slid open, and he sighed deeply. He had been afraid that there would be an override operable by the monitor, and the doors would remain closed.

It was necessary to turn his back to the attendants while he used the key. He heard the slap of feet, and he wheeled. Two men were coming after him, and the others were spreading out.

They slowed down but continued to fan out. A current of slightly cooler air touched his sweating back. He turned again and ran out through the double doors into the hallway toward the first door through the short hall and then the second door, which was sliding open. Since he had not applied the transmitter of the key to the outer door locks, he knew somebody from the outside had done so. He hoped it was someone who had not been warned.

At that moment he heard Simmons' scream, "It's not a weapon, you fools! It's my key to the other place!"

The outer door opened all the way, and Wang started to step inside. From his expression, he had not been warned about Jerry's escape. Jerry rammed his fist into Wang's face and brought the sack-wrapped, fluid-heavy arm up as he spun. Wang tried to use the heavy briefcase he was carrying as a club, but Jerry's arm caught him on the side of the head and knocked him down. The water burst out of the sack from the sealed end. Jerry himself fell over Wang and slammed his head against layered paintings of white arcs and twelve-rayed figures on the wall, then he was up and running. He tugged at the sack and got it loose and let it drop behind him. A nurse yelled and jumped aside, and Jerry rounded the corner and sped down a long corridor.

He was lucky. The policeman on duty at the entrance had turned away from the door to answer one of the phones set in a niche. Jerry ran past the admittance desk and through the door, which was sliding shut, having just admitted four people. He got to the door, squeezed through it while the cop yelled at him, and he was out into the public corridor.

This had dark yellow carpeting and bright green edging and red phoenixes seeded everywhere. Seeing it, he knew he was on the Thirteenth Floor, and while he wasn't very familiar with this floor, he knew what turns to make from here to get to the elevator banks or the escalators. Every floor was constructed exactly alike. He got into a crowded elevator just as its doors were closing. He was dripping wet down one side, and he was breathing heavily. Some people muttered protests or sarcastic comments, but he paid no attention to them. He pressed the emergency button for a stop at the next floor below, despite the cries of some that this was an express. He got out just as the power stopped; the doors were open enough for him to force himself through, though he could feel the loss of some skin on his back.

He sped down the corridor away from the elevator banks. If they had been stopped it was only because Marks had put out an alarm. The police on every floor would be looking for him, and they would have been given a story by Marks which would make them ignore whatever Jerry said. He'd be delivered to Marks and handed over with minimal questioning. He might even be anesthetized immediately to ensure that he didn't attack anyone.

At the far end of this corridor were escalators for carrying people up to the thirteenth and down to the eleventh. They would be stopped but he could easily run down them if the police hadn't gotten to them. He was hoping they weren't anywhere in the neighborhood yet, though they undoubtedly were on their way. And so they were. He heard a whistle behind him, looked back, and saw two policemen on trikes speeding toward him.

But there were no policemen at the tops or bottoms of the escalators. He plunged down one, sliding his hands on both railings and using them to keep from falling. He got to the bottom just in time to see three cops, each on a trike, come around a corner far down the corridor. They were three hundred yards away and so he took the corridor at the bottom of the escalator. He raced along it, turned at the first corridor, went down it until he came to another cross-corridor and turned left. He had passed about thirty people in this short space, and they would tell the cops they had seen him.

But this corridor was bare of people, so he turned into the seventh door he passed. This was the twenty-fifth century but seven was still a lucky number, and he wasn't going to scoff at superstition in his need.

The apartment being a twelver also influenced his decision. Though the door was no larger than any other, it was further away from the other doors than it would have been if it had been the entrance to a four-person dwelling. In the atrium was a rotating clock on top of the nose of a plastic seal in the middle of a small fountain. It told him this was 15:27:33 on a Monday.

A Hole in Wednesday

He drank deeply from the fountain and went into the living room. He passed a man and a woman lying on a sofa. Neither seemed inclined to take notice of him. He went down the corridor and into the stoner room. He was very glad the place was relatively deserted.

Inside the quiet twilit room, he slumped against the wall. Now that he had gotten away from Marks, and wasn't likely to be caught immediately, Marks might decide to call off the cops. He would know Jerry might emerge later, get hold of a reasonable cop, and tell his story before being hauled off. If some of the police decided to investigate, they'd put Marks in a bad spot. The police would check out the violent ward, and they'd find any number of men who didn't belong on Monday, unless Marks got them out of there. He was probably doing this now. But where would he put them? In some stoner room where they could wait until things cooled off? Not that Marks would be able to keep them there for long. If he didn't return them to their respective days on time, then they'd be subjects of manhunts.

But how much could Jerry rely on any of that? Marks obviously had power and influence, and if the number of people and range of professions he had met in the recreation hall were any indication, it was possible Marks would have police on his side. Perhaps even hounds. In this case there might not be such a thing as a reasonable cop; and it was guaranteed there was no such thing as a reasonable hound.

It also occurred to Jerry that Marks, on Monday, would not be named Marks. He had no idea what his name really was, since no one had addressed him as Marks beyond Jerry himself. Or Marks could be Marks on Monday and every other day. There was no cross-checking among days; the hospital records for each day were kept separate from the other days. These would be available locally in the CIC bank and federally in Wheeling.

Or if Marks didn't have enough police in his back pocket, he could call off their hunt, saying he had caught the escapee. Then he would put his own organization to hunting Jerry. He should be able to figure out that Jerry's refuge was within this area. A house-to-house search could be done on the sly, though it could also run into some difficulties. Unless, of course, Marks had access to dome-wide surveillance as well.

Too many things could happen. As before, too many things were unknown. But one way or another, Jerry had to act.

He went to the great storage cabinets and opened the door of one. He didn't know whether or not he'd hide in one, since Marks knew about his original hiding place. Perhaps he could hide under one of the beds. Later, he could sneak out to another place. The trouble was that when it came time to get back to his own stoner, he was going to find the Gallows waiting for him. They knew he had to come home, or else face a daybreaking charge.

But he might be able to justify what he had done if he could expose the Gallows to enough people. Surely there were still people in power who would not want to destroy their own society, or would fight to protect their own livelihoods. And he could prove that what he had done did not originate from psychotic motives.

For some reason this cheered him, though he was not optimistic about getting past Marks' men. The Gallows or the police might be searching room by room for him, possibly using building surveillance or tapping into personal security or computer cameras. For all Jerry knew, they could have a portable transmitter to activate the drug needle fixed to his wrist and he would be knocked out before he knew they were coming. He had to do something swiftly to keep out of their hands.

He went into the stoner room and stopped short.

It took Jerry another heartbeat to figure out what was odd about the stoners: they were all different. Not basic differences like colors or designs layer-painted onto the cylinders the way people did, the way pre-Dayworld people had different kinds of beds, but the cylinders themselves were fundamentally different, as if they were early experimental models.

Some were vastly different sizes, others orbs instead of cylinders; some were thinly sheathed and others so thick they resembled submarines; others were windowless; others were solid capsules with no apparent places for wires or ports for receiving energy for the stoning field and timer, while a few had so many wires and receptors they obscured the capsule itself. One—or possibly more, it was difficult to tell under the circumstances—had been completely disassembled and had pieces sprawled across a horizontal drafting table in what seemed to be total chaos to Jerry's untrained eye.

The bizarre sight made Jerry forget his predicament for a moment and he wandered from stoner to stoner, intrigued with a mix of historian's curiosity and dark fascination. But none looked like antiques. In fact they all looked as if they might have been constructed yesterday. If they were old they had been as well preserved as if they had been placed in stoners themselves.

Maybe they were, Jerry thought. Stoning technology was often used to protect precious items as well, particularly in private collections. But if these were museum pieces, why were they here? Or was a resident of this floor a collector of prototype stoners?

Jerry was jolted back to his dangerous position not by police or Gallows bursting into the room, or a resident, but from a voice Jerry didn't recognize:

"Well done, Mr. Carson. You have led Galapagos on an excellent chase. But now it is time to return to Marks and surrender."

Twelve

Jerry felt caught in a three-way trap. Behind him, the old stoners—if they were old, rather than some bizarre new experiments. Before him, the door leading back out to where an unknown number of authorities were hunting him. And then that voice from all around him, though in the dim room Jerry saw no evidence of speakers, or any kind of computer or other terminal capable of producing sound.

"Where are you?" Jerry asked the air.

The voice chuckled. "Directly ahead of you, I hope."

"Who are you? The Shadow?"

As he asked, Jerry walked around the room again seeking a weapon, and finding nothing or nothing he could fabricate in short order, he increasingly felt that hiding was useless. There was nothing present to hide in but the cylinders and other-shaped stoners, but he couldn't take the chance of any of them being active, or if they were, their functioning properly. One small mistake in the field could be catastrophic, something Jerry was forcing himself to consider after a lifetime of conditioning that no such problem could ever occur with the stoners.

"I've tracked your progress in escaping from Galapagos," the all-surrounding voice told him, "and I find it impressive, particularly the simplicity of using fluid to negate the kill frequency. Galapagos had taken measures against a more technological jamming but obviously never considered something so basic. Ironic, really, considering their stated goals of breaking away from technology."

"I won't join you," Jerry made himself say. There, it was out. "Stone me if you must. There may be problems with this world, as you say, but nothing so wrong we have to destroy everything we've built."

"I have no intention of destroying this world, Mr. Carson," the voice told him. "I am not with Galapagos, but part of an organization nearly as old as they are and dedicated to destroying them. Likewise we oppose the ever-increasing invasive surveillance of our so-called 'organic' government through the stoners and other means. But Galapagos has, as I'm certain you've guessed, infiltrated every level of society—they have been at it since the beginning of the New Era, and before, when it was clear which way the winds were blowing. They have the advantage of being skilled at daybreaking, as you have also no doubt witnessed by now."

"If you're opposed to them, then help me escape them!"

"Mr. Carson, let me spread out the facts as they exist at this moment so you'll know where you stand—or fall. By your first night in Galapagos' custody they would have learned everything about you, starting with your home address and your marriage to Linda. Your home is no longer a sanctuary. Any attempt to legally leave NYC will involve processing a request that one of their people will see somewhere along the line and intercept. Any attempt to leave illicitly will be watched for by all means of surveillance. And as they are masters at altering identity, any attempt by you to alter your own would be caught immediately."

Jerry deflated as if some reverse stoner field had robbed his body of all solidity. "Where are you?"

"If you mean how are you hearing my voice, Marks had a microchip implanted within your skull as a means to monitor you at all times. Primarily your emotional state, which will be broadcasting to him right now like an old air raid siren, but to an extent it may also be used as a tracking device."

"Tracking! Then they know where I am!"

A Hole in Wednesday

"Not precisely. First of all, when you belong to an organization that distrusts technology so thoroughly, sometimes you are bound to make mistakes with technology. The chip's primary duties are for mental and physical surveillance of a more long-term variety, by which I mean to record patterns Marks and Galapagos might find useful later."

"Can they use my bioreadings to determine whether or not I'm lying?"

"Possibly, but I suspect they would prefer other more invasive means like Truth Mist. Marks himself has a substantial ego, however, and is more likely to trust his own observations than technology. As for tracking, the chip isn't specifically meant for that purpose. Why bother, when the needle in your wrist is all the guarantee of compliance they believe they need? It can be homed in on like a wireless radio signal, but you are in a shielded room. For the moment they cannot track you with any precision at all."

"Shielded?" Jerry looked around at the strange chambers again and wondered if they might be operating after all, and somehow creating an electromagnetic dampening field of some sort. Or even something more destructive, like the old electromagnetic pulse weapons used in the twenty-first century, which would explain the lack of other electronic devices in the room. "What do you mean?"

"There are security devices in the room creating a static field blocking surveillance of any kind, or any unauthorized transmissions in or out."

"But I'm hearing you," Jerry told him, then his stomach knotted with realization. "I'm hearing you through a chip the Gallows implanted."

"Gallows?" The voice chuckled in a way that did not strike Jerry as at all friendly. "Yes, it was Galapagos' chip, and our ability to hear each other means the shielding in your room was placed by Galapagos."

"Then they can hear us!"

"No. Another fault in their chip technology. I'm piggybacking on their signal, and have attuned its vibrational frequencies to emulate my voice. I am also the one who initiated the remote code response allowing you to open the door into the room."

Jerry rubbed his eyes as if the scene of the stoners—of everything that had happened to him since his baleful decision to daybreak—would rub away too. When this didn't happen, he gave the door a long stare. "Will you help me get away from them, then? Never mind what you said about not being able to escape. I just want to get out of this building, and then I'll think of something."

Jerry expected to be scolded, and soon decided he would have rather had a scolding than what the voice said next.

"The only way for you to escape, Mr. Carson, is for you to surrender to Galapagos and join them. Though the room is shielded they did have your general location before you entered it, and are searching this floor room by room. I estimate you have ten minutes, no more, before they find you."

The dimness in the room seemed to go black for a moment. Jerry had to grab the edge of the table with the chaotic stoner parts to stay standing, and grabbed it hard, hurting his hand, to use the physical sensation of the table to keep himself grounded, not to mention conscious.

"Maybe you could explain to me how surrendering and joining them are the same thing as escaping? If you've been fighting them as long as you say, you know how insane they are! And how dangerous!"

"We are well aware of all of this and more, Mr. Carson. But we have been fighting them for three subgenerations. They will not fall in a day, or a year, and possibly even much longer if we wish to preserve the civilization we have built. Because, you see, they have infiltrated so many places that taking them all out at once would leave too many holes, and the edifice would collapse."

"I don't understand how my joining them will do any good . . ."

"We need people to fight them from inside, Mr. Carson, and fill those holes as the holes appear. You have proven your resourcefulness even against many obstacles, not the least of which is yourself—your fears and indoctrination may be substantial, but you have already demonstrated yourself proficient at overcoming them. Join Galapagos . . . the Gallows, as you appropriately call them . . . learn their training, watch who and what they move to where, and tell us everything you can."

"And who are you? I know you told me you want to destroy Galapagos, but what do you believe, whoever you are?"

"If you require a name, you can call me Oscar Diggs."

Jerry laughed cynically. "You want me to call you after a wizard whose powers were nothing but technological hokum hidden behind a curtain and smoke?"

"Think of it as a man who proved to others that the resources they needed to fight evil were already within them. But my name is not important. Our organization believes all things in this world have core components, and anything can be destroyed or undone—or built—when those components are arranged the right way."

Jerry decided to call the organization behind his nameless voice the Reductionists.

"And so," Jerry said, "you've spent four hundred obyears trying to take apart the Gallows piece by piece?"

"If we tried that, Marks and his people would simply fill in every piece we removed. What we mean to do is rearrange and rebuild those pieces to turn Galapagos to our own ends—and wreck their intentions to wreck the New Era. We are particularly fond of the technology and benefits of this world, and wish to see those things preserved. We ask now that you join Galapagos, and in doing so, join us."

"Whoever you are—"

'Your time is short, Mr. Carson. As I tracked you, I am also tracking your pursuers. I estimate you have no more than five minutes before Marks or the police locate you."

Jerry felt his resolve wavering. But just as he did he remembered another major problem, and shook his head as if the voice could see him. "Even if I do give myself up, Marks will know I'm not sincere about joining them the moment he puts me through the narcohypnotic test."

"Then you must be sincere. To start with, we can prevent your wife from having any further miscarriages."

Jerry felt swelling hope in his chest in spite of himself, though that hope possessed a cold core. "This is what we wanted, as the Gallows well know . . . but it may not be enough. I have to be . . . reasonably certain you are who you say you are. If I have any doubt that this isn't just a test by Galapagos, that doubt will surface in the testing."

A pause. "How much do you know about Theodora Maria Ashkenazi Caird Carson?"

"My grandmother? I . . . very little. She died when I was young."

"Do you remember her ever saying anything about evolution? Survival? Perhaps the Galapagos? Or . . ."

"*Gallows*," Jerry remembered. "She used the word gallows." And she was always angry when she said it.

"She was a mole for us. Theodora and your grandfather both. From early on, before they went into the domes and the stoners."

His grandparents were first-gens in the domes, Jerry remembered. Jerry knew still less about his grandfather, who died subyears before he was born. But he did remember his grandmother never wanting to talk about the stoners or the New Era, to the point where she would leave the room altogether if she could.

"Theodora and I were close for a long time," the voice said with what almost could be a trace of wistfulness. Though, Jerry knew, if the voice had any training in psyche evaluation and rehabilitation, he would have likewise been trained in vocal and emotional manipulation to bond empathically with any subject and build an artificial connection between them. "She was part of my family. I don't mean by blood but every other way that is important. But she refused . . . certain benefits of working for Galapagos, including their gene therapies. She could still be alive, but working for the Gallows was so repugnant to her, even as a spy, she chose against it. For her, much as it grieves me to say so, it was the right choice."

"How will this help me pass the truth tests?" Jerry asked. He wondered how much of his five minutes had passed. Maybe there were police or Marks himself right outside the apartment door, seconds away from bursting in.

"Even in the New Era, Mr. Carson, there are few guarantees. But I can make you some promises. I will promise you Linda's genetic issues will be corrected. I can promise you that I—and you, I imagine—will do everything in our power to destroy Galapagos. And I will tell you anything about your grandparents you ask of me. Including their service against Galapagos, and how it led to you being where you are today. If you join us, I will give you immediate allies in our fight. But I remind you that your window of opportunity is nearly ended."

Jerry let out a long breath. He could not stay trapped. No matter what the voice said he must do, Jerry was certain if he could slip out of this tightening noose, then he could figure out something to get away on the next step. And the next, and the next after that.

His legs felt electrified, psyching themselves up to take the steps outside the shielded stoner room, then one foot after another back out into the corridor.

"Who are you?" Jerry asked again, the door out seeming to approach him inexorably of its own accord. "What do I call you, your organization?"

"We call ourselves the Family. For to a great extent, this is what we are."

By the time the voice finished, Jerry had reached the apartment's last door. He watched his hand reach to the knob, turn, pull. The walls were featureless but pulsing gently when he stepped out into the hallway, a signal meant as an alarm to residents to stay in their apartments.

"Take the stairs immediately to your left," the voice said.

"Why?" Jerry said. "I thought you wanted me to surrender."

"There is something we need you to do first."

That didn't make any sense to Jerry, but if it meant a chance at escaping instead, then he would run.

The corridor was empty. The residents, having seen the pulsing walls whether outside or inside their apartments, would have locked themselves into the safety of their rooms.

"Down," the voice told him. "Down as far as you can go."

Jerry obeyed, this time, hoping the order would not prove to be personal irony.

Thirteen

Jerry lunged into a different world.

On the surface nothing appeared different. The twelve flights of stairs he bounded down were nothing more than stairs, although the walls were still blank and pulsing, devoid even here of the paintings and entertainment programs that normally filled the spaces and the minds of those who passed on the escalators. The light seemed a little dim, which could have been the result of the alarm or Jerry's constricting blood vessels forcing tunnel vision on his eyes, he couldn't tell which. But the world he left behind last Wednesday was gone, forever irretrievable, and the farther downward he ranged, the deeper his drowning in this black and unimaginable unknown felt.

And helpless fury. Fury at himself for daybreaking, for learning things he could never unlearn. Fury at himself for managing to connect the timer with Linda's miscarriages. Fury at Marks for dragging Jerry into a thorny net that mortified his flesh with every move, and fury at the Reductionist voice in his skull that resumed speaking the moment Jerry burst into the stairwell.

"Now having cast your lot with us, Mr. Carson," the ubiquitous voice told him, "we have a job for you."

Jerry didn't reply, partly because he was having trouble breathing, partly because he was concentrating on not tumbling the rest of the way down the stairs, and partly because the statement only added to his fury.

"At the bottom of these stairs is another exit across from the public one. You will take it. In doing so you will also add significantly to the time you are given to evade pursuit."

Jerry had thought he was in good physical shape, but was exhausted enough when he reached the bottom of the staircase and already so used to running downward he stumbled over the last step, nearly falling into the door the voice had described. But there was no obvious way to open the door, no keypad or frequency receptor. Only a small dark bubble atop the door frame which Jerry recognized as a biometric scanner for entry access. It was a sure bet the scanner would refuse to recognize Jerry, and more than one failed scan, if that many, would trigger an alarm.

"How do I . . . ?" Jerry began, but a whirring emanated from the door as it slid open just enough for Jerry to slip sidelong through.

"Proceed," the voice said with infuriating calm. Jerry complied.

These halls and the stairs the voice directed him through were sheathed in white metal, bright with sourceless lighting but without pulsating walls, and no artwork or vidfeeds either. It was as if the labyrinth was sentient and wanted to be as nondescript as possible, forcing any unauthorized person to guess blindly as to their location and purpose. The only indication this buried place was used by human beings was an alphanumeric designation on each otherwise featureless door, and the name *Burroughs* at every intersection.

There was a slight downward angle to the floor, barely noticeable but after a few lung-wracked moments Jerry was sure he had descended enough to now be several stories under the building. Into the underworld figuratively and literally, then; some back corner of his brain wondered how far and long his Tartarean descent would last, this Faustian trade of one devil for another. But then, if his grandmother truly had been a spy, it seemed she was one long enough to still be so when Jerry was around, meaning subdecades, not a prospect Jerry relished, and the thought only served to fuel his mounting anger.

A Hole in Wednesday

He wondered if the corridors were shielded as well, if his emotions as well as his location were hidden from Marks. It seemed logical, particularly given the voice's comment about gaining more time. But Jerry didn't want to gamble any more than he had to on whatever additional time he was given, and in just a few seconds he was back at a full run and turning every which way, ever downward, as the voice in his skull snapped directions.

Now and again a door blocked his flight. Those requiring key-frequencies to open popped open automatically, no doubt at the Reductionist's command. With others, Jerry punched in each code as the voice recited it to him.

The door designations switched from alphanumeric to a name with a number attached, but not using any logic Jerry could determine. He reasoned these must be more secure areas and each designation represented a code. Then at one door exactly like the others, which was to say completely blank aside from the non-revealing designation KRUBERA-7208, a dark cavern opened before Jerry.

When he entered it was completely black, for just an instant, but long enough for him to hear his footfalls absorbed by a vastness of which he was only instinctively aware. Light found him slowly, rising up from the floor like cold white lava as more melted down the walls. All of the multiple sources of light coalesced on Jerry and followed him as he obeyed the instruction to continue moving forward. The farther he walked the more his illuminated island reached out with probing tentacles to touch objects around him, surrounding him, filling the Brobdingnagian abyss.

Jerry realized with horror that he was in a stoner chamber—but one where the growing light was touching hundreds of cylinders, which seemed to be made of gray paper, mounted horizontally and vertically for stories above him on thick silver rods into the darkness and silence.

In the darkness beyond he sensed thousands more, all with the feeling of their not being opened or even touched in an extremely long time. Longer than Jerry's own lifetime. None of the stoners he could see were empty. Each had a nameplate, with a chip Jerry guessed would provide scanners with the occupant's personal information, along with their illness or crime.

"And now, Mr. Carson," the voice said, "we begin adding some pieces to the whole, and rearranging those already in place."

Jerry found himself barely able to breathe again, but this time it had nothing to do with exhaustion. He was walking slowly among the stoners, the chase relegated to the backmost corners of his overheating brain, with a near-reverence he could not explain. A few names stirred something familiar in his mental corners, but looking at the faces did nothing to help. These stoners barely had more than small viewing slits rather than the large windows of those in the rest of the NYC domes, so all they afforded was a glimpse of the face and none at all of any clothing.

"What do you want me to do?" Jerry asked, then said it again when he realized he was whispering.

"These are prisoners, Mr. Carson. Political prisoners. I will give you names, and you will free them."

Jerry placed his hand on one stoner. It felt cold, as if the unfortunate person within was literally frozen rather than having the quantum energy of their bodies halted. But he recognized the graven waxen image of a face characteristic of the stoner field.

"What did they do?" He couldn't shake the feeling that they had been in these cylinders—and this cavern—for longer than he cared to imagine.

"These you will be freeing were early opponents of the stoners."

Jerry stopped suddenly, feeling as cold in his chest as the cylinders' metallic doors did. Now he knew why the names were familiar—he had just read about them a few submonths before in *Early Objections to the Stoner*. "They've been here for three sub-generations," he said. "Three hundred and fifty obyears. Buried this entire time?"

"They have. As you will be entombed in a nearly identical subterranean chamber should you refuse Marks' offer to join

A Hole in Wednesday

Galapagos. Which is an idea I trust now you will not be foolish enough to seriously consider."

If I needed sincerity to pass Marks' narcohypnotic test, Jerry thought, I'm saturated in it now. I would do almost anything to keep from winding up in one of these stoners for . . . who knows how long? Till the end of time, for all I know.

"I don't understand," Jerry admitted. "If these people fought the Dayworld from becoming reality, why wouldn't Marks free them? And why haven't you freed them already?"

"To answer your first question in an overly but necessarily simplistic way, being an opponent of the stoners does not automatically mean they sympathize with the destruction Marks is seeking. As for why we never have freed them before . . . finding someone to side with us who is already inside this building has been exceedingly rare. And frankly, Mr. Carson, you were the first one to make it this far without being caught. Or terminated."

Jerry had to take a few long breaths before he could speak again. "What am I to do?"

He meant that in a dozen different ways, but the Reductionist narrowed it down to a request for instructions. "As I said, Mr. Carson, I will give you names. No need to waste time searching. When you speak the name aloud, the proper cylinder will be transported to you, wherever you are."

As the Reductionist gave Jerry names, Jerry spoke them aloud—first in a cautious yell until the voice explained he could speak in a normal tone and still be recognized. As each name was announced, a maglev platform scooted away into the darkness, sometimes far enough away that its high-pitched hum and glimmer from its lights would disappear, returning a moment or several minutes later with an unopened stoner. A robotic crane lifted the cylinder out of the maglev and deposited it horizontally on the floor. Each cylinder door bore a special lockpad requiring a code Jerry would need to enter manually, though the Reductionist advised Jerry not to open them yet.

"Why not give them as much time as possible to acclimate?" Jerry asked.

"Swift acclimation may not be in their, or our, best interests. These are very strong-willed people, as you may imagine since they protested the New Era right to the moment they were led to their stoner prisons. For their safety and yours, they must be as compliant as possible if any of you have a hope of escaping. Some might resist otherwise, or even muster the spirit to penetrate back into the building and fight their oppressors. They must escape now so that they will be given the tools they need to give their fight a chance of success."

"Where is Marks now?" Jerry wondered, looking back toward the door where he came in, which was nearly invisible with Jerry and his illumination having moved so far away from it, much farther away than Jerry realized until that moment.

"Still several floors away, but distance is no longer relevant. He will not have thought it possible for you to get where you are, and there is heavy shielding over the entire chamber both from electromagnetic technology and the city bedrock. But there will be a digital record made in real time of these prisoners being released. If for some reason he or someone else in Galapagos happens to scan the records now, they will find you immediately. But there is no alert system, so it may be submonths or longer before the breach is discovered."

"Or right now," Jerry said.

"All of those we wish freed for the time being are before you," the voice said in way of reply.

There were twelve cylinders arranged in three rows of four. They contained six men and six women. Despite being antiques, the stoners looked exactly like the ones Jerry and his neighbors used, making Jerry wonder again about the strange stoner or stoner-like objects he had discovered earlier. He shoved that wondering away for another time, though, as he began entering the open code for each cylinder in its lockpad. Ten of the twelve had the same code, but two—marked SANDRA PHOENIX VON HENTZAU and LEONID FYODOROV MITROKHIN—each had a unique combination.

Jerry was walking among the open cylinders and the blinking

A Hole in Wednesday

occupants when an arm clenched around his throat and pulled him back.

"Where am I?" a gravelly male voice at his ear demanded.

Jerry raised his arms with hands outstretched. He almost gave his name, then thought better of it. "I'm here to free you. I . . . I am a mole in Galapagos. I work for a group called the Family." He swallowed hard, an effort with the arm pressed into his throat, and continued, "Let me go, if you want to get out of here instead of going right back into the stoner."

The arm held fast for another moment, but finally released. Jerry turned cautiously to see a tank-like form who wore an obsolete green military dress uniform and a long challenging glare. Jerry recognized the face twice over. Not just from the visor slit in the stoner marked JAMES ERECH GARRISON, but also the vid he had watched recently in *Early Objections to the Stoner*, of the final protest at the White House before it was broken up by bullets. Garrison had been one of the protest's ringleaders, despite being an active duty colonel in what had then been the United States Army.

"I don't know this Family or Galapagos," Garrison said, looking around, "but I remember who shoved me into . . . what the hell did they call those things . . . that *stoner*. And I'm familiar with most of the people you've awakened here. What year is this?"

"2440, Colonel Garrison. Which is to say, three generations, subjective generations, into the Organic political system implemented when you were taken prisoner." There was a sharp gasp from another prisoner, a red-headed woman with icy blue eyes, who was halfway in the process of climbing out of the stoner marked Von Hentzau. Jerry remembered from his readings that she had been a scientist of some sort.

"Where are we?" asked Von Hentzau.

The one whose cylinder was marked Mitrokhin chuckled. His name also sounded familiar, then Jerry placed it from the book too. A Mitrokhin had been the chief director of the Russian State Library and tried to save it from the destruction during the second revolution that burned through Russia in the 2070s. He had failed.

149

This fellow didn't look like a librarian, though, but a hawk-faced wrestler. Then again, if this was the same Mitrokhin, he had tried defending the library's millions of books and thousands of historical artifacts in hand-to-hand combat.

His chuckle had been unpleasant. "We are in the future," he said with a Russian accent. "The one we tried to stop. What else matters?"

"Manhattan Dome. New York City," Jerry clarified. Or so he hoped. He also hoped no one would ask him about the specific building, since he wasn't sure of their location himself, which wouldn't play well with claiming he was a Galapagos mole.

He knew he had to throw his whole gamble into his next words. "All you need to know for right now is that I am here to free you. I will lead you out of this place, but we do not have time for longer explanations, or for you to do more than what I realize is blindly trusting me."

"I'm out of that hellish machine," the redhead said. "I want out of this godforsaken place too, wherever it is. I'll follow you out."

Garrison reached for his belt but then hesitated. Jerry wondered if he was going for a weapon that would have been confiscated long ago. "I am never going back into a stoner," the officer said, "and I will do whatever it takes to make that happen. But whoever you people are, you should know that if you leave me out, I'll do whatever I think needs to happen to get my world back."

The Reductionist began feeding Jerry directions while Garrison talked, so now Jerry had to cut off the group's talking to tell them, "Follow me."

The directions led the motley group out of the chamber hundreds of meters away, and back up a slight incline. The keycoded door Jerry was told to enter opened with a small breeze and more darkness, but a string of lights hanging from the rounded cement ceiling illuminated a dozen long and wide metal steps descending into what looked like an old unfinished subway tunnel. That impression was solidified by flaking paint on the closest sloped wall reading WEST 14 STREET.

A Hole in Wednesday

The tunnel was not uniformly straight or level, and it branched off many times, sometimes every few paces. A few of the tunnels bore street names but others were nothing but blank cement walls, and Jerry suspected these did not run parallel with any streets above but rather went off on their own ways, to what ends and purposes he couldn't guess. If not for the voice in his skull he would have likely become lost in short order, even though he was certain they did not go more than a few blocks.

As it was, he knew they had made so many twists and turns in this labyrinthine underworld, automatically lit from above only for the length of the thirteen people spelunking through it, that he would need the Reductionist to lead him back too, if this was what his disembodied benefactor had in mind. Jerry was certain the voice did plan to lead him back, though, having already insisted his only way out was to find a way in to Marks' organization.

Then they began working their way up.

None of the tunnels or stairs here were named, and Jerry suspected they were beneath a particular building. Though at this point where that might be, aside from still in Manhattan, he could hardly guess. For all Jerry knew they could be right next door to Galapagos and the voice was hiding this location by leading the group around in circles, in case they were captured or Jerry spilled the whole adventure under narcohypnosis. But he was in deep now, in every sense of the meaning, and the only way through was forward. Or at the moment, still upward.

At last a door opened before them as if prodded by the hand of an impatient ghost. The room was dim even after the group entered, a few small, soft lights slowly coming alive grudgingly but miserly about surrendering any details. The room was featureless except for a few wall-mounted screens—real physical screens, not morphed into the walls themselves like everywhere else—that were turned off.

"Welcome to the first step of your escape," the Reductionist said, "and your retribution against those who imprisoned you."

It took Jerry a moment to realize the voice was coming from speakers built into the ceiling rather than the chip built into his head. Everyone was looking up, now, though Garrison the officer and Von Hentzau the scientist were also constantly surveying the room as if awaiting an attack, which perhaps they were. As the voice continued, a few of the twenty-first-century anti-New Era resistance had furrowed brows and a look of familiarity pulled just out of reach.

"Most of you should remember one another from your days fighting the New Era, but for those who are new to each other . . ." He proceeded to name them off one by one. The list reminded him again that he had run across most of these people before in the pages of *Early Objections to the Stoner*. Some had been more violently opposed to the coming Dayworld than others, but all had, in a way literally, given their lives fighting it. Whoever the Reductionists were, they had gained allies Galapagos would have a challenge reckoning with.

"And the man who led you here," the voice said, "I will just call Wednesday."

After Jerry's Day, of course. None of the others would have been confined to Days, having only gone into their cylindrical prisons once the first people began entering the domes and cubes. And if they did not know his name, they would not be able to give him away to the Gallows if they were recaptured.

The door they entered had remained open; another at the far end of the room directly across from it slid open now. "Those newly freed, come through the door I have just opened and meet this new world you rightly fought so hard to prevent, and in doing so rejoin the fight."

After the others disappeared through the nameless door, the voice that had called himself Oscar Diggs with misplaced whimsy said, "Wednesday, you will return to Galapagos."

As Jerry expected. But still the truth of it hit like he was whacked in the gut with a battering ram. He stood for a long while after the others had advanced amid his procrastinated retreat, hoping somehow the Reductionist would change his mind or Jerry could find another alternative to suggest . . . or even to flee. But again, as the voice had so brutally explained, flee to where? Not to home, not to anywhere inside the dome, not to anywhere outside. There was no recourse.

A snatch of poetry claimed his thoughts for a moment: *Home no more home to me, whither must I wander? Hunger my driver, I go where I must . . .*

"And then what? How far into their ranks am I to try penetrating?"

"We will decide this based on how you perform over the next few obweeks or months in Marks' physical outdoor training. If you prove yourself worthy and finish the training—worthy of Marks and our people as well—then we will determine where you go from there. But Marks and his Gallows, as you so appropriately called them, will not be the only ones observing you. We will also have a spy in their camp who will, if you survive and succeed in joining Galapagos, become your handler. In the meantime the spy will mark your progress—or lack of it—as well, and report back directly to the Family."

And let them know if I go too sincerely over to the enemy side, Jerry guessed. And then deal with Jerry Carson fittingly as a traitor. Not that Jerry had much of a choice now.

But no, that wasn't quite true, some instinct told him. He wasn't sure where the instinct's message was coming from—perhaps innate stubbornness, perhaps something primal and ancient scraping its way to the surface upon the first real challenge to Jerry's survival. Either way, it insisted he always had a choice. Jerry must seize the power to control his own actions regardless of the circumstances.

Wherever the source of his determination, Jerry found a wellspring of strength to voluntarily choose the path laid out before him and kick his way through. With the Stygian beast swallowing him he held out his arms to find its fangs and yank them out before they sliced him open. He would do what the Reductionists demanded of him. He would do what Marks and the Gallows demanded of him.

He would use the beast's fang to slice open its own belly from the inside.

Then, when Jerry had built up his muscle, and climbed his way up, and knew the warp and weave of the web he had found himself in, he would begin making demands of his own.

Jerry stepped out of the screen room, ignored the whoosh of the door closing behind him, and advanced with an unfaltering step toward his reunion with Marks and the hunters.

Fourteen

Jerry was surrounded by nothingness, or what at first appeared to be nothingness. If he concentrated, tried to send his senses outward, he realized he was in a giant space much like the stoner prison buried deep beneath Manhattan—with nothing making itself known when you first walked in but a small pod of liquid light. Here, as then, he decided to walk forward. As he did details resolved themselves, and he realized he was outside, but not outside the Manhattan Dome. A vast verdant land stretched out beneath an endless sky above of the sort he hadn't seen since serving in the Nature Rehabilitation Corps out on the Illinois prairie.

Was he in Illinois again? It was possible, for the land here was flat as far as he could see, though the perspective kept shifting so he wasn't at all sure how far away the horizon was.

The more he remembered Illinois, the more the landscape became filled with grass as high as his hips and waving in the wind. He could hear and smell poetically burbling water, reminding him of crossing the little Spoon River on his way to the mighty Mississippi.

The only thing he was certain of was that he was alone, and even this certainty was shattered when a voice addressed him.

"Why did you run, Jerry?" it asked. "Why did you try to escape?"

The voice was friendly almost to the point of being comforting. But something in the back of his mind was simultaneously issuing vague warnings.

"I was afraid," Jerry said truthfully. The sound of the water nearby was soothing, although his not being able to see it was odd.

"Afraid of what?"

"Of the world you want to create," he answered. Now he could see the water. Like the Spoon River, it threaded shallowly but vigorously through a thin copse of trees among a sea of grass, between hills so low as to be almost invisible.

"I can understand your reservation," the voice said amiably. "It is, after all, utterly foreign to the existence you have always known, in fact the total opposite, and a complete departure from the paradigm you have always been taught and benefited from. Yet you returned. Why did you come back?"

Before Jerry could answer he felt a touch on his arm and a presence behind him. This presence whispered in his ear, ("Be careful, Jerry, what you say from here on out. None of this is real.")

The voice was female and familiar. He slowly realized it was the voice of his Grandmother Dora, Theodora Maria Ashkenazi Caird Carson, only stronger and without the raspy voice of age. There was a certain braid to her accent, a twisting of cords of old world and new, and when he grasped for that cord it felt more solid than anything else around him.

("This is a phony joint creation between you and Northpath Marks," his grandmother's form told him, "a world you create around yourself based on drugs he injected you with, Truth Mist, and hypnotic suggestions. You must not tell him everything. Only enough for him to decide he will bring you back.")

How are you here? Jerry wondered. He didn't believe in ghosts or supernatural phenomena and was well aware of the probability of drug-induced hallucinations. This felt different—although he really had very little to base the feeling on, aside from some teenaged experiments with soma and a narcotic gum that was the psychedelic rage for a short while.

"Genetics," he said aloud. "Are you in my genes?" Or perhaps the compartmentalized logical part of his brain still operating, in tandem with genes. Memories of past human beings, especially direct ancestors, still locked away in his brain through morphic resonance?

A Hole in Wednesday

As much as genetics had rammed its way into his life recently, her presence here, born from his carrying a sizeable portion of Theodora Carson's genetic code, made a certain kind of sense.

The voice, Marks' voice, answered, thinking Jerry was addressing him. "An astute observation, Jerry. But first you must answer me, and you must answer me truthfully: why did you come back, Jerry?" Marks sounded more determined this time, less amiable. "Did you realize at last that escape was impossible? Did you bow to the inevitable?"

("Do not try to hide your doubts," Grandmother Dora said. "Doing so is impossible. But you must convince him that you found something appealing in greater measure than doubt. You must find something you want, Jerry. A reason *you* want to join the Gallows.")

"I wanted . . ." Jerry began.

"Yes?" Marks asked.

". . . A child . . ."

"I already knew this, Jerry. As did you. Yet even so knowing, you ran. You made it out of the building. Perhaps to freedom—and yet you stopped. What brought you back? You must tell me the truth, Jerry."

Outside.

But Jerry hadn't made it outside. He remembered now. He went through another door, a door less taken, and that made all the difference. Yet as far as Marks knew in his tracking of Jerry, it made no difference at all. Down a rabbit hole where everything was mad, but was Jerry mad now? No, he was under an induced influence of a narcohypnotic TM cocktail, in the power of a man whose voice projected everywhere as an illusion. Yet he couldn't even tell the difference in his scans between Jerry leaving the building versus going into a deeper shielded portion of it. And here, now, he was outside, in a place far from any dome, so rare in the world it might have been Wonderland.

("And why did you create this?" Grandmother Dora asked him. "This landscape in particular? A world outside with no domes or cubes in sight?")

"I wanted out," Jerry let slide off his tongue.

"Out of what, Jerry?" Marks pressed. "Out of the building? Out of Galapagos? Then why did you come back?"

This place, though an unreal landscape of his own mental creation, was drawing Jerry as much as the thought of the wild places beyond the cities did. Drew him and terrified him in equal measure, that is. When he first stepped onto an airplane outside of Manhattan Dome, then off the plane onto natural, dirt-grown prairie grass beneath the Illinois big sky, he had been terrified.

Some part of him remained terrified. The part craving the security of the domes, the Daily benefits, the controlled seasons and the access to whatever food or knowledge or entertainment he wanted. But another part knew these for the wombs humanity never left now, not for long. Artificial environments using safety and entertainment to mask a slow wasting process stultifying humanity.

Marks was right on that one point, Jerry allowed. Humans were creatures of Nature and could not totally barricade themselves from it without some negative consequence in the most fundamental biological sense. And without real challenges of the sort the New Era had virtually eliminated, there could be no growth, only stagnation.

"I will ask you one more time, Jerry," Marks said. "Why did you return?"

He surveyed this artificial world around him. Though artificial, it was the most natural place he had known in his adulthood. The wildlands of his dreams. The utter contrast to the giant stoner prison he had just seen, both in a literal way and in the metaphors that had constructed the human body over millions of years of pre-New Era evolution.

"I wanted outside," Jerry said.

"Outside?"

"You told me Galapagos trained its people by taking them outside the domes. Into the wild spaces. I want to go outside. To a trackless realm where I am forced to learn to survive without a dome. I realized you were right—I tapped something in myself when I broke Days, and then when I ran from you. There is more inside me than I knew. I want to find out what. I want the challenge of learning how strong I am, and then let my body decide afterward what it needs."

Jerry heard Marks say, "Bring him back."

The prairie vanished, but he still was not in a dome. He was surrounded by trees, not the tamed and manicured kind in the Parks, but growing wild and rampant, tall and straight or crooked, smooth-barked or gnarled, with leaves of all varieties of shapes, and all bathed in orange light born from a campfire nearby rather than a lantern. There were stars overhead, real stars rather than lofty visual projections. They arced because they were in open sky and not on the ceiling of a dome six thousand feet above the ground.

There was a pressure in his right arm. Jerry turned to see Marks' assistant, Buster Donnelly, wrapping a bandage around Jerry's arm where the assistant had just withdrawn a drug needle.

Marks was a few paces away, close enough to be heard but far enough away to prevent contact if Jerry had grown violent. Others stood just at the edge of the firelight, equal parts light and shadow, none with faces he knew.

The past days rushed back into his head now with the narcotic memory barrier down: the slow march back to Marks, the hunters' weapons drawn, Marks' command for them to give Jerry safe passage. Jerry giving his decision to join Galapagos. More obdays in edgy waiting while Marks monitored Jerry's chip, perhaps also looking for biological signs of deception, until Tuesday's residents were made sleepy with a gas injected into the ventilation system.

Then, once the Tuesdays were in their stoners and the gas cleared, Jerry sneaking back into his stoner while Marks' people took the dummy. A day spent wholly with Linda. He had been warned not to tell her about his new "position," but instead rattled off a well-practiced genuine-sounding explanation about a temporary job in another city allowing genetic medical benefits, but no, he didn't know for how long.

A sad and hopeful farewell, with Jerry giving Linda a long look which in itself made her concerned in a way he was not permitted to alleviate.

Jerry spirited out of his apartment shortly before midnight by cops who were in Galapagos' back pocket, and then a private windowless car taking Jerry and a half-dozen other recruits into the Appalachian mountains of what had once been Virginia. A reborn wild place, an easy place to dispose of Jerry if stoning him indefinitely proved impractical, he reasoned, and far enough from NYC to make escaping back there virtually impossible.

Perhaps. Or perhaps not. Jerry wondered just how resourceful he might truly be by the conclusion of this training. Provided he could last all the way through it.

Jerry knew he was here, now, because when he revealed to Marks about wanting the challenge of finding out how strong he was, if he could survive without the domes, he was telling the absolute truth—one only recently realized. The lure of the wild had overpowered the terrors and doubts completely. Jerry wanted to find out what he was capable of, good or bad, greatness or evil.

More immediately, if he was capable of helping to destroy the Gallows from within. Here, on this mountain, in a forest that had survived the brutality of the old world, was Jerry's own barbarous cauldron.

He dove.

Fifteen

The great insatiable maw of primeval time opened and beckoned.

Its billions of years of evolution mocked Jerry Carson in the form of the endless landscape rendering him less than an iota, he who had been raised in a climate-controlled dome.

He was beneath its notice. He could shout till his lungs bled, wave his fist or spear or quantum slider, but the mountains had seen his like come and go countless times and found nothing in him to even bother judging, much less find wanting. All of it mocked him for nothing more than having the reckless nerve to breathe.

Jerry had expected to see some green, spreads of trees, and other such natural beauty. He had known Marks' training camp was set in a reclaimed wildland. He hadn't expected the wildland to swallow him in a sea of hundreds of organic—true organic rather than born from the New Era—square miles.

And it all, Jerry knew—this Jerry Carson who had never trod more than a few miles from NYC's domes except during his protected Nature Rehabilitation submonths in Illinois, who had never been long outside at night under stars that could unsettle the strongest of dome dwellers—all he could witness from the precipice where he stood almost naked against the vastness both literally and in his soul was but one small corner of the planet and sky. These green mountains fading to blue as they stretched to the horizon, not the tallest of all of Earth's mountains by far. The curve of the horizon was perhaps sixty or seventy miles away, but with thousands more miles beyond. The visible stars were only the smallest fraction of what was even in the Milky Way, one small orb of their neighborhood, a few thousand light years in circumference, amid a galaxy a hundred thousand light years long.

And Jerry trembled, as was proper when presented to his master.

Two recruits were already practically catatonic with severe Nature Shock, so quickly Jerry hadn't even learned their names yet. Half of the remaining twenty-four were visibly afraid of being completely outdoors indefinitely. So far Jerry's two tent-mates, Venn and Vanwoerden, showed no signs of terror or catatonia, but he was more concerned with keeping himself together.

One of the recruits, a lumpy and somewhat clumsy fellow named Beta Graham, who had spent most of his adult life working in NYC's sanitation departments, was the happy fellow Jerry had seen ambling out of the mysterious hospital interrogation-operating room. Jerry still wasn't sure what if anything had been done to Graham back in NYC, but was intensely curious to see how Graham would hold up in isolated wilderness training.

Marks called their training area Camp Natufian. Jerry recalled that its name came from a prehistoric people who, unlike their contemporaries, settled down into a sedentary lifestyle before the invention of agriculture. Marks' primitive reserve where he had settled his latest batch of recruits for training of every sort was spread across dozens of square miles of multiple mountaintops.

Layer by layer the recruits were stripped naked of posing and pretension, along with any preconceived notions of what they were signing up for. They were allowed no cosmetics, and those with any decorative implants beneath their skin had those implants removed. Whatever clothes they wore to the camp were confiscated and replaced with simple brown ones, woven from real cotton, capable of acting as camouflage in any season—above the waist came tunics or shifts, and for below trousers or wraps to be used as a dress or kilt. They allowed the passage of air to the skin, to keep in warmth in cold weather, without the aid of built-in artificial mechanisms and electronic biotrickery.

On their first morning they were lined up before Buster Donnelly, who ruled the camp in Marks' stead, the voice of the Gallows while the ringleader was away. He ordered them to strip and place their new clothes at their feet.

Everyone hesitated at first. "Strip now, or leave now. But if you are so weak you must leave now, right at the very beginning, you're walking back to your homes. If you can survive getting out of these mountains at all."

Jerry had come this far, and was not about to be tossed out at the beginning. He was the first to pull off the plain clothing, and he even folded it on the ground.

Proving that being the first at anything is always hardest, the others followed Jerry's example. When everyone was naked, Jerry's own feelings of shame passed. With all naked none were naked, as it were. But some of the women had superbly fine forms and he found his crotch reacting as if it was joyous over being freed of its clothing. He had to force himself to face forward but at least he wasn't the only male with this issue.

Donnelly, likewise, stripped down, tossing his clothes away as much to make his point as to get them out of the way of his pacing before the line of recruits. His form had the lean muscles of the Native Americans who had lived before the coming of the white man, suggesting tawny strength and a hearty but lean diet.

"What you see of yourselves now is all you are. Not the clothes you wear or the chromes you paint your faces with. If you cannot find a way to survive in the new society Galapagos is bringing with only what you have right at this moment, you will die quickly but not easily. But we will teach you how to survive, if you have the strength of will. Strength of mind and muscle will follow."

He told them to put their clothing back on, then gave a curious order: after being issued their choice of primitive weapons like spears, wooden bows, knives, and hatchets, along with a spade, their first day and night was to be spent exploring all the thousands of acres of Camp Natufian, to range out as far as they could go, and then come back by sunrise the next morning.

Jerry hadn't understood the order at the time, but now he did. Donnelly and the camp masters, as the individual trainers were called, were not the masters, nor even was Marks. Nature would shape and forge them into Natural Men and Natural Women. Nature was their ultimate master. Exactly what Marks believed, after all. This was just Marks' first method of making this lesson sink inextricably into their brains.

His wanderings had led him miles from the center of Camp Natufian. The landscape was mostly wooded as far as the eye could see and might have been so since antediluvian times, for all he knew, except for the traces of humankind that survived the centuries since the New Era by hiding where no one would think to look. A crumbling asphalt road ran along the mountaintops, often coming close to the edge as if built for people to see the wonders around them but without leaving their vehicles. Traces of stone foundations and stone fences were reclaimed by the woods.

Jerry had even stumbled across a cemetery but most of the stones were unreadable. The etchings in the marble were mostly gone, while the fieldstones looked to never have been carved with names at all. The only name to survive, and that just barely, and covered in lichens, was carved into granite. Jerry scraped aside the lichens. The date and first name were worn into oblivion, but he thought he could make out the name of Carson.

He lurched back. That whoever was buried here was related to him seemed statistically unlikely, but . . . he knew nothing about his family before his grandparents' generation. Which was to say, nothing about his own history more than a few obyears before the New Era. So it was possible this was some distant forbearer who lay unrecognized and, until now, unremembered atop a mountain whose name Jerry didn't know. More importantly, this was someone who had called this wildland his or her home, so much so that they chose to spend the rest of time here. For them Nature . . . nature . . . was to be learned and respected, a partner, but it was no enemy, and no god.

A Hole in Wednesday

Where Jerry had felt like an insignificant speck shortly before, now he realized he had a place here. Indeed, the longer he stared at the old grave, ancestor or not, the more he realized that this could be more his place than it ever would be Marks'.

Then his explorations led him to what might as well have been the end of the world.

The precipice Jerry stood before was as real as anything breaking through his consciousness and paradigms now. He stood on a granite slab jutting out from the edge of the mountain, stratas of green stone lining the cliffs behind him, with a steep drop into a river far below. Two other mountains pressed into each other before him, but there was a wide gap opening to his right, the north. While he stood staring at the mountains immediately before him and untouchably far beyond, the sunny sky darkened and he could see a sheet of rain moving in, toward him. Thick clouds of rolling gray flashed lightning just beyond the mountains opposite him, then burned through the torrent to scorch the peaks.

Gales swept up the mountain as the storm's vanguard, almost knocking Jerry off his feet at first. The clouds overtook his position at the precipice but he made himself stay put, embracing the wind and rain and everything they might teach him. This was the outdoors he had dreamed of, after all. The wildness he had secretly longed for even as he felt confused and embarrassed by the longing.

He had not dreamed his first night at Camp Natufian. But why should he dream? He was in the wilderness that had filled his waking dreams. He was living out history instead of it coming into his dreams. Or at least the subtle sort of backstage history which never made it into the Museums.

Thunder roared and its echoes drummed through the mountains like a herald formally announcing the storm.

Despite the day's heat, the rain was cold, and it slapped his face sharply. This was no dome storm. No dome storm would ever be so fierce and frightening. Such rainstorms still existed in New York, of course, but the sounds of their violence outside were muted by the domes.

"Isn't it beautiful?" a woman shouted from nearby.

He hadn't noticed her sitting there on the far edge of the granite outcropping, until she cried out in a sort of frenzied ecstasy. Rain poured down her face but there was such terrified joy there too that he imagined she might have been crying beneath it all.

She was so transformed he almost didn't recognize her, but this was Ele'ele Venn, one of his two tent-mates. She was petite and lithe almost to the point of elegance, with copper-gold skin and black curly hair. She wore the bottom of her cotton tunic tucked into the neck like a twentieth century beach teen.

Jerry found her immediately alluring. Though he loved Linda and still found her physically and psychically attractive in their monogamous marriage, he nevertheless couldn't help but feel drawn to Venn. Even without cosmetics she was radiant. It was a pity, Jerry thought with private honesty, that she was vying to be one of the Gallows.

For a moment, Jerry could almost believe in God. Despite his native atheism, the government disavowing the existence of God, and no doubt Northpath Marks concentrating all of Galapagos' divine belief into the multitudinous aspects of Nature without need or regard for an anthropomorphic figure reigning over the universe, there was a beyondness here he couldn't begin to fathom.

"I never imagined anything like this," Jerry admitted. "I was in the Nature Rehabilitation Corps for six submonths in Illinois when I was seventeen. But those were reclaimed patches. Plus the whole time I had access to all the latest technology, and was never far from help if anything went wrong. This is . . . the entire world, and we're standing atop it."

"I thought I was an artist," she shouted above the storm, "but my art is nothing compared to this! Nothing I ever do again will compare!"

A rain-soaked silhouette clasped Jerry's arm and pulled him back. "You may never do anything again if you don't get away from this spot," a voice broke through the storm.

The robust newcomer was his other tent-mate, a South African Organic Union native named Piet Hluphizwe Vanwoerden. He was as square-jawed as a 1950s movie hero, broad-shouldered and barrel-chested, and already muscled without Camp Natufian's help, but he moved as swiftly as a cat. He had a brutish look but his eyes only thinly hid a shrewd intelligence.

"Come, both of you, this way," he said. "I have built a shelter."

Jerry's eyes must have revealed that he was wondering how Vanwoerden found them, because the South African said, "I followed you. You almost seemed to know where you were going. Perhaps you did and did not realize it yourself. Ha ha!"

He led them deeper into the woods. "This can't be safe!" Jerry cried. "Aren't you supposed to avoid sheltering under trees in a thunderstorm?"

"Where would we go around here that there are no trees? Come inside. We'll be low."

Inside a cluster of trees, mostly oaks and chestnuts, Vanwoerden had built a shelter across the low-hanging branches using pine boughs and curled strips of birch bark. It was dry and blocked most of the wind. All in all it was an impressive thirty feet long by fifteen feet wide, much larger than their tent, where they would practically be sleeping side by side.

"When did you build this?" Venn asked with wonder.

Vanwoerden nodded to Jerry. "While he was reading gravestones. I always find it useful to have an extra place to go to in case I need one away from where everyone expects me to be, ha!"

The storm passed within an hour, but the clouds magnified the darkness and laid it heavily over the mountain. The three recruits surveyed the sodden land before them as well as they could in near total darkness. But Jerry noticed patterns around him: the silhouettes of trees, different sounds and the ways they interacted with and reverberated off objects.

The sounds were increasing. There were the meanderings and scufflings of small animals, the hoot of an owl, a return hoot—inviting or challenging, Jerry wasn't sure—the yips and barks of foxes, and the screeching of what sounded at first like a woman, but which Venn told him was a bobcat. She didn't appear discomfited by their wild neighbors in the least.

"These mountains are theirs again," Venn said, "now that people have lived inside the domes for almost four hundred years. They may never have seen humans before."

"How will they react to us then, do you think?" Jerry asked.

"There's no way to tell without us learning empirically. I imagine they'll regard us with great caution—or if not, they certainly will once we begin taking to these woods more often, and start hunting. We may have bigger brains than them, but right now they're smarter. They're on their home turf and they've had centuries to practice what we're just starting to learn."

A rustling noise in the brush nearby startled and unsettled Jerry. This one sounded as if it was caused by a large creature and he would have been perfectly happy to start back for his tent, where he was required to be by the break of morning anyway. But Venn and Vanwoerden stopped and listened instead.

"Do you suppose . . . ?" Vanwoerden started but did not finish.

"Wouldn't that be amazing?" Venn answered equally cryptically. She pressed farther into the brush, opposite the direction Jerry yearned to travel.

Despite the subtle but distinct noises their passage through the woods made, muted by the wet but obvious as far as Jerry was concerned, the rustling ahead continued unabated.

When it seemed as if they must be right on top of the creature, whatever it was, Venn and Vanwoerden stopped and tried peering through the darkness. The moonlight was reasserting itself, and found a slice of opening in the forest canopy enough to nudge their vision toward the behemoth shape undulating before them.

The bear's muscles rippled as it walked and dipped its great head down to the ground in search of food, or perhaps sniffing out the intruders' whereabouts. Its sight might not have been that good, something Jerry remembered reading once, but there was nothing wrong with its sense of smell. Its head lifted suspiciously at the first whiff of its first humans, and regarded the frail but undaunted new creatures about twenty feet from it. At least Venn and Vanwoerden were undaunted, Jerry thought, but he was remembering how frail the human body could be against something with large teeth and that outweighed him by hundreds of pounds.

A Hole in Wednesday

"Black bear," Venn said. "*Ursus americanus*. Probably *Ursus americanus americanus*, the Eastern Black Bear. They're reasonable creatures overall. If it was a grizzly we'd be in serious trouble . . . but those were in Alaska, or are, if there were any left by the end of the twenty-first century."

"Shouldn't we be quiet right now?" Jerry asked.

"This isn't a mother guarding her cubs. Just don't make any high pitched sounds or sudden moves. As far as the bear is concerned, we're all just looking for supper."

But the bear no longer appeared to be seeking food. He was growing increasingly agitated, more visibly unsettled every time he looked at the humans.

The creature stared at Jerry, then sniffed the air. Some understanding passed into its mind as reflected in its intense gaze.

Something sparked in Jerry's mind, aware of the creature's understanding at some primal level that he had never tapped into while living in the dome.

"He knows," Jerry heard himself say. "He knows who we are and why we're here. That we've come to take back the rest of the world."

The bear growled, then roared, towering up on its hind legs over even Vanwoerden. A white crescent moon marking blazed across its hirsute chest. Below it was a wide fresh red gash with blood only barely dried in its matted fur.

Jerry knew he had no weapons but a knife he had belted to his waist more out of curiosity than thinking he would require it. Venn likewise had a knife, plus a hatchet. Only Vanwoerden had come prepared to any extent, with a wooden recurve bow and a quiver full of stone-tipped arrows provided by Donnelly, but Jerry wasn't certain how effective they would be against a full-sized *Ursus americanus*, as he was thinking of it.

The bear roared again and charged them as Vanwoerden nocked an arrow in his wooden bow. Jerry and Venn were able to leap out of the way but only because the creature had centered its attention on the bow-wielder, slamming into the South African with an audible *crack!* of wood. Vanwoerden had managed to get off a shot. The arrow protruded from the bear's shoulder muscle over its left front leg, but the beast wasn't impaired despite the wound.

The three humans—intruders, Jerry thought—spread out as if they had planned it, but the bear wasn't about to be distracted from Vanwoerden. This time Vanwoerden had his knife out and he tried thrusting it into the bear's head but only managed to open a gash when the bear looked away. It rammed its bulk into Vanwoerden, dropped its paws on the human, and clamped his teeth down on the back of Vanwoerden's neck.

He didn't bite through, as easy as it might have been to snap the human's head off, but Jerry met the sight with a determination rising alongside his fear. He guessed that Venn had told them not to make a high-pitched sound as this would sound to the bear like a prey animal crying out in fear and attract the bear's unwanted attention. They already had that attention, so Jerry desperately began wailing and making as many sudden motions as he could manage.

The bear let go of Vanwoerden, turned on Jerry, and charged at his new target. Jerry braced himself for the impact with his own knife out, but doubted in those seconds that he would even have the scant luck Vanwoerden did.

A spear flew into the bear's side hard enough to jolt the animal out of its charge. It roared with pain added to its anger and earlier wound, and whirled to face this new attacker. The man who had stepped into harm's way was enormously tall and stocky, rock solid, a head higher than Vanwoerden, in his early thirties, with a hooked nose and a glare as intense as his ursine opponent's. Jerry recognized him as one of the camp masters, though he didn't know the man's name.

Their new savior notched another spear in an atlatl, something Jerry had never seen outside of a museum, much less in use. He didn't even realize anyone still knew how to use such a prehistoric weapon. When the bear charged, the camp master flung the spear out of the atlatl and drove it deep and straight into the white crescent on the bear's chest. It skidded and fell hard, snapping the spear.

A Hole in Wednesday

But it wasn't dead yet. The camp master approached the animal with caution but no hesitation, yanked the first spear out of the animal's side, and plunged it two-handed into the heart. The bear moaned, shuddered, and died.

When the three recruits' trembling subsided enough for them to breathe, Venn asked, "What could have wounded a bear like that?"

"One of you," the camp master snapped. "By which I mean one of the recruits. A human being. Someone with the skill to use a metal blade in close quarters against the bear and escape unscathed."

"Hunting?" Jerry asked.

"This isn't a hunting wound, Carson." He placed one hand on the creature's thickly furred side. "Someone riled it up before you found it, and it recognized your scents as the same, or close enough, as what agitated it before. Three scents this time, so it assumed you were coming to finish it off."

He pulled the spear from the creature's heart and pointed it at the recruits.

"Which is the sort of thing you will learn to recognize by the time your training is done, if you survive, and don't wash out," he continued. "Including learning to hunt. An obmonth from now, if you last that long, you'll only be eating and drinking what you can hunt and forage for yourselves. For now, no death here should be wasted. We'll carry the bear's carcass back to the camp to eat."

"No wasteful killings," Vanwoerden quoted.

The camp master nodded sharply. "My name is Gilbert Ching Immerman. You will obey all the camp masters' instructions without fail or delay, but you will obey mine foremost of all. Because I am the one who will be training you. I will be the one forging you into the world's next chosen generation."

Sixteen

Jerry knew that somebody was trying to kill him.

He didn't know why, though he entertained many possibilities. But he knew how.

The Gallows had strange training regimens at Camp Natufian. Sparring in caves. Sparring under waterfalls. Sometimes partners were tethered, hand to hand or foot to foot, or in some cases even hand to foot. Sometimes they would have to fight while each holding an egg, and the first person to let his egg get broken was the loser. Unusual, and recruits often came out injured, but there was nothing overtly sneaky about those exercises.

Yet as he trained, Jerry realized that his mind turned less toward the Reductionists' point of view, and more toward the holistic. So he started noticing patterns born out of what others might see as randomness or coincidence.

During the weeks of the vertiginous mountain training thus far, there had been traps laid here and there, small things but potentially lethal. Equipment sabotaged like a half-cut rope Jerry used to scale a rock cliff. Luck and some of his growing skill had saved him there. Fortunately he found that he could spot ledges and crannies and hand-holds naturally, including those others might miss, and happened to be at an ideal spot to clench close to the rock when the rope snapped and plunged into the granite maw of the ravine far below.

He wondered if whomever had riled up the black bear that attacked them had done so on purpose, meaning to stoke it into going after the next hapless recruits who happened upon it.

Another day, canteens of fresh water awaited Jerry and his tent-mates at a time outside when their trainers normally provided such. Jerry, already suspicious from the other incidents, decided to pour the water onto the grass. He nearly used the grass inside the tent as an experiment, but decided against that in case either of his tent-mates were the saboteur, and might get suspicious. He picked a spot close to the tent but mostly out of view and dumped the water.

While Jerry waited for the results of his experiment, he snatched up Venn's and Vanwoerden's as well, though tried them in different spots. He tried Vanwoerden's first. There was no reason for testing the canteens in that order, except maybe for Jerry having a subtle ancestral prejudice that the male was the greater threat. Of course, history proved many times over that the female could be just as much a viper in silk robes. Venn had demonstrated repeatedly in physical training that she seemed to possess an endless font of endurance.

The experiment proved inconclusive. The grass suffering the test of his canteen browned and burned within an hour. The grass used for his tent-mates' water looked unaffected. But that didn't prove that Vanwoerden or Venn were the culprits. Jerry could simply be the target of someone else, or perhaps—this seemed likely based on the supposedly random nature of the sabotage—that the saboteur poisoned one canteen without knowing exactly whose hands it would end up in. And if Jerry's ultra-caution should save him, as it did, a poisoned canteen might be intended to generate suspicion between the tent-mates.

Whatever the truth, Jerry decided that from now on he would draw all of his own water or do without.

A run through the woods with Vanwoerden, who loved to run and frequently jibed Jerry about his lack of running ability, saw his warning instincts flare up suddenly when they came upon a patch of leaves on the ground that didn't look quite right. Vanwoerden had pulled ahead as he always did and had all but flung himself into the trap before Jerry burst forward and grabbed the back of the South African's shirt to pull him back.

But Vanwoerden had too much mass and velocity to be pulled back so easily, and both he and Jerry pitched sideways into a sinkhole covered over with twigs and leaves. Jerry caught a glimpse of sharpened woodened stakes below as they tumbled.

Had they run full-out into the pit they would both have died immediately. Or at least been gored immediately, with death possibly waiting as they lingered in agony first. As it was, Jerry's reflexes had turned them away enough that when they tumbled they could pivot and grab the side of the pit, though Jerry heard Vanwoerden cry out in pain as they thrashed about for purchase.

The sinkhole was twenty feet deep and they were both hanging from the side. Jerry had managed to miss the spikes, though one menaced him from directly below. Vanwoerden, farther ahead and faster, had a bloody two-foot long slice up his bare left leg. When Vanwoerden put that foot against the pit wall he grimaced and left behind a spot of blood. There was a hole in the sandal that Jerry guessed penetrated through to his foot.

Jerry had grown to be as good a climber as Vanwoerden was a runner, particularly after the incident with the severed rope. He managed to get his elbows over the top with a single heave, then cast his leg over and pitched forward and over the rest of the way. He turned and looked at Vanwoerden. The South African was still struggling and the pain was stealing away the color from his face.

For an instant Jerry thought about leaving the man in that position. In that instant he considered the possibility that Vanwoerden still could be the saboteur, just going to great lengths to hide his involvement, to the point that it amounted to self-mutilation.

But after his first flash of terror began to subside, Jerry decided that the idea was ridiculous. Jerry had pulled Vanwoerden back himself. Now he grabbed one of Vanwoerden's arms and pulled again, this time with his tent-mate grunting as he put his own muscle behind his survival.

When they were both finally out and several feet away from

the pit, Vanwoerden cried, "Who would do such a thing? And how could they?"

That last question was a practical one rather than one of morality, Jerry knew. The Gallows' recruits had little free time, and the camp masters less so. A twenty-foot deep pit filled with a dozen sharpened wooden poles and camouflaged, all done by hand, would have required an intensive and time-consuming effort.

"I've noticed things," Jerry finally said, then related the various anomalies.

"*Ja*, as have I," Vanwoerden said. "But this is far above and beyond someone slicing into a rope. Were we the targets, do you think?"

"I doubt it, if you mean us specifically. Someone else might have chosen to run through this forest path first. For that matter, the rope and poison could have been distributed to others. Others among the recruits did fall ill afterward. But in these savage circumstances, hundreds of miles from the nearest dome, illness to one degree or another is not an uncommon occurrence."

"As I said, Carson, this is far above and beyond," Vanwoerden told him. "This would require a great deal of planning, never mind the execution. This is an obvious trap that cannot be faked to look like an accident. This one was meant to be noticed."

He glanced away, and Jerry followed his look. Vanwoerden was studying the wound on his leg. He stripped off his cotton shirt, tore off one sleeve, and bound the rest around the wound with a handful of kudzu vines. The sleeve became a medical wrap for his injured foot, and Vanwoerden slipped a thick wad of grass between his covered foot and the sandal.

But who was supposed to notice the trap? Not the intended victim, at least not until it was too late. That would leave surviving recruits, the camp masters, Buster Donnelly, and Northpath Marks himself. Maybe it was meant as some sort of message, or to make the recruits and the camp masters suspicious of one another. Perhaps even to send Marks a clue that the organization had been infiltrated.

Which, of course, Jerry had done. But since Jerry was nearly a victim himself several times over, it didn't seem that he was the one suspicion must fall on.

He felt he could safely rule out the Reductionists as well. They had work for him to do, so planting traps at his feet hardly made sense.

A moment later it occurred to Jerry that he and the saboteur might be on the same side. But then he shook the idea away. Jerry had no intention of being on the same side of a killer. Especially one who had, by design or accident, tried killing Jerry as well.

Another idea hit him. "If the killer wants to be noticed, then let's make sure he—or she—isn't."

"What do you mean?" Vanwoerden asked.

"When the saboteur comes back, he'll find his trap dismantled. But he won't know who did it. So any of us in the camp could be on to him."

"You want to fill it in? We don't have time. Or the dirt." Vanwoerden nodded to his leg. "And I'll admit I'm not feeling up to that kind of labor at the moment. But I see what you're shooting at, Carson. Why don't we just take the spikes?"

The South African grinned, and his cheeks flushed a bit ruddy. "We each take six and hide them somewhere. Then we'll have our own spears if we need them. I'll help."

"You need to get that leg stitched up," Jerry told him. "And people will certainly notice your wound."

"I'll stitch it after I get my spears. As for the wound—you cut me during sparring. A great coup for Jerry Carson, ha ha!"

Vanwoerden was in no shape to help with the spike withdrawal directly, so Jerry made a snap decision. "I'll get them out. You help me in and out."

Vanwoerden was strong, and while he rested his leg and foot, he had no trouble wrapping a muscular arm around Jerry's waist as Jerry was dunked into the pit six times, pulling up two stakes per plunge.

"I'm guessing you do not suspect me of being the saboteur," Vanwoerden said when they were done. He nestled a formidable pile of spears in his arms.

"That still leaves too many suspects," Jerry answered.

As much as who, Jerry wanted to know why the saboteur was going about the nefarious business. The rigorous physical training offered the perfect forum to release his mind to work the problem over and over. It demanded his physical body be completely subject to the camp masters, but left a small box tucked away in the back of this brain at liberty to mull over the problem. Likewise it roamed his mental chambers as he fell asleep and as he awoke—both of which sometimes took a long while with no speeder to induce the process.

There were many suspects but no obvious culprits.

His training-battered side was quick to blame their camp master, the brutal—though probably only brutal from the standpoint of his soft life in Manhattan Dome—taskmaster Gilbert Ching Immerman. Immerman took a special dislike to Jerry, Venn, and Vanwoerden. Immerman had boundless energy and accompanied the recruits on their scheduled group exercises, never getting so much as winded, at least not enough that he had to stop yelling at them.

Immerman, however, seemed to be ruled out as the potential assassin by virtue of the fact that he *was* constantly with them, usually running ahead of or beside to goad them. Severe as he was, Jerry welcomed Immerman's presence because if some trap awaited, particularly something large like a tiger stake pit, he might trigger it first.

Assuming, of course, that Immerman wasn't accompanying them to make sure a trap sprung successfully.

Marks' proxy, Buster Donnelly, came and went, spending days at a time watching the training, though never commenting, and never giving anyone more or less attention than anyone else. It was probably foolish to peg him as the culprit, though. He could have finished or permanently stoned Jerry at any time. And if he was waiting to see if Jerry betrayed them, or tried to find a way to escape, why try killing him?

There was, of course, the spy the Reductionist had told him about. But why would the spy turn assassin? Perhaps he or she was watching carefully to see if Jerry truly turned to the Gallows, with orders to kill him if he did. Jerry had worried about not being able to fool Marks and the narcohypnosis test, but what if he was doing too good a job of acting the part of the good ultra-Darwinist?

Ironically, the attempted killings were having their own unintended educational consequence. Jerry was learning how to recognize patterns. And in doing so, he realized he was naturally skilled at it.

As wild and chaotic as this mountain was, there was some order in the mountain itself and its temporary residents. The outcroppings and cleavage in the rock faces he climbed. The lay of the forest floor and when a pile of leaves did not appear quite the same as the rest. The martial arts moves the camp masters used, and the ones the recruits used as their skills increased. A flattened patch of grass or broken twig where recruits had passed. The routines among the camp masters, occasionally varied but moving into a recognizable pattern with each shift, and after only two weeks Jerry could predict their whereabouts with complete accuracy.

Thus he realized he could rule out the camp masters as culprits, including Immerman. If anything they were more strictly regimented than the recruits, who had thin patches of free time now and again between training and at the end of the night—while surveilled, no doubt, through their own chips and other means, to see if they still complied with the program. The small lethal traps like a cut rope and poison could have been accomplished by anyone, but a staked pit would require more time and effort.

The camp masters had access but, ironically, not time. The recruits might have time, particularly during survival exercises where they were unleashed in the woods for days at a time to fend for themselves—and against each other if needs be—and this likewise gave them access. The knife, spade, and hatchet meant for building shelters and hunting traps would be sufficient to construct a large trap, if incredibly labor intensive. Still, Jerry's definition of "labor intensive" was changing rapidly from what he could have imagined in the dome.

He could even create his own tiger stake trap if necessary.

And now, on his first day in the next survival stint alone in the woods, hidden among the throng of trees growing wherever they pleased instead of to the dictates of the Park attendants, hosting animals of all sorts who lived by the dictates of the wild instead of being curated by specially licensed animal producers for the dome's green spaces, Jerry crouched in the brush as if in ambush, and realized he had spent no short time while contemplating doing exactly that.

A trap for the hunter. A lethal pre-emptive strike to test the mettle of his tormenter, and if someone else just happened upon it, well, then . . .

He froze the thought, horrified, before it could run its course. This was not the person, the creature, he wanted to become at either the hands of Galapagos or the Reductionists.

But if he wished to bring down Galapagos, and have any kind of future, and for Linda to have any kind of future, this was, for the time being, a path he would have to walk beside if not directly on. These past weeks since his daybreaking had taught him about dark men and dark thoughts. He could not save himself or anyone else by blinding himself to the shadows still lingering in the New Era.

He located a gnarled ancient oak tree marked with a single pale line where he had stripped off a slice of bark. The oak was grandiose in its splendor, perhaps older than the Dayworld itself even without the benefit of spending six days an obweek in a stoner, and yet its aesthetic qualities were not why Jerry had chosen it. Its thick trunk was mottled with whorls and bulges allowing for climbing. Its multitude of branches were generous enough to offer places to lie in wait, to stand, to hide objects, and to hide himself nearly everywhere among them.

He got the idea from another pattern he noticed. No one among the recruits ever looked up, to the trees or otherwise. None of the caches they were ever charged with finding in their exercises were up, just hidden in brush or buried. As far as Jerry could tell, while their bodies were outside on a mountain, the other recruits' brains were still back in the domes—where trees were nothing more than ornaments in parks, and the sky was a polymer arch more than a mile above them.

Jerry climbed the tree to the first tier of branches, then the second. There he had cached a recurve Kickapoo bow made of Osage wood and a rawhide quiver of hunting arrows tipped with chert arrowheads. He hung the quiver on his shoulder, and climbed further. At an altitude of sixty feet he was completely camouflaged from anyone on the ground, yet a break in the leaves gave him commanding views of the forest. He could see several of the recruits. Now his crouching in ambush was intentionally what it appeared to be. He slowly laid down across a branch about half as wide as he was, in an area with no other branches close at hand to restrict his movements, and watched.

And in watching so intensely, did not notice the figure watching him until it jumped and slammed into him from above.

The heavy blow to his back stunned him but his reflexes were already honed to act automatically using any tools at hand. Now this meant swinging his bow at his attacker's large silhouette. The attacker slapped it away and jabbed a fist into Jerry's chest, sending Jerry reeling backward across the large rough limbs, tottering but not falling. Jerry ducked the next swinging punch but, still a little off balance and too conscious of the ground far below, did not jump back or block fast enough when the attacker sent a booted foot into one of Jerry's knees. Jerry buckled and the next punch connected with his chin and sent him over the limb and downward.

He plunged ten feet before he tossed aside the bow and hooked his arms around another limb, though it seemed like a hundred. This fungi-covered limb bounced, and Jerry could tell at once it was dying or already dead and not the safest of perches. But there was now nothing between him and the ground thirty feet below.

And as it was his attacker, revealed in the dim light of dusk as his camp master, Gilbert Ching Immerman, vaulted down to the edge of the limb and loomed over Jerry.

"You're the assassin!" Jerry cried, scrambling to find a better perch on this worst of branches. Worst, of course, except it had saved him from falling, but now he could see his weight striking into it had left a noticeable crack between Jerry and Immerman.

Immerman placed his booted foot over the crack.

"No, Carson. But it is perspicacious of you to determine that one of your number was trying to kill you."

He leaned closer to Jerry while increasing his weight on the crack. "I realized it some weeks ago. And I determined—through patterns, as I suspect you have, eyeing you as I have been—who the would-be killer is. I sent word to Dr. Marks. It seems one of our recruits is a hound."

"If it isn't you, then tell me who it is!"

"If you cannot determine the identity on your own, then you are a fool who deserves to meet whatever fate these days have in store for you instead of seizing your own fate and twisting it to your own ends. But you recognized the sabotage, so you possess the capacity to ferret out our hound before he does you in."

Jerry was breathing heavily and speaking was a struggle, but not the hardest he had encountered through the fierce extremes of his training. "If you won't tell me who it is, then tell me why you haven't stopped him!"

"Why should we? When the domes fall, his kind will spread out everywhere through the world like a virus. Those who follow Galapagos must learn to recognize them, because they will not always reveal themselves, and then deal with them by any means necessary."

"A necessary killing?" Jerry snapped back.

"Would you not think so, if he threatened your life, or those you loved? Perhaps you should kill the killer first, your opening move in this slow but methodical murder of this New Era that is so deserving of death. But first you must determine the killer's identity."

"Which you won't tell me!"

"But I will offer you a hint. Your profile portrays you as an avid reader, Carson. So you should understand your clue. If there is anything harder than a poor author trying to write a great book, it is a great writer trying to write a poor book."

A Hole in Wednesday

This spun round in Jerry's already spinning head, but he couldn't snatch it still or make sense of what little flashes he did spot.

"Perhaps in this matter," Immerman said, "as in other things, you perform better under pressure. Think, Carson!" He slammed his foot down repeatedly. "Think!" *Crack!* "Think!" *Crack!*

Jerry felt the limb bounce and shake, then sag, a splintered brown wedge appearing where the crack had been.

What did Immerman's riddle mean? What was the quote he had once read by a famous author advising those just starting out . . . write bad books. Everyone starting will write a bad book. Give yourself permission to write badly. But if you write enough . . .

"Think!" *Crack!*

. . . Sooner or later the writing won't be so bad, then better, then good, and maybe someday great . . .

There was the sound of a gunshot in Jerry's ears. Not from a gun, though, but the branch as it broke halfway free and was suddenly vertical, with Jerry's thoughts broken just as surely as he clamped his arms around the branch and fell with it, swinging. He began climbing up the limb, his feet searching for a purchase far below. Yet the back of his mind continued working.

An author who has achieved greatness, his mind told him, will find it distasteful at the very least, and most likely impossible, to write something poorly. He can try to, pretend at the game. But something will give him away. The flourish of a sentence. A few intense words that lesser authors would not have the courage to use. An unimaginable twist of plot . . .

As he reached the top, only a handhold from salvation, Immerman was there, boots ready, knife in hand poised where he could plunge it into Jerry's hand. Immerman raised the blade with the admonition, "Think!"

And then Jerry knew. Along with having a better idea of the risks he had dived into.

This time, the risk was breaking off a smaller branch from the larger one he clung to so precariously, which he jammed upward straight into Immerman's crotch. The camp master didn't drop his knife but he did *Whufff!* and stagger back, giving Jerry just enough opportunity to grab the safer end of the limb and haul himself up.

Immerman was now a dozen feet away, red-faced and knife pointing at Jerry's chest. Close as they were, it wasn't close enough, and the limb not wide enough, for Jerry to avoid a killing blow if he took the offensive.

"Answer," Immerman told him. "Give me an idea for how you plan to find the saboteur!"

Jerry did.

Immerman gave Jerry a long look, then laid the knife on the limb and said, "This field exercise ends tomorrow. And tomorrow, Dr. Marks will be arriving. So tomorrow will be your do or die, Carson, literally. Because once the killer knows you're on to them, with Dr. Marks judging you all, they will need no more reason for discretion. You might have five minutes to decide what to do once the killer is revealed, if you're lucky."

Then Immerman clutched the oak's thick bark and descended downward free-handed. In just seconds he was on the ground staring up at Jerry for what Jerry wondered might be the last time before the confrontation with the assassin.

This wasn't the only confrontation he was careening toward, Jerry knew. Just as great if not greater, he was preparing to face the best or worst of himself. He was on a stage, only playing a role—a role full of sound and fury, yet signifying everything to him personally. If he did break the killer's fourth wall and the revelation made the killer desperate, Jerry wondered if he could immerse himself in his own part long enough to kill the killer. Or if hesitation, perhaps even morality, would cost him everything.

Tomorrow, and tomorrow.

Seventeen

Once Jerry decided on his course of action, he was impatient to get it over with, no matter the outcome. He had read accounts of soldiers in the days before the New Era saying how waiting for the battle to start was worse than the fighting itself. Now he understood.

He had thought sleep would be impossible the last night of the field exercise. But he slept nevertheless, as those soldiers had slept whenever and wherever they were able, as if his body had known what it needed and wrung sleep out of Jerry's jangled nerves.

Immerman had made no promises to Jerry about setting up the circumstances from which Jerry could try to single out the traitor in their camp. He had said nothing at all, except for lowering Jerry's bow and withdrawing from the forest. But as the reveille horn roused the recruits from their sleep, Immerman ordered them all to run up to the top of the Bald—what the camp masters called a treeless domed hill just beyond the camp overlooking the seemingly endless Appalachians to the western horizon—and into two lines facing each other. He announced that they would now be testing each other in hand-to-hand combat.

There were twelve recruits left of the original twenty-six. The others had dropped out, overwhelmed by the rigors of the training, or fallen too ill, physically or psychically, to proceed.

Or maybe the traitor got to them—killed them or done some incapacitating injury, perhaps, as each was already gone by morning reveille. Either way, the result was the same. The fourteen were probably permanently entombed in the stoner chamber by now, or dead.

Marks had arrived, unnoticed by the recruits until he made his appearance at the Bald's round peak. "Based on what your camp masters have told me, and what I have watched so far, I am almost satisfied with your progress," the doctor announced. "Proving yourselves to be stronger than all of those who will be around you in the cities would satisfy me. But I want to be more than satisfied. I want you to exceed my expectations.

"There are those who would say Galapagos is planning genocide. It is the New Era committing the slow genocide of our species, while you and I are trying to stop the patient from bleeding to death. All we are doing is nothing more than pushing society to its limits. If it is stronger than I believe, then it will survive our poking and prodding. If it is as weak as I am certain it is, then it will collapse, and we will move into what is left.

"If we are not strong, then we will not survive either—but we must.

"There are three components of the universe that must be faced and embraced for humanity to be free and under its own control: reality, the knowledge of why reality is truth, and change. But there are likewise a trinity of forces acting against humanity: governments, religion, and technology. The government of the so-called Organic Commonwealth of Earth mandates that only the government can decide what is reality and truth, and only through the help of the government can you change. They put a boot on your neck, watch and record every moment of your life, and they call it a social contract! It calls religion superstition because religion is the only force capable of successfully counteracting government!"

Marks' voice rose, pitched toward greater anger. "And yet the leaders of religion obscure our necessary components of life and freedom as well! They claim, like government, only they can interpret reality and truth, and the only changes you are to make are to conform to what they say—or that you are not allowed to change at all. That nothing changes, and all of the universe itself must stay static." He shook a fist. "But this is not the way of life! You trade a lifetime under a boot heel for the hope of something better after your life here is over!

"Technology by its nature does not seek to control, but it is equally insidious because it gives the false illusion of putting control in our hands. It promises you can use it to find reality and truth. It whispers false promises that you can use it to enact change!"

Marks had riled himself into such a righteous froth by now that Jerry wouldn't have been surprised if the ground beneath them started shaking.

"All of these are false gods and true evils in equal measure," Marks declared. "The only way you can learn truth and reality, and the only way you can bring yourself true change, is to find those things within yourself, from your own instincts and your own primitive natures.

"Our New Era of convenience and abundance has rendered humanity's two greatest instincts, survival and problem-solving, nearly extinct. Anyone who is to survive in our society after the domes must possess these so deeply they can never be rooted or burned out. Some have told me they believe we no longer possess these instincts. The New Era has bled them out of us, they say. I believe they cannot be completely lost. Somewhere deep within us yet resides our Old Stone Age savage, and it is the one we must now heed if we are to save what is left of our world.

"We do these things not for greed or self-aggrandizement. We must possess these if humanity itself is to survive. Show me today that you are worthy and capable of being humanity's saviors."

With you as chief savior, no doubt, Jerry thought. Even Marks' position on the Bald, atop a peak above the clouds and mountains and the rest of the Natural creation, was calculated to appear messianic. He wanted to be the Supreme Councilor of a world with no World Organic Council.

"How will we do this?" Marks continued. "You build the biggest cage for the biggest predator. But the people of the New Era are already in their cages—the domes, and their own psyches. All we need to do is become the predators ourselves.

"Do not see the world as you wish it to be," Marks concluded. "See it for what it really is, if you would change it. Accept, plan, and act. Accept what you see, plan for it, and then act swiftly and decisively."

That much Jerry agreed with. He accepted Marks' power to make his dark vision a reality. What he saw ahead of him, if Marks had his way, was more bleak and grim than the false Utopia implied in Marks' demagoguery. All Jerry saw ahead of him was the crumbling of civilization as humanity had known it since people first built homes and set their words to writing, replaced by a brutality of which Marks was the supreme leader.

It was the planning and acting where Jerry faltered. What could he possibly do to stop the Gallows' world from coming about? His only allies were the dubious Reductionists, and the only one of those he had spoken to had half-seriously suggested Jerry call him after a false Wizard.

But Immerman's presence now reminded Jerry of far more immediate concerns.

The camp master paced along the two lines, eyeing the recruits up and down, his face hard but otherwise giving no hint about what he was thinking. "All of you have strengths, and all of you have weaknesses," he said. "Some of you don't know one or the other, and some don't know both. Each of you will be paired first with someone who opposes you with a strength to your weakness. Find your strength and defeat your partner. Fail to identify your weakness, and you will lose."

Immerman glanced at Jerry for the barest instant, then looked over them all with a single tenebrous stare.

"You will each fight until one surrenders. If neither surrenders, you will fight until one of you is no longer able to fight, by whatever force this requires. But surrender will come with punishment. For this first bout, anyone who surrenders will be required to go the next three days without food. Future bouts will increase the penalty. The camp masters will neither comment on your fights nor intervene in your matches under any circumstances."

There was Immerman's answer to Jerry's plan. If Jerry was able to fight the killer to the other's point of desperation, the killer now had permission to use lethal force to silence his target.

The idea Jerry suggested to Immerman in the tree the night before was as simple as it was deadly dangerous. Up until the point they joined the Gallows, all of the recruits presumably had soft and basic city lives. If they'd had any instruction in martial arts it would be as Jerry had, nothing used in combat against an opponent determined to win at any cost. Jerry had gotten a taste of this during his first days of daybreaking. But even in his fearful desperation, those skirmishes had been less of a challenge than what he had faced these past weeks on the mountain. And Marks had admitted that none of the recruits gave the Gallows the hassles Jerry did. So Jerry thought it likely the lessons to fight the recruits were receiving was the first real martial training they had ever known.

All except for one. The hound in hiding, the asp in the wooded shadows, taking small strikes until the opportunity to launch a large one. If he or she truly was a hound then their training would have been far more advanced and progressed than what the Gallows put them through. This would be elementary school stuff. Jerry suspected the hound could probably beat down any of the recruits, Jerry himself included, but would be hiding those skills in order to appear as a novice.

Here was where Jerry's idea to Immerman during their decisive confrontation came into play. As a great author could not truly write a poor book without some traces of the greatness peeking through, neither did Jerry think a hound could go on forever hiding skills that would have become ingrained into reflex. They would be muscle memories tapped without requiring conscious thought, Jerry reasoned, if genuine danger immediately threatened. Jerry intended to threaten immediate danger to induce the desired, or perhaps not so desired, results.

There was, of course, the lesser danger of the hound surrendering before reaching their climax. But in the meantime Jerry would take note of each of his opponents' fighting patterns, particularly whenever Jerry threw a move into the mix wholly different from whatever he had been using before. If he suspected he was facing the killer, he might make a move that could inflict serious pain or damage if successful. He would pay close attention to the countermove, then the counter to Jerry's counter, and in particular if his opponent employed any contrivance not included up to that point in the Gallows' training.

"Face your opponent," Immerman commanded, and Jerry did, along with everyone else up and down the line. Were they going to start their sparring right here, side by side?

Only now did Jerry see flaws in his plan. There were eleven other recruits, for one thing. Statistically it wasn't likely Jerry would fight all eleven to find his tormentor, but it was equally unlikely he would locate his quarry on the first try too. It was most likely he might have to engage in a substantial number of duels, and quickly if the previous weeks' regimen was any indication, which would leave him tired and probably not doing his best and quickest thinking.

Also, his first opponent, eyeing him as warily as he eyed her, was his tent-mate, the slight golden-copper-skinned woman, Venn. She was typically brusque and aloof, and usually unforgiving. But she was also tenacious, which Jerry admired and respected, and her unforgiving nature was aimed at herself as much as anyone else. Jerry found himself liking her over the weeks they spent together. He hoped she was not the hound.

You can't think like that, Jerry admonished himself. Think like a soldier. Defend yourself no matter who your opponent is.

"Fighting stances of your choosing," Immerman said. Another nod to Jerry's idea. The opening stance itself, and the opening moves, could be telling. The camp master stepped back to where the others watched on impassively. "From this point on, none of the camp masters will have any involvement in these contests except to assign your opponents."

A Hole in Wednesday

For a few moments there was an interminable silence. Jerry began to sweat under his arms, down his chest. The day seemed hotter than he remembered. He and Venn stayed poised before one another as if they would be locked in that near-embrace but never quite touching until Nature wore down the mountain they stood atop. Out of the corner of his eye he noticed other recruits glancing at one another, wondering what to do. He wondered if the hound would be patient, or impatient and glancing around, or hiding whatever was felt at the strange delay.

Then Jerry realized the delay wasn't strange at all, but a test. No more involvement except choosing opponents, Immerman said. This included giving the order to begin.

Jerry took the initiative and lunged.

She reacted swiftly but a half-heartbeat too slowly. That gave Jerry enough time to sweep her leg as he struck rigid fingers at her sternum to throw her further off balance. She went down but was lithe enough to spring back up into a fighting crouch, and Jerry knew that in just a matter of seconds he had already lost the opening advantage.

But it hardly mattered. Venn had grown strong during their training, but was still too methodical. She fought like a scientist attacking a particularly troublesome theory that didn't quite hang together, with a set series of steps ordained by some higher secular authority, one after the other systematically, abandoning each one as it didn't work for the next in a series Jerry could predict before the sparring even started. Against many opponents, and certainly against nearly anyone used to life in a dome, she would be effective. But Jerry was already learning to launch and react without thought, while Venn thought too much. In less than two minutes she was on the ground with Jerry atop her and her neck in the crook of his elbow, squeezed until he knew her vision was blacking out, along with her consciousness. She slapped the ground to surrender.

Jerry jumped back immediately. He had worried that perhaps Immerman made Venn the opponent first because she was the hound. But their fight only confirmed Jerry's guess that she could not be. Based on her fighting style, along with everything she did through the past weeks, she was too methodical, too invested in planning every detail. Most of the hound's sabotage was necessarily by opportunity because the recruits often did not know what they would be doing from day to day. Intelligent as she was, and physically quick, Jerry did not think her adaptable enough to be the saboteur.

Nor were the next three people Jerry tussled with. One was his other tent-mate, Vanwoerden, the old-fashioned Boer from the Southern Africa Ministering Organ, who almost seemed incapable of any move not involving his brute strength and muscles two rungs above everyone else. Speed was Jerry's ally fighting Vanwoerden, but the Boer put up a greater fight than the others, enough that he and Jerry were evenly matched, until Jerry locked his whole body around Vanwoerden in a wrestler's grip Vanwoerden couldn't escape. From there Jerry inflicted a series of painful but otherwise harmless nerve blows on him, the same ones he had used to take down his two other opponents between Venn and Vanwoerden.

Those two, and to a lesser extent Vanwoerden, had been relatively simple take-downs. There was always the possibility they were playing at weakness, but his instincts analyzed their moves and turned up nothing suspicious.

The next two, fought after a short break where the camp masters allowed rest and water but no food, dug in and scrapped harder. They were more of a match and Jerry was on the ropes several times, and so upped his game, striking with harder punches in more sensitive places, teetering on the edge of but never quite spilling over into fighting dirty, and he wondered if he had some crazed look in his eye—which was entirely possible, he supposed—because both eventually seemed to quit fighting as much out of fear as pain.

His seventh opponent was the shuffling Beta Graham, the one Jerry had seen in the hospital right after being taken by Marks. Jerry's instincts screamed out a warning before they even faced each other.

A Hole in Wednesday

Jerry wasn't sure how Graham had come to be recruited, or why, or for that matter, exactly how he had managed to last in the Gallows' training for so long. Graham was fifty or fifty-five, named Beta for being a second child, once a corridor cleaner who switched to getting a PhD in Mystery Stories of the Twentieth Century. He arrived at the camp pudgy, but his fat had burned away and his muscles toned quickly. But his shuffling was still endemic. His moves still sluggish in any particular exercise the camp masters threw at them. Though he was persistent enough to always finish what he was made to do, he was always struggling. Yet his determination had seen him through thus far, until he was now facing his fourth opponent of the day—fewer than the faster Jerry, but more than Jerry would have given him credit for.

He shuffled into a half-clumsy fighting stance, feet placed not quite in line with the shoulders, the crouch not quite far down enough, showing just a little too much chest. If anyone else had met Jerry with that stance, Jerry knew at this point he could take the opponent down relatively easily. With Beta Graham this was simply the way he opened.

The truth hit Jerry first in the second before Graham struck: Graham had a pattern of sorts, in having no pattern. He did nothing different, every single time, no matter who he was fighting, or what he was doing. The same shuffle, the same stance, the same slow struggle with each exercise, the same as he had from the very beginning despite losing weight and toning up. In fact these days he possessed a chiseled look as if his body had remembered muscular was its normal state, the pudgy a temporary aberration. In Graham's desire to hide his real skills he had overcompensated, and was pretending to be the exact same man who first came to the mountain camp.

Jerry's flash of revelation saved him. Graham obviously saw awareness in Jerry's eyes because the older man didn't bother hiding his motives now, at least not from Jerry, whose lurch to one side just barely dodged a fist that would have thundered straight into his windpipe and crushed it. It would have looked like an accident yet been within the rules of the no-rules contest.

Jerry would be dead and Graham's identity would be safe, or so he thought.

Now both had the others' measure and there would be no hiding, no obscuring, no dancing around. Graham was no pushover and any ineptness on Jerry's part would be punished severely, probably lethally.

That thought made Jerry hesitate for an instant, but no more. He stepped back a few paces to make Graham work for the next move, which Jerry wanted to see. He saw an eyeful, and then nothing out of one eye at all, as Graham jutted at him like lightning and in a single stroke battered Jerry's left eye, though luckily Jerry had moved himself back far enough to keep from losing the eye altogether.

Beta Graham the laggard was gone. The hound showed its fangs and claws, plainly marked with the stains of past kills.

"I've seen the way you fight, Carson," Graham told him. "You're a sneak fighter. I know the way you work, and it won't work on me."

"I've seen your work too," Jerry told him. "The traps and sabotage. So far they haven't worked on me either."

Jerry was trying to goad Graham, but he might as well goad a rock. Hounds took their names not just from their ability to find things, but their reputation for being completely at the service of their masters. Like a faithful dog, they did as they were told within a completely amoral framework. They could accomplish great good; Jerry had heard many stories of hounds risking their lives to save people involved in accidents or disasters. But they also had a darker reputation as the deepest agents of the World Organic Council, to the point where all their life records were locked tight upon becoming hounds. Jerry was well aware now that they would follow more sinister orders with equal tenacity.

Graham's flurry of punches were like a manic windmill, if the windmill's blades drove the wind. Jerry just barely dodged them, leaving little room to block or return.

By the time he returned the punches Graham was already gone, flanking Jerry fast enough that a dodge only meant Graham's punch to the side of Jerry's head hit at half strength instead of enough to crack his skull. As it was Jerry was dazed, but he still had the presence of mind to drop and throw out a kick that connected with Graham's right knee, the leg the hound led with.

Graham sprung back on his left leg, reassessing his target. Jerry willed the mountain to stop spinning around him. But he still needed another moment.

Everyone was watching now. Whatever they said would be heard by all.

"Was I your specific target?" Jerry asked to buy time, and because he was intensely curious. "Or a bystander in the way? Or did you mean to take out all of the Galapagos recruits eventually? I can't believe even a hound would be capable of that."

Graham answered only by launching a punch aimed squarely at Jerry's throat. Jerry ducked slightly, enough to let Graham's chest make contact with Jerry with enough power to let Jerry pull them both back into a roll that ended with Jerry's boots connecting with Graham's head.

Graham flung himself backward again, putting distance between the two of them and this time holding it. But still he said nothing. What was he waiting for?

Jerry had his answer a second later, when Graham flicked a chert knife from his boot and flung it at Jerry.

The pain in Jerry's left shoulder where the blade struck was immense, but not crippling. During the course of lying awake at night thinking about the anonymous killer, he suspected that sooner or later there might be a projectile attack—in ambush, though, not in front of everyone when the camp masters had eliminated the rules.

So along with bow and arrows and rawhide quiver, traps, and the plethora of other survival gear they had learned to make, Jerry had fashioned himself a deerskin tunic that would slip easily under his camp-standard nondescript cotton shirt. He'd kept it hidden in the same oak with his bow until before sunrise this morning. Graham threw the knife with such power that the tunic hadn't prevented the blade from lodging in Jerry's shoulder. But without the tunic it surely would have gone into bone or all the way through.

Graham lunged again the instant the blade made contact. His eyes went wide with shock and pain when Jerry yanked the knife from his shoulder and jammed it into the side of Graham's neck.

Graham staggered back, shock replaced by anger. He pulled the knife out of his neck and covered the wound with one hand. It was only as he did so that Jerry understand what he had just done.

No decision, only action. No intent but defense. Yet the fact remained, he had given the killing blow. Whatever was left of the Jerry Carson who had not yet decided to daybreak was long behind him now.

"Was I your target?" Jerry demanded. He still wanted to know.

Immerman stepped toward Graham, who had somehow managed to keep his feet. "You might as well talk," the camp master told him. "We know you are a hound. We know you were placed here intentionally. Who were your targets?"

Venn and Vanwoerden flanked Jerry with concern. Venn offered an arm of support. Jerry realized he needed it.

Immerman ripped Graham's hand away from the wound and placed one of his own hands there. "I can save you or let you die, Graham."

"I only chose the best as targets," Graham said nonchalantly. His mission, then, which he went about fulfilling without pleasure or regret or remorse. "And I alone choose when I die, Immerman ever-man. *Hassasin*," he spat.

Graham's body seized and then the hound dropped, dead.

Immerman spun on his heels and approached Jerry.

"What just happened?" Venn asked.

"Code word," Immerman said. "A self-programmed kill switch in his brain."

"Hassasin," Jerry repeated, his own history lectures taking hold amid shock. "The order of fanatics who were promised paradise if they killed their masters' enemies. It gave us our word assassin."

A Hole in Wednesday

And yet he fired off the word at Immerman as if accusing him of being an assassin himself. And what did "ever-man" mean?

"We'll bind your wound," Immerman told him, then took in all three of the tent-mates in a glance. "Then I will have a discussion with all of you in my tent in one hour. You're excused from exercises for the remainder of the day. The other camp masters will deal with Beta Graham."

As Jerry followed Immerman down the Bald, he heard a voice behind him—no, in his skull—that he had wondered if he would ever hear again.

"We have a new job for you," the Reductionist told him.

Eighteen

"Tell me how you did it," Immerman said as he jabbed the needle into Jerry's shoulder.

Jerry gritted his teeth. The needle was small and expected, Immerman personally threading the stitches into the wound Graham left. No enduraskin here, and just alcohol in the wound rather than antibiotic treatment, although the camp master might make an exception if a lethal infection took hold. Yet at the moment it felt as painful as Graham's chert blade embedded in his shoulder.

Maybe he was feeling especially hypersensitive since the Reductionist's voice reappeared via the chip in Jerry's head for the first time in weeks. Jerry was definitely on edge now, between that, Graham's attack, and Jerry's killing of Graham in the sparring. Jerry didn't forget how it was Graham speaking a code word that triggered a signal in his brain to do the literal deed by creating an almost instant catastrophic metabolic collapse. But Jerry went into the battle knowing either he or Graham would likely be dead by its end, so even if he hadn't put Graham's chert knife into the hound's neck, Jerry still would have felt responsible in no small measure for affecting the killing stroke himself.

"How I did what?" he asked.

"Determine that Beta Graham was the saboteur," Immerman answered between stitches. "Obviously you deciphered my literary clue. I watched you track the fighting patterns of each of your opponents. Why Graham?"

Between stabs of localized but intense pain, Jerry told him, "Graham knew what he wasn't supposed to."

Immerman responded with a long look that bordered on amused. "As you say. Knowing what you are not supposed to, then, is clearly dangerous no matter your level of experience and caution."

Jerry didn't reply this time. Instead he looked around Immerman's tent in an effort to distract himself from his ongoing surgical procedure. One glance could take in everything as the tent was appropriately spartan. Two chairs, one of which Jerry sat in while Immerman stood, a small folding camp table between them, a larger wooden table that could be broken down into multiple pieces for quick moving, and a bulky wooden chest that would not have looked out of place on a pirate's galleon except for the modern biometric sensor mounted where an iron padlock would have dangled.

Jerry wondered less than idly about the chest. Immerman hardly seemed to need much. Some supplies, a way of communicating with Marks, weapons more than likely, and the camp master would be set to live anywhere.

"What was Graham's mistake?" Immerman asked.

Jerry considered this for a moment, knowing that if Immerman wanted an immediate answer he would have said so. He wanted Jerry to think it through.

Overconfidence in facing what he considered an inferior opponent? But Jerry sensed something larger lurking, of which overconfidence was a mere symptom.

His weakness. That's what Immerman was hunting for. The martial duets had been paired based on weakness versus strength.

Then Jerry had it. "He was inflexible. His training was broad and deep, but it saturated him to the point where nothing else would fit."

"Every situation he encountered was classified based on his own understanding," Immerman agreed. "But aren't we all guilty of this?"

A Hole in Wednesday

"To an extent," Jerry allowed. Another stab of the needle. Jerry wondered if the timing of answer and jab was coincidental. There was no time pressure to answer, but Immerman was not a taskmaster who would let a recruit ponder at his leisure. "But with a hound the training is conscious. An action is taken regardless of morality. They are trained to take a specific action, or to choose from a limited range of actions, as a specific consequence of a specific instigating action. There is no room for creative thinking. No room for improvisation."

The pain ceased and the needle was placed inside a cloth on the table. Immerman walked behind Jerry.

"When he faced you he was taking a multiple-choice test in which all the answers he was given were wrong," the camp master said.

"It shouldn't have mattered," Jerry remembered. He tried focusing his memory on the fight itself rather than, again, the outcome, which struck Jerry deeply as gruesome even though it was nearly as clean a death as mortally possible. "He was better trained than me. He was more experienced. He had no qualms about killing."

"You hesitate to kill. You still do."

Jerry tamped down the lingering malaise of taking another human life so he could continue functioning. Graham may have initiated the termination code word, but it was Jerry, in the haze of pain and heat of combat, who plunged the knife into Graham's neck for what was almost undoubtedly a mortal wound.

His mind was no doubt still in shock. The turmoil would come in the middle of the night, perhaps. Or in the next life-or-death fight, which Jerry thought increasingly likely. Perhaps he would hesitate, and then he would be the one with the knife in his neck.

Jerry would only kill in self-defense. He considered no other kind of killing to be justified. But he suspected this was not the answer Immerman wanted to hear.

Finally Jerry said, "Unnecessary killing is wasteful."

"'With consciousness comes clarity'," Immerman said, quoting Nietzsche.

"With experience comes clarity, and with clarity comes further experience," Jerry said, though he couldn't remember where he had heard that before. "Are you saying Graham was more experienced but a more limited thinker?"

"Graham had a base set of mandatory reactions he could not deviate from," Immerman explained. "And all of them involved killing anyone, or otherwise silencing anyone, who compromised his mission."

Jerry wondered if this was the real reason Immerman hid his knowledge of Graham's identity. Perhaps he was afraid Graham would target him first.

Though any of the camp masters had a better-than-even chance of being able to handle a hound. Yet Jerry still pondered the situation. Had he been placed in the position of the sacrificial pawn? Or was Immerman waiting to see if Jerry made it far enough across the board to be Queened? If so, he had moved one square closer. Of course, every square closer meant greater danger. And unlike even the most novice chess player, Jerry could not see what waited more than one square beyond, if that far.

"Yet you used your strength, Carson, wittingly or otherwise," Immerman continued, "to defeat him. What is this strength?"

"I've learned to notice patterns, and I could see the patterns in his fighting. The actions he took were based on knowledge he was not supposed to have."

"Incorrect. That is a facet of your strength only, and one which I led you to, not the core. At your core are the two instincts Dr. Marks knows are nearly extinct in humanity: survival and problem solving. You, shaped on our forge, are the exact kind of man Marks wants to populate the world after the New Era is brought down."

Jerry wondered if his mysterious Reductionist on the other end of the clandestine Gallows chip broadcast was listening in on any of this. The voice had spoken nothing more beyond the single line about a new job, then gone as silent as if Immerman's tent possessed a static jamming field. Jerry was sure there was no such field, only that the Reductionist was more interested in eavesdropping than ordering.

A Hole in Wednesday

There was another voice though, also a male, but this one came from outside the tent. "Camp Master Immerman! Recruits Vanwoerden and Venn requesting permission to enter!"

"Carson, stand," Immerman told him, and Jerry obeyed. "Vanwoerden and Venn, enter," he called out. They lined up at attention by Jerry, and Immerman told them to gather around the table.

"All three of you suspected we had a spy," Immerman told them, facing them. "Carson was the first to determine his identity. Why? Because he was the only one to initiate active measures to draw the spy out, while the two of you decided on passivity, waiting for the spy to make a mistake or be caught *in flagrante delicto*. In some cases your continuing observations would have been the correct course of action, but this spy would not have made a mistake. He needed to be triggered."

Immerman turned from them and walked toward his wooden chest in the corner of the tent.

Jerry knew he was being vain, but he was hoping for some sort of positive response from Vanwoerden and Venn. An acknowledgment of a job well done at great risk, or perhaps even a little admiration. But all he saw from them out of the corner of his eye, and felt radiating at him, was wariness.

Curiosity pulled him away from his tent-mates when Immerman placed a hand on his trunk's biometric sensor, which simultaneously read the DNA in his hand, the rhythm of his pulse, and the sound of his breathing—the first to verify that the lock was being opened by the proper person, the other two used as a life-log to prevent a crook from using a severed hand or deeply unconscious Immerman to open the chest.

Even with the trunk lid up, most of the trunk's contents were shrouded, except for a small box and a long bottle. The box, a simple carbon composite much like part of what made up Manhattan Dome, he placed on the camp table. The bottle was champagne with an ancient label. In his other hand Immerman produced wooden cups, as if the four of them were medieval warriors about to partake of mead before a battle.

Immerman popped the cork and poured champagne into each cup. "Consider this your graduation ceremony. Congratulations. You are now full-fledged members of Galapagos."

The three recruits—former recruits now, Jerry supposed, wondering again if his disembodied Reductionist was listening in and perhaps taking notes of details, including arcane ones flying past Jerry—glanced at one another with some uncertainty. Jerry shared their uncertainty. Was that it? Would they simply head home, Jerry to Manhattan, Vanwoerden to Johannesburg, and Venn to wherever she came from? Would they be given assignments? Jerry wondered foremost when he would be allowed to see Linda again. Perhaps that would be his graduation present.

Immerman was not immediately forthcoming. "This is champagne old enough to be the genuine article, from the Champagne region of France, before Champagne's ground was too poisoned to grow grapes, or anything else," he told them, sipping his own and gesturing for the others to follow his lead. They did so on command. "It was an excellent year even by the standards of the world before the New Era, and far superior to anything made since in this era when most anything bubbling alcohol is labeled 'champagne.' Drink it as a taste of what you will help bring back."

He finished his cup, set it down, and did not refill it. Jerry was more judicious with his, as was Venn, though the South African finished his with gusto and continued holding the cup, expectant.

Immerman smiled faintly at them, an expression which, on Immerman's visage, Jerry found unsettling.

"Left on its own the champagne would have suffered a slow decline, until now it would have been undrinkable. From time to time over the generations it has been kept in a stoner field. When we bring the New Era to a close, we will be able to make something like this again instead of having to consume our old treasures, among many other things."

He refilled the former recruits' cups, but not his own. Jerry wondered if he was participating in some ritual he had not the slightest inkling about. Something primitive and only one step over the line of civilized from antediluvian savagery. Or perhaps he was just overblowing things, still heady less from alcohol than the shock of the thudding force of jamming a knife into a human being's neck.

"Dr. Marks was pleased with your performances today," Immerman said almost formally. "Particularly you, Carson, your identification and neutralizing of the spy. From today forward, the three of you will be trainers, a new position second only to the camp masters in our hierarchy, several of whom are being sent back to the cities for various recruiting missions over the next few obmonths. Each of you will also receive these . . ."

He opened the carbon composite box on the small table to reveal three black hand-sized tablets stacked within. Jerry had never used one but he recognized them as Scouts, devices meant to be easily programmed to the designs of its owner. These were the SN-2056-634 models with probabilistic quantum computing, nanodiamond qubits, and self-isolated Turing-busting artificial intelligence algobrains. The ones Jerry had seen demonstrated in the Museum could also be used as communicators, research databases, and biological scanners both of the owner's physical and psychic well-being, along with determining the locations of others, either as random searches for anyone nearby, or trackers anywhere within a dome-sized area based on pre-programmed DNA sequences.

No doubt Immerman had one. Perhaps this was the way he or another camp master determined Graham was the hound. For all Jerry knew, they may have been watching him on their Scouts when he dug the staked pit or snuck into Jerry's tent with the poisoned canteen. He wondered how often the camp masters had watched him with their Scouts.

Immerman told them each to take one of the devices.

"The DNA of the new recruits will be programmed into your Scouts," the camp master told them. "The rest of the programming is at your discretion. By tomorrow night at sundown I want each of you to have come up with ideas for training the new recruits, and what you will be volunteering to do to lead them.

Also, do not think your own training has ended. I also called the three of you here to say you will still be training with me, and answering to me."

Jerry had sensed a calm in Immerman up to now. As he spoke there had been a certain elegant rhythm to his movements and the cadence of his speech, almost a melody, though less Mozart than the harsher undertones and clashing musical paradigms of Stravinsky's *Rite of Spring*. The patterns of speech and movement told of a balanced man of grace who was duty-bound to shove himself through a broken window to get where he was going, coming out on the other side bloodied but without a breath of complaint. Now something shifted, and while Immerman seemed to stand on rough, uncertain ground with his metaphorical torn and bloodied clothes and flesh, the previous preternatural calm descended upon him again.

Immerman refilled his own cup, though he took only the barest sip. "Things are moving forward. Dr. Marks believes your group of recruits is the most promising thus far, and as he watches you train others he will be deciding what positions to place you in, and where."

"Manhattan?" Jerry asked without thinking.

Immerman gave him a steady look. "If you continue exceeding Dr. Marks' expectations, Carson, I suspect something close to home for you can be arranged. A man who fights for his family is as powerful as one fighting for the world entire, as I well know."

For an instant he was staring a thousand yards away, or perhaps a thousand miles, beyond the endless mountains and into an abyss Jerry could hardly begin to see into. Then he was directly in front of them again both physically and in psychic presence.

"The timing of this group's superiority is also fortuitous," Immerman said. "I am not privy to the plans Dr. Marks has for beginning the implementation of Galapagos' long planned-for incursions to bring the world into our line of reordering. But I am aware he has made some sort of breakthrough, and the work will commence soon. All of you, if you satisfy him, will be on the front lines of the end of the New Era."

A Hole in Wednesday

Again, Jerry felt wary glances on him from Vanwoerden and Venn. Did they not trust him? Were they jealous? He wasn't certain. He didn't think they wished him any ill intent in a dangerous fashion. But some distance had opened between them, and he couldn't measure this new gulf.

Immerman dismissed them. Vanwoerden and Venn left together, beelining back for their tent without waiting for Jerry. Jerry hung back more as he tried to take in everything from the last few hours. He only barely succeeded, but for that matter, he only barely wanted to succeed. For the moment he preferred his mind to be in a quiet oblivion. It was more restful, and rest was what he wanted most right now.

But his mind was not naturally restful, and it refused to change now no matter what Jerry wished.

"A breakthrough," he murmured aloud. "Something allowing Marks to move all of his insane plans forward."

"This is your next job," the Reductionist's voice at last returned. "Marks has a special project he never strays far from for long. The Family has learned that since Marks will be with you in Virginia for an extended period of time, he will be bringing all of the records of his work with him on his computer. It is called Project Dantian."

"What is this project?"

"You don't need to know yet, Mr. Carson. Simply locate the file on his computer, break the encryption, and submit the contents to us."

"Simply?" Jerry snapped. "I don't know anything about encryption. I don't even know where to upload the files to. And that's assuming I can even get close to the computer in the first place, and for long enough to do anything with it."

But the voice was silent again, and Jerry was aware of footfalls behind him. Casual steps, not caring if they were heard.

It was Immerman.

Jerry almost panicked, wondering how much Immerman might have heard. The camp master was as inscrutable as always, then the edge of his mouth quirked up a little, as if he had all the knowledge in the world—or at least, knew everything about Jerry Caird Carson that he needed to know.

"I have a story for you, Mr. Carson," he said. "There was once a master and a student in China, many centuries ago. The student had come to the master pledging to do whatever must be done to learn from the master. He promised he would do anything the master told him to do. So the master gave him a test. He ordered the student to hang over a cliff, holding onto a limb sticking out of the cliff by just his teeth, with his arms hanging free and to not grab the branch for any reason. Then the master asked a riddle. 'Why did the Buddha go from India to China?' I don't want you to answer the master's riddle, Carson. I want you to tell me whether or not the student answered at all."

Jerry stared at the camp master. The story made no sense. If the student answered the riddle, he would plunge to his death. If he didn't answer or he grabbed the limb, thus saving himself, he would fail the test.

Immerman presenting the koan to Jerry made no sense either. It certainly didn't answer Jerry's worry that Immerman might have overheard him talking to the Reductionist. Jerry felt a sense of layer upon layer of risk and intrigue he was unaware of, with each layer successively piling on top of him until he was nearly suffocating.

A shadow of dark amusement passed over Immerman's face.

"If you have an answer, Carson, whether you believe it to be right or wrong," the camp master said, "do not hesitate to tell me. The master and student alike can learn a great deal from such answers."

Nineteen

The next few obweeks for Jerry were about education. Meaning, for the Gallows, an even more brutal regimen than he had endured as a recruit.

First there was increased physical and martial training to work through. This included learning to be proficient in more technological weapons than they had been allowed before, lethal gadgets like sliders rather than Neolithic stone daggers and pre-Columbian Osage bows.

Jerry never won a single sparring match with Immerman. The camp master was too fluid to reveal any patterns. He also had a habit of cheerfully switching to a new set of moves whenever Jerry thought he'd figured Immerman out, as if Immerman had spent several lifetimes learning a menagerie of martial skills.

More difficult, not something Jerry would have expected, were the mental and psychic tests as well. Learning the ins and outs of the Scout was simple though the little machine itself had a devious number of potential functions limited only by the user's imagination. But the newest members of Galapagos were also put through strange puzzles of various kinds, with a multitude of rewards and punishments for their solutions or lack thereof. Some were simply logic challenges, while others openly provided passive glimpses into the user's psyche.

It was a strange sensation, this dichotomy of his brain pulped into jelly while being made sharper. His body grew stronger with every bruising and battering, like an ancient red-glowing sword being folded over and over again in the forge. Every obday took him farther from the Jerry Carson he had been and toward another one he was uncertain about. But he made himself hold fast to his moral core, and his determination of doing this for Linda and the world that would burn if the Gallows had their way.

But other tests were more invasive. These, thanks to a demon's brew of narcohypnosis and Truth Mist, were fully sensory holographic scenarios gauging everything from reflexes to moral boundaries.

Jerry decided early on that knowing these were simulations, he would have no moral boundaries. He did whatever he was instructed to do, although he knew a total conversion so relatively quickly would seem unrealistic, so he did offer an instant or full moment of hesitation when instructed to do something utterly reprehensible, such as the torture of a child or a fatal quantum beam blast to the belly of a pregnant woman. Sometimes he would allow Immerman to repeat the command a second or even third time, with the admonition that this was a necessary inhumanity rather than a wasteful one the Gallows so often claimed to avoid. But ultimately Jerry would always follow through.

If he needed any further evidence of the Gallows' insanity, the psychic training and conditioning he knew it to be should have been absolute proof. The Gallows themselves, however, were not satisfied with this evidence of Jerry's loyalty.

The first time he saw Marks close up since leaving the dome was when Immerman called Jerry into his tent and Marks was there. Jerry had been keeping an eye on Marks, and was sure the demented doctor was likewise eyeing him. But whether he had been paying Jerry any special attention, Jerry wasn't sure. He wondered now if he would find out the hard way, and what that learning would cost him.

Marks studied Jerry while closing the distance between them. "Camp Master Immerman informs me you have done well in the psychic testing thus far, Jerry," the doctor said. "I am not yet convinced."

A Hole in Wednesday

The palm of his hand slapped on Jerry's neck, a move Jerry now could have countered easily, part of his most basic training, except for the shock of who was doing it.

A narcohypnotic patch. And everything went black.

But only for a moment.

Jerry Carson opened his eyes. His knees bent slightly in the conditioned reflex to keep him from falling as his muscles suddenly lost their tension. However, he could not fall, since the cylinder was so narrow his knees and back would wedge him at once on his downward slide.

He pushed the door open and stepped out. He had to reorient himself after a vivid dream of being out in a wild land far from Manhattan, being pushed to his physical and mental limits and tested in horrific ways he could barely comprehend, or even remember now that he was awake.

He went to Linda's stoner. Five minutes had passed since his chamber had revived him, but she still had the statue face of full immersion in the field. It was taking longer and longer for her stoner to release her, and Jerry was concerned. Concerned enough that he might . . .

Linda's stoner sparked. Smoke of various colors whirled up and away from the back of the chamber like magician's handkerchiefs all tied together endlessly, but this time the trick with the woman in the sealed chamber went horribly wrong. Linda did not scream because she could not, since her lungs and throat were still immobilized by the stoner field while her head and brain were released.

Amid a room filling with smoke smelling strangely of nothing at all, Jerry frantically searched the room for something he could use to get her chamber open even if he had to smash in the window, which was supposed to destone the occupant as a safety measure.

He found a quantum slider, but even its lowest setting would slice right through the transparent metal and straight through Linda's head as well. Instead he aimed at the door's seal and fired, ignoring the throbbing in his head of years of inculcation that the stoner was sacred and must not be tampered with under any circumstances, hoping it would be enough . . .

He pushed open the door of his stoner chamber and stepped out. Linda's opened at the same time and they greeted each other with sleepy smiles. Linda was reflexively reaching for her speeder when her eyes went wide and Jerry whirled around to see a stranger with a nebulous face he couldn't place lunging for them with a stone knife.

The attack was clumsy and Jerry deflected it easily. The reflex came without thought but a second afterward he was ablaze with anger. This stranger tried to attack him—worse, tried to attack Linda! When the stranger lunged again Jerry caught his arm in a basic two-handed hold, twisted the man around, and Jerry cracked the arm in half.

Linda screamed. The scream triggered something in Jerry as if she were being attacked despite the fact that the attacker was writhing on the ground. He yanked the stone knife from the stranger's hand and opened his throat.

"You killed him!" Linda yelled.

"He would have killed us," Jerry tried to explain, but Linda backed away.

"You don't know that!" she protested. "He might have been trying to scare us! To get us to stay quiet while he robbed us. I've heard stories around the dome . . ."

Jerry felt his fury turning inexorably toward her. The knife was still in his hand. He was aware of its power. He remembered vaguely that this was not the first time he had killed with such a blade, and he knew he was capable of it again. If Linda thought of reporting him to the Psychic Bureau . . .

But why would she? What made him think she could possibly do such a horrible thing?

("Guard your thoughts," a familiar woman's voice whispered to him. "They are watched. You are watched. Say nothing to me. I can keep your feet on the ground, Jerry, if you will but listen to me.")

His Grandmother Dora. She was the voice. He couldn't see her but he could feel her all around him, as if she was a part of his blood and bones. In a way, he supposed, she was. Jerry dropped the knife and as he did so, he remembered where he was. Not back in his apartment in the tower and Manhattan Dome, but some wild place in the Virginia mountains, in Immerman's tent, buried in a narcohypnotic fantasy thanks to the power-hungry madness of Dr. Northpath Marks.

The scene reset again. Jerry stepped out of his stoner. Linda did likewise, smiling at him. But Jerry remembered. This was not real. He was not, as much as he desired this to be true, by Linda's side. He wondered what the next test of this drugged delusion would be.

He did not have to wait. Marks himself strode into the fantasy with a slider aimed at Linda's head.

"Step aside, Jerry," Marks told him. "Linda has been spying on us through you. Her punishment is execution."

Jerry did not step aside. He did not move at all. He was paralyzed with doubt again. This must be a simulation. But what if it wasn't? What could he do?

"Who are you?" Linda cried.

"You know me well enough, Linda," Marks told her, "and I know you well enough to know bad blood runs through your veins, about the flaws in your genes, and the weakness of the thoughts in your mind. She was born your enemy, Jerry. She just didn't realize it until you joined us. She must die or all of us, including you, and everything we have worked for will perish."

Jerry looked at Linda and saw nothing but fear. No pattern indicating any dissembling or fakery. Marks' body language was nothing but purpose. He would kill Linda.

Including in the real Manhattan Dome, Jerry realized. He would come into their home and kill her. He would kill anyone, no matter what he said about necessity. He would murder, then rationalize a necessity after the fact.

"Are you sure of this?" Jerry asked.

Marks smiled thinly. "You know me by now well enough to know, Jerry, I say nothing if I am not absolutely certain. This woman will doom Galapagos if she lives."

"Then you have my answer," Jerry said, stepping between Linda and Marks.

He heard Linda gasp, and Marks squint in surprise with reddening cheeks, and Jerry was quick enough to yank the slider out of Marks' hand. For an instant he pointed it at Marks, then swung on his heels and fired it point blank at Linda.

"Jerry, I love you!" she screamed in the ghastly moment she survived after being struck by the slider while it shredded her substance at the subatomic level. The slider had been on a lower setting and would rip her being apart with agonizing slowness. Even knowing this was a dark fantasy, Jerry couldn't take watching her suffer for what seemed like hours. He forced himself to level the slider at her head, seeing in her eyes how she was still conscious of what was happening, and fired it on a higher setting. She disintegrated instantly.

Jerry stood frozen with the slider still held out from his chest. He hoped Marks could not see him wince when he fired, or at her realistic hysterical declaration of love for him, or how his arm trembled when he lowered it.

He hoped this was only a simulation.

"Bring him back," he heard Marks' voice say from a place other than the Marks standing before him.

Jerry was lying stiffly on the ground, legs together and arms tucked hard against his sides. Marks hovered over him in one of Immerman's two chairs. Immerman himself stood behind Marks, and there was a black look in eyes focused on Jerry for the heartbeat before he noticed Jerry looking at him.

"Interesting sequence of events," Marks said. "First a shot to the heart—poetry, Jerry?—to fulfill your duty. Then a shot to the head for mercy. Perhaps as a recognition of the love you once shared?"

Jerry didn't answer. His whole body was soaked and trembling. He didn't trust his voice. He didn't trust anything about himself right now, and feared if he took any action it would be drastic—either against himself or something useless against Marks or Immerman.

"Your day is complete," Marks told him, rising to his feet like a surgeon who had miraculously restored life to a dead patient. "Rest and relax, Jerry. You will resume your normal training tomorrow."

A Hole in Wednesday

Education followed education. Physical, mental, psychic, and now Marks was spending part of each day indoctrinating the newest members of Galapagos as well. Instead of speaking from a dais or podium like a true demagogue, he would arrange a circle of chairs or logs or just have them sit on the ground, as if they were in a group therapy circle. There he regaled Jerry and those who had been his fellow recruits with the corruption of the natural human being by the New Era, an end to the evolutionary dead ends of the Dayworld, the stultifying of human progress, an escape from the "escape from freedom," but by Marks' strongest-takes-all definition of freedom.

But Jerry had already decided, from the moment he was forced to kill Linda—and it felt like a killing for all it had been a simulation, for he had felt the quantum beamer in his hand, the crackle of energy flowing from it, the heat from the blast taking apart Linda's corporeal form rapidly but not rapidly enough to bear anything resembling mercy—that this education would go both ways.

They constantly tested him to learn about him. Both Marks and Immerman had said so outright. So very well, he would learn what he could about them. He would watch them, spot their patterns, form three-dimensional pictures of their psyches.

He began training himself intensively in the ways and wonders of his Scout. He made this his nightly ritual no matter how tired and battered, physically and mentally, he was by day's end. He had never been especially astute at technology; even the Nova, the first basic quantum computer he looked at now and again at the Museum in NYC, he had considered beyond his abilities. But the Scout was more than scanners and networked databases, it was programming, and programming had a logical pattern to it he was beginning to fathom.

Spurred on by the vision of Linda being partially destoned and the physical havoc wreaked on her, he also used his Scout to teach himself Stoner technology. This he did carefully, only accessing information about them after he had learned to encrypt his requests and search incognito. He didn't know who might be watching him, but there was no point in taking chances that were manageably avoided.

That the Reductionist spy was still out there, though, was not a question. Possibly related, when Jerry checked on each of his caches to make sure they had not been found, one of his hidden spears had disappeared. It seemed unlikely Vanwoerden had taken it, with six of his own to choose from. Whether or not it was now with Jerry's covert judge remained to be seen.

He was also still curious about the bizarre alternate forms of stoners he had discovered when on the run from Marks. Yet so far, nothing he learned about stoners among the substantial information he dug up and committed to memory gave him any kind of clue about the other ones' purposes.

Nor did he have much of an answer when the Reductionist voice would echo in his skull once or twice a week asking him about his progress, and urging him to hurry up and steal the mysterious Project Dantian file off Marks' computer.

Jerry discreetly searched for references to Dantian using the Scout network. There were a lot of references to it, but none were helpful. Apparently it was an Asian reference to energy centers within the body tapped into for meditation, exercise, and other activities. But Jerry wasn't sure what those would have to do with Marks' project. Translations of Dantian, such as "elixir field," were likewise unhelpful.

At one point the voice broke into the middle of a run Jerry was taking up and down the steep hills of the Gallows' mountain camp, a ten-mile run with fifty pounds of equipment wrapped up in a backpack he lugged. Jerry was alone and far from anyone else in the camp, and exhausted both from the training and what he felt was a wall his progress had hit in educating himself about stoners. The last thing he wanted was an anonymous taskmaster added to the mix, demanding what Jerry still thought was impossible.

"When can you retrieve it? Time is growing short," the voice insisted.

"Tell me what Project Dantian is," Jerry said.

"You don't need . . ."

A Hole in Wednesday

"This is my price. I'm not just getting you that file. I've been gathering a lot of other valuable information about Marks and the others here. Tell me what is in the file you want, or you don't get the file or the other intelligence I've gathered."

This was part bluff, but partly true as well. Maybe he didn't know anything the Reductionists didn't already know, but he wouldn't pass up the possibility of cashing in a bargaining chip if the Reductionists thought he had one.

There was a silent moment, the only noise Jerry's heartbeat throbbing in his ears, his heavy breathing, his boots crunching soil and leaves and twigs in an unbroken rhythm.

Then the Reductionist told him, "It is a collection of biological formulae that could be capable of transforming the Gallows' recruits into super soldiers."

Jerry wasn't sure if he trusted that answer or not. But he knew it was the only one he would get, so it would have to do for now. And even if it was false, there might be some grain of truth buried deeply within it.

Another dozen things flashed through his mind like the sun-dappled shadows flickering on his sweat-soaked body from the leaves above him. He might be able to use the Scout to steal the file, but he still didn't know how to decrypt it. Though the Scout might be able to assist him in that endeavor.

Or how he could get to the computer in the first place. Or how to escape back to Manhattan if he needed to—or what to do there once he was back, if he ever got back.

Though the mind, he reminded himself, was a potent weapon as well, and he was feeling the florescence of his mind well underway. There would be a solution. He only needed to reason it out.

Out of that mix, though, a single question found voice almost unbidden. It was a question born of the new confidence from his training that he didn't realize, until that moment, he possessed. Like it or not, he was turning into a weapon, just as the Gallows intended. But a weapon could be subtle rather than blunt. A needle rather than a nuke.

He shot the question at the Reductionist, "What am I allowed to do to bring the information back to NYC?"

"Anything necessary," the voice answered, this time with no pause.

Jerry's run stopped suddenly. "Even break cover? Reveal myself to all of Galapagos?"

"*Anything you must.*"

Jerry said nothing further in response. He resumed his run, turning back toward the camp.

TWENTY

When Jerry stepped into his tent that night he nearly walked straight into air shaded dark blood red. A horned skull hovered waist high off the ground. Just beyond the holo-scene, Ele'ele Venn sat cross-legged on her mat wearing only a loincloth of white cotton bright against her copper-gold skin. She hardly noticed Jerry enter. Her rapt attention was divided between the skull, which was facing her, and the Scout in her hand.

"The painting is complete and rendered with a one hundred percent level of realistic pan-level accuracy," her Scout announced. It used a woman's voice sounding halfway British, and half mild but almost bewitching Southern American. "Would you like to run a molecular comparison between the original and the recreation?"

Venn looked at Jerry when she answered. "That will not be necessary. End 3D visual and store in Scout memory." The floating holo-painting disappeared.

"Who was that?" Jerry asked.

"TAMARA," Venn told him.

"It looked like a Georgia O'Keeffe painting."

"It is a Georgia O'Keeffe painting, down to the molecular structure of the original. 'Cow's Skull on Red.' The original in the Museum of Phoenix Dome has been scanned and is publicly available on the networks. Every iota of paint cataloged to atomic superstructure, even the arrangement of the brush stroke structure by molecular positioning. Available for anyone who wishes to recreate it. The recreation I just built was done with the Scout's TAMARA program—the Trompe-l'oeil Art Modeling And Recreation Algorithm."

"It can recreate any artwork?" The seed of an idea was germinating in the back of Jerry's brain.

"Any artwork that has been scanned," Venn told him, "which the Scout can also do. Or it can take elements you have scanned, such as layered colors of a particular sunset and the texture of a newly budded leaf you find especially attractive, and create something original to you. Think of TAMARA as a master painter and calligrapher. She could create beautiful artworks of her own as many users have her do, while also, as human calligraphers do for the Days' political and business executives, replicating official signatures on invitations and cards."

"May I have a copy of the program?" Jerry asked. The seed has just broken the soil with its first shoot, though that bit of green was only tiny so far.

"You never struck me as an artistic type," she said. Then, "You'll need to open your Scout's permission for a share specific to my device."

Jerry entered his passcode on the visual display and then let it scan his wrist for bio-verification. "I've discovered a great many things about myself while we've been in this camp," he said truthfully. "Things I never would have considered important. Or thought myself capable of."

There was a flash of wariness in her eyes. Jerry recognized it. It was the same one she and Vanwoerden turned on him when Immerman announced that he had ferreted out Graham as the hound. But then something softened. She stretched out her hand, and Jerry placed his Scout in it.

The wireless upload to Jerry's scout took only a moment, and then she handed his Scout back. Jerry retreated to his own mat—though "retreat" was a bit of a misnomer since the mat was only five feet away from Venn's—to study the program. Vanwoerden entered the tent as Jerry began, but no one said anything to the other. They had a mutually beneficial arrangement similar to the kinds necessary in a twelver, with so many people packed together in one space: all three-way interaction was by unanimous agreement. Otherwise two would take themselves outside, or all three tent-mates embarked on their own actions individually and quietly.

Vanwoerden had obviously been out running with a pack again, his favorite "free time" activity. He came in smelling of water but not soap, which was still considered a luxury in Camp Natufian. While Jerry and Venn worked with their Scouts, Vanwoerden tested his reflexes by using two fingers to catch any fleas that sprung off of his skin. He shredded them between sharp fingernails.

Jerry correlated TAMARA's programming with the Scout's and found that they were mutually compatible. Not a surprise, since Stoneburner was the standard programming language used in the Scouts and across many of the world's networks. It could be as simple or as complex as necessary. An artificial intelligence was built into the program coding itself which took the measure of its user, placing the user on a scale ranging roughly from complete neophyte to preternatural computing genius. Then it offered up its programming structures and logic accordingly, combining the user's desire with their programming and item-generation skill level.

Jerry had been a complete neophyte when Immerman first handed him a Scout. But the device's logic was built with inherent patterns he could spot and utilize. After a few weeks of experimenting with a range of programs in Stoneburner, he had a good handle on getting the Scout to do what he wanted through his own personal designing.

As he was opening TAMARA's program he ran across Immerman's koan again. Jerry had placed its text on the top of his Scout display to keep the riddle in the forefront of his mind. Immerman did nothing casually so there was a meaning behind the koan. Of that Jerry was certain. But he still couldn't reason out Immerman's intention, much less the answer to a riddle where passing the test would mean death, and the only way to survive was to fail.

Jerry put it aside to concentrate on the task at hand, as he had done a hundred times already. The artistic programming was ingenious. Jerry had expected it to be strictly art-focused. That is, only concentrating on the basics necessary to replicate or create new art works, the way a painter might have nothing more before her but canvas, easel, paints, and brush. But Tamara—he started thinking of the program as a name rather than an acronym—was vastly broader.

It appeared to be constructed around the same AI algorithms that Stoneburner had built in. Into that AI had been fed everything but the kitchen waste unit. Not just physical art and rendering subroutines but music, literature, mathematics, plus hard sciences such as physics and chemistry. There were even storehouses for philosophy and religion. Many of them were tied together in unusual and unexpected ways—at one point he stumbled across links interconnecting biology, anthropology, and classical poetry, which led a path to twentieth-century science fiction. It was as if the programmer—or the AI within the program itself—realized that art in a vacuum was sterile, but had to be fed with an entire life outside of the artwork in order to blossom.

The more Jerry studied the Tamara program and mingled it with the knowledge and skills he had gained in Stoneburner, the more his idea blossomed. By midnight he realized how he could steal the information about Project Dantian from Marks' computer.

And as with his confrontation with the hound, Jerry decided the worst part was waiting. So he decided not to wait.

He spent the wee morning hours customizing Tamara for the task, along with inputting a new set of passive Stoneburner commands into the fabric of his Scout's hardware.

He paid for his lack of sleep the next day during the physical training sessions, which proved as intense for him as his trainees. Like Immerman, Jerry preferred staying close to his charges in order to share whatever suffering they were enduring and enjoy whatever enlightenment they snatched from their ordeals. He would almost forget they were Gallows' disciples—though he never let himself completely forget.

A Hole in Wednesday

But that night, when his portion of the training had ended, Jerry fought the urge to tend his bruises and sleep, and made a beeline for Marks.

There was no tent for Marks, but a log cabin just beyond the edge of the camp proper and near the old road winding across the mountaintops. It was luxurious by the standards Jerry had grown used to in the camp. But it was still simple and rough, and symbolic, harkening back to the pioneers. The logs and roof tiles were real, not simulated wood, bearing the cracks of aging. It could've predated the Dayworld. Likewise the stones in the foundation and chimney were real stone. The only thing giving the cabin a modern appearance was the cement filling the spaces between the logs.

Two guards were posted at the cabin, one at the front door and one at the back. It was likely there were technological defenses too, buried in the simple-appearing structure or made to appear as part of it. Jerry hadn't actively scanned the cabin, since that would likely set off an alarm. It was unnecessary anyway since Jerry didn't plan to enact any real mischief yet. But his Scout's passive sensors did detect a low amount of energy radiating off the structure consistent with an outward energy projection of the sort a defense mechanism would use.

This despite Marks' protestation of how the Gallows' Natural Man needed no dependence on technology. But Jerry had the chip inside his skull to prove Marks would not shun technology altogether. There were even the little hints, such as Marks' unfinished cig going into a stoning field to keep it from burning down. So Jerry approached cautiously and observantly. But he also made sure to approach with confidence. He was surprised to realize that in some measure he really did feel as confident as he played at appearing.

He announced himself and the guard at the front door waved him through.

There were only two rooms. The front door led to the larger, though it was "large" only in comparison with Jerry's tent. Ten broad paces would suffice to navigate its length. It was sparsely furnished, with the only non-basic item being Marks' desk at the back end. Marks looked up without surprise from the desk and his computer. The doctor was sitting facing the door with his back to the log wall.

"Do you have something to say to me, Jerry?" Marks asked nonchalantly.

"I have a great deal I wish to say to you, Dr. Marks," Jerry admitted. "But most of it can wait for another time. There are two things I want to say tonight in particular."

"Prioritizing is important, and not a skill many master thoroughly. But one we do take pains to teach in our camps. Demonstrate for me how well you've learned this."

Jerry offered Marks his Scout, which had Jerry's chosen text featured on its display. He said nothing as Marks closed his computer and then looked the Scout over. "This is the training regimen you've devised for those in your charge, I take it?"

"Yes, Doctor. Camp Master Immerman has served as much of my template. I want to do for the trainees as he has done for us—training to think and observe, to use logic and solve puzzles, be they mental or physical, alongside strengthening our bodies. Camp Master Immerman has approved this overall, but I wondered if you had any further advice."

Marks nodded and handed the Scout back to Jerry. "It is important for the physical training to come first. The body must be molded to its peak abilities. The mind will follow, in fact be strengthened as the body is conditioned."

And be more receptive to what you want to fill the mind with, Jerry thought. The physical training, he knew from history, was intended to break someone down and build them back up. Make the body a soldier, which was to say, a weapon. A certain level of intelligence and initiative was required for a soldier to survive a dangerous situation. But beyond that, for more than just a few select people, too much intelligence and initiative could lead to overthinking orders, questioning them, and perhaps even disobeying. Marks fitted into this mold of what he wanted from his soldiers as much as any general from history.

A Hole in Wednesday

But a truly good military force was one which did not seek to stifle those who were the most intelligent, but rather place them where they could be most useful. Make them a part of the structure. Deepen their investment in it.

Sometimes politics and bureaucracy had interfered. But Jerry suspected this would not necessarily be an issue with the Gallows. If Jerry could bend the ear of the dictator, he might get himself into a good position much more quickly.

"The mind will follow," Jerry agreed.

"And this is relevant to the second thing you wished to tell me?" Marks asked.

Marks would also, Jerry knew, be psychologically analyzing Jerry's every word, move, tone, and flinch as Jerry spoke.

"Yes, sir. Since you took such pains to recruit me, and since, as you said, I gave you so much trouble in the process, I wanted to be forthright about where I stand with Galapagos."

"I appreciate forthrightness."

"What I am doing is not just for Galapagos, or its goals. I am also doing this for myself. You were right about me. There were a great many resources within me I was unaware of and left untapped. Many I would have never even believed existed. I have gained strength and mental alacrity. I have gained confidence and a much better measure of my abilities. I like the person I have become. And I want to see how far I can go."

Jerry wasn't sure for a moment how much Marks could read from Jerry's statement and body language. But all of his words had the advantage of being truthful.

Jerry did like what he was learning about himself. What he was capable of doing—even if it meant being capable of killing as a need for preservation. It had not been cold-blooded murder. And he would likewise defend Linda if the necessity arose. From a certain point of view he was defending them both right now.

Next he hoped he was capable of carrying out the Reductionists' order to steal the Project Dantian file. What happened in the next moments would determine whether or not he got the chance to try.

At last, Marks smiled faintly. "You have reached a new level of understanding about what Galapagos is truly about, Jerry. The individual is as important as the goal in the long scheme of things. No individual ever won their rights or freedom by passively accepting what was given them or floating on the tide of circumstances. Fighting has always been the human condition, and you will need to be strong when we are ready to bring down the curtain on the New Era. And when the body is strong . . ."

"The mind will follow. And choose to follow Galapagos."

Marks frowned. "I do not intend to have slaves or slavish followers. Galapagos will be comprised of individuals serving a common cause. Slavishness posing as culture and the Thirteen Principles is what created this doom for humanity in the first place."

Jerry offered what he hoped looked like a sincere nod. "And my resourcefulness was lurking deep inside me all along, waiting to be brought out. If I had been able to take the PhD classes in Self-Knowledge . . ."

Marks laughed. "But you weren't allowed to, Jerry! I discovered this when I looked into your records. The Bureau of Population Social Construction constantly scans records and biorhythms trying to identify those just such as yourself, those who could possibly pose some kind of threat to the New Era, and marks them. If they try taking a Self-Awareness program, which would open the possibility of them discovering their latent abilities, the BPSC takes extensive but subtle measures to ensure they never enroll. New job offerings suddenly appearing, or the like. Anything to keep the would-be deviants otherwise occupied. They actively seek to keep extraordinary people buried."

Without thinking, Jerry asked, "Did you know Theodora Carson, Dr. Marks?"

Marks looked at him oddly and Jerry wondered if he had overplayed his hand. Grandmother Dora may have been a spy, after all. And at this point, decades after her death, her true role within Galapagos might be well known.

But if so, why go to so much trouble to recruit Jerry, even

with his genetic profile? Revenge? Or could the reality be that she had been a loyal follower of Galapagos after all?

Finally Marks said, "I only knew your grandmother for a short time when I was young. But our time together was more than enough to realize she was remarkably self-aware, tapped deeply into the morphogenesis of her time. She knew how to fight. She will live on for generations. Now I must return to my work."

Marks said no more than that, answering without answering. Instead he opened his computer, let the biosensor scan his fingertips, and began attending to work Jerry could not see. Jerry felt pressing the matter would be a bad idea, and saw himself out.

Unbeknownst to Marks, Jerry hoped, the Scout now possessed the key to getting into Marks' computer. Jerry was ready to spring just as soon as he could get close to the computer for a few moments.

Yet he still felt like the student in Immerman's koan who faced the dilemma of hanging over a cliff by nothing more than his teeth biting into a tree limb. And opening his mouth to answer any question posed to him, right answer or not, would be fatal.

Jerry slept despite being wound up with anticipation. But he still did not dream.

Twenty-One

Programming the Scout to execute Jerry's unusual requests worked with astonishing speed. It was as if the Scout itself was a mischievous old mythological Trickster who'd been locked away for centuries in a cave and finally given the chance to make trouble again.

Jerry supposed the AIs were programmed to be helpful. This one not only anticipated Jerry's wishes but bounded ahead, offering up back-end programming suggestions as shadowy as any twentieth-century film noir villain and as robustly bold as Sidney Greenstreet. When Jerry started the programming he began with a natural language sort where he would tell the Scout what he had in mind and watch the device synthesize programming code to execute the user's wishes. But by the time Jerry was inputting code directly the Scout itself would finish lines, complete sequences, and run its own simulations unbidden as if it gleefully anticipated the havoc they were about to wreak together.

Obviously the Scout was ready. Still Jerry hesitated.

Daybreaking had been one thing. There was a very real chance of getting caught, but psychic rehabilitation likely would have been the worst punishment. Killing Graham had been a necessary act in the heat of the moment. But now he was planning on taking on the leader of an apparently vast and deeply connected network only on the faith of his new skills and an anonymous voice coming from a chip in his head.

"This is madness," Jerry said to himself more than once. But then, the whole life he had found himself in was madness. This was only a different and broader sort of madness than he was already growing accustomed to.

The impatient Scout only responded by occasionally flashing the line *Waiting to execute*.

Then the storm came.

The weather in the mountains during the interminable, prowling objective summer, which dragged on for weeks instead of the subjective days Jerry and his body were used to, was as fickle and changeable as a toddler in a room of toys and sweets. Sunny skies one hour wouldn't guarantee the next hour wouldn't rage with thunder and deluging rainstorms. Jerry had learned to train under sun and storm alike.

But this storm would be different. Jerry could sense it. His Scout had even taken it upon itself to run a weather-watcher in the background, constantly running algorithms based on a mix of cloud movement, air pressure, and more arcane factors Jerry's mind, still partly living under a dome, could hardly fathom. But his instincts and the Scout came to the same conclusion. This would be no sound and fury lasting less than an hour and then moving on or dissipating. This storm was already announcing itself with horizontal wet winds and the promise of pouncing on the mountains and lashing them for the better part of a day.

More than enough time and cover for Jerry to strike.

Even as the downpour was starting and its rotating winds whipping at the tents, Jerry filled his pack and prepared to run. The weather and its implied threats were enough for even the running madman Vanwoerden to flash Jerry a funny look.

"Punishment," Jerry told him and Venn. "You'd best leave me be if you don't want to join me."

"Come back alive, Carson," Venn told him.

"Or at least in good enough shape so we don't have to go out in this horrific mess to rescue you," Vanwoerden added.

Otherwise they left him alone. Running across the trails with a full fifty-pound pack, no matter the time of day or night, was a common punishment in the camp. None of the former recruits-cum-trainers had been made to endure it, but Jerry guessed right about his tent-mates not hindering him. They could be made to share it if they did. They likely were wondering what he did to deserve being flung out into this beast of a storm. They also thought nothing of it when he took his Scout with him.

The full pack wasn't just for show. Jerry loaded it with everything he would need if he had to flee after stealing the Project Dantian file and somehow make his way back to Manhattan Dome. As it was he knew he could survive the hundreds of miles he would need to trek to get there, even with the coming of objective autumn. He was more concerned about Linda's well-being, and what could happen to her in the time it took him to get back.

But he was learning to trust his gut. And his gut told him what he was doing was the only real way to protect them both, or as much protection as there was left in his situation. And he could contact her with his Scout if need be, and do so without being traced. He would tell her to run. He would tell her to leave the dome—if she had the courage—and meet him outside.

From there . . . he would figure out the *from there* when he got there.

For now, he had a cabin and computer to break into.

The ground-pounding storm didn't stop the innermost sentries from manning their posts. Jerry did nothing to hide himself from them, but the storm did the work for him. They had their own Scouts stowed away someplace dry and didn't realize he was there until he was right on top of them, then they looked equally startled to see him on a punishment run. But they didn't try to stop him either.

The outermost sentries were spread more thinly. Just to keep in practice, Jerry went off-trail and ran through rugged woods. His footfalls were muted by the soaked leaf blanket covering the ground. Those guards never knew he passed them.

He only paused for one moment, long enough to find a relatively dry spot, pull out his Scout, and execute a program casting his "ghost" somewhere off on another trail, while masking his DNA from anyone doing nothing more than passive scans. It wouldn't work if they were close by and looking for him specifically. But unless someone realized he was up to something, it would be enough to keep him cloaked.

One more sprint brought him to the edge of the forest in sight of the cabin, though out of sight of the single guard manning the front door. This one, a burly fellow a head taller than Jerry, wasn't intimidated or less alert for all the lightning and wind. He remained standing, his eyes occasionally sweeping the sodden darkness, and his Scout out and active.

Jerry would not be able to sneak past this one. So he must hide in plain sight and take him by surprise instead.

"What are you doing here?" a voice next to Jerry cut through the rain.

It was one of the outer sentries, one of Marks' men rather than a recruit, who had apparently decided to patrol in the rain instead of standing still until he sunk into the mud. "Punishment run," Jerry told him.

"No it isn't. I would know if it was. And you're way off the trail. You're not supposed to be here. This close to the cabin . . ."

Understanding dawned in the sentry's eyes a half-second before Jerry executed a practiced move of flinging the backpack off of his shoulders and slamming it into the guard's head in a single whirl.

The guard staggered back but wasn't down. This was one of Marks' bodyguards, after all, not a green recruit, and he wouldn't go down easily. But Jerry knew he had to make the fight fast, before he wore out, or before the guard could signal danger to the cabin.

Jerry feinted a run for the cabin, and as he predicted, the guard physically put himself between the cabin and Jerry. A glimpse beyond the sentry showed the guard at the front door doing his normal surveillance but noticing nothing wrong. So far his bio-masking program was working.

Nothing the Scout had in its bag of tricks, though, would ward off the sentry who was now a human windmill of kicks and punches. Jerry was able to deflect them but just barely. The sentry had already betrayed all of his own patterns, however. He was quick and strong but stiff, used to finishing opponents quickly through sheer swift force. A tougher opponent exhausted his repertoire. More predictably, he kept placing his body between Jerry and the cabin.

Jerry lurched to one side as if stumbling, then ducked a roundhouse kick, and made another run for the cabin. That attempt was fake. He didn't want to follow through because of the crater, half filled with water, in the ground directly ahead where the trunk of a giant oak had been before it fell. The sentry, intent on beating Jerry senseless, leaped blindly into the big hole and tangled his feet in the dead oak's roots. Jerry leaped on him and took the sentry out with a vicious fist to the head. Binding and gagging him, and tying his hands to one of the massive roots—one out of the hole so he wouldn't drown—was only the work of a few more moments.

With the most immediate threat neutralized, Jerry took another moment to scan the cabin. The Scout registered the guard at the front door and another at the back, but no one else inside. He could specifically scan for Northpath Marks' DNA, thanks to the passive background collector program he ran when he handed Marks his Scout days before.

The Scout registered Marks as being alone in Immerman's tent. Jerry put his muddy pack back over his shoulders, and walked toward Marks' cabin.

"Hello the house!" Jerry called.

"Who's there? State your name!" the guard challenged.

"I'm here to see Dr. Marks!" Jerry said, using the words as a delay to close the distance.

The guard was all suspicion when Jerry stepped up onto the porch, but did not move from his spot by the door. "Dr. Marks is in the camp," the guard said.

"I see," Jerry said, then shot a fist into the guard's throat. Another fist in the nose and a knee to the chin was sufficient to put the guard down. Any noise they might have made was covered by the storm, though Jerry made hardly any noise at all when he dragged the guard into the cabin.

Convinced of his own superiority, no doubt, and that of his guards and computer security, Marks' computer was sitting on the desk at the far end of the cabin's main room, albeit closed and locked with the biosensor. The Scout told Jerry the guard outside the back door was still in place, unaware of what transpired just on the other side of the cabin but, thanks to the storm, what might as well have been miles away.

Now Jerry stared at the computer, which was in effect his toughest enemy of all. Guards were one thing, but speed and force here would do more damage than good.

On Marks' computer's biolock was a muted rainbow of lights, which intentionally followed no pattern at all so as not to give thieves any clue about how to break through the program. Jerry assumed that despite all of his protestations about technology, Marks would have supremely effective security on his lock.

The obvious route for a thief would be to steal the configurations of Marks' DNA and other chemical and physical traces, as Jerry had done when he handed Marks his Scout, to emulate them and fool the lock into thinking it was Marks himself rather than a series of electronic ghosts emulating the lock's owner. But being the most obvious path, it was the one the computer would take the stiffest security measures against.

And Jerry could not assume he either had the time or the luxury of multiple tries with a fake electronic Northpath Marks to break into the computer. Marks could return at any time. And it was likely multiple failed attempts to break into the lock—maybe no more than just one—would set off an alarm, or even erase all of the computer's contents.

Which is how Jerry had come up with his other idea.

"Tamara?" he asked.

"Ready," responded Tamara's half-British, half-Southern American voice on his Scout.

The biolock on Marks' computer would be constantly running to prevent anyone from taking the machine. But in so doing, it would ignore anything inorganic so as not to constantly set off alarms. Thus it didn't consider Jerry's Scout to be a threat when the display screen, and thus uploader, came face to face with the lock.

"Tamara, upload 'Marks' Masterpiece' to computer biolock," Jerry said.

"Engaged," Tamara responded.

Any program specifically designed to pretend it was a human signature would likely be recognized as such by the most basic security on a biolock. So instead, Jerry encoded all of the bioinfo he stole from Marks not as a faux human being, but as an artwork. Being an artwork rather than a cracking program, the biolock interpreted it as non-threatening, in fact irrelevant, and ignored the program's entry. Which meant Jerry and his Scout were able to slip the program past the security measures of the lock's front end into the brain of its back end.

The lock's back end surveyed the human signature presented to it and found a perfect molecular match with a Northpath Marks who was apparently feeling quite smug and pleased with himself. It relayed a command to its front end to unlock.

Rainbow lights turned green across their small board and Jerry flipped open the computer.

Marks required a password for entry. And here the Scout and Tamara, working hand in hand, would come through again. With Tamara already slipped into the computer's brain through the biolock, "she" would now turn toward creating an artwork out of Marks' entire system, including any security objects dealing with the passwords and encryption. Once the artwork was complete, the Scout would scan it to retrieve both Marks' password as well as the encryption algorithms to render the Project Dantian folder readable. Or failing that, Jerry could pass along the entire thing wholesale to his mysterious Reductionist voice and let them work through the process at their leisure.

Or that was the plan, anyway, before Marks walked through the door from the side room with a wolfish smile stretching his face.

Twenty-Two

Jerry realized he was being ridiculous, even panicking, by looking at his Scout. But it still registered himself as the only living presence in the cabin.

"You aren't the only one who knows how to mask a DNA bioscan," Marks told him. "I've been in the room next to you during your entire clandestine mission, while I left a Scout behind in Immerman's tent that pretended to be me. If you look closely at your Scout you will see 'I' am still there."

Jerry took his Scout in hand protectively, but left the computer open—though he was sure Marks wouldn't fail to notice for long. Jerry hadn't yet been able to copy anything off Marks' computer, but Marks might not know that. Jerry held the Scout close to his chest as if guarding it with his life. Which in fact he was doing, Jerry thought, as the device was his only key to getting back anything resembling the life he wanted.

Marks made no move toward Jerry or the computer. He did not call in the guard from the back door. He was now the larger, faster, and stronger cat. He could pounce at any time. In a moment he would. But he wanted Jerry to know terror and helplessness first.

Except Jerry wasn't helpless. Marks' own training regimen guaranteed that. He just needed to find Marks' weakness.

Jerry lunged. The next thing he knew his head was cracking

against the desk and Marks' knee jabbed into his ribs. The next thing Jerry saw was Marks looming above him as Jerry lay bruised and winded on the floor.

"That won't work, Jerry," Marks told him. "Who do you think taught Immerman and the other camp masters? There have been a number of attempts on my life and obviously none of them have succeeded. The sins of the father are legion, but he has learned to exploit all of them in one fashion or another. Now shall we discuss this problem between us like reasonable men?"

Jerry realized he had dropped the Scout during the all-too-brief scuffle and reached for it. Marks did nothing to stop him. Jerry used the desk to pull himself back to his feet. He and Marks faced each other across the desk as if they were an ordinary doctor and patient.

Jerry hadn't learned anything about Marks' fighting ability yet, aside from it being considerable. For the moment he only needed to get close enough to Marks' computer to upload Tamara's invasively retooled program. The Scout was running Tamara to image Marks' computer files.

"Some time ago," Marks said, "we detected a Galapagos implant being used to communicate with the outside. Or more probably, someone on the outside was 'borrowing' the chip to communicate with someone here. I'm jamming this cabin to prevent any unauthorized broadcasts, by the way, so your friend will not be able to communicate with you, or you with him."

"That was the real reason you came to the camp," Jerry realized.

"I never have only one reason for doing anything, Jerry. That would be inefficient and wasteful. It did, however, determine the timing. As I was saying, these unauthorized piggyback transmissions were encoded well enough to prevent us from tracing the source. I suspect this is being done by my nemesis, an organization called the Family . . . Ah, I can see you recognize the name. So my suspicions are correct."

Jerry fully came to his feet, ready for another go at Marks, but the doctor simply shook his head. "You should know if I am injured in any fashion, as unlikely as the possibility is, an alarm in my Scout will send guards rushing to this cabin. You'd be a fool to try."

Jerry smiled. "You were the one who said I'd given you a harder time than anyone else."

So far Jerry and Marks were still alone. But Jerry didn't want to bank on that not changing any time soon. And he was certain any physical move he made now would be useless—or worse than useless if Marks was telling the truth about the bio-alarm. He had to at least buy time to copy and transmit Marks' computer data, and preferably find a way to incapacitate Marks in the process.

What about the spy? The Reductionist had told him there was a spy in the camp. Someone who would be Jerry's handler for the Family. But Jerry still had no clue who that could be. And he also didn't want to bet on any rescues, particularly since Jerry did such a thorough job of making his disappearance seem like nothing more than an especially grueling punishment run.

Marks continued, "I see your breaking into my cabin and into my computer, both very intrepid moves on your part, as having their source in one of two possibilities. Possibility one, the Family is coercing you somehow, perhaps using Linda against you. Or two, you have been working for them all along. But everything about you, Jerry, your body language, the emotions you psychically radiate, tells me the second possibility is the correct one. Which also leads me to wonder how you managed to fool the narcohypnosis and Truth Mist."

Jerry said nothing. Even if he wanted to talk or was made to, he wouldn't know what to say that wouldn't make him sound insane. Though he caught himself being tempted to reveal it anyway. It was possible Marks, madman though he was, had the training and knowledge to explain what had happened, some physical explanation rather than a supernatural one.

He quickly decided the price of knowing wasn't worth it. It would reveal too much. And besides, Marks might figure out a way to counteract it if it was some method others could use against him.

How much time had passed? Tamara would need at least five minutes to make a complete copy of Marks' computer. If he could hold out long enough, and if Marks didn't shut his computer first.

Marks was staring at Jerry with a mix of anger and fascination. "Of course, intrepid though you are, Jerry, your actions will not go unpunished. And despite the fact that I am the director of NYC's Psychic Rehabilitation Department, in many cases, including yours, I do not believe in psychic rehabilitation."

He pointed a sleek silver quantum slider at Jerry. It had been modified to create a narrow cutting beam, Jerry noticed—the sort of alteration capable of slicing off fingers or limbs or hollow out organs without disrupting the entire body's quantum substance.

"A necessary death?" Jerry asked. His mind was still thrashing around for an escape but finding nothing. "Wouldn't that be wasteful?"

"I'll have you answer a number of important questions first, including the one I just posed to you. Then it will not have been a waste. But what I don't understand is . . . why. You accept the things I have told you are true. You sympathize with my beliefs."

"I don't accept anything you believe," Jerry said. But he had to force himself to say it.

Marks smiled faintly. "Of course you do—though you may not realize it fully yourself yet. There would be no other way to fool the narcohypnosis and TM if there hadn't been at least a seed of sympathy. You not only survived my training regimen, by which I mean both metaphorically and literally, you thrived, Jerry. You leaped into it wholeheartedly. You were telling the truth when you told me you liked what you had become and want to see how far you could go. You have me to thank for your self-realization, Jerry."

Marks leaned over his desk with an intense stare Jerry couldn't look way from. "Be honest with me. Would you go back to your old life now if you could? I don't mean just going back to Linda, but exactly the way you were before. You would not, would you?"

Jerry didn't answer. He couldn't. Marks was right.

"There, you see? I would not have recruited you, Jerry, if I didn't see your vast potential and I had any doubt you could be brought to our cause. You know humankind isn't meant to live in domes. You know we are not meant to live only one day a week out of seven. You've felt it! Once you reconnected with the way you were supposed to live, you became a completely different person!"

Red anger seized Jerry at the last words for some reason he couldn't fathom. But Marks was right. He knew Marks was right. Maybe this was why anger blinded him.

Whatever the cause, Jerry's anger sent him flying over the desk with his hands clutching Marks' throat.

Jerry's weight sent them tumbling over Marks' chair and onto the floor. For the barest instant there was fear in Marks' eyes. Then it was gone, but it had been enough. Jerry felt himself reinvigorated by that most elusive and dangerous of beasts, hope.

Marks grabbed Jerry's hands and yanked them back by their thumbs, shooting an agony all the way up Jerry's arms that made him break his grip. Then Marks had Jerry by the throat and against a wall. Jerry's feet were off the ground.

"I can't make you understand your own mind if you refuse to understand it yourself," Marks said calmly, though he was winded. "But I will have my answers."

He slammed Jerry's head against the log wall and threw his dazed opponent to the ground. "Computer, summon Immerman," Marks said, pacing and kneading his fingers together.

Jerry was only fully regaining his senses as the tall, stocky form of Immerman wove through the room. Jerry tried coming to his feet. He succeeded but was wobbly. He also knew fully well he had never defeated his camp master in any sparring contest.

With both Marks and Immerman facing him down, Jerry knew his situation had probably gone from mostly hopeless to impossible. But he was still standing under his own power. The Scout he had dropped on the desk when he went after Marks the last time was still there, and if Tamara had finished her recording, it would now be on Jerry's Scout. There had to be a way out, if Jerry could just find it.

"I have discovered," Marks said to Immerman though he faced Jerry, "that your charge, Jerry Carson, was able to fool our narcohypnotic procedure. I want to know how. This time, I'm afraid we must seek the truth from him more invasively."

Immerman said nothing. Instead he gave Jerry what looked like a questioning stare.

Was he waiting for Jerry to offer up the truth himself, before a procedure could permanently destroy Jerry's mind? Assuming Marks let him live, which Jerry didn't want to make any bets on.

But no. Jerry knew Immerman after all the months in the mountains. He knew his camp master's pattern. Immerman was indeed waiting for an answer.

There was only one question Immerman had asked Jerry which remained open-ended.

"I will fail the test," Jerry said.

"What test?" Marks demanded, his face flushing. "My interrogation will hardly be a test, Jerry."

"Continue," Immerman said.

"If I answer the master while I hang from the branch over the cliff," Jerry said, "no matter what answer I give, right or wrong, I will fall to my death. So I choose to not answer. In not answering I fail the test, but will survive—and thus survive to take other tests in the future."

"I see," Immerman told him.

Marks narrowed his eyes at Immerman. But as Marks turned toward him, Immerman landed a single hard punch to the back of the doctor's neck. Marks dropped.

"This test you have passed, Jerry Caird Carson," Immerman told him. He handed Jerry his Scout with one hand and clutched Marks' computer with the other. "And I will be your handler."

Twenty-Three

Immerman slammed his foot into a floorboard next to Marks' head. One end of the board swung upward, revealing a small space underneath containing a wooden shaft topped by a stone arrowhead. Jerry's missing spear.

A sea of relief at what appeared to be Jerry's reprieve was abruptly drained by cynical skepticism. Everything with Immerman, after all, was a test.

Had the spear been there the entire time? Had Marks brought him here to be killed by his own weapon—or had it been meant to frame Jerry in some way that would make him a fugitive in two worlds?

The room spun sickeningly in a way that had nothing to do with his injuries. Ripples of panic spread, but his mind also raced with calculations. He'd been ready to die only moments before. It seemed a simple, inescapable certainty. Now every outward expanding ripple seemed to represent untold lives to be destroyed by his failure, pulling him faster and faster toward their collective doom, the final casualties an almost academic equation multiplied by the product of time. Jerry wondered if he had become the product of improving their striking ability.

But Immerman? What was this? The pardon from a death sentence, another test, or a frame-up? Or a coup, as Jerry was well aware was all too common in history at the beginning of many movements? Would Immerman tell everyone he'd caught Jerry in the act of attacking Marks, too late to save their leader, but in time to make sure Jerry's punishment was swift and absolute? He looked at the camp master and waited for Immerman's strike, in whatever form that would take.

"Wood and stone wouldn't show up as a weapon on Marks' scanners in a cabin with wooden walls and a stone foundation," Immerman told him.

He raised the spear above Marks' chest but Jerry grabbed it when it was halfway down its death plunge.

Immerman flashed him a black look and hissed. But Jerry could not allow a murder in cold blood to take place right in front of him—even if the would-be deceased had been about to do him in a few moments before.

"The alarm!" Jerry cried, the quickest pragmatic reply he could come up with. "Marks told me—if he's injured in any way, an alarm will alert the guards to come here."

"I've already injured him, though perhaps not seriously enough to summon help." Immerman glanced once at his Scout to determine they were safe for the moment. Then he began feverishly typing on Marks' computer. Beside them his Scout was uploading something.

"What are you doing?" Jerry asked. He was casting nervous glances at his own Scout, waiting for the hammer to drop—or Marks to rise back up like some indestructible leviathan to destroy them both.

Several bioblips on his Scout angled toward the cabin and accelerated.

"A little bit of corruption," Immerman answered. "A virus to infiltrate the files for Project Dantian and everything medical on Marks' computer. If he discovers they've been tampered with and tries syncing them with his backups, it will corrupt the backups as well. It could set Galapagos back years."

"Some of the guards have been alerted and are on their way," Jerry said.

"Then watch the doors if it makes you feel better. I already took care of the one at the back door, by the way."

Jerry ran for the front door a second before it burst open and the first guard rushed in. Without thinking Jerry grabbed him by his collar and head-butted him, then whirled him around and smashed him through the shuttered window and out. Lightning flashes and booms of thunder intruded into the cabin, and rain swept onto the wooden floor.

Jerry sidled to the window to keep watch, keeping within the room's shadows. "Why didn't you just do this before? Why use me to get to it?"

"You weren't the first person we recruited, only the first to get this far," Immerman said. A red light flashed on his Scout display. "I never thought of using an art modeling routine. But as it was, I had infiltrated high enough into Galapagos' organization to be wary of risking my position."

"You've risked it now."

Immerman chuckled. "Getting our hands on all of the research for Project Dantian is worth me losing my place in Galapagos ten times over. The address to send it is ready on my Scout. Even if we die in the next five minutes, we'll have won."

"Dying doesn't feel much like winning to me," Jerry said. But he linked his Scout to Immerman's.

"Take a look at the long view, Carson. People used to talk about the glass being half full or half empty. Think of the glass as already broken. That way you will enjoy the glass more while you have it, and accept it more when the glass finally does break. Because sooner or later it always will."

"You were the one who talked to me on the Galapagos chip, weren't you? Even when you were here in the camp?"

"Here in the camp I would program the AI in my Scout to speak with you, using the same artificial voice. But in a sense, yes, you conversed with me on every occasion."

Jerry's Scout obediently started transmitting the stolen files to a location the Scout told Jerry was in Manhattan, which put it close to both Galapagos' secret headquarters as well as whatever building the disembodied Reductionist led him and the anti-stoner refugees to shortly before Jerry turned himself in to Marks.

Before Jerry could respond to Immerman's fatalistic philosophy, his Scout gave a subtle warning bleep. The Scout's AI already knew Jerry well enough to know the human would want to be informed about any anomalies it discovered, anything that broke or didn't fit a pattern. Now it found an anomaly in Marks.

Immerman was finished with Marks' computer and left it open. Marks was stirring now and drew Immerman's attention, but not Jerry's as Jerry scrolled through all the possibilities the Marks anomaly might entail.

Immerman pulled a long knife out of his boot and placed it against the mumbling Marks' throat.

"I should have done this decades ago, Doctor," Immerman told him. "Not a mistake I'll make again. You've tormented my family long enough and now we're finished with you!"

"Wait!" Jerry yelled as he yanked Immerman's arm away from Marks.

Immerman lashed a punch into Jerry's sternum hard enough to send Jerry flying back a half-dozen feet.

"This man has killed members of my family, Carson!" Immerman said. He poked his knife into Marks' neck. "And more friends than I can count! Including your grandfather. I will not let your weakness spare him when he deserves any death I give him!"

Jerry struggled to breathe, and more importantly, talk. "Chip," he managed to spit out. "Marks' head."

"What are you talking about? Why would he put a chip in his own head?"

Instead of trying to say more against the pounding in his chest, he slid his Scout to Immerman's feet. Immerman looked at the display and cursed.

"It's linked to a quantum bomb built into his sternum," Immerman murmured and yanked the knife away from Marks. "Set to detonate if the chip detects Marks is dead or has suffered a mortal wound."

Jerry took a deep breath and ignored the burning beside his heart. "Enough to obliterate the whole camp and kill everyone in it." He glared at his master-turned-handler as he came to his feet. "You break your own glass, Immerman. But you don't have the right to smash everyone else's on this mountain."

A Hole in Wednesday

Immerman returned Jerry's glare. "Even if it means saving far more lives later?"

But Immerman thrust the knife back into his boot. Jerry watched him do it, and only saw the guards rushing the cabin through the sheets of rain out of the corner of his eye. By the time he whirled to face the onslaught they were rushing into the front door and more through the side.

Jerry's fists and feet began flying to halt the attacks by Marks' would-be saviors. Immerman throat-punched the last one who got close, then realized all of them were down. But his Scout warned more were coming, many more. Even he and Immerman together wouldn't be able to handle the horde about to sweep over the cabin.

But maybe the Scout could, Jerry realized.

He scanned all of the biosignatures surrounding the cabin and saw they all had chips in their heads just as Jerry did. His Scout was already familiar with the chip's layout, and so it was just a matter of hacking into the Stoneburner programming, if he had enough time before being overrun.

There wasn't, Jerry knew, even if he kept the program as basic as possible. It would take him about two minutes longer to program than he had before the next wave of guards burst in.

But the Scout's AI had a good handle on Jerry's psyche by now, and even more on its own capabilities for mischief. It completed the program in a fraction of a second, laid out on the display screen for Jerry's approval.

What sound do you want? it asked.

In the middle of his own breathless adventure, though Jerry might not have thought it as such at the moment, his mind jumped back to some of his favorite twentieth-century pulp adventures he had grown up watching on his books and TVs. He typed in a name. The Scout approved it from its audio library just as half-a-dozen guards broke in through both doors.

Jerry pressed a button, and all of the guards howled and collapsed with hands to their ears.

"What did you do to them?" Immerman asked with the detached curiosity of a man who just realized he has been spared.

"I ordered the chips in all of their heads—all of Marks' guards' chips everywhere within ten miles—to set off a high-frequency radio burst. Tarzan's yell looping over and over again at the equivalent of one hundred and fifty decibels, but you can't cover your ears or run away. But it won't last long."

Jerry retrieved his Scout and pressed a few more buttons of a pre-programmed escape mechanism. "I'm running my DNA ghost program. If anyone tries tracking us their Scouts will be clouded with dozens of false human signatures."

As Marks' hands felt around him for purchase to rise, Jerry delivered a kick to the head that sent the doctor back to the floor.

Jerry grabbed his pack and ran with Immerman out into the storm.

Jerry wanted to head for either the old road or the trails he knew so well now. Immerman refused. "Everyone else knows the road and trails. And I have a faster way out. Which we're going to need if we're to beat Marks being able to transmit a warning back to Galapagos in NYC." He pressed a button on his Scout's display. "And it's being prepared for us now."

They ran through the downpour, which hadn't let up in intensity or thunderous noise, toward the edge of the mountain where a half-severed rope once nearly sent Jerry plunging hundreds of feet into a ravine river, and plunged him into something equally dangerous instead.

Even mostly blind from the weather, Jerry recognized the spot Immerman brought them to, a small clearing ringed with mountain laurel and waves of other thick-leaved plants, to know they were only a few hundred feet from the mountainside. In fact he remembered there was a path open to the precipitous drop straight from here.

The ground was rising.

The whole forest floor canopy was elevating and then dropping away like a sodden blanket. Which it was, Jerry saw. A hundred-foot long camouflaged tarpaulin with foliage growing atop it.

A whirring sound, noticeable when next to the canvas but lost just a few paces away, emanated from inside. After a few more moments it lifted slowly but wholly off the ground. Beneath it were folded slabs of a fiberglass-looking polymer. As the inflating canvas rose the polymer stacks did as well, unpacking and spreading out until they formed a long box with a door on one end and what looked like small windows lining the sides, with slits in front and back.

Jerry at last understood what this was: a small personal zeppelin to lift them up and away. But up and away into a chaotic tempest of lightning and fifty-mile-an-hour gusts.

"I'll take my chances getting back to NYC on foot," he told Immerman.

"By which time Linda will be dead," Immerman snapped back.

The whirring Jerry heard was a rapid electrolyzer. It emptied small tanks of water into itself to break the water down into its hydrogen and oxygen components. The hydrogen to fill the bag and give it lift, the oxygen into storage in case the zeppelin needed to flee to a high altitude with thin air.

"You're as insane as Marks!" Jerry yelled over the storm. "Do you really mean to take us up in that contraption? Into this storm?" All Jerry could see in front of him were visions of the *Hindenburg*'s flames eating the airship as it came crashing to earth.

Immerman was watching intently as the zeppelin grew increasingly fast to its full cylindrical size. It nearly filled the clearing. The gondola below the rigid bag was off the ground now, but only by a couple of feet, and almost fully extended. Immerman ran his hand along it. "There are helium pouches inside emptying into the zeppelin while it fills with hydrogen. They'll put us safely out of the flammability limit. Then it will just be a matter of piloting her through the storm and around the mountain peaks without crashing. But I'll take care of the flying."

"If we're hit by a direct lightning strike—"

"The outer skin has the same carbon nanotubing as the domes and cubes. They act as capacitors so if we're hit by lightning, the electricity will channel into the airship's batteries. Multiple strikes and any other excess will be discharged back into the air."

Before Jerry could protest further he realized the zeppelin had ceased inflating. It was ready to go. He saw to his dismay that the gondola below was also finished, but as he feared, it was small, only really meant for one person. And only four feet tall, so Immerman would need to stretch out where he was belted down, lying on the floor, to access the stick and all of the instrumentation. Meanwhile Jerry would be pressed up against a wall or corner, trying to make do while the storm and turbulence did its best to toss him about.

Each side of the gondola was marked AUDEAMUS.

"May we dare," Jerry whispered, and crawled in through the gondola's back door behind Immerman.

It wasn't quite as bad as he expected. Space was tight, but there were hooks he could use to secure himself with the flex-rope he brought in case he needed to climb during his escape. The storm was already lurching the cabin to and fro, but he managed to get himself roped in the wedge behind Immerman. He even withdrew his Scout, and kept it clenched tight against the bucking.

The zeppelin rocked back and forth against the tree tops. But the bag held and soon they were over a ravine stretching into a deep blackness Jerry couldn't see due to the night and rain. The winds tried to throw them right back against the mountain but Immerman was a more skilled pilot than Jerry expected. He aimed the *Audeamus* into the wind like a ship on a rogue wave, and sailed upward.

The mountaintops were almost invisible, but Jerry could make them out as vague shapes black against a slightly less black sky. "Do you at least have radar?" he asked as they skimmed perilously close to a peak. Close enough so one wrong turn or stiff wind could drive them into the granite top and shred them.

"I have it," Immerman said. "I won't use it. Radar can be detected and tracked."

"Marks already knows where we're going," Jerry pointed out.

"No sense in painting a target on us while we're en route. Bigger than the one we already have, of course, which is damn large enough."

A Hole in Wednesday

The whole cabin rumbled and tumbled, and shook hard enough in the buffeting air Jerry feared it would be shaken apart. The thunder was close and rattled the zeppelin's ribs and windows. The lightning was close enough to be blinding even through the slits of windows.

He caught an unexpected pang telling him he would miss Venn and Vanwoerden. He reminded himself once again that they both were the Gallows' creatures now.

Jerry realized the only way he would get through this without going insane himself was to distract himself. He put his back to the window and woke his sleeping Scout.

He considered sending a message to Linda. He brooded over the wording. How to convince her to get out of the dome, urgently but not in a way that would panic her?

He settled on something simple. *Sorry I haven't been able to write. I don't have much time now. But I wanted to tell you I'm coming home. Meet me in Melville Park . . .*

The park outside the NYC domes, one of their favorite places. He named an early morning time, hoping he could make the date. Or that he would still be alive by then, or otherwise in a position to let her know if he was forced to cancel.

Then he hesitated. The Scout told him today was Thursday, a little past 2:00 A.M. He would be sending a message outside of his Day, handing over hard evidence on a silver platter that Jerry Carson was a daybreaker. An alarm could be raised. The message might never find Linda at all—or worse, she could be implicated as an accomplice to his crime.

He saved the letter in his drafts folder. Even with no obstacles to sending the message, she wouldn't see it for another six obdays anyway.

Which also meant if Marks decided to take revenge on Linda he would have six full obdays to enact it. Suddenly the *Audeamus*, for all its pitches and rolls while it wound breathlessly through the mountains just below the peaks, no longer seemed like such a bad idea. If they survived the flight they could be back in NYC in a matter of an obday.

After Linda, there was only one thing on Jerry's mind enough to distract him from the horrific flight: Project Dantian.

He'd set his Scout to working on decrypting the file as soon as it was imaged in its memory. *What did I steal?* he wondered.

The Scout reported 9% of the files were decrypted. But when he tried opening them the Scout locked up. Amid the cacophony from outside he heard Immerman's Scout beep.

"Don't bother trying to look at the files yet," Immerman told him, never taking his eyes off their window lifeline just a few inches beyond his hooked nose. "You'll get to see them when you've done more work for us. In the meantime I've remotely disabled your Scout."

Anger gripped Jerry's mind. His immediate reaction was to lunge at the strapped Immerman and beat him either senseless or until he surrendered the passcode that would return control of Jerry's Scout to him. Of course this would guarantee crashing, since Jerry couldn't fly the zeppelin. But calm quickly returned, and with it remembrance of another one of Jerry's Scout's AI initiatives.

"Reroute," Jerry said aloud. The Scout's full display returned. "Enact Turnabout."

Immerman's Scout beeped frantically and then went dark.

Jerry's fears about Marks finding him out had bled into the Scout's AI. So over the course of the first fortnight the Scout belonged to Jerry, it took it upon itself to construct a second "spare" brain completely off-network. When Immerman—or anyone else—tried shutting the Scout down remotely, the second brain would "Reroute," kick in to replace the primary brain and in less than a billionth of a second, piece itself together from hundreds of files tucked away in hidden objects scattered among the device's quadrillions of nanodiamond qubits. Once assembled it could use Jerry's Turnabout command to follow the path of the offending remote user's command link back to the source.

"Your Scout is now disabled," Jerry reported to Immerman. "Until you tell me about Dantian."

"Do you really want to play this game, Carson?" Immerman demanded. "My Scout is our guide through these mountains. Do you want me flying blind in this tempest?"

"I doubt we will be. I can't imagine you wouldn't have a backup navigation system embedded somewhere in your controls you could use without a traceable uplink to a computer network. You were the one, after all, who always had us make plans on top of plans in our training. You wouldn't want to chance not being able to use your getaway if your Scout was taken or otherwise unusable, and the normal GPS could be tracked."

Immerman looked ready to rip Jerry's throat out.

Jerry faced him squarely.

Then Immerman laughed.

"You've proven again what I've believed all along, the one philosophy Northpath Marks and I share," he said. "Our Dayworld and stoners are stultifying humanity and dampening our intelligence and our drives, but even just a short time away from stoners, with certain types of training, can produce extraordinary results. You were my personal test case, Carson, and you did better than I hoped."

"So you'll tell me what I want to know?"

Immerman considered. "I think we have a dharma link, you and I. So yes, I'll tell you. When I'm not trying to prevent us from crashing."

Still looking out the front window, Immerman continued, "I'm going to tell you a story. It begins in Illinois on June 10th, 2037. The day I was born. To spare you from having to do the calculations yourself, particularly since I spent part but nowhere close to six-sevenths of that time in stoners, this works out to my being one hundred and twenty-six objective years old."

Twenty-Four

Immerman spoke in patches between thunder and wind gusts, the echoes of both drumming through the mountains, the maniacal patter of rain everywhere on the zeppelin, and as he said, the frequent moments when he had to concentrate his focus solely on keeping them aloft and alive.

But dark mile after mile, the tale—tall tale, Jerry thought at times—of Immerman's life from 2037 to 2440, United States to North American Union to North American Ministering Organ of the Organic Commonwealth of Earth, was related if not necessarily made wholly clear.

"My father—who had a different surname than the one I wear now—was a geneticist, so you could say it was the family business," Immerman explained. "We lived in Illinois. My father worked at a small lab in Peoria, which was close enough to major centers like Chicago and Saint Louis for business purposes, but on the edge of thousands of square miles of farmland. Or what had been farmland before much of it was ruined or otherwise made fertility-destitute by the blights and superbugs—diseases, I mean, evolved to resist the almost monopolized treatments. The third leg in this trinity of desolation, as the World Organic Council has harped on frequently over the subyears, was unscrupulous genetic modification. Genetic modification of plants and animals had been challenged for decades by then—obdecades, remember, as there were no stoners yet—but the worst of the lot dug in against the legal and moral challengers, and paradoxically managed to thrive all the greater for all the obstacles.

"My father was an ethical man. Far more so than I am, I suppose, though the times are much different now. His ethics cost him substantially. He was recruited by an organization whose descendants you have become intimately familiar with, called Galapagos Biotech. Their specialty was forced evolution through genetic modification, and they were a multinational corporation with tentacles stretching into numerous places around the planet where regulations were relaxed, or ignored with a sufficient amount of *baksheesh*. He refused their offers. He also knew enough about their operations that they feared he would expose their more nefarious practices to the world. So like a jealous, abusive lover, they decided if he would not come in on their side, he would work for no one at all.

"They set out to ruin the literal fruits of his labors first. They were partnered under and over the table with the leading multinational agricultural corporations, which likewise had deep roots in genetic modification, which only grew deeper but more covert with every assault. They mounted attacks against uppity farmers by 'planting' evidence in the way of their patented seeds in the farmer's fields, then sued the farmer into oblivion for trademark infringement.

"They did this to my father, which also meant he was fired and blacklisted. At the same time their agents stirred up the anti-modification's more radical elements, those who blamed the blights and superbugs on companies like Galapagos with no small justification. By this time even the radicals had been infiltrated, and Galapagos' competition mostly bought out, particularly the competition opposed to modification. The undercover operatives incited the radicals to the point where they destroyed my father's lab in Peoria, all his records and organic samples, and then came out to our farm—it was halfway between Peoria and the Mississippi River, you may have seen its corpse while you were with the Nature Rehabilitation Corps—they came and burned the test fields there too. For good measure they likewise lit up our house, and destroyed the crops in all the neighboring farms for three miles around us."

"What happened to your father?" Jerry willed himself to ask.

"He was eventually poisoned. It was made to look like he died from the results of his own work."

At this point in the narrative the zeppelin sailed into a brutally turbulent portion of the storm, and it seemed to the tossed and battered Jerry that it took the rest of the night to push through. At one point he tried pulling out his Scout to get a look at the weather patterns immediately outside them to have some kind of idea how long he would have to suffer the shaking, but one hard knock sent the Scout out of his hands and sliding down to the far end of the cabin and out of Jerry's reach. He would have to unstrap himself to retrieve it, but for the time being he was unwilling to take such a risk.

Even before they were out of the vicious pocket, Immerman resumed his autobiography. Jerry found strange comfort in the fact that his handler felt secure enough in his piloting skills to navigate and reminisce at the same time.

"As I said, Carson, genetics were the family business. As soon as I was done with my graduate courses at Bradley U., which I had by the time I was twenty thanks to starting early, I went to work for a company researching and selling genetic therapy. I did not use my birth name when I started college, but transformed into Gilbert Ching Immerman. By graduation I was a promising young anti-senescence biologist, which is to say, I was looking for ways to halt aging. I didn't know at the time that the company I went to work for was one of many secretly under the umbrella of Galapagos Biotech. All I knew was I was being paid a lot of money, with hefty bonuses for every major breakthrough.

"Eventually I did learn who my true employer was."

"Yet you kept working for them," Carson said. "Why would you? How could you, after what they did to your father?"

"This was before your time, Carson. By the early 2060s the world was suffocating under the weight of its human population and all of our excreta and ejecta and effluent detritus of seventeen billion people, before the great travails of the next two decades reduced the number to eight billion, which was still too many for the ruined world. But even at the time, the best and worst genetic modification companies alike could not manage to save enough of the world's crop production to feed us all. And both were blamed for the failures—even when those failures were caused by other factors. Industrial pollution, chemicals in the landscape, and then fallout from the first nuclear exchanges in Kashmir and on to the opening of World War Three, before the war cast down most of our higher technology."

"I was a history teacher, don't forget."

Immerman scowled back at him. "History is automatically sanitized in the minds of those who never lived through it. You forget most of our advanced technology was destroyed within months of the onset of World War Three. Most engines and computers were wrecked by electromagnetic pulses. Much of the world's fuel supply was eaten by oil-destroying nanorobots. The few planes that survived couldn't fly, as they became easy targets. Tanks had to be fueled by nuclear engines, or coal, on the rare occasions coal could be found. It got to the point where combat was carried out with swords and crossbows. And whenever new technology was invented, it was something like the quantum slider, heaping new horrors upon the old.

"Add all of this to starvation and pollution, and you'll understand how when Wang Shen, who began his conquests as the Chinese Communist Party chairman, overran the world and created the first world government, it wasn't just because his army was so much larger and stronger—it was because the survivors were weakened and exhausted. They couldn't fight. And when Wang Shen's son Sin Tzu turned against him, along with Communism and capitalism alike, and converted his father's world government into the New Era of stoners and the World Organic Council with its alluring Thirteen Principles, those weary and hungry people thought of it as their last best hope for salvation."

"And along with other scientific disciplines, people turned against genetic modification of any sort," Jerry guessed.

A Hole in Wednesday

"So zealously it would make the Inquisition seem like diplomats. The research we did could have helped grow more food, but it was never allowed. The ancestors of the Hinxton Decrees, which outlawed genetic research into life extension, came first. Then the floodgates opened."

"Which meant everything you had spent your life working for was now illegal," Carson said.

"Everything my father and I both had."

"So you made a deal with the Devil."

Immerman shrugged in a way that managed to be eloquent even though he lay flat on his stomach and strapped to the cabin floor.

"Faustian bargains are often the only solutions when the world is falling apart and your survival is at stake. Don't fool yourself, Carson. You have proven yourself to be a superior human being, which you are to be commended for. But superior by twenty-fifth-century standards only. You are still a child of the domes with no gut understanding of the world before. And I still believe the work I did then was for the ultimate benefit of humanity, as is that which I do now."

The zeppelin lurched again, struck by multiple lightning bolts blacking out the cabin's electronics for a heartbeat. It pitched forward and down. It lost altitude quickly and Jerry hardly noticed his Scout flashing by him again before it was already gone. The drop was violent enough that Jerry might have been thrown into the controls too if not for being strapped to the wall.

By the time Immerman regained control of the *Audeamus* a few seconds later, Jerry knew, as surely as if Immerman had planned the plunge, those seconds were more than long enough to conclude that he likewise would have done nearly anything to survive at the moment, get back to Linda, return to anything resembling a normal life.

"To get alive out of the darkness and the storm," Jerry said aloud. He suddenly felt he knew Immerman a lot better.

The Scout had slowly made its way back to Jerry, who clutched it tightly.

"The last two decades before the population of the world went into the stoners in 2084 were darkness and storm," Immerman said. "The Devil is greedy and doesn't want to destroy the world. The longer Judgment is put off, the more souls he gathers. Galapagos, twisted though it was, was not invested in letting the world be destroyed. I let myself be gathered into Hell because I thought I could work my passage to Heaven."

"Then why did you leave?"

Immerman waited a long time before answering. "It left me. We were working on creating an elixir that would cure many if not most diseases, and extend life both through elimination of those diseases and by directly regenerating the body's DNA. But despite our progress, some key element was missing. The elixir worked on some people, but others it sickened. A few died after taking it. We couldn't figure out why. Then we learned the hard way we had a thief. He stole all of the research, wrested control of the entire organization, then went off in a different direction, starting with firings and then outright purges, including me. Whatever he did apparently broke through a wall and has been more successful, based on the Gallows' communications we have intercepted."

"Northpath Marks was your thief," Jerry said.

"And he ascended to be its undisputed despot."

"So you're left with the atomic bomb problem. The Manhattan Project scientists didn't want to create an atomic bomb but they were afraid the Nazis would get it first. Thanks to Marks, you have to develop your elixir, regardless of what ruin you think it might bring, so the Gallows don't have an atomic-bomb sized advantage."

"You see the conundrum."

"But you had some success, if your claim to be over one hundred obyears old is anywhere close to being true. Is that why Marks didn't recognize you when you joined . . . rejoined . . . the organization?"

"My features have been altered greatly in the duration, both physically through surgery and, thanks to my own life-extending work, down to the genetic level to a great degree as well. But ah, we had wild successes! We developed numerous treatments, injections, and even partnered some of our work with cybernetics. The Gilbert Ching Immerman you see is a result of those treatments and yes, in a few cases, there are artificial parts within me. But there was nothing miraculous."

"The fact that you appear thirty-five years old seems miraculous enough."

"We've hit walls. None of those treatments can be used more than once. The cybernetics could replace certain parts, but did nothing to slow aging, and we never broke through where you could replace everything with machinery—if anyone turns themselves into a cybrid. What Galapagos was searching for—*is* searching for—is a one-off treatment. They want a single permanent cure for growing old."

"So Project Dantian is genetic life extension. How much of their research did I steal?"

"All of it. *Dan t'ian.* The Elixir Field. The Center of Energy. Places of regeneration. Places where, say certain Eastern religions and medicine, they manifest as centers of *qi*, the life force energy. The work I started and took underground in the years before the Dayworld became reality. If Marks and Galapagos have been successful, however, they will possess a literal elixir possessing life force energy of one sort or another. It will permanently regenerate DNA and the body."

"So you could live outside the stoners from day to day without ever appearing to age." Then Jerry remembered. "The elixir is why the Gallows muckety-mucks I met in Marks' office said daybreaking wasn't a problem for them."

"A fringe benefit. If the immortality elixir succeeds, you could theoretically live forever."

"Why would you want to?"

Immerman gave him a long, withering look over his shoulder. Jerry realized he had spoken without thinking, but every instinct told him being deathless was a horrific idea. He saw the appeal of a vastly extended youth, especially being in the best shape of his life now. He had found a new lease on life even if the means were dastardly. He did want to extend his lease for a long time. But the idea of existing on and on, obcentury after obcentury, was abhorrent. After a time, what would be the point?

When it was clear Jerry would not say more about it, Immerman told him, "Sometimes we are presented with a job to do which cannot be accomplished in a single lifetime. I've had more than the naturally given share of years already, and I am still far from being finished. And I protect my family. Couldn't you imagine, Carson, living forever if it meant keeping watch over your family?"

If I ever have descendants to watch over, Jerry thought.

Then a horrific realization hit him. "So if Marks succeeds in his necrotic nostalgia for the pre-New Era world, combined with this immortality elixir, he would be the eternal Supreme Councilor of the apocalypse."

Jerry's Scout emitted a warning bleep.

"Check it, since you've managed to bust my lock," Immerman said. "And don't forget to unlock mine when you're finished."

Text flashed over the display. Jerry told him, "It says it's been analyzing the hazards of our flight through the mountains . . . and if it is going to die it wants to die with a name."

"Are you to name it, or has it picked its own?"

"It wants to be called Coyote."

Immerman barked a laugh. "With the jobs ahead of us, we could use a Trickster's help."

"Coyote sometimes helped, and sometimes did harm," Jerry recalled. "But the Coyote stories typically warned what you were not supposed to do."

"I already said times are different now."

The storm retreated at the same time the night did. Their northeastward flight through the Appalachian mountain corridor became peaceful with the daylight, if no less urgent. Immerman pushed the throttle forward as far as it would go. The zeppelin still was occasionally buffeted by the damp wind, but the passage was now rough rather than potentially lethal, and all of the mountains walling them in were in clear view.

A Hole in Wednesday

Jerry had also been paying close attention to Immerman's working of the controls. He was certain he could take over if something happened to Immerman. He wasn't as certain how to land—though he imagined his Scout, Coyote, would have suggestions. It was opinionated about everything else.

When Jerry grew tired of visually learning the controls, he shifted to his window slit and looked down. What he saw shocked him.

Everything was green.

Which was the last thing he had expected.

The overpopulation and pollution spread across the Earth had precipitated the need for humanity to move into the domes and cubes. Vast stretches of land were laid waste, devoid of sustaining power of any kind for plant or animal. Immerman had said so himself, about the catastrophes rendering much of the American Midwest untenable in his long-ago youth. Jerry had seen some of the lingering environmental wreckage during his time with the Nature Rehabilitation Corps in Illinois, though most of his own work had been mop-up. The hardest restoration tasks had already been accomplished by then.

What stretched below him was a bright and fertile swath of land as far as the eye could see. Most of it had been reclaimed by forest sometime in the past. But the forests looked healthy. Now and again he ran across grasslands, and what seemed to be stretches of wild grains, even the occasional orchard.

What he did not see was any evidence of humans. He had expected the lack. They would all be living in high-rise towers in the cities now. But if what he saw of Eastern North America out the zeppelin window was any indication—and where he had been living in the Gallows' camp bore this out—there would be plenty of room to move back out of the cities.

Immerman followed Jerry's gaze and seemed to read his mind. "Being out has changed you, Carson. As it was supposed to. You're longing for those vast trackless lands again already, aren't you? Perhaps thinking you and Linda can carve out a place for yourself somewhere among it? It's a noble dream. But if we do it now, we'll bring down the same ruin on the world we did before."

"I thought you wanted to eliminate the stoners," Jerry said. "This was the one philosophy you had in common with Marks, is what you told me."

"I didn't mean migrating back out into the world. I have no intention of giving up the technology we have already achieved, as Marks claims he wants—to try forcing ourselves backward from the evolution we have achieved so far. And think, Carson! If the immortality elixir becomes a reality, then until we evolve our sensibilities further, we will visit destruction on the planet a hundred, a thousand times worse than what drove us into the stoners."

"I won't believe that no one aside from the licensed farmers ever goes out there."

"You're right. Others do, on the sly. The elites of the world."

"Then more of the planet has recovered. And it's the playground of the people who are in control."

Immerman flashed him an impatient look. "There is a simple solution. Work in the Family. Eventually you may become one of the elite."

Jerry's Scout bleeped another warning. "Maybe it's changed his mind about what name it wants?" Immerman asked.

But this time the alarm was more urgent.

Jerry scanned Coyote's text alert with mounting horror. "The AI knows I'm from Manhattan Dome and took it upon itself to follow news from there. There have been two explosions there. The Columbus Circle Power Station and Union Station. Both are wrecked with hundreds of casualties. This is Marks, isn't it?"

"It's highly improbable that two strategic attacks immediately following our theft of Galapagos' elixir research would be otherwise. One blast to cripple Manhattan's primary power supply, and the other to disable the main transport artery out of the dome."

"Columbus Circle provides my apartment's power." Jerry had a sudden fear for Linda's safety. NYC had never experienced a blackout in his lifetime. "Will the power station explosion mean the stoners won't be activated or deactivated?"

"No. The stoners are unique in being fed power directly from the dome's own external nanotube capacitors when stoning and destoning their inhabitants. Marks' primary target is most likely NYC's World Organic Council Headquarters in the Upper West Side. And no doubt to sow as much confusion and panic as possible. The question is whether or not Gallows has its claws sunk deep enough into the Powers That Be to take control of the dome's power nexus as well."

"How long before we're back in NYC?"

"We're two hours from a safe house, a farmhouse on Long Island, where we'll land the zeppelin. From there, another hour."

Jerry and Immerman's Scouts clanged simultaneously, alerting them to a high priority message coming through.

Jerry already knew who the message would be from before he read it.

Your betrayals and theft of Project Dantian have forced my hand. –N.M.

"Forget the safe house!" Jerry said. An ominous foreboding gripped his stomach and sent cold tendrils into his heart. "Fly us straight to the city!" If necessary they could hitch the *Audeamus* to a zeppelin tether at Seeger Airfield just across the Hudson River. Doing so would alert Marks to their location and leave the zeppelin vulnerable if they needed it to flee the city, but Jerry hoped the time they saved would be worth the risk.

The zeppelin banked and put the easternmost mountains behind it. For all the speed it was making it might as well have been drifting lazily on a random breeze as far as Jerry was concerned. All of his instincts, all of the skills he had discovered at noticing patterns and connecting their traces to a greater whole, warned him they were still not going fast enough, they would arrive too late to stop whatever scheme Marks had put in motion, and Jerry should brace himself for the worst of possible outcomes.

Linda, wait for me!

The fact that this was Thursday, and Linda was a Wednesday trapped in her stoner beyond any kind of warning he could send her for another six days, refused to stop nagging at Jerry.

Twenty-Five

Manhattan was a circus of horrors.

After so many obweeks spent in the starkly quiet and depopulated natural outdoors, Jerry was overwhelmed by the cacophony of colors, noise, and artificiality saturating every foot and footstep. He went from dozens of people to hundreds of thousands on this Thursday evening, and the millions more he knew lurked inside the stoner chambers in their domes. All the noise and fuss they stirred up beat against his head, even with the electricity out all over Lower Manhattan and probably well beyond.

He might have been almost swept away by it anyway after being thrust back in so jarringly. But add to it all the chaos of New York's first terrorist attacks since the twenty-first century—three subgenerations ago—and the panic it instilled in a population which thought itself safe and insulated, and racing up Park Avenue become more challenging to Jerry than anything he had done in Marks' camp.

While his legs pumped down the road on Immerman's heels, Jerry forced his mind to quiet and focus. Jerry had grown used to the stillness of wilderness isolation at Camp Natufian, and then his mind had been completely focused on getting to Linda during the flight, then when he and Immerman stole a boat to cross the Hudson and used Immerman's Scout to open a service passage into the dome. Now being back in Manhattan was assaulting every sense and nerve he had. But he couldn't join the rest of NYC in panicking. He couldn't afford to be confused and bewildered. He had trained his mind and psyche along with his body, and now he must put his training to use in what was really the middle of a war.

"You're going the wrong way!" Jerry shouted at Immerman as his handler bolted onto East 30th Street, away from Jerry's apartment.

Immerman stopped and grabbed Jerry's arm. Immerman might be one hundred and twenty-six obyears old, but he wasn't sweating or so much as flushed from all the running.

"Marks is impatient and hunting bigger game," Immerman said. "And if he bags it, his trophy will be the ability to control anyone he wants to. Let's go, Carson, it isn't much farther."

The tower Immerman led him to was a high-rise like any other around it. It might have been the same one his journey through the subterranean tunnels leading the ex-stoner prisoners to the Reductionists took him. But above ground, and with so many people crowding the entrance floor of the building, whose front doors were frozen open in the blackout, there was no way to tell.

Jerry assumed they were going to go underground but the doors to the lower levels were immobilized by the power outage as well. Jerry and Immerman passed one after the other but none appeared to have manual locks. "How are we going to open them?" Jerry asked.

Immerman pressed forward but cast an answering glance toward the throngs of people still surrounding them. Jerry took the hint and stayed silent.

At last they were out of the human morass of the streets and inside the high-rise. Jerry caught himself relaxing at once, the way he once would have if he had been able to come back to NYC immediately after first experiencing the then-unsettling world of natural, uncontrolled mountaintops.

"We have to find out what Marks is up to," Immerman said, beelining for a door looking as sealed as all the others, "and there's only one place we can do that. You've been there once already, but you've only seen the outer shell, not the inner mechanisms which help the operation turn."

He held his Scout display against the door's dead electronic biolock's receiver, and the Scout set to buzzing. The lock and the biosensor above the door came back to life. He was feeding them power wirelessly from the Scout, Jerry realized.

The door recognized Immerman and allowed them entrance.

The corridor plunged downward from there. Jerry recognized the passage by its utter featurelessness as one he had run through before, or at least its identical twin, complete with alphanumeric designations on the otherwise blank and windowless doors. It also took him a moment to realize the lights were working.

After a few hundred descending feet, one new feature appeared which Jerry also recognized: a bronze plaque on the wall reading BURROUGHS WING. It was a real physical object rather than an electrolayered painting. And the murals on the walls beyond of wild forests and tropical jungles, one of which contained the ruins of an ancient stone city, were likewise painted on with real pigments rather than scanned into the wall's visual crystal exterior. One hand on the walls proved to Jerry they didn't have viscrystal facings at all.

Immerman stopped in front of a door marked B-205. This corridor likewise had power and the door opened to him immediately without the Scout's assistance.

Jerry knew he had been here before, only through the door on the opposite side of the room. It was the room with the banks of antique quantum computers where the Reductionist's voice in his head—then still Immerman personally—led him with the ex-stoner prisoners.

Then it was as dead as a tomb except for a single light in the ceiling. Now the whole room was ablaze with power. Every light was on and every computer was active. There was one giant Christmas tree light-like console filled with rounded monitors, metal switches, and numeric dials like something out of a twentieth century pulp science fiction movie, and a single swiveling chair placed before it which Immerman took for himself. The dozens of old personal computers—all S-Wave Novas, the first personal quantum computer, Jerry remembered from his trips to the Museum—filled shelves flanking the console from knee-height to eight feet off the floor.

"This is your secret headquarters?" Jerry scoffed in worried frustration, Linda still foremost in his mind. "An oversized closet full of junk?"

Immerman rounded on him with such a black scowl Jerry thought his handler would pounce on him. But Immerman got control of himself, and said in a level tone, "These are all linked to form a supercomputer as powerful as anything the World Organic Council—or Galapagos—has in NYC. Or possibly anywhere in the world. They have been modified to communicate with any computer or AI in the city network, but the city's computers don't have enough backward compatibility to track my computers back here. None can except the only other computer set-up like mine in the NYC domes."

"Marks' computers," Jerry said. "What is he up to?"

"That's what I was working on discovering when you interrupted me with a stupid comment."

Immerman returned to the flashing console. Every flipped switch and turned dial changed displays on some of the S-Wave Novas, which either showed pictures from around the NYC domes or various computer readouts. Some of the readouts were in Stoneburner, so Jerry could pick up enough bits and pieces of them to realize the computers, like their human operators, were frantic.

"It's a virus," Jerry realized. "Marks has uploaded some kind of control code into the city network. It's similar to what Coyote's AI uses to design his own initiatives."

Immerman nodded. "Only far more malignant and pervasive. It's gotten into the heart of the NYC Control Authority. Taking out the Columbus Circle Power Station forced enough security to reroute that Marks has been able to go around it—and help is coming in from outside slowly, thanks to the Union Station destruction. And it looks like the virus will execute . . . damn!"

A Hole in Wednesday

"What is it?" Jerry felt the foreboding knot of terror forming in him just as it had before in the zeppelin.

"No!" Immerman shouted. "Even I didn't think Marks wouldn't be that mad! But he's doing it . . ."

Jerry shoved Immerman away from the main console display and read the scrolling Stoneburner code. It came in a hundred different pieces from a hundred different nodes and nexuses, but they all pointed to a single pattern.

Marks was taking control of all of the millions of stoners in Lower Manhattan.

Including Linda's.

"We have to stop him!" Jerry shouted, and ordered Coyote to begin an uplink to the stoner network. "This is Stoneburner. I can reprogram it!"

"There's not enough time to reroute all of it, Carson," Immerman snapped, "and his program has infiltrated the system too deeply. It's already implementing."

"Implementing what . . . ?"

But the code told the story with cold and cruel impassivity. A third of the cylinders were destoning their occupants not in a quarter of a nanosecond but over the course of minutes, shredding their molecules as they went. Another third were destoning only partially, which meant people across Lower Manhattan were waking up in excruciating agony because parts of their bodies were still frozen. And the other third were destoned normally but in chambers staying locked tight, so those occupants would suffocate in minutes.

"There's too much," Immerman repeated. "We'll never rewrite most of it even if we can break into Marks' programming."

Jerry leaned into the console, feeling as if the whole world was a whirlpool sucking him deep into the ground. His mind and body's automatic reaction was to go insane with rage to pull him out of the sucking maw. But again, he forced himself to quiet his mind and focus.

"Then we save Linda," Jerry said. "Isolate her stoner from the virus."

"Agreed. I'll look for Marks, or at least the path he's using into the city's computer network."

It was only when Jerry started swarming through the city's stoner programming that he realized he wasn't sure how to seek Linda's stoner in all of Lower Manhattan's millions, or even a particular building. Every building, terminal, and stoner was given alphanumerical designations as long as twenty characters. Cold sweat dripped into Jerry's eyes. He was going much too slowly.

"Coyote, I need your help!" he said. "Can you translate these ID tags?"

Jerry's Scout jumped to work. Its display screen flashed blocks of images back and forth as it sought Jerry's building and then scanned the ID tags of each stoner within faster than Jerry could follow.

"There!" The Scout had given him visual confirmation of his apartment's cylinder room, and Jerry's eye went straight across the twenty-eight cylinders to Linda's. The room was almost completely dark, though, thanks to the power outage. But Jerry could see Linda's eyes were closed.

His heart seized. He had seen her eyes closed in her chamber, all the times her stoner was delayed. But her face was not the impervious statue of somebody in the stoner field. It was colorless, bloodless flesh.

"Linda!" he shouted at the Scout as if just trying to awake Linda through it from a speeder sleep. "Linda!" he cried again, as if he could open the stoner door, or restart her vital functions.

He shouted as if she could hear anything at all.

Jerry rounded on Immerman. "Where is Marks?"

Immerman was pale and his hands on the console trembled. "They're all dead. Everyone in every stoner in Lower Manhattan. Marks murdered them all. Three million people."

"Where is he! I'm going after him, Immerman. I'll find a slicer and blast him out of this world, or if I can't find a slicer I'll crush his neck with my own hands!"

Immerman turned to him but didn't quite face him. "He'll kill you if you try any kind of frontal assault, Carson. He'll see you coming from the whole city away and be ready for anything you try."

"The whole city . . . ? Is he here?" Jerry felt the insane rage returning, saturated with terror for Linda. He grabbed Immerman by the collar, ignoring Immerman's physically superiority and being the only one in a position to help, and slammed his fist across Immerman's jaw. "Tell me!"

Immerman roared a roar drowning everything else out in Jerry's ears. He threw Jerry into a computer shelf solid enough to feel like it cracked Jerry's spine as he bounced off and plunged to the floor. Then Immerman grabbed him again and slammed him into the shelf once more.

"He killed my wife!" Jerry screamed. "You can't stop me from killing him!"

"And he killed my daughter! Linda was my daughter!"

Jerry felt all of his resistance to Immerman fracture in an instant. "You're lying. Linda's father died before we were married."

"Linda's father is one hundred and twenty-six years old with the body of a man who's thirty-five." Immerman fought to control his heaving breath. "How long was he supposed to stick around being practically ageless? Linda's mother knew, but she wanted no part of the Family by then, nor for Linda to know anything about my true existence. I made my persona of Linda's father disappear before Marks could swoop down and harm her. But I only delayed the inevitable."

Jerry realized Immerman still clutched his collar and broke free from him, moving a few paces off. He wanted to fight, to scream, to wail, to thrash his fists at the whole universe for such a vicious theft of Linda's life and the life Jerry had wanted to plan with her. All useless. The only thing left was stopping Marks.

"Where is he?" Jerry demanded again, though with a quieter and colder note than before.

"He was here in the city before we arrived. He didn't have our need for stealth."

"Why did he do this?"

"To instill fear. Next he will use the terror he has caused to seize control of the governments of all seven Days. But there is a chance of stopping him if we use our heads and move quickly enough."

Jerry's Scout cut in with an urgent klaxon.

"What is it? Marks?" Jerry asked as he scooped the tablet into a white-knuckled grip so tight Coyote might have cried out if it could feel pain. "I don't understand this readout, Coyote. What does this mean?"

Immerman took the Scout and looked it over. "It means two people were stoned in Linda's chamber, Jerry. Linda . . . and a fetus. Your child. My grandchild."

Jerry wailed. "Then he's killed my life twice over. My wife and the child we would have had!"

Immerman shook his head wildly. "Linda died from her stoner field only partially destoning her. Everything from her chest down is still stoned. The fetus is still alive."

Jerry choked, and worried he was choking on hope. "Can we save it?"

Immerman jabbed a few buttons on the display. "It's only a couple of subweeks old. And the stoning field is unstable since it only covered part of her body. But if we can preserve the stoning field around it long enough to implant it in another womb, there is a chance. Though the time spent doing so means we will probably lose Marks."

"We won't lose Marks," Jerry said. An idea flowed into his brain like glowing lava. "He won't let us lose him. While we're still alive—and while we have his research on the immortality elixir—we're still a threat. What are you willing to do to protect your family, Immerman?"

"Anything necessary," Immerman answered. "And you, Carson?"

"Anything I must."

Twenty-Six

The subways were shut down since the Union Station explosion. But it was only a mile-and-a-half from East 30th to his apartment in Gramercy Tower at West 20th and 21st, and Jerry and Immerman knew the cresting panic flooding over Manhattan meant they could both run faster than trying to take any wheels through the chaos on the roads. The distance was nothing more than a quick run at Camp Natufian. But this time Jerry was fueled by grief and his hope the stoner field protecting the miniscule flicker of life within Linda's womb would last until they arrived.

"If the field has shut off completely, the backup battery will hold at least until we get there," Immerman had told Jerry just after they burst out of the Thirteen Principles Tower. "Whether it will hold long enough to get Linda back, I don't know. This is also assuming Marks' virus didn't affect the battery as well. Either way, we're going to need to cut off the receiver on her stoner to take the cylinder."

"But you got what you wanted, didn't you, Immerman?" Jerry said, not noticing he had pulled ahead of his former trainer. "You and Marks both. An end to the Dayworld. Nobody will go back into their stoners tonight. They'll be afraid to in case this happens again. And every stoner room in Lower Manhattan is full of corpses."

"I wanted the end of stoners eventually," Immerman agreed,

"and I have no qualms about a violent disruption to do so. But nothing of this magnitude, and not yet, with eight billion people still on the planet. And definitely not on Galapagos' terms."

They reached Gramercy Tower in fifteen minutes and Jerry shoved his way in with Immerman close at his heels, ignoring the screaming and wails and shouted protests of, just as he guessed, people who said they were never going into the stoner rooms again, rooms that would feel like tombs even after the bodies were cleared away. The power was still off, and nobody knew what was happening and hardly paid any attention to the two frantic men running through their midst and to the nearest stairs.

Eleven stories later Jerry was at his apartment door, fumbling with the Scout to power open the door. As fast as he had run, though, he stepped inside with care, as if Linda was only sleeping after a long day at the Folk Library and he didn't want to wake her.

He forced himself to step into the stoner room.

Twenty-three of the twenty-eight stoners were filled but not a single occupant was living. Beside Linda were the Washingtons, both of whose faces were twisted in rictuses of agony. Linda's face, though, now that Jerry could see it close up, only looked like she really was sleeping.

Jerry let Coyote scan her cylinder. The stoner field was three-quarters operational, meaning everything from Linda's toes to halfway up her chest was encased in that impenetrable motionless force for however long it lasted. It ceased midway up her heart and so severed her body at the chest, including cutting the heart in two. Jerry allowed himself to hope that her death had been instant and painless, instead of thinking that in a way, the same thing had now happened to his own heart.

Immerman pointed to a small row of blue lights across the stoner's status display. "The battery still has almost a thirty percent charge. We might be able to get her back in time."

"Only thirty percent? Why would the battery not be able to hold a charge for six full days, in case the power went out?"

"The stoner fields don't need to draw power once they're activated just so long as they encompass the whole body, remember.

A Hole in Wednesday

And also because the power has never gone out in the whole time Manhattan Dome has existed. I have no intention of eschewing most of our technology as Marks does, but we have grown too dependent on it. And right now there's no telling when the power will come back—or what people might become afraid enough to do in the meantime. Here, take this," Immerman told him, handing Jerry a slider.

Jerry stared at the weapon lying cold across his palm, then he gripped it tight. He had become fairly proficient with it in Marks' camp. He'd never before seriously thought about using it in anger, but now he had every intention of using it on Marks the instant they met again.

At the moment, Immerman was using his own slider more pragmatically. This was the one Marks had pointed at Jerry, with the adaptation to narrow the beam to a line thinner than a razor, and now Immerman was using his quantum razor to dissect the transceiver that received the wireless stoner field energy, and constantly broadcast back the stoner's status, without damaging the cylinder's structural integrity and thus jeopardizing the field.

Even with the proper tools it would have otherwise taken an hour to disconnect, more time than Jerry and his child had. But removing it would, Jerry hoped, eliminate the virus from the stoner. It would definitely mask the stoner's location from anyone seeking it.

"How will we get it down the stairs?" Jerry asked.

"We won't. We'll drop it down the elevator shaft."

"Drop it! You can't! Linda . . . she'll . . ."

Jerry stopped short, realizing how stupid he must sound. The stoners were sheathed in nanopolymers that were unbreakable except from slider beams. The battery was built inside the door so that it would likewise be undamaged by physical trauma. The field itself would protect Linda's child. And in case of a power disruption, elevators retained reserve power long enough to return to the ground floor and open the doors, so there was no chance of the stoner hitting a car halfway down and being stuck out of reach.

Immerman was looking at Jerry without judgment. "We'll

need a service elevator with open access to the shaft, preferably one stopping one floor below ground level. Do you know one? Jerry!"

"Yes. Yes! Let's just get her out of here while we have time."

The stoner was surprisingly light, thanks to the nanopolymer's ability to retain maximum cohesion despite being only a few molecules thick. What it covered was little more than a sheet of copper. Most of the weight they carried was Linda's one hundred and forty pounds. But the stoner itself was still eight feet long and three feet wide, and would have made for cumbersome carrying under the best of circumstances.

Immerman used a knife he'd kept hidden until that moment to create a wedge in the elevator door, and then he yanked the doors open to reveal the empty shaft. Once the cylinder was upright, Jerry hesitated, feeling foolish again. Linda was dead, she would feel nothing. And yet Jerry still couldn't bring himself to push the cylinder into the narrow maw.

Immerman understood and did it himself, hurriedly pulling the door closed again to spare them the sound of the impact below.

"Now how do we get her out?" Jerry asked.

"There's the usual medical storage facility for the tower's clinic below the ground floor, yes? Take me there, then follow my lead."

Electronic security was non-existent with the ongoing power outage—an event thought impossible a few hours before—plus there was only one guard in the storage unit where the tower kept, among other things, gurneys used to wheel out someone still in a stoner in the case of a field being necessary to preserve the patient long enough to reach a specialized hospital. By the time the guard jumped to his feet from his desk just beyond the storage room door, Jerry and Immerman had sliders aimed point blank at him.

"We're taking a gurney," Jerry told him. "And an ambulance," he added, which he knew would have a charger the stoner battery could interface with. "If you let us knock you unconscious without resistance, there will be a lot less pain."

Twenty-Seven

"Welcome to Alphabet City," Immerman said.

Immerman's quarters were more than the room of cold computer screens Jerry had already seen, B-205 in the Burroughs wing several stories below East 30th Street. It was a honeycomb of networked rooms elaborately decorated in stark contrast to the blindingly plain earlier corridors. The floors were covered in seafoam colored plush carpeting thick enough to muffle footsteps and incorporating a multitude of gold spiral designs resembling some ancient alphabet.

All of the rooms were elaborately and luxuriously furnished. Some made Jerry feel like he was back in the Museum. This room an overstuffed Victorian parlor, that one a cushioned Raja's palace, then a Roman bath with heated and frigid marble pools. Others boasted the brightest—and most garish, Jerry thought after his time in Camp Natufian—modern décor. Many rooms were filled with people who took little to no notice of Immerman and Jerry's passing. The walls were covered in paintings (real paintings, not holo-layers, which confirmed Jerry's belief that the place was full of daybreakers) of elephants, rhinos, and other long-dead large animals the Natural Rehabilitation Corps was attempting to genetically resurrect.

Everything was spread out across a long and multileveled distance below the high-rise. There were multiple exits far-flung enough to allow passage into different wings, or more tunnels like the one that had led him and the stoner escapees to B-205. Some of the doors had permanent metallic plaques saying which wing they exited to: Asmodée, Burroughs, Clemens, Diogenes, Erinyes, and so on. Others remained anonymous, or were to Jerry. Whether or not they overtly identified their destination, they had carvings etched permanently into the doors (still another sign pointing to this honeycomb being full of daybreakers) and a phrase, typically in a foreign language and not always a living one, stenciled above each door.

The unending apartment retained electrical power. Jerry suspected this was self-generated not just for emergencies, but also not to draw attention to Immerman's private warren.

Immerman led him through the domicile menagerie to a small arch-ceilinged, reverentially quiet and dim room in the Diogenes wing. There Jerry and Immerman wheeled Linda's stoner and reconnected it to a transceiver of Reductionist design that would wrap Linda's body in a complete, stable stoner field, but not transmit a location.

"We need to find out what's happening in the world," Immerman said as he led Jerry through the labyrinth, "and how people outside NYC are reacting to Marks' attack. We'll be back in the Burroughs wing for that. In many cases we'll also be able to remotely feed power to cameras in Manhattan."

The more he walked through the corridors the more Jerry became convinced that the Reductionists might be every bit as powerful as Galapagos in this dark underworld of sub-government elites. There was no other way to explain how Immerman was able to command such a vast piece of the most valuable subterranean real estate in Manhattan, and as a daybreaker no less.

"Who are you on Thursday?" Jerry asked.

Immerman halted at a biosensored door marked B-612 without answering. The length of the door was filled with an etched and brightly painted carving of the ancient Egyptian ibis-headed god Thoth, inventor of writing, scribe of the underworld—perhaps a literal underworld in this case since Jerry was several subfloors below Manhattan's streets—who could see the secrets in men's hearts, and was the arbiter between no fewer than three major battles between good and evil. Thoth wore a necklace of bright lapis lazuli and a loincloth woven of reeds made from papyrus, a plant now extinct in Egypt.

Above the door was carved the Latin phrase *AD VITAM AETERNAM*: "To Eternal Life."

Jerry expected the door to Immerman's inner sanctum to open on some sort of library or laboratory or both. Instead Immerman revealed a technological wonderland running for hundreds of equipment-filled feet. In a few cases there were slots for old S-Wave Novas like in B-205, and basic atomic clock strips featuring every time zone, but most of the equipment was more advanced than anything Jerry had ever seen.

Some were obviously quantum computers, both personal and large scale supercomputers big enough, Jerry figured, to contain every piece of information in the world. There were rows of interlinked Scouts, glowing crystal boxes of artificial intelligence processors, scanners of both planetary and cosmic weather, seismic monitors, fusion capacitors releasing small wafts of cold smoke, holistic communication gatherers, voice encoders—probably where Immerman spoke to Jerry's chip while they were still in Manhattan—and telephones and radios of every sort plus what Jerry could only assume were unknown communication devices based on their proximity to the others.

The room would have felt uncomfortably warm before his training. Jerry couldn't imagine how much power was required to run all of these systems. Had it been on the dome grid, somebody definitely would have noticed, drawing attention Immerman undoubtedly wanted to avoid.

Oddly, there were stoners on the far end of the room. Except like those he saw when first on the run from Marks, these were a variety of shapes and sizes, including one shaped like a coffin looking like it was made out of gray paper. None appeared to have a familiar field transceiver.

He wondered why they were stored in the war room. Maybe to keep them close to the pinnacles of technology the room offered.

But unlike when he ran across Marks' unusual chambers, Jerry understood better now what they represented. "They're experiments. Creating a stoner capable of generating its own field independent of the activating burst of power from an exterior source. You're doing the same thing as Marks. Why? To be able to stone someone and make them permanently disappear?" As long as a stoner was linked to a primary field generator you could track it down later even if you dropped it in the middle of the Pacific Ocean or a deep crater on the Moon.

"Only under absolute necessity. But more accurately, we are trying to build our own so if Marks succeeds in building one, we can determine how to stop it—or find someone he wants to disappear."

Immerman paced restlessly in front of rows of monitors showing news broadcasts from around the world. "We can discuss that later. For now we need to be here. This is our war room. From here we can plan how to strike back at Marks. In the early days of the New Era it was devoted to air defense, but now it serves every surveillance need I could possibly have."

"Everything in here is linked, one way or another," Jerry guessed.

"The ultimate supercomputer. You asked me who I am on Thursdays. My name today is Richard Huxley Beauchamp. I am NYC's Information Officer—which I'll admit among Family is a subtle way of saying I'm the chief government censor. As Winston Churchill said, 'In wartime, truth is so precious that she should always be attended by a bodyguard of lies.' My position every day of the week is, in essence, the chief bodyguard who directs all the others. And every day of the week you could say B-612 is my home office.

"From here I can monitor the entire planet. The AI's decision-making capabilities scour the world for information and their collection gatherers harness it from every medium and bandwidth, along with making critical decisions about what I should see based on ranking. Everything, critical or not, is fed into the individual supercomputers' storage with each item cataloged in multiple ways. I have the same hunting and storage capacity as the World Organic Council's LifeLog system, which records every communication everyone makes from childhood to death—although those belonging to hounds and Council members are locked so tightly upon ascending to those positions that only the Council members themselves have access to those records."

"This will find Marks?" Jerry asked, once again allowing himself a modicum of hope that was quickly overwhelmed by the need for bloody revenge.

"This will find anyone eventually. Finding Marks might not be the problem, despite his not wanting to be found and his having nearly the same technological capacity we do. The problem will be getting to him through the extra security he will inevitably surround himself with. He will use the attack as an excuse . . ."

"But it's because he knows we'll be gunning for him," Jerry finished.

Coyote vibrated mutely in Jerry's hand. *I can access the Life-Log from here!* it flashed in a perpetual scroll across its display. *Can I read it?*

-Mine will be dull-, Jerry typed back.

I thought so, but I had other Logs in mind to poke into.

-Self-serve buffet. Just be ready if I need to call you back.-

Sí, jefe!

Immerman turned away from the bank of public channel screens with an increasingly unhappy look. "I'll be back shortly. Carson, I want you to watch what's happening out there until I return. If you notice any patterns, or anything significant otherwise, tell me at once."

As if ignoring the tragedy in Manhattan, or more likely seeking to calm people and make them believe everything was back to normal, the screens displaying public streams showed nothing but normal programming. Some pumped out the Eastern philosophical stories of Pao Chang Abrishamian, whose words and voice were like moonlight glittering on a sea in the middle of the desert, putting one in mind of the domes being oases. Others played the soothing jazz of Arthur Link Ozam or the cityscape tones of Bocuma Xax so popularly piped into the Museum and other public buildings, to relax the psyches of anyone too unsettled by the terrorism. The private screens were something else entirely, but nothing showing any obvious patterns.

Which in itself could be significant, Jerry thought. The more he watched the screens, the more it seemed as if someone was intentionally supporting the quiet chaos—almost orderly chaos if that wasn't too much of an oxymoron—outside NYC in order to disguise any patterns. Marks, most likely, fomenting disorganization as quickly as Immerman was likely trying to clamp down on information and channel it.

Then three significant things happened simultaneously.

The private feeds held reports of two murders of prominent officials: Wang, head of the Psychic Rehabilitation Department in Los Angeles State, and his Central Illinois Cube counterpart, Mbala—the two other psychicists Marks had Jerry meet with in his office after Galapagos caught him.

The third feed was from Dallas Dome. Crowds that were angry or fearful or both had taken to the streets. Somehow guns had reemerged and the mobs were threatening insurrection—the official news sources did not say as much, but it was plain to Jerry and probably anyone else watching. Jerry zoomed in on one particular face at the head of the mobs and recognized another one of his freed stoner prisoners, Colonel James Erech Garrison, who had led what became the last mass protests against the stoners in the late twenty-first century.

Jerry called Immerman back to B-612. Immerman returned to the war room transformed.

The simple cotton tunic and slacks he had worn before, which was practically the uniform of the Gallows at the camp, were replaced with a flowing saffron-colored robe wrapped around his stocky, muscular frame. His leather boots were replaced by ornate Roman sandals latticed around his feet and ankles. Kohl was applied to his eyelids, black on top and green below, half Egyptian pharaoh, half old-time special forces soldier.

He waved a hand over an optical sensor on a control panel beside Jerry, and a portion of the floor slid away for a computerized chair to appear. The entire chair pulsed with light and was a single nerve center of computerized implants, buttons, monitors, and wiring.

A Hole in Wednesday

When Immerman sat, pulsing tendrils reaching out from the back sought his head and hands and attached themselves with tiny leg-like filaments to his skin. The filaments and tendrils themselves glowed with hums and warm light like old computers coming to life. It was the first time Jerry had seen a stim-chair: the tendrils provided either moderate drugs or electrical impulses to strategic points of the body to keep the user awake and sharp.

Immerman the plain soldier was gone. Immerman the elite government official had taken his place.

A gray Siamese cat infiltrated the war room, obviously recognized by the biosensor, and jumped into Immerman's lap. A chipped tag hanging from the cat's collar identified the animal as Kane. Kane didn't seem to mind that both of Immerman's hands were vertically typing away on holographic keyboards floating above the chair rather than stroking fur.

His midair keystrokes started shutting down public channels across the world one by one, replacing them with innocuous entertainment programs or musical scores. "This room has complete Organic cutoff capability," he explained. "From here forward I will control what people see, if they haven't seen too much already."

Immerman sighed at the images beaming on the private streams, and few remaining public channels he hadn't altered, from Los Angeles, Chicago, and Dallas, but his eyes glittered with malice. "I didn't see Wang's and Mbala's murders coming. But breaking that triumvirate means Marks is gathering the entirety of Galapagos and its resources under his sole control—and will use them as a further excuse to fortify his own security. As for our Colonel Garrison, I freed him because I wanted his twenty-first-century military mind and experience, but he is more independent than I expected. I suppose he believes he is helping us. But I've already spotted four Galapagos agents provocateurs in the crowd. Marks will simply use this to convince the World Organic Council of the need for a clampdown. But we have assets of our own in Dallas and among the relays forwarding these broadcasts."

"Family?" Jerry asked.

"All Family. Some are even other children of mine—and a few grandchildren. Our Family is large, but know Linda was no less precious to me because she had many siblings, nieces, nephews, and cousins. I'll avenge her as if she were my only child."

Jerry felt his heart burst at the thought of Linda again. He had almost been able to let events sweep him away from thinking about her to distraction. Maybe they could again, for now. He did not have time to mourn yet. They had work to do.

"How many people are protesting in Dallas?" Jerry asked.

Immerman answered, "Our sensors count fourteen thousand, two hundred and seven. More are joining them, or will if we do nothing . . . ah, there. Colonel Garrison has snatched at Marks' bait."

The insurrection steadily tipped over into violence. Wave after wave of the armed mob surged, then rioted, still led by Garrison, who was shouting things Jerry couldn't make out above the tumult of thousands of other shouts. Windows were smashed, police were pushed back. Smoke poured out of windows.

Screens around Immerman changed scenes—either Immerman himself or other Family members blacking out the news coverage from what other sources were calling "The Battle of Dallas." Immerman scowled at the name.

Most of the screens went dark for an instant, then reappeared with Northpath Marks' face.

Immerman leaned forward, face black. "'And just as I'd taken the highest tree in the wood, and just as I was thinking I should be free of them at last, they must needs come wriggling down from the sky!'"

Alice in Wonderland again, Jerry thought. Except his rabbit holes continued getting darker, narrower, and increasingly treacherous. And now he was pulling countless innocent people in with him.

"Is he going to claim responsibility for the attack?" Jerry wondered.

"Why would the savior of the day admit responsibility for what he is saving us from?"

Marks smiled placidly and explained in a calm voice that he

had personally used psychic profiling to identify the terrorists, and they were being rounded up while he addressed the cities. They were rogue elements, he said, including the freed Colonel Garrison, whom Marks named, living outside the cities and trying to destroy society and the New Era.

"So he admitted responsibility," Jerry said, "but only we know it. I thought he would have named you, Immerman." Or me, he thought.

"He wants to deal with us himself. But he admitted nothing. He issued no more than a broad swath of accusations which could be made to fit anyone the World Organic Council deems a threat to society. We may become the targets, or somebody else who the Council finds inconvenient."

Jerry looked at the clock strip for NYC on the wall. It glowed a few minutes before midnight.

Cameras revealed people throughout the city were still refusing to reenter the stoners. But now the police, hounds, and every other governmental authority was starting to play hardball as the chronological barrier approached. The hounds were even wielding opalescent sliders to back up their threats.

Mostly, though, loudspeakers were calling out exhortations to patriotism side by side with stoking fears about people losing their cherished lifestyles. Others rubbed salt in the wound caused by the idea of law-abiding citizens breaking their most fundamental law by becoming daybreakers if they stayed out of their stoners. The NYC envoy for the World Organic Council himself addressed a nervous crowd gathered in the plaza outside the Council's Morningside Heights office complex, between the statues of Louis-Sebastien Mercier and Pyotr Alexeyevich Kropotkin. The statues were unlit and the animated paintings normally playing across the crystalline plaza floor were dark below everyone's shuffling feet.

Just as it looked like NYC might still break into open rebellion, electricity across the city was restored. The would-be rebels were soothed as fast as if they had been chloroformed. Jerry wondered if the timing of the power restoration was intentional.

One by one most of the dome and cube residents were

calming down like soothed sheep who are finally convinced the wolf has been satiated, and stalked away. Jerry didn't know about Dallas as the beams from there had completely stopped. He assumed that meant more force to stop the Battle of Dallas had been deemed necessary.

Some force was still necessary in NYC. Once midnight passed, police and other temporal agents—anyone with permission to cross days—rounded up the remaining daybreakers and coaxed or forced them into stoners. The daybreakers who gave the most trouble were herded into the emergency stoners found everywhere throughout the city.

And here I sit, Jerry thought, *watching everything and doing nothing.*

From what he was seeing on the monitors there was no pattern emerging, except that everywhere across the cities people had been soothed one way or another back into complacency by assurances of control being restored, and when they awoke the next subday—and they would awake—everything would be as it was before. Immerman was broadcasting more refined versions of the assurances for Friday's population outside the affected area, words of hollow comfort.

Jerry picked up his Scout and thumbed through the displays idly. Marks had successfully launched his attack but the results were not necessarily unfolding with the chaos he would have desired, so he might have a hundred other things to worry about besides Immerman and Jerry. This seemed to be bolstered by Marks not pinning the horror on the Family.

But Jerry was not done planning revenge. Marks was obsessed, unhappy with the current state of the world, but above all he put himself as the highest priority with no immediate second. And one thing could draw him out of the most secure hiding place and deepest machinations: a successful immortality elixir.

Jerry chose a time when Immerman was deeply involved with his frenetic continent-wide damage control. Even Immerman's cat had given up on its master and wandered off. It was possible, of course, Immerman knew exactly what Jerry was up to and was curious to see if his guest could get into the system. Or perhaps he was, like he had done in the camp, testing Jerry's initiative. But Jerry meant to act regardless.

He perused the computers until he found an access terminal to the internal databanks. Once Immerman's zeppelin had escaped the storm and Jerry felt reasonably certain of his continued survival, he and Coyote had worked out a way Coyote could trace back a path through Immerman's computer security while those computers were downloading all of the Project Dantian files.

The computer escorted Coyote deep enough into the network to find Project Dantian. It was running Marks' files in a checkpoint comparison to Immerman's research, called Senephage. Coyote mirrored the terminal screen so Jerry could turn the screen off and browse with less chance of Immerman figuring out what he was up to.

He wasn't sure what good he could do. Immerman was the biologist, not Jerry, and he had been working on the elixir for decades. But then, Immerman had been thrust into circumstances too quickly to reflect on what they had absconded with.

What Jerry was seeing now of the stolen material was so much scientific gobbledygook. "Do you understand any of that?" Jerry asked Coyote.

All items are referenced in my memory, Coyote told him. *Some are stranger than others. It's quite the mish-mash, pieces of thirty-six different jigsaw puzzles thrown into the same box.*

"Thirty-six? That's an awfully specific metaphor." Jerry was darkly amused over Coyote learning metaphors.

It isn't arbitrary. Each item is tagged with a single letter or number. Though the items don't show any relationship to each other just because they have the same marker except for being under a broad category like "biology" or "cybernetics."

"So he also rearranged and randomized everything in case someone managed any unauthorized decryption. All the pieces are here, but thrown together willy-nilly. Analyze everything," Jerry said. "In the meantime, show me visual representations of what is running."

There are three billion items to analyze.

Jerry choked.

Coyote was already carrying out the order in visual form so rapidly the screen showed Jerry's human eyes nothing more than a nebulous orb resembling an atomic cloud. But even at the Scout's speed, with no notion of the range of analysis—whether they were looking for a combination of just ten items or a billion—there were so many potential combinations, the Earth might burn to a cinder from the engorged red Sun before Coyote hit the correct one.

There must be an encryption within the encryption. There had to be—too many items were the same thing, as far as Jerry could tell, or almost exactly with only slight variations. Marks wouldn't flood his files with so many random items unless he had a simple key to unlock the right ones in the proper order. And thirty-six markers was an infinitesimal number for three billion items.

Three billion. Why did that number nag at his mind?

Then he remembered: three billion was the quantity of DNA strands in a human being. Maybe a clue in itself.

"Coyote," Jerry said, "analyze only the items marked with the letters A, C, G, and T." Those were the "letters" assigned to the genetic code.

Of course, assuming all markers filed away an equal number of items, cutting the potential combinations from thirty-six markers to four still left over three hundred million items to analyze. Still the work of years.

More encryption, then. A puzzle within a dilemma within an enigma.

Jerry fretted his brain over the next layer of Marks' secrecy for a while, then decided in frustrated exhaustion to try something else and let the back of his brain work on it. "Coyote, show me a sampling in visual representation of the most repeated items among what we already know has already been accomplished with Project Dantian."

Pictures he could figure out, and they might help him notice something missing or amiss. Coyote knew Jerry well enough to make the pictures childishly simple, like a scalpel slicing into a double helix to indicate genetic editing tools.

Marks' research, Jerry decided, was either brilliant or horrifying. The Gallows had created a genetically enhanced synthetic bacteria acting as a repair system, multiplying rapidly in short bursts when needed, then all but one or a handful dying with the survivors hibernating in hiding the rest of the time. The problem Marks ran into was the same one Immerman did with his similar research: it didn't always work, and sometimes did great harm, even when theoretical models projected it should be successful. But instead, any subject, animal or human, taking the elixir had a fifty-fifty shot of creating what felt like severe flu. A few times the bacteria would multiply out of control until it supplanted the normal bacteria and cells, killing the host.

Meanwhile, Coyote had determined somehow that the successful Project Dantian had a better than 90% chance of containing one hundred and ten thousand elements, if one included pieces of wholes like genetic strands. The Scout began recording elements it had higher than 50% confidence were part of Marks' successful elixir.

Jerry rubbed his eyes, having trouble thinking. He needed sleep but wouldn't let himself. "Wait, why are you breaking down elements into individual items from a whole? And what does that even mean?"

I did not do this, Coyote replied. *Marks enacted his own filing system this way. It means if, for instance, you count a genetic strand as "one," you count it as the number of letters in the strand's code. Because . . . well, I don't know why he did.*

Suddenly Jerry knew. "Because that fits his next encryption layer!" he said. "His third encoding was based on his own DNA." Which Coyote had thanks to Jerry's trick of getting Marks to hold the Scout. "Correlate the markers with Marks' own unique genetic strands. Make the letters match up in order."

The fuzzy orb instantly disappeared from Coyote's display and was replaced by hundreds and then thousands of visual icons weaving together one by one not unlike a growing double helix. It only took Coyote a few minutes to connect all of the elements of the immortality elixir in their proper order.

Or nearly so. There were fuzzy gaps in places, pieces that didn't seem right or didn't fit correctly. The top-heavy load of information about viruses, for instance, made no sense.

"More encoding to figure out," Jerry groaned.

I don't think so, Coyote told him. *I think this was Marks' failsafe. A few pieces of his genetic record are missing. Marks knew you used me to copy his DNA record as part of your trap, and it seems likely others may have tried the same thing before, so it is probable he masked a few parts of his genetic code in order to fool bioscans. The decryption connected enough elements so a human mind, particularly one that had been laboring over this elixir for decades, could fill in the missing pieces from memory.*

"Then we've gone as far as we can go with what we stole," Jerry realized. "From here on out we have to figure it out ourselves."

Coyote gave a warning buzz. *There's more. I found something unsettling in the LifeLogs. We need to talk.*

The words blurred. Not from any defect in the Scout but Jerry's all-too-mortal eyes. He rubbed those exhausted eyes for the hundredth time and wondered how long it had been since he had slept. Over forty-eight hours. Probably longer. His brain was swimming too much to count. He envied Immerman the stim-chair.

So at first he wasn't sure he saw what he thought he saw when he heard the door swish and he looked up. But there could be no doubt when they stepped into the war room's light, both figures staring straight at Jerry.

Ele'ele Venn and Piet Vanwoerden had found him.

Twenty-Eight

Jerry jumped out of his chair and readied himself to face down Vanwoerden and Venn. He knew he could beat either of them in single combat if he had to, having done it once already, but he was less sure about how to deal with them as a pair, even with Immerman present. And how did they manage to sneak into such a secure facility?

Immerman calmly commanded the stim-chair filaments to withdraw from his skin. Then he stood and made a single nod conveying more respect than most bows. "Excellent, you made it back. Did you have any trouble getting away from the camp?"

Vanwoerden guffawed. "Hardly any at all. It seemed to us you had already done the heaviest work for us." His accent was no longer South African Boer. It struck Jerry as more Russian.

Venn withdrew a nameless ID card flowing with colors around her picture as if the card was made out of a liquid rainbow. "Do you need to put this to use with your work here?"

"Only if absolutely necessary,' Immerman told her. "I may have a greater need for you to use it later."

Then Venn stared at Jerry. She moved toward him lithely with a faint smile, and took his arm in the same way Immerman did. This seemed to be the limit of Reductionist displays of affection. "It is good to see you again, Carson. I am glad to see you escaped Marks' grip."

Jerry pulled his arm away. "Not all of us did."

Her accent wasn't quite the American-Polynesian mix from before, rather more of a German-Frisian. But at the moment he didn't care. The stirred-up memory of his survival when Linda died, combined with the realization Immerman had lied to him, stoked a furnace of anger inside him and shoved back his weariness.

"You told me there was only one spy in the camp, Immerman," Jerry snapped.

"You inferred there was only one. I told you there was a spy in the camp, who would be your judge and handler. There was no need for you to know at the time that we had two others in place as well, particularly in case Marks tried to slice open your brain to pull out anything you knew. Marks knew one of you was a hound, and obsessed over his incomplete knowledge, so Graham's presence meant the spies had the perfect cover. Particularly since Graham would have just as soon considered us all threats to the World Organic Council and killed Family alongside Galapagos."

The answer made sense, but Jerry was not mollified. "Are they Family? How do you know you can trust them? They did an awfully convincing job of being Gallows back in the camp."

Venn's laugh was delicate to the point of ethereal. "So did you, Carson, up until the moment you assaulted Dr. Marks and stole Project Dantian. In fact you performed your part so skillfully we had our doubts for a time about your loyalty to the Family. But Immerman continued to order us not to make any moves on you without his say so."

"And you met them before Camp Natufian," Immerman continued. "Only under different names and faces. Vanwoerden you knew as Leonid Mitrokhin. And Venn was Sandra Phoenix Von Hentzau."

"The ones I freed from the stoner cavern?" Jerry said. "So they've only been Family for as long—or as short—a time as I have!"

Immerman replied, "They were Family before I was even born. Mitrokhin is my uncle. And Dr. Von Hentzau is my grandmother."

"Then how . . . ?"

"As to their youthful appearance, it is more than appearance, but a result of early experiments with our immortality elixir, the Senephage. The restoration of DNA was one of our first goals, turning back the clock, though it had more failures in human trials than the version that only slows aging rather than reversing it. Mitrokhin and Von Hentzau were successes, though of course this only drew more attention to them when they turned against the coming New Era."

"And how do they look completely different?" Jerry asked.

"They don't. Remember, you didn't see them for very long, and most of what you saw of them was in dim light in the tunnels and then Burroughs B-205. You'll notice their builds are the same if you think back, the facial structure nearly so, and their skeletal structure would be exact if you had X-ray vision. Their faces were altered somewhat with surgery to look like their new pre-chosen identities, while changing hair and eye color were basic cosmetics. Along with skin tone, too, though Von Hentzau—fair redhead to swarthy Polynesian—required somewhat more work with her melatonin. Then they were identity-fused with their alternate identities."

"What does identity-fused mean?" It sounded unpleasantly permanent.

"A DNA infusion to the point of being nearly a transfer. Much of their old DNA was swapped, surgically rewritten, for DNA resembling their new identities—those who were real people but were no longer around, having either died, disappeared, or something otherwise taking them out of the societal picture. This was one of our early Senephage experiments—instead of repairing DNA, replace it entirely. Overall it failed, enough so and long ago enough that Galapagos probably would no longer consider it when checking out their new recruits. But I already knew it had worked for my uncle and grandmother, who are now Piet Vanwoerden and Ele'ele Venn as far as the rest of the world—and Galapagos—is concerned."

Jerry examined his two former tent-mates closely. Immerman was correct about Jerry only having the most glancing acquaintances with Mitrokhin and Von Hentzau. But he did have a sharp memory. As he overlapped those memories with the man and woman standing before him, he could see the ghosts of their old identities floating over their faces.

"In case you have forgotten," Vanwoerden-Mitrokin said, "you saved my life. Even should I be working secretly with Marks, I will not betray someone who holds my life in his debt."

"And we told you the truth about being early stoner protesters," Venn-Von Hentzau said.

"I remember your names from history," Jerry allowed. "Though I don't remember much of what you did."

"Likely because it has been excised from your history books," Mitrokhin answered. "As the Museum proves, no one can completely eliminate history from memory, for traces always linger, but they are the largest traces. The details can be made to be forgotten given enough time, or filled in with untruths and fairy tales. I know this, because for a time I was the Chief Director of the Russian National Library in Moscow. My great-grandparents dealt with the Communists; I dealt with those who brought on the New Era."

Jerry turned to Venn, who struck him once more, as she had their first night on the camp's mountaintop, with how elegant her form was, though he knew firsthand the strength hidden just beneath the surface. "And you? What did Sandra Phoenix Von Hentzau do in the world before the stoners?"

She looked pained. "I helped create the stoners."

At Jerry's own surprised look, she went on, "We, the scientists, never meant them to be used as they have been. But of course, when did scientists ever have any say in how their creations were exploited? I originally envisioned them as a way of allowing people extra time after a critical accident, or if they had a terminal disease—perhaps even being stoned until a cure for the disease could be found. It could maintain precious objects with near-perfect invulnerability. The National Archives in Washington D.C., ironically, used its first stoner field to preserve the Constitution. Perhaps somewhere deep below ground it still does."

"But it didn't take long for the world governments to come

up with the use the stoners mainly have now," Jerry remembered from *Early Objections to the Stoner.*

"The blink of an eye," Venn agreed. "Perhaps they already had the idea while the work was still experimental. They certainly decided from the first published research to stone prisoners and other undesirables. I tried protesting in the only way I could, which was to stop all my work and even abandon scientific research altogether. I had not started in science—my original dream was to be an artist. But I had a natural talent for electromagnetic theory, and in those days being both scientist and artist simultaneously was frowned upon. I left New York City and became a painter in the New Mexico desert and tried withdrawing from the world."

Her face twisted into an agony of grief. "But the world found me again."

The four-century-old weariness in her expression bled into Jerry's exhaustion and overwhelmed him. He could no longer fight sleep, but he didn't stop trying. He retrieved the icons of double helixes and chemistry tubes on Coyote's display, but everything swam together in a blurry mess which likely would have exploded if they were the real substances they portrayed.

"Project Dantian?" Venn . . . Von Hentzau . . . asked. "Have you worked out how Marks succeeded?"

Jerry shook his head, making the room swim around him. "There's still a missing piece."

She smiled faintly. "I discovered one truth as both a scientist and an artist, Carson. Nothing is missing—we just haven't found it yet."

"That doesn't make any sense," Jerry said through a cotton mouth. Maybe it sounded like nonsense because he was so tired, but he didn't think so.

"Everything you need is already out there, if you can find the right thing and put it in its right place. This was true with my research on the stoners, and this is true when I decide what brush and colors to use in my paintings. Everything has its companion. There is no lock without a key, and no canvas without paint."

Jerry was vaguely aware of Von Hentzau leading him to the

horizontal experimental stoners in the back of the room and easing him into one.

"Go to sleep, Jerry," she whispered. "You will think more clearly when you have rested. You will see what is right in front of you so much more clearly . . ."

Coyote bleeped a warning. Jerry had learned to pay attention to those bleeps, but he only got so far as seeing the Scout found something about Von Hentzau's LifeLog before the text blotted into unreadability.

The inside of the stoner Von Hentzau brought him to was lined with something soft and Jerry felt himself sinking into it even as the slightly more awake and logical part of his brain screamed a warning that she was reaching for the stoner lid. He used the last of his strength to reach for her, or to stop the lid from closing, but it was too late and his fingertips only bumped into the transparent metal window.

Her face appeared in the window looking down at him with what seemed to be sadness for a moment, then vanished. Then everything else went away too.

Jerry dreamed.

At first Jerry thought he was walking through the Museum. But the hallways were dim and mostly empty, and he was the only one in the entirety of the vast complex. What light there was flickered on and off in patches across the floor. Then he realized flickering was born from amorphous shapes floating above him in and out of the light emanating from a ceiling too high above to see.

Some of the shapes slipped out of sight when he tried to pin them down with a stare, but others resolved into the same chemical, genetic, and other biological shapes Coyote provided that had bedeviled Jerry since his first looks at Project Dantian and Senephage. Double helixes danced twirling waltzes locked hand in hand for a four billion year-old song but sidestepped out of reach when Jerry tried cutting in. There were strange creatures here too, beasts with five or six legs, long necks, and polygon-shaped heads lacking eyes. Jerry vaguely remembered seeing those somewhere before but couldn't imagine where, or what they even might be.

A Hole in Wednesday

He couldn't reach the DNA or the creatures, but the creatures drifted effortlessly onto the air-turned-ballroom floor where the double helixes went on about their reveries until the creatures had them surrounded. On the fringes several giant turtles with android human faces, which might have been the extended family of the Mock Turtle from *Alice in Wonderland,* stood up on their hind legs.

"Tortoise!" one of the Mock Turtles cried.

"Yes, because a turtle lives in the water, and a tortoise lives on land," Jerry remembered.

"Tortoise because he taught us," said the Mock Turtle angrily. "Really you are very dull!"

"Taught you what?" Jerry asked. "And who, Marks? Immerman?"

"Why don't you find out for yourself?"

Jerry went for his Scout, but it was busy interrogating the DNA.

Even half-aware he was dreaming, Jerry couldn't believe what he saw next any more than the Mock Turtles or Tortoises did: the polygon-headed creatures clasped to the dancing DNA, jabbed the helixes with tentacle-looking extensions protruding from their bellies, and whirled away with the DNA as a threesome . . . Or was it still a twosome, since the double helixes were considered one unit? Either way, the dancing continued unabated. If anything it sped up frenetically as if the DNA had been waiting for the creatures all along. Then the Mock Turtles stepped in too, turning the whole procession into gracefully tumbling triangles, and once all the creatures and androids arrived and joined their partners, the double helixes multiplied a thousand-fold.

Jerry jolted awake. He was lying on his back staring up through the stoner window showing only soft pulsing hexagons of sensored ceiling panels. He reached this time not to shove open the stoner door but to try grasping for the dancers again and the beautiful music swiftly fading away as if trapped in another stoner far out of reach.

Maybe, thought the part of Jerry's mind still nestled in the dream, I could hear the music again and see the dancers if I go back to the place where I saw them. The Museum . . .

The Museum. Then Jerry's mind, wide awake as was his body, remembered where else he had seen the multilegged creatures. And they fit the DNA as the perfect dancing partners in Project Dantian too. After determining the stoner was unlocked—of course it was, or else he would have suffocated—he ran a few genetic simulations on Coyote and howled with joy when all of the disparate puzzle pieces locked into place. More so, Coyote was running simulations showing the elixir could cure all of humanity's worst diseases and ailments.

This time he did shove open the stoner lid. "Eureka!" he shouted for fun and dramatic effect, and the others in the room—Immerman still tentacled to his chair flanked by Von Hentzau and Mitrokhin—jumped at the sudden clamor. "I know the missing piece of Project Dantian! We have the elixir formula!"

But instead of looking pleased, Von Hentzau looked what Jerry could only describe as being horrified. "Why are you awake?" Then more quietly as she came within a few paces of him, "Jerry, don't get out of the stoner . . ."

"The Scout network just went down," Jerry heard Immerman say. "Marks must have his hands on a kill switch."

There was a rising wail of frightened voices. Not from those in the room, Jerry realized, but the screens tuned into the Battle of Dallas, which Immerman had camera access to even when the rest of the planet did not. A heavily armed force of temporal agents had stopped the swarming mob and pushed it back with bullets and slider beams opening up on the crowd. Even amid the colorful thousands Jerry could pick out Colonel Garrison in his old-style camouflaged U.S. Army uniform, so he saw Garrison cut in half at the gut by a beam.

"We tried reason," Northpath Marks' voice overlaid the images, "and to persuade them of the terrible wrongness of their course of action. We pointed out to them that they were being exploited by those who would see the best elements . . . the best nature . . . of our society destroyed. But they would not listen, and now they are suffering the inevitable consequences of their misapplication of their negative energies."

A Hole in Wednesday

"Can you track his broadcast?" Jerry cried.

Immerman's hands flew across the buttons on his stim-chair. "The signal acts like it's coming from multiple places. The strongest are from Confucius Tower and the city's broadcast studios on the top floor of the Empire State Building. But there are at least two dozen other relays claiming to be the origination point."

Marks' voice continued, "We hope all of those who are protesting against us will reconsider so force will not be necessary, but we also understand and regretfully accept that there are those who are incorrigible, unable to be reached with psychicist help, and must be dealt with harshly through corporeal means. And to Citizen Jerry Carson, if you are able to hear me, you should know you helped me decide the location of the retribution. Never forget this."

It wasn't until Marks' last three words that Jerry realized there should have been no such narration, from Marks or anyone else, broadcasting out of Immerman's covert camera feeds.

"He's a lot closer than the Empire State Building," Jerry realized, too late.

The front of the room exploded.

Twenty-Nine

The flash dazzled Jerry's vision for a few seconds. But what he thought was an explosion had been soundless so his ears were fine, and he recognized crackling sounds as electrical surges while the equipment in the room was being fried.

When his vision cleared he could make out the unmoving forms of Immerman and Mitrokhin. He wanted to check to see if they were still alive but saw at once the flash hadn't been from an explosion, but the surges' massive arcs that were jumping from shelf to shelf destroying the precious computers, monitors, and every other piece of equipment as if their very nature attracted the bolts.

A second later he realized the arcs were heading toward him and Von Hentzau and were about to sweep over them.

"Get in!" Jerry yelled at Von Hentzau as he grabbed her and pulled both of them into the stoner he'd just come out of, with barely enough room left to yank the lid shut behind them.

The electrical bolts rushed over the stoners. Experimental though they were, Jerry knew from the first sight of them that most, including the one Von Hentzau eased him into, were sheathed in a standard nanotube covering almost as impervious to damage as the stoner field itself—including from electricity. The room and stoner went dark except for the white flashes Jerry could see through the small round window in the chamber door.

After a moment the bolts stopped, leaving behind smoke, an acrid burning smell, and dim flickering lights from the wounded ceiling panels. Plus two shadowy shapes still unmoving at the front of the ruined war room.

Jerry shoved open the stoner lid. Smoke curled around him. Reflexively he swished it away with his arm but it was everywhere. There were no fire alarms or suppression mechanisms going off, so those must have been damaged as well.

"I'll check on Immerman and Mitrokhin," Jerry told Von Hentzau as they climbed out. "See if you can get the door open."

Immerman was unconscious but alive. Jerry realized the stim-chair had saved him. The chair itself was completely insulated and the filaments were designed to allow only a certain mild amount of electricity to flow through them, blocking any potential surges. There was a single round burn at his hip, which had also blasted right through the Scout that had attracted the arc. But Coyote's bio-readings of Immerman looked strong and hopeful.

Mitrokhin was badly burned, having been hunched over computer consoles just seconds before the sabotage occurred—and Jerry was growing increasingly convinced it was sabotage, if for no other reason than the highly protected room's hundreds of pieces of equipment were a total loss, beyond any accident that could reasonably have occurred. The Russian needed medical care soon. But how could they help him? It seemed likely the saboteurs were close by.

Mitrokhin grabbed Jerry's arm. The Russian struggled to rise out of the smoke. He wielded a slider in one hand and an old fashioned silver Colt revolver in the other, no doubt with all six bullets in place. For an instant he pointed both at Jerry.

Then smoke cleared from his eyes, literally and metaphorically, and he lowered them. "You have come to the same conclusion I have, yes?" he croaked. "This was no accident, no?"

"No, no accident." He joined Von Hentzau pulling open the door. The ceiling tiles were pulsing red in a repetitive sequence of three slow bursts, then three long ones. Jerry wasn't sure what the sequence meant exactly, but it was clearly an alarm. He also didn't want to bet on anything but it meaning that Immerman's lair was already infiltrated.

A Hole in Wednesday

"Marks," Immerman said groggily. He tried to sit up in the stim-chair but didn't quite succeed. "He gambled this would destroy our copies of Project Dantian. He doesn't realize we still have it on the Scouts . . ." He trailed away, staring hard at Jerry.

"I still have it," Jerry said. "Including a copy of the simulation revealing how the immortality elixir works."

"Then take it and go, Carson."

The two surviving Scouts, Jerry's and Von Hentzau's, buzzed warnings.

The voice coming from each tablet was from Marks, who was transmitting directly to their Scouts despite the Scout network being down. Jerry noticed Marks was blatantly, probably braggingly, using an emergency government breakthrough channel to get the message through.

"To the traitors, I hope all of you remain alive," the doctor said. "I desire to deal with you myself. By now I imagine your control center has been wholly eliminated, since I am no longer tracking Immerman's interference across the media spectra. But I can see from what is freely transmitting again that my initial effort has failed. The lion's share of this population of sheep has gone back into the stoners either willingly or by allowing themselves to be forced back."

Jerry glimpsed a set of bioreadings on his Scout indicating several dozen people raiding the north side of the subterranean complex, and warned the group.

"Go out the door by the stoners," Immerman told him. "It'll put you farthest away from the government agents, and take you to a tunnel leading you the farthest from 30th Street, to lessen the chances of them watching any tunnel exits they may have discovered."

Jerry started helping Mitrokhin unhook Immerman's stim-chair filaments, but Immerman pushed him away. Even weakened and burned, he still had a great deal more strength than Jerry expected. "Your Scout is the most important thing now. More important than any of us."

"Go where?"

"The World Organic Council Headquarters in Morningside Heights. From there you can plug your Scout directly into the Scout network and send the evidence of Marks' treachery to anyone."

Where Coyote had bleeped an alarm before, now it blared a klaxon.

At first Jerry assumed this meant the AI was becoming more agitated, but when the warning persisted, Jerry looked at the display. Coyote had found something nasty in Marks' files: a double-bomb. The first stage would release a swarm of flingers sufficient to wipe out all the electronics in every NYC dome. Once those were away, the second stage, a nuclear portion, would explode with enough of a blast to entirely destroy whatever dome it was cached in.

Jerry told his companions about the Scout's discovery. "But where would the bomb be?"

"Most likely in the Upper West Side," Mitrokhin guessed. "Destroy the World Organic Council HQ there. Certainly not here in Lower Manhattan, based on Marks' last message."

"Then we go to the Upper West Side," Von Hentzau said.

Jerry felt himself tugged both ways, between rushing to the rescue and wanting to stay—Linda and his unborn child were still here, he remembered. But the agents were closer to her now than Jerry was.

It's not there, Jerry thought, remembering Marks' last message. "He said I helped decide the location. I wouldn't have any reason to pick there, not personally."

"Then where?" Venn asked.

Jerry's mind raced. Mitrokhin was likely right that it wouldn't be anywhere in Lower Manhattan. Or anywhere in Manhattan at all, since any such explosion would bring all of the borough's dome down on their heads.

Then his mind snapped out an idea. "The Museum. The one in Brooklyn. The one I enjoyed going to so often, and where Marks' people caught me."

"Then go there first, Carson!" Immerman said. "Above all, keep your Scout away from Marks! He'll be here in moments."

A Hole in Wednesday

"How do you know he's here himself?"

"Of course he is. His ego wouldn't allow him to let others capture me. When he said he wanted to deal with us himself he meant it literally. And most of all, remember one thing we taught you at Camp Natufian: always use your environment as a weapon."

When Jerry placed his Scout against his head Immerman shouted, "What are you doing? Why aren't you leaving?"

The pattern of Marks' attack was falling into place for Jerry, and he spoke as surely as he had about anything in his life. "I'm scanning my chip so I can reactivate it. Marks will know the sabotage destroyed your copies of his research here in B-612 but he won't be as certain about backup copies independent of this room. He may also suspect I've got evidence of him being behind the stoner virus—and he'd be right. I'm going to let him know I have the research on Coyote—I'll transmit it all back to him, including the segments I altered to show I figured it out—along with my recordings tracing the path of the stoner virus back to Marks, which I also plan to transmit to agents of the World Organic Council."

"You can't transmit anything from the Scout, not till you get to the World Organic Council," Immerman said. "The whole network is down."

"Then once I'm well away from here I'll reactivate the Gallows chip in my head so he can track me."

"You would use yourself as bait?" Mitrokhin asked. Just the effort of speaking must have cost him greatly, though he hid his effort under his wrestler's bulk well. "Protecting you until we are out of this morass will repay my life debt."

"No, Mitrokhin. You and Immerman get out of here if you can. We need to scatter. I know how Von Hentzau thinks and fights—she'll be enough of a partner until we can get to the Museum." Provided he could figure out a way to get all the way from Lower Manhattan to Brooklyn without being caught by Marks. Or any other agents, for that matter.

Immerman's smile was wolfish, full of teeth. "I've stowed weapons and ammunition beneath my chair, in a case acting as a Faraday cage to protect them from the chair's electrical charges.

There will also be Scout pouches too. Take whatever you can carry that won't slow you down. Then get out of here, and find someplace to hide in the spaces between the teeth. Someplace so dangerous... for anyone else... they won't want to look for you there."

Jerry grabbed three weapons each for him and Von Hentzau, two pistols and a slider. But then he froze. Now that it came time for action he was unable to force the image of Linda in her stoner out of his mind, or Coyote's tiny spectral dot indicating the child in her womb, or the bitter clawing in his gut rebuking him for abandoning her yet again.

Finally Von Hentzau grabbed his hand and yanked him toward the rear door and nearly off his feet. That snapped him out of his dark reverie and set him to flight.

In just a moment they were out of the luxuriously furnished and painted areas of Alphabet City and running through the featureless white corridors he was becoming so familiar with. Von Hentzau said a code word that shut off all the lights behind them, as well as lights they passed under once they were through those lights' section of corridor.

"I've disabled the lights," she told him. "They won't turn on again without the right reactivation code word. Marks may be able to track us through these passages with scanners, but we don't have to make it easy for him to follow us."

The corridors were wide, the floor free of obstacles. Yet their escape felt harder than any forest run with a full fifty-pound pack at Camp Natufian. But then he was only running for his life in an abstract way. Now it was literal, and every step took him deeper into the rabbit hole. While he might eventually get out of the tunnels if they could stay far enough ahead of Marks, he doubted he would find his way out of Galapagos and the Family ever again.

He had naturally expected the corridors and then the utility tunnels they found themselves in to go up, streetward. They continued down instead.

"Where are we going?" Jerry asked, recoiling at the echo of his voice bouncing into the darkness.

A Hole in Wednesday

Von Hentzau's gaze darted back and forth as they passed through tunnel after tunnel. "No matter how good your Scout is at masking your bioreadings, Carson, once we approach West 14th Street and Galapagos' headquarters, their bioscanners are powerful and sensitive enough to detect us within a mile. Both of our DNA profiles are in their databases and no doubt they're set to an ongoing passive scan looking for us so we don't get too close to their home base."

"They won't detect us underground?"

"They probably will. But these tunnels are laid so thickly and in such a convoluted fashion that even if they detect us on the outermost fringes of their scans, it would take them so long to get down here we should have time to get away."

It was an excellent theory, Jerry thought, right up until the moment Galapagos agents who were already stationed in the tunnels opened fire.

Jerry and Von Hentzau's Galapagos-trained reflexes flung them into covering alcoves on either side of the tunnel. Just ahead and above the Gallows' positions, WEST 14 STREET was painted onto the colorless cement wall much like the one he saw while rescuing Von Hentzau and the others. So he had already run at least sixteen blocks underground, though there were still miles yet to go before they reached the Museum.

He was hardly winded, though, and secretly blessed Von Hentzau for making him sleep. Otherwise he would've likely been too slow and then a corpse, either from the agents infiltrating Alphabet City or the ones, four according to Coyote, who'd just taken shots at him.

Those agents were still taking shots. They were using guns, though, not sliders, which was a blessing in itself. Sliders could cut straight through the cement walls they took cover behind. They could still have quantum weapons held in reserve. But using them might also bring down the tunnel ceiling on all of them, so the agents would likely be judicious with them. So he had to find a way to take the agents out before they got desperate enough to use sliders.

After firing off a couple of shots of his own he whipped Coyote out of its sheath and scanned their attackers to see if their skulls were chipped. They were. But when Jerry tried to send a feedback wail into them like he had to the camp agents, he was blocked.

Von Hentzau saw what he was up to. "They'll have expected you to try that trick again," she told him between shots at them. "You can't do it a second time. We need to find another way through."

Jerry quickly surveyed the tunnel. There was little to nothing useful. Old worn walls, alcoves like the one they had ducked into, and various cables to carry electricity to the city. Nothing more than a basic utility corridor seeming devoid of humans treading through the passage for subyears.

Then Jerry remembered Von Hentzau's comment about the complex layering of the tunnels, and set Coyote to scanning all of the subterranean layers within a few hundred yards of them, including up and down. Coyote took the initiative and showed Jerry first the layout of the stretches of tunnels ahead of them, beyond the attackers, and then what it thought was the most interesting layer of them all: one right below them.

It also showed twelve more bio-blips closing in on them from behind. Coyote estimated both ends of the tunnels would be blocked by enemies in another six minutes.

Jerry put away his pistol and aimed the slider at a distant point straight down the hallway, intentionally well away from the attackers, and fired a beam on lower power. The attackers' yells were fearful and indignant all at once, but none of them responded with a retaliatory beam.

"What are you doing?" Von Hentzau cried out just under the echo threshold.

Jerry transmitted a detailed picture of Coyote's scan to her Scout, resulting in a look accusing him of insanity. It occurred to him that he was about to make them endure one of the very few things they had not trained for at the camp, since all the surface water in Camp Natufian had been in small, shallow streams. But he could see no alternative they could carry out in time.

A Hole in Wednesday

Von Hentzau started to protest, but a few bullet ricochets made her shrug instead. "If we miss the exit, or you didn't beam a big enough hole at the end of this tunnel, we're dead," she told him.

"We're dead if we stay put, so brace yourself and hold your breath." He secured the precious Scout in the pouch belted at his waist as best he could.

Coyote's scan proved the tunnel was probably older than the Dayworld itself, and not well maintained in the last four centuries, and firing a slider beam at the walls and ceiling would likely bring a respectable portion of the ceiling down on all their heads. But it also indicated the floor was equally vulnerable. Jerry fired at it directly behind them, away from the attackers, at a rough angle calculated by Coyote. In two seconds the slider had not only broken through the floor but also ruptured the conduit beneath, and water and broken cement gushed out of the floor.

Before New York City was a metropolis of domes, Manhattan was veined with rivers both above and below ground. Modern civilization fought a constant struggle with nature to barricade those rivers from the city streets, using tunnels, conduits, and pumps to prevent the rivers from reclaiming their ancient dominance over the island. One such conduit ran through a tunnel directly under Jerry and Von Hentzau, and now its branch of the Manhattan rivers was a geyser through the breach. In seconds the water was already up to Jerry's knees, with the rate it was filling the tunnel increasing as the water pressure widened the hole.

Angry shouts of surprise from their attackers turned into alarm. Yet they held their places.

By the time the water reached Jerry's waist he realized again, as he had in his fight with Beta Graham, that while he was capable of killing in defense, he had no wish to do so if it could be avoided. "Get out now while you can!" he shouted at the attackers. "The flood won't stop until the tunnel is full!"

He gave them a few seconds to answer. When they didn't, he fired a mild slider beam at the wall near one of their positions. The wall broke apart and brought down a few chunks of ceiling with it, including on the head of one attacker who squawked in startled pain. They took the hint and launched into the rushing water.

"You may regret that," Von Hentzau said as she lifted her chin above the waterline.

"Shooting the wall, or letting them go, or both?"

Then Jerry looked up, alerted by the sound of the ceiling cracking from the wall Jerry's beam had just hit. Chunks of cement fell into the new river as the cracks reached both toward them and upriver.

"Dive," Jerry told her, and they did.

Jerry had seen the shapes of their attackers flee into the torrent and assumed they had all tried to escape. As the water swept him ahead of Von Hentzau, one of them sprung from the spot where he'd taken cover and now waited in ambush, as well as he could kick off from the crumbling wall into the water, and wrapped himself around Jerry's head to force him under.

Everything went dark and silent. His head pounded from the pressure as his lungs tightened, but this attacker was trained well, and had his arms wrapped tight around Jerry's neck, cutting off any air Jerry might have been able to snatch even if he could get above the surface.

Jerry's vision constricted and he could feel his existence constricting at the same time, being cut short in great swaths with every breath he was unable to take. He knew he was only a few seconds from blacking out entirely and he reached for the pouch Coyote was in, thinking with his last thoughts that somehow he might get it to Von Hentzau so she could save the data and bring down Marks without Jerry's help. The attacker realized what Jerry was up to and reached for the pouch himself.

But in doing so he released one arm from Jerry's neck and all the pressure with it, and Jerry used the sudden respite to twist his weight around at the same time he bunched up his body and rammed one foot into the attacker's head. Jerry went up above the surface and the attacker went under. But the attacker's hands were still close enough to grab Jerry's neck and throttle.

A Hole in Wednesday

He only stopped when Von Hentzau slammed a chunk of former ceiling into the side of his head. Blood pooled in front of Jerry despite the rushing water, and the attacker sailed away.

"Are you all right?" Von Hentzau said as she clung to his arm in an attempt to keep them together. "The Scout, is it safe?"

"Yes and yes," Jerry called back. He hoped the Scout was safe, at any rate.

Enough of the ceiling had collapsed, and was still collapsing immediately behind them, to take out most of the tunnel's lights. But some remained, and Jerry could see the hole that his first beam had made and a dim light from the ladder shaft just beyond that would take them back up to the street.

Then he cried, "Look out!"

The ceiling collapse had reached them and Jerry saw a ten-foot length giving way right overhead. Jerry shoved Von Hentzau out of the way and the slab came down between them. She was beyond it but now it had wedged itself in the tunnel and Jerry found himself underwater again as the torrent pooled behind the slab.

There was no time to think. No time to find another way out. He pulled out his slider, hoping it was still set to a moderate beam, hoping Von Hentzau was not immediately in the beam's path, and fired point blank into the top of the slab.

It disintegrated instantly and sucked Jerry and a new rush of water through it. The ceiling collapse was ahead of him now, reaching the hole in the wall before he did. There was no sign of Von Hentzau. He hoped she was already on the ladder, not disintegrated or swept past the ladder, which would mean a protracted drowning instead of quick quantum obliteration.

He lengthened himself out in preparation to flush through the hole and reached one arm upward to grab the bottom rung of the ladder, when a chunk of ceiling struck him in the head.

The blow stunned him enough that he couldn't grip the ladder, but not so much that he couldn't see it and his only hope of getting out of the tunnel slide past him.

The Scout pouch yanked away from his side, and with another

tug Jerry was yanked along with it. Toward the ladder, where Von Hentzau hung from a lower rung, one hand on the ladder and the other gripping his pouch strap.

He saw hesitation in her eyes. Hesitation, Jerry realized, about whether or not to take the Scout and go, leaving him to die deep under Manhattan's streets, or to save him too.

He thought for an instant that he must be imagining things. The cement that clocked him must have done more damage than he realized. But no, the hesitation was there. Yet another pattern filled in for him, and Jerry felt his naiveté about Von Hentzau sweep away as if carried off by the subterranean flood.

At the same time, Von Hentzau hooked one leg around the ladder so she could grab Jerry with her other hand, and she pulled him up from the frothing water.

"Can you climb?" she asked him.

He nodded. Nodding made him dizzy, but he summoned a well of strength he knew would be enough to manage the four storey ascent.

He made sure to let Von Hentzau climb ahead of him so he could keep an eye on her.

After what seemed like hours, but must have been no more than a few minutes, she pulled a lever on a square metal plate just above her head. Pushing the plate aside let a shaft of dim but welcome blue-shaded black evening light penetrate the shaft.

Then they were out, and rushing away from the street and out of sight toward the doubtful but marginal cover of an open-ended alley between nearby buildings.

The city was almost completely quiet except for speakers and vidscreens trying to relax the handful of people on the streets by playing soothing tracks. The latter made it seem like the streets were filled with invisible people and vehicles. Jerry found himself missing the city clamor once more.

He pulled Coyote from the pouch—the Scout was perfectly dry and responded with what would have been a happy chirp from a human—as he had it run a diagnostic while also scanning for any bioreadings obviously heading in their direction.

A Hole in Wednesday

"Is the Scout all right?" Von Hentzau asked.

Jerry sealed it back in the pouch without answering.

"You really did figure Project Dantian out, didn't you?" she continued. "You were going to tell us how, or what you learned, before Marks found us."

When he still didn't answer she reached for the Scout pouch. Jerry slapped her arm away, then grabbed her collar and slammed her against the alley wall.

"Why would I reveal such an important secret to a hound?" he demanded.

Thirty

"I'm not a . . ."

Jerry responded to Von Hentzau's unfinished denial by grabbing her throat and squeezing, though not nearly as hard as he knew he could.

"Are you even really Immerman's grandmother?" Jerry said. He snapped the words out in hesitation over snapping her neck.

"Yes," she croaked. "Everything . . . everything he told you is true . . ."

"And everything you told me? Or did you lie by omission?"

He realized he was squeezing her throat too tightly for her to talk now, and released the pressure just slightly. A faint red returned to her ashen face.

"I'm not a hound . . . wait!" she cried when Jerry squeezed. "Sandra Von Hentzau is not a hound. Ele'ele Venn is."

"You are Ele'ele Venn," he reminder her, though intrigued by the distinction in spite of himself.

He felt her trying to shake her head. "The real Venn is in a stoner somewhere . . . stoned by Immerman. Maybe even in the cavern where you rescued us. The cavern below Alphabet City," she added.

That surprised Jerry enough to make his fist around her neck almost spring open. He hadn't realized the stoner cavern was beneath the city's most famous tower too.

If she was telling the truth. Knowing what he knew of the Dayworld now, the prison cavern's placement was appropriate. But Jerry was still far from convinced that anything she said at the moment was more than uttering anything which might save her.

But it rang true with one thing he had already guessed: the real Ele'ele Venn had been targeted long before Sandra Von Hentzau was destoned as a prospective match for Von Hentzau's physical structure. Particularly one who already must have had an inside track with the Gallows. There had, after all, been only a few days between Von Hentzau's rescue and her appearance at Camp Natufian. Even Immerman, for all his resources, would likely have found it impossible to retrieve Von Hentzau, peg Venn as a target, kidnap Venn, and do Von Hentzau's physical alterations and DNA infusions in less than a week. Everything must have already been prepared in advance, awaiting someone who could free Von Hentzau and the others.

The real Venn might even be in Von Hentzau's old prison stoner. Immerman would likely think it some sort of karmic justice alongside it being a pragmatic choice.

"And then Immerman secretly pulled strings to get Venn assigned to Camp Natufian," Von Hentzau continued.

"But you, Sandra Von Hentzau," Jerry said, "led Marks along with other government agents to Immerman's hideout. You did the hound's work even if you want to claim you aren't a hound from a certain point of view."

"I didn't know I was leading them. They were probably scanning for my DNA. For the mix of mine and Venn's. They must have figured out my ploy after Mitrokhin and I took off from Marks' camp. Something so distinctive could be read by their scanners through Immerman's shielding."

"That may be so," Jerry allowed. "But you were the one who planted the flingers responsible for destroying all of Immerman's equipment."

"How did you . . . ?"

"How did I figure out that the electromagnetic expert, as you admitted to being, would know the most lethal way to destroy electronic equipment? And could also build the twenty-first-century nanobombs that would fling themselves from computer to scanner to sensor, destroying everything as they went, but be programmed to only limit themselves to what was in the war room? Then get them into such a high security area? I know they didn't go outside B-612 because the alarms still worked, letting us know when Marks' men penetrated Alphabet City."

When Jerry reached the next part of his deduction, he felt his pressure on Von Hentzau's neck slide away slightly. "And you knew the surges were going to happen. That was the real reason you wanted me to sleep—and why you picked the stoner you did for me as a bed. With the lid closed, even unsealed, it would be resistant to the electrical surges. But you let Immerman and Mitrokhin face the surges!"

"I thought they would both be protected by Immerman's stim-chair. Mitrokhin went to a computer panel the instant before the flingers went off."

Jerry's heart hardened again. "You planted those flingers in Immerman's inner sanctum right before Marks sent us his last message."

"His message was about the bomb, Jerry, you know that," Von Hentzau insisted. "Marks calling right afterward must have been a coincidence."

"No, it wasn't," Jerry realized. "He said he was monitoring Immerman's media interference. He must have tracked the location of B-612, and then his scans registered the flingers powering up. So he decided to send his message then. But you knew he was coming," he repeated. "So you wanted me in the stoner."

"I knew he was hunting us, and I also knew you would be in no condition to escape if they found us," Von Hentzau replied. "I didn't think they would—but then I never assume anything will go according to plan. But I meant, how did you know I was a hound instead of simply one of Marks' plants? Those identity records are kept carefully guarded."

"While others are locked to the point where only World Organic Councilors have access to them—specifically your LifeLogs.

Ele'ele Venn's LifeLog required Councilor access. Which meant she is . . . or was . . . either a hound or a World Organic Councilor. I doubt she was a Councilor, if only because she then would have probably been impossible to replace."

Here was the alarming piece of information Coyote had discovered when it scanned the LifeLogs, which Jerry would have known hours earlier if he hadn't fallen asleep in the stoner as Coyote was attempting to warn him.

Jerry felt a warm prickling in his chest and realized she was pointing a slider's targeting laser directly at his heart. He released her neck and stepped back.

"I know I'm not as good a fighter as you," she said, "but this slider in my hand means I can punch a hole the size of my forearm in your chest before you can throttle me to death. So listen to me, Jerry, and since I now have tipped the odds, I have no reason to lie to you."

"Tell me the truth, and then kill me? Like you were thinking of letting me die when I was being swept through the tunnel?"

She looked genuinely pained. "Venn the hound was under orders to kill anyone working for Immerman if it gained her an advantage, though not Immerman himself. Immediately before I left for Camp Natufian this programming was implanted in my mind through narcohypnosis. My 'dual' mind, Venn and Von Hentzau, meant I could usually control it . . . but for an instant, in the right circumstance—the shaft—my programming almost kicked in. I could've taken the Scout and left you to drown."

"I doubt Coyote would've given you anything," Jerry said.

She gave him a confused look at the name, then continued, "The World Organic Council and their hounds want Immerman's— and Marks'—research. Then to kill anyone with knowledge of Project Dantian or Senephage once both of those were in the hounds' hands."

"Because they want it for themselves, and nobody else. Just like they have the rest of the planet outside the cities to themselves. But then why did you destroy all of Immerman's equipment?"

Instead of answering directly she said, "I did not know the

government would kill the Scout network. If I had I would have left the computers operational so we could have sent the World Organic Council evidence of Marks' treachery. But I also did not want to disable the proximity sensors. I wanted everyone to know Marks was coming to give you and Immerman and the rest a chance to escape."

Light dawned and illuminated more of the pattern. "But not the research on Dantian," he said. "You didn't want them to have it either."

"Don't you see, Carson? I don't want *anyone* to have the immortality elixir. Once I knew Marks and the hounds were coming I activated the flingers to destroy Immerman's research. Even if I had been able to bring myself to let you die under the streets, I would have smashed your Scout to qubits and let the pieces drown in the tunnels with you. It's my fault there are stoners in the world. I'm not going to be the agent who also unleashes eight billion immortals on a planet that's only just begun to heal itself from the damage their great-grandparents inflicted.

"And on a world," she added, "where those eight billion are constantly monitored by a few hundred. Everything they do recorded on camera, everything they write and say archived in their LifeLog. With any dissension or protest met by psychic rehabilitation at best, or murder, as Colonel Garrison discovered . . . or permanent imprisonment in a stoner. You saw the stoner cavern. Hundreds of thousands of people just from NYC alone who have been entombed, for obcenturies in some cases, and will likely never be reanimated—even if the government wants to bring them back, the sheer numbers make such a recovery impossible. This is one thing Marks, Immerman, and I all agree on. Whether we live outside the domes or not, we should be able to live freely."

He glanced at the slider still pointed at his chest and calculated his chances against subduing her before she could fire. Those chances weren't very good. He could beat her in a hand-to-hand fight, but she had done well enough in Marks' training camp to guarantee any attack he made would end with his disintegration.

But would an attack even be necessary? Almost certainly, if

she had any suspicion of his intention to go through with giving Coyote to the World Organic Council.

Unless he could somehow make her hesitate.

He decided to throw at her the one thing which had made him hesitate and ultimately decide on his course to follow through with Immerman's plan.

"Let me tell you how the immortality elixir works," he said.

"No."

"It's only right that you be the first to know, since you were the one who filled in the missing piece."

He could see her curiosity was sparked, and pressed, "No key without a lock, you told me. No canvas without paint. The part of the Project Dantian elixir you ingest was only the key. The lock was somewhere else—already inside your body."

Von Hentzau gasped. "DNA!"

"*Artificial* DNA. A dual integro-compound, an organic and manmade nanocomposite blend made into a 47th chromosome, constructed in part using the subject's own genetic material, containing all of the material necessary to repair the DNA itself along with boosting the body's own immune and repair mechanisms. I remember reading about Human Artificial Chromosomes in the history books."

"But they never got far enough," Von Hentzau said. "A lock with no key. If the artificial DNA is the lock, what is the key?"

Jerry envisioned the strange multi-legged, long-necked, polygon-headed creatures from his dream. He hadn't connected them with anything in the waking world until he remembered where he had seen them before: the Museum's appropriately named Galapagos exhibit. Which Jerry figured was itself a signal to the Gallows members in NYC about the Dantian breakthrough.

"Bacteriophages," he told Von Hentzau. "Viruses that infect bacteria. It sounds destructive—sometimes it is, because the virus often destroys the bacteria or other cells—but they've also been used since the twentieth century to cure diseases. Many kinds of bacteriophages evolved with humans, so they can be sent into the body without triggering an immune response."

A Hole in Wednesday

Her face flushed with realization. "Dantian's bacteriophages are genetically engineered and would target DNA infused with the 47th chromosome. But target to do what?"

"Send encoded information into the DNA. The 47th chromosome would have built-in multitasking instructions to alter the DNA of various cells and bacteria throughout the body into holistic repairers that team with latent stem cells, making them capable of repairing anything in the body. They would start with telomeres in the DNA, which regulate DNA replication. But theoretically they would eventually be taught to repair things as complex as an eye or a limb alongside going after any aberration, like cancer, or to repair normal wear and tear. In the case of cancer and hostile microscopic invaders, the bacteriophages would slice them apart and recycle their genetic material to put it toward a more beneficent use."

"And the people without the artificial chromosome—they were the ones getting sick?"

Jerry nodded. "Or someone without specific DNA markers already present naturally, like members of Immerman's literal Family. Without an Immer-gene or the artificial chromosome, the bacteriophages were accidentally destroying the DNA their tubular cores penetrated. The body would eventually either get sick and then fight off the bacteriophage or let it keep doing its work until the patient died."

Von Hentzau sighed. "It is brilliant, but too brilliant, Jerry. Don't you understand why it all has to be destroyed?"

"It isn't true immortality, Sandra. It extends life by a factor of seven—which is appropriate considering the subject would be living seven times as long by existing in all seven obdays."

"Still much, much too long."

"But there's so much more to it! With this technology, medical science will have leaped ahead generations. This delivers the cures for cancer, heart disease, strokes, and every major infirmity on the planet on a silver platter . . ."

This was what finally made him hesitate about destroying the information himself. Dantian provided automatic repair structures for genetic predispositions for all of humanity's major ailments, plus countless other applications. Immortality or not, it could mean an end to human suffering.

Von Hentzau pointed her slider at Jerry's pouch and the Scout inside.

The pouch kept out water easily enough, but no substance known to twenty-fifth-century science could ward off a beam built to disrupt quantum vibration itself, hence why the weapon was outlawed, officially at least. In a few more seconds Coyote would cease to exist. And possibly part of Jerry's leg or waist with it.

"It's been found once," he told her quickly. "It can be found again. Once people know a thing exists they keep working toward it. It's only a matter of time before Dantian is rediscovered."

"I'm willing to settle for buying time," she told him. "Maybe by then society will have evolved to a place where we will be more responsible. Or we will possess terraforming or interstellar travel to settle on other planets . . ."

"Do you really believe that?" Anger rose inside him. Couldn't she see what had been so obvious to him nearly since the start of his ordeal? "We're stultified. We're devolving, not evolving. Our minds are shrinking when they should be expanding toward infinity in all directions. And there's been no substantial scientific progress for two subgenerations. There aren't even any scientific exhibits in the Museum postdating the stoners. We're farther away from breakthroughs like interstellar travel today than we were in the twenty-first century."

"My fault! And all the more reason to destroy Dantian and Senephage!" Von Hentzau insisted.

Her unhidden anger was mostly directed at herself, Jerry thought. She felt helpless and out of place in this world far beyond her own culture. Her anger and helplessness were about to translate into a beam that would destroy the elixir's formulae.

Unless he could rechannel it. "All the more reason," he carefully countered, taking one step forward and ignoring the slider pointing at his chest again, "we need an ethical hound like Ele'ele Venn on the inside, working her way up the ranks until she's in a position where she can change what needs to be changed."

In one last gamble, he withdrew the Scout from its pouch and offered it to her.

He took a deep breath and spoke through a mouth dry with nerves. "If you still think I'm wrong, then destroy it."

He ignored Coyote's alarmed chirp, which strangely was harder to ignore than the weapon aimed at him. "But you'll get a lot farther rebelling against this world and changing the government toward something better if the rebel is one of the authorities. Maybe someday one of the elite."

Her hand on the slider quavered, but it didn't drop. "They know I'm a traitor. They know I ran from Marks."

"My Scout holds evidence that Marks is the traitor and the terrorist, remember? How far could Ele'ele Venn rise in the world if she throws him to the World Organic Council?"

Coyote's alarmed chirps grew in frequency and, if possible for a machine, panic.

Finally Von Hentzau lowered the slider. "Relax, Scout. I'm not going to destroy you." She looked at Jerry with a plaintive mix of resignation and hope. "I'm really not."

The chirping continued unabated. Jerry looked at the display.

"He wasn't fearing for his life this time," Jerry said sourly. "If you've made up your mind for certain, Sandra, tell me now. Because Coyote was trying to warn us that we've got twenty bio-blips closing in from all directions."

Thirty-One

"We'll split up," Von Hentzau said as the bio-blips were closing a wide circle around them. The closest was three blocks away and coming up fast in a vehicle. "Upload your evidence about Marks' stoner virus into my Scout in case we get separated, or one of our Scouts is destroyed. If I can get to the World Council NYC Headquarters, I can upload it directly into the city network."

"You'll have to get back to the Upper West Side," Jerry reminded her. "Most of Marks' people are between here and there."

"And you'll need to find a way to cross to Brooklyn. We both have our work cut out for us."

Both Scouts bleeped intruder proximity warnings. Night was falling, but a virtually empty Manhattan meant Marks' agents could use even the most basic Scouts to keep tracking Jerry and Von Hentzau.

They ran northeast, putting them farther from Brooklyn, but also taking them away, if to a lesser degree, from the World Organic Council Headquarters in Morningside Heights so as not to give their pursuers a clear idea of where they were running.

After a few twists and turns they were hoofing it alongside Kropotkin Canal. Jerry knew they were closing in on Gramercy Park and what had been his home before his fateful daybreaking, but he put that out of his mind. It was more than he could take right now to add remembering the corpses of his friends and the other Days' residents on top of running for his life.

"This is ridiculous." Von Hentzau stopped and looked around. "We need a vehicle."

The street was completely devoid of people, though Jerry knew the emptiness wouldn't last long, as their pursuers were closing in again. He pointed at a short and sleek orange-pulsing police car. "Over there. If we can use it nobody will question a police car racing through the streets. But even if I had my ID, this isn't Wednesday. The car won't let me in."

Von Hentzau's fingers produced as if by magic a metallic silver card that bore hypnotic flashes of holographic colors around her photo, but no other identifying information.

"Ele'ele Venn's hound ID," she said. It was the card she had produced when first entering Immerman's sanctum sanctorum. "It will get us any vehicle, and it also acts as a temporal passport across all seven Days."

"Won't Marks be able to track your using it in this car?"

"So what? He already knows where we are anyway."

The police car opened obediently but Von Hentzau pulled Jerry toward the driver's seat. "You drive. I don't come from NYC, so you know the city a lot better than I do."

Once they were in, the vehicle shut the doors automatically and wound seatbelts around the passengers. Von Hentzau pressed a few buttons on the dashboard console and it came to life with an array of lights. A tac-screen below them turned on a fraction of a second later and displayed several intercrossing lines. When Von Hentzau turned a dial the lines shrank until Jerry realized he was looking at a map of Lower Manhattan.

"What are the pulsing dots?" he asked.

"Other temporal agents. Or at least the transponders in their vehicles. Most seem to be clustered into roadblocks. This will tell us where they are, except maybe for hounds, so we can try avoiding them." The barricades made for a convoluted trip to Brooklyn, but there were a few paths available.

Jerry's foot was heading for the accelerator when the back windshield blasted in on them.

A Hole in Wednesday

Jerry glanced behind him just quickly enough to see three temporal agents leveling large caliber guns at the car, all of which together would have been enough to violently shatter even the police car's protected uberpolymer flexiglass. It didn't look like any of them had a slider but if they did, he and Von Hentzau were finished, and he didn't want to take any chances.

They were firing at the tires but so far the nanofluid covering the rubber was holding, though it wouldn't for long. With violent crime so rare the protections were only basic ones and would only last a few moments. But until then the car was as good as an armored vehicle. Jerry threw it in reverse and he heard the tires screech as he slammed the accelerator and aimed the car at their attackers.

They scattered but kept on firing as they retreated like the professionals they were. These were not agents who would send Jerry and Von Hentzau to psychic rehabilitation. Being caught and cornered by them would be a death sentence.

Jerry swung the car around and accelerated away onto a side street, trying to put as many buildings between himself and Marks' people as he could. Driving, like swimming, was not covered in the training at Camp Natufian. But the point of the training had been adaptability to any situation. His physical and mental reflexes had been sharpened and made to conform to the needs of the critical moment. And he had the whole of an almost completely abandoned Lower Manhattan to practice.

"Jerry, we're on 14th Street!" Von Hentzau warned.

"It'll take us to the highway," Jerry said.

"It'll take us right past Marks' headquarters first. His headquarters is in Mayor Tower. Their sensors will pick us up doubly, our bioreadings and the stolen car. And we won't be hard to spot since we'll be nearly the only car on the road."

Jerry hesitated, but only for a few seconds. What he had in mind would require handing his Scout over to Von Hentzau when he was still uncertain about her intentions with the precious Dantian research. But she needed the evidence of Marks' treachery, and while he was driving he needed her help to bring up the biomasking program he had designed back at the camp.

But what he had in mind once he got to the Museum, he would need to do alone. And he would need his Scout back.

They raced past Mayor Tower, the glittering monolith whose base filled several city blocks. So far the road was clear, with nothing on the tac-display.

"Jerry, look out!" Von Hentzau cried.

Jerry spun the wheel and the car skidded sideways toward the line of police and other temporal agents' cars blocking the next turn. "They weren't on the display!" Jerry cried indignantly.

"They're working for Marks," Von Hentzau said. "Unofficially. So they wouldn't show up on any official scan."

The car idled while he forced himself and his breathing to calm. He and Von Hentzau stared across the empty two blocks between them and the roadblock as the police and agents stared back at them.

"They may not be here specifically for us," Jerry said. "They may be here at Marks' order to protect him and Galapagos." It wouldn't be the first time the police had been used as private security for a large corporation even in the New Era. But the words rang hollow.

They deflated entirely when a woman in a flowing blue trenchcoat and the silver-sheened face of an overt hound stepped away from the roadblock and aimed what could be nothing but a crimson slider at them.

"Go!" Von Hentzau yelled.

The beam fired as Jerry shot the car forward and it blazed a wide tunnel through the trunk, but missed the tires and electrical cables. Jerry angled the car deftly down yet another side street, but heading south again, before the hound could fire a second time.

"Why didn't she destroy us?" Jerry wondered. "She hit us squarely enough that if she'd upped the setting we'd be nothing now but quarks. Along with my Scout, which I thought they wanted destroyed anyway."

"Maybe Immerman escaped?" Von Hentzau said. "If so, Marks may think he can use us as bargaining chips to get to Immerman."

A Hole in Wednesday

"Would Immerman surrender himself to save us?" Jerry asked, though he was pretty sure he already knew the answer.

Von Hentzau confirmed it. "Not for us. For the Scout and Project Dantian, he would at least consider it."

"He already sees our glass as broken," Jerry muttered.

He handed her his Scout. "Do the uplink. And while you're copying the evidence, upload my biomasking program too. We're still going with your original plan of splitting up, but as far as Marks is concerned, I'll remain with you. Run the program the instant it's ready."

"You mean, mask your real presence in the car while my Scout broadcasts a fake presence of you in the car?"

Jerry grinned. "Exactly. Marks might look for a signal of the program starting at the time we mean to split up, but not while the car is still zooming madly down the streets of Manhattan." That notion had come from Coyote. Maybe Immerman was right about a trickster being a helpful partner.

"There's another program running here too," Von Hentzau said, then her jaw dropped. "You're not seriously considering doing that once you get to the Museum, are you?"

"You designed these stoners, Sandra. You can tell me better than anyone—would my plan work?"

"Work? It would work too well, Jerry. If nobody could figure out a way to approach you afterward, you might make yourself a prisoner for a thousand years!"

Jerry knew that. The shaking in his hands as they gripped the steering wheel was a reminder of how well he knew it. But he didn't see any way around it.

"I know I can't go against Marks head to head," Jerry told her. "He's too strong, too fast, too skilled. I have to lay a trap. But I don't know of any other trap he might fall for than the one you're looking at. Do you?"

She started to reply, then huffed and looked back out the windshield. "No, I don't." She was silent for a moment. The whole of Manhattan around them was silent except for the whirring of the police car's engine and the occasional screech of tires as Jerry banked at turns or dodged the odd car left in the middle of the road.

But the farther Jerry drove, the closer he got to the Museum, the more he realized he accepted the fact that he might have to sacrifice himself to stop Marks. Yet if he did succeed in stopping Marks, the murderer of his wife and future, and the lives and futures of three million others, it would be worth it.

Jerry was seeing his own life as a glass already broken. He would enjoy these last moments now while they were laid out before him like a banqueting table.

He thought again of Immerman's koan of the man hanging by his teeth from a branch jutting out of a cliff.

Answer and fall to his death, or not answer and fail the test?

This was one test Jerry could not fail. But Zen was also a branch, as it were, of Buddhism, and another acceptable answer to a Buddhist, or at least to Immerman, might be one Jerry only now considered.

"Let go of the branch," he murmured, "and finish the test in the next life."

He glanced at Von Hentzau, whose fingertips were sliding back and forth across Coyote's display. She didn't seem to hear him. Just as well, Jerry thought. She already disliked his plan enough as it was. But she also knew he was set, and it was necessary enough that she wouldn't try talking him out of it.

"Done," she said, then looked at the transponder locater on the dashboard with an increasingly unhappy expression. "The Brooklyn Bridge, Manhattan Bridge, De Blasio Bridge, and Staten Island Ferry all have checkpoints." Which meant they were nullified as exits to Brooklyn. The dome access tunnels allowing passage back and forth between Manhattan Dome and Brooklyn Dome under the East River were likely closed as well. The lights were on in the *Halve Maen*, the scenic tour riverboat docked at the South Street Seaport and named after the ship Henry Hudson sailed into New York Harbor in 1609. But Jerry suspected the boat was not for hire at the moment.

"More water," Jerry grumbled. "And the river is four thousand feet wide."

A Hole in Wednesday

"Maybe a little less after your antics in the tunnel," Von Hentzau answered, laughing at the look he gave her. "This would be the time to split up, then."

"I suppose so. What will you do?"

"I'll lead them on a merry chase around the tip of the island as if I'm looking for a way off. Eventually I'll make my way back to the Upper West Side if I can."

"Good luck, Sandra."

"There is no such thing." She handed Coyote back to him. "Your bio-masking should hide you long enough to reach the Museum—or whenever you decide to reactivate your chip." She gave him a peck on the cheek.

Anyone scanning the car's motion would not have seen it slow down as it raced along the East River, because it didn't. Thanks to Jerry and Coyote's stealth program they also would not have seen, unless they were looking directly at the car, the driver's side door fling up and open and one figure jumping into the water below while the passenger lithely slid into the driver's seat. By then it was dark enough that the unblinking cameras on the bridges and piers almost certainly would not have seen the first figure swimming toward the Brooklyn Bridge and then climbing up a tower to make his way across the underside of the deck to Brooklyn.

Thirty-Two

Brooklyn had been a shock to Jerry with its teeming hordes of people after quiet Manhattan, as much as the bustling Manhattan was after Camp Natufian. Now Jerry was drowning in silence again, in the dark cavernous spaces of the City Museum. It was closed for the night, but its locks proved ineffective against Jerry and Coyote's linked determination.

Only the occasional emergency lights high above and at his feet were on as midnight approached. Jerry let the darkness be, preferring the shadows. What little he could see and the sounds around him, along with his memory of countless trips to the history and science complexes, provided all the navigation he needed.

His focus tunneled as narrowly as his vision. Stop Marks. End Marks one way or another. This moment was all there was and those tasks were the total sum of Jerry's existence. Once more he found the waiting for the confrontation to be the hardest effort. He wanted it done one way or another. But he was more determined than he had ever been for anything in his life that it would end his way.

See the glass as already broken. Jerry was ready to smash it himself if necessary. But only if Marks went with him.

Galapagos Island was motionless as if all its creatures and the ocean itself were sleeping. The robots were indeed sleeping and the ocean was calm, until they would rouse again at six in the morning, daybreakers by design. Sand crunched beneath Jerry's feet as he wove in and out of the silhouettes of giant tortoises, each big enough for Jerry to sit on, under the pale light of the holographic moon, left just below the ceiling as an emergency light of its own. Coyote had muted its own sensors as Jerry scanned for any sign of nuclear radiation. But so far there was nothing to detect.

The bomb could be tightly shielded. But Jerry increasingly worried it wasn't here at all. He could have guessed wrong. If so, then millions more would die, starting with him. Fair penance for him, since he blamed himself for the deaths of Linda and six Days' worth of human beings in Lower Manhattan already. But he refused to let another slaughter happen if he could stop it.

Where was the bomb?

Coyote unmuted itself and chirped an alarm. It still hadn't detected a nuclear signature. Instead a dozen bioreadings had appeared out of nowhere surrounding Jerry, some just a few feet away.

He dropped behind a tortoise but didn't see or hear anyone. Someone definitely knew he was there, though, and sending out false readings to confuse him. Probably to mask his own presence, too, by hiding himself among fake numbers.

Coyote figured out the problem too and went back into silent mode. It buzzed in Jerry's hand when it located the bomb. The radiation had stayed hidden until Jerry was standing right on top of it—or rather on the floor between the bomb and Jerry's feet.

He froze as if he'd stepped on a land mine. Without a sound he moved his thumb to a button on Coyote's display to have his device seeks the means of disarming the weapon.

Dropping to his knees again, Jerry chanced a look at the display. The bomb's image was in one corner; much of the rest of the screen was taken up by the dozen bioreadings, most of which were moving in random patterns. One was right on top of Jerry and lunged at him the instant before Jerry sprung out of the way.

Both men went tumbling into the sand locked together. Jerry got in a glancing blow on the figure's jaw but his attacker slammed a double-fisted punch into Jerry's cheek that flung Jerry and Coyote across the island. Lights flashed in front of his eyes and half-blinded him to the attacker leaping to his side and sending a kick into his ribs that rolled Jerry across the sand and toward the edge of the exhibit, and still farther from the bomb.

Marks stepped into the fake moonlight and laughed. "I left the clue specific to you, Jerry, because I knew you, of anyone in Immerman's pockets, would figure out where I placed the bomb. And I hoped you would, too. You're still giving me trouble. But not as much as I would have expected after your time in my camp. I am disappointed in you."

Jerry felt around the sand for Coyote, but the Scout was nowhere in reach or sight.

As soon as Marks stepped toward Jerry and out of the light Jerry vaulted straight up from the ground and tackled Marks with his fists flying. The ambush managed to surprise Marks for a moment, but the madman's jaw and chest and stomach all seemed to be made of iron and he absorbed Jerry's blows one after another with hardly more than a *whooof!* from the ones that hit most solidly. A single punch from Marks put a quick end to Jerry's attack, though, and in one motion Marks sent Jerry down with a kick to the knee, broke the head and neck off a robotic tortoise, and slammed the head into Jerry's temple.

Jerry reached for his pistols. One was gone, probably lost in the underground river. He only got the other one in hand long enough for Marks to snatch it away, just as he simultaneously took Jerry's slider with a lightning-fast sleight of hand. He pointed both at Jerry for an instant. Then dropped the pistol, obliterated it with a slider beam, and snapped the slider in half with his bare hands.

"You believe you have something to fight for," Marks said in the tone he might use to prove to a teenaged patient that he understood why the teen was rebelling. "I'll remind you of the bomb in my chest. While it would not wreak nearly as much havoc as my nuclear plan, it would still have a devastating effect in both physical and psychic terms. But ah, you need more convincing, even so? Have a look above us, Jerry."

Jerry didn't care what Marks was about to show him but it gave him a chance to grab back the wind knocked out of him. The exhibit's holograms of Galapagos bacteriophages—the real islands', not the Gallows'—appeared and floated over their heads. Then they vanished and the forms of Immerman and Mitrokhin appeared, their bodies beaten badly and tied to chairs surrounded by temporal agents. Even if Immerman had taken the new immortality elixir, Jerry doubted he would heal fast enough to prevent a lethal beating.

Marks studied Jerry closely. "You see? And my people are already closing in on Von Hentzau. We'll have her shortly too."

The holo-image switched to a firefight just outside of the former Cathedral of St. John Under the Dome. Von Hentzau was firing pistols and the occasional slider beam from the wrecked police car, but it was clear she was surrounded and couldn't hold out much longer.

But she was still holding out. How long she could, how long Jerry could—those were the immediate questions. Marks looked like he could keep going like this for obdays.

Marks regarded Jerry for another moment until Jerry leaped again, but this time his punches never connected. Marks dodged them easily, grabbed Jerry, and banged his head into a tortoise shell, then punched Jerry's ribs and kidney and threw him back, farther away from the bomb.

"Or I suppose this could all be revenge," Marks continued, pacing as he once had in his office. "I suspect your wife's murder is more on your mind than the three million other people in the dome. This is only natural, Jerry, and perfectly understandable. You knew Linda intimately. The others—are all statistics. The trick is to see them as such before pulling the switch. Or how would Immerman put it? Three million glasses already broken." Marks chuckled.

Jerry found moving more difficult than last time by a factor of ten. His head pounded. His ribs were bruised, with a couple probably broken. The strike against his knee was starting to make itself known and his leg trembled when he put any weight on it.

Holding out seemed increasingly less like an option. The holo of Von Hentzau below the cathedral still ran, just to torture Jerry with the sound of gunfire and the increasingly desperate look on her face.

There was no way he could save her directly, or Immerman and Mitrokhin. He would have to take out Marks and then somehow get word to the right people that Marks was the terrorist.

If he could hold out. If something would distract Marks. Or if Jerry just had a sign he wasn't as alone in all of this as Marks wanted him to believe.

Coyote understood all of those needs.

There was a flicker of motion on the island behind Marks, not far from the bomb. One of the robotic tortoises was dipping its head, and when the head reemerged in Jerry's sight it was holding Coyote, and then placing the Scout on the polymer tortoiseshell.

Then it began to walk away.

Watching them distracted Jerry enough for Marks to land another superhumanly strong punch for good measure across Jerry's jaw, putting Jerry on his back.

Marks kneeled beside him. "There is one thing I'd like to know, Jerry. How did you fool my narcohynposis? I've figured out Immerman's trick already. He did want to rejoin Galapagos, with all his heart. It never occurred to me, of course, to ask during the procedure whether or not he wanted to rejoin in order to take over the whole operation himself. But you—I suspect you plotted against me all along, and yet you spoke under the procedure with complete sincerity. How did you manage it?"

Jerry fought answering for a moment, both not wanting to tell Marks and because any jaw movement sent out flares of pain. But again, he wanted to buy time.

"My grandmother helped me," he said. "She told me what to answer."

"Ah, do you mean Theodora Caird Carson?"

Jerry nodded, which brought more pain. He spat blood into the sand.

"Dora was an extraordinary woman, as I told you. She worked for me—and against me, I suppose—subdecades ago, when I confiscated Immerman's elixir research. She was the one who identified me as the spy. Yet as extraordinary as she was, she still would not have supernatural means of helping you. And as misdirected as you have become I doubt even you believe she was helping you from beyond the grave."

"Genetics?" Jerry forced himself to ask. Anything to keep Marks talking. "Part of her genes still residing in me?"

"A biological explanation is not outside the realm of possibility. Of course . . ."

Marks considered for another precious moment. Coyote and the tortoise were well along on their trek out of the exhibit and possibly the building entirely. So much for trusting tricksters, Jerry thought.

"There is another intriguing possibility requiring no spectral explanation," Marks said. "A few people have the capability of dividing their brain into segments. Metaphorically, of course, but still as effectively as if you took a scalpel to the gray matter. Similar to multiple personality disorder, but in a controlled fashion. Each part contains a different identity. A very few of the most superb daybreakers are adept at this and become a different person for every day they walk through. Of course the risk is that insanity awaits at the end of that road if the personalities start bleeding into one another—or even interacting with one another."

He waggled his finger at Jerry. "Your vision of Theodora Carson during the narcohypnosis—which is what I am certain you experienced—was the result of your brain compartmentalizing and turning for help to a different personality during a time of great tension and duress. You accessed 'her' personality in order to answer my questions however you wanted, for it was not Jerry Carson who was answering, but Theodora Carson, who had no such impositions placed upon her. Perhaps she appeared for genetic reasons, perhaps she is a singularly strong figure in your mind, perhaps she was nothing more than a ping of morphic resonance. But either way I'm not sufficiently curious to let you live long enough for me to reason it out."

As Marks finished the examination he noticed Jerry looking

elsewhere. He glanced over his shoulder to follow Jerry's stare and shouted, "No! Get back here!"

The robotic tortoise Coyote had activated and hacked into was now nearly all the way out of the exhibit hall with Marks' electrobike engine-sized bomb propped up on its back.

Marks ran for the slowly fleeing giant tortoise, turning his back to Jerry in the doing.

Jerry struggled to his feet one more time, and he suspected it would only be one more time. A small horde of hand-sized brown and red lava lizards, *Microlophus albemarlensis,* was eyeing him as if with living curiosity.

Coyote must have switched them all on after hacking the runaway tortoise. They wouldn't approach him—their fail-safe, like the ants he had encountered before in his first daybreaking flight, had programming to prevent them from being harmful to people. So he couldn't use them against Marks. He wasn't certain why Coyote would activate them.

Then he was. A Galapagos albatross, *Phoebastria irrorata,* was pecking away at the floor where the real bomb was still hidden. This likely was not true albatross behavior, be it a Galapagos strain or otherwise. But it was behavior not considered harmful to visitors and so the system allowed it. And the renewed nocturnal activities and noise of the exhibit's animal robots were cloaking the albatross' critical mission.

Marks figured out the ruse a few seconds after Jerry did by launching himself at the tortoise-back bomb and passing through the Tamara hologram of it Coyote was projecting. He stumbled over the chair-sized animal, snatching for the Scout but missing.

A tortoise body with Coyote for a head, Jerry thought. Now it really is a Mock Turtle.

Marks recovered his footing quickly but still took just long enough for Jerry's good leg to slam a blow into Marks' knees as the doctor had done to Jerry moments before. When Marks pitched forward Jerry landed both fists against Marks' face and neck in a double blow that staggered Marks but wasn't quite enough to knock him off his feet entirely.

Jerry watched with horror as Marks' bloody and swollen face broke into a wicked smile and then disappeared into stars as Marks' fist made contact with Jerry's face hard enough to send Jerry sprawling back to the floor.

Jerry began crawling toward the next exhibit, a canyonland diorama from South America but otherwise much like the one he'd used to flee the Gallows last time. He felt completely helpless but hoped if he could get into the twisty passages he might be able to buy himself enough time to recover. Just the few seconds he was allowed was enough to already start bringing a modicum of strength back into his muscles.

And somewhere in the last moments he had taken hold of Coyote again. The Scout was displaying a map of the nearby exhibits and asking which ones Jerry wanted him to hack into, while a series of albatrosses were working their way into the Galapagos floor.

"Fokker him," Jerry whispered to Coyote.

He could feel Marks watching his exposed back the way a bored cat watches a new little creature slipping into the house. Just a little farther . . .

Marks decided not to give Jerry that chance. But instead of hurrying to shorten the gap in distance and the gap between Jerry being able to stand again or not, he walked arrogantly, approaching Jerry only when he was at the edge of the canyon. Not close to the nearest exhibit entrance, though. Between Jerry and the twenty-foot drop was a ten-foot high transparent polymer fence built to withstand the press of a crowd without falling over. Even at full strength Jerry wouldn't have been able to knock it down.

Marks hauled Jerry to his feet and slammed him against the fence.

"I do regret this, Jerry," Marks said. "I regret I couldn't turn you to my camp. Even just a few men and women like you would assure our victory."

Jerry rammed his head into Marks' forehead, only to have Marks shove Jerry's head back into the unyielding fence. "Sooner or later you have to give up," Marks said.

A Hole in Wednesday

Then the doctor turned his head toward the sound of an approaching engine. His eyes swept the doorways but he saw nothing. Only when he finally looked up did he see the red Fokker Dr.1 triplane, the one most associated with the Red Baron and used as the Baron's own plane in the World War One exhibit, heading toward them. A plastic Baron Von Richthofen complete with leather helmet, goggles, and Iron Cross sat in the pilot seat.

"Is this your attack?" Marks laughed. "They don't have bullets, and you can't hack their self-isolated human protection programs."

"It doesn't need to attack you," Jerry said. "That's my job."

A second later the triplane crashed into the fence twenty feet from Jerry and Marks, sending fence and men and plane into the canyon. Jerry twisted at the last second before impact to put Marks closer to the fence, then the bottom when they slid down the sloping wall and hit the ground twenty feet below.

They were showered in debris, including a broken wing strut that had landed a few feet from Jerry's left hand. He grabbed the strut and swung it across Marks' head like a baseball bat.

Marks yanked the strut out of Jerry's hands on the second swing and struck back. Jerry ducked his head fast enough to dodge what would have been a knockout blow, but it caught his right arm and sent a jab of agony up the bones and then nothing at all. The arm hung useless at his side.

"It is ironic that my training is what is keeping you from being dead by now," Marks said as he stepped back and wiped away blood pouring down from the new gash in his forehead. One of his eyes was swollen shut and Marks was trembling, but unlike Jerry, still on his feet. "But now I am late for a very important date."

He climbed up the sloping wall, unsteadily but without faltering. Once on the top, on the high ground, with Jerry caught inextricably in the valley below, he pulled a quantum slider from a pants pocket and leveled it down at Jerry.

But before he could fire something caught his attention. "Now what . . . ?" he shouted, and saw what Coyote had been plotting all along. The real nuke was being lifted up into the air and away toward the main exit by a flock of Galapagos albatrosses.

Coyote hadn't specifically said where he planned to take the bomb, but he knew Jerry's plan to trap Marks once and for all—if Jerry lived long enough—so Jerry had a pretty good idea.

Marks braced himself to run after it then stopped short when he heard another plane engine heading straight toward Marks.

"Did you hear nothing I said, Jerry? The robots won't let visitors come to harm. It will veer away before it can crash into me."

Jerry pressed a button on Coyote's display as the second red triplane flew into the exhibit hall above the albatrosses and a heartbeat before the plane would have banked off.

The plane's engine shut off while still on a collision course for Marks.

Marks had only just enough time to bring up his slider and slice the plane down the middle before the steel remains plowed into him.

The "pilot" may have been pseudo-protein but the plane was real enough, an exact replica of a Fokker down to the full tank of combustible fuel, a luxury allowed to the Museums. Jerry heard the plane violently disintegrate with a canyon wall-shaking roar that sent him scrambling to press himself against that wall when smoking and burning meteoric remnants rained into the canyon. The roar was matched by extremely well-simulated screams of pain and terror from the AI "residents" of whatever exhibit was above, their bodily pieces joining the torrent of metal and chunks of wall.

But Jerry couldn't tell if one of the screams was Marks', or if any of the severed limbs and pounds of flesh originated with the doctor. All of the body parts oozed a thick reddish fluid, which in the robots' cases would be lubricant. He spotted chips and wires and servos protruding out of some, but others had their revealing places hidden under debris. Jerry would have to go over the top to find out if Marks was finally neutralized.

It took him a few minutes to work his way back up to the top of the canyon rim. The smoking red halves were only a few feet apart and smashed up against the ruins of an Andean mountain village. The collapsed wood huts had caught fire but the fire suppression systems were already streaming thin jets of water at the last smoldering embers. Jerry stared at the wreckage of plane and exhibit, waiting for confirmation that Marks was dead and Jerry's original plan, which still seemed desperate despite what he'd just been through, was off the table.

He got no confirmation. Pieces of broken Andean house wall stirred beneath the plane's cockpit. He hesitated long enough to see the arm come out holding the slider that aimed and fired a lot less wildly than Jerry would have hoped.

He jumped out of the way and the polymer fence behind him rippled and blurred and then vanished out of existence.

Jerry ran. It was only sheer luck Marks couldn't angle his firing at Jerry once Jerry was away from the wall, but Jerry wouldn't be able to get close enough to Marks to do anything without Marks killing him with the slider first. He understood now that Marks would not stop chasing Jerry until forcibly stopped.

So as Marks steadily freed himself from his burial beneath village and triplane, Jerry ran for the place Coyote's hacked albatrosses were taking the bomb, and where Jerry knew he must have his final confrontation with Marks.

He reactivated his chip to make certain Marks could follow him.

Thirty-Three

Near silence and darkness again. Although this time the darkness was as much from Jerry's dimming vision as the dim Museum lights, and the silence was punctured by the blood throbbing inside his skull almost loud enough to drown out everything else. But he could still see the shadows cast by the fifty antique stoners lining the walls like coffins in nineteenth-century photographs. And even through the pounding in his head he could hear the faint humming of the power keeping them ready to use as if no one nowadays had the courage to disconnect a stoner, even if the cylinder was nothing more than an artifact.

Jerry's whole ordeal, the circumstances leading him here, and leading to the deaths of so many, had started with a stoner. Or more accurately, the lack of one, since his first step on this path was stepping out of one when he was supposed to be stepping in. Now it seemed it would all end with a stoner too. Or more accurately, fifty at once.

He passed the sign warning that the stoners were unreliable antiques. Jerry hoped the sign was right.

The little bomb was sitting out in the middle of the exhibit room, as if mocking the contraptions supplanting it as—Jerry was sure Marks would think—the technological device most threatening to civilization. It represented a cold and hard tumor in the center of the immediate universe. Jerry went cold looking at it and the softly blinking row of red lights indicating everything with the bomb was normal. It was ready to go off and shred millions more lives.

He fought the temptation to jump into one of the stoners. The temptation had been dogging him since the very first moment of his daybreaking, of course. But this time it was spurred on by the bomb a few feet away from him. The idea was silly. The stoner field wouldn't protect Jerry against the heart of an atomic explosion. The stoners themselves would be destroyed in a billionth of a second too.

The temptation was still there nevertheless. A way out. An escape. But Marks had only left him one way out which didn't involve dying. And Jerry didn't consider dying an option when the entire Brooklyn Dome would perish with him.

Four robotic albatrosses guarded the nuke. They looked ridiculous and would scatter the moment Marks got close to it. But Coyote insisted there was one more way they could help during this final showdown. His surprisingly clever Scout AI had been helpful above and beyond so much, Jerry wouldn't second guess it now.

Instead of jumping into a stoner, Jerry shuffled to one after the other, opening their doors as he went. Coyote synchronized the stoners' timers.

"Are you ready?" he asked Coyote when he was finished.

The Scout bleeped.

"All right then. Don't free the bomb's flingers under any circumstances. But rearm the nuclear bomb."

By the time Marks limped into the doorway of the exhibition room, slider in hand, clothes shredded and body laced with angry red gashes and purple welts, Jerry was on the far end with Scout in hand. Marks scanned the room with his own Scout.

"This has been a fascinating experiment, Jerry, in survival and competition across multiple terrains and situations," Marks told him. His voice reached out as if from a deep place, another universe, or perhaps an underworld. It sounded more feral than human. "But I'm tired of it now. If there can be one Jerry Carson, there will be other extraordinary individuals, and I have a better idea of how to mold them into what Galapagos needs after our jousting."

"You can see your bomb, Marks," Jerry said, "if you want to come get it."

"Is this supposed to be a bluff? You can threaten to kill me all you like, and tell me how I've left you nothing to live for, but I know you won't take all of Brooklyn with us. And I don't believe for a moment you won't fight to your last breath. Otherwise you would already be dead."

"I've locked anyone else out of the bomb's matrix but me," Jerry said. "If you want to retake control of it, you'll have to come get it."

"Against you and your army of bird robots, you mean?"

Marks chuckled. There was a liquid gurgle in the laugh, and he braced himself on the doorframe. But he was still too dangerous to confront physically again. Jerry was in even worse shape than Marks. One reason Jerry was on the far side of the room wasn't just to lure Marks in, but also because it had empty wall space Jerry could use to keep standing.

"And my Scout," Jerry said, holding up Coyote with a shaking hand.

"Ah yes, your resourceful AI. I must say you worked wonders with it. I saw how you penetrated my stoner virus. A few more minutes and you might have stopped it. But I'm not interested in your device or your programming abilities."

"But you are interested in Project Dantian," Jerry said, "and my Scout contains the blow-by-blow record of your virus infiltrating the city network. You know I'm telling the truth if you've managed to capture Von Hentzau, because her Scout would have archived the same information. Maybe you wiped it off hers. If so, then my Scout contains the only proof you were the Manhattan stoner terrorist." Jerry waved the Scout back and forth. "But first you have to come and get it."

Marks took one step inside, then stopped and narrowed his eyes.

"You badly want me to enter this room. But you won't blow the nuke. So why the invitation?"

Jerry shrugged. No more than that basic gesture ripped pain through his broken ribs and collar bone. He would definitely lose another all-out fight now.

"You're the doc, doc. You figure it out. We can keep going back and forth if you like instead. That's okay by me. The longer you wait the more I recover from our brawl. And every passing moment increases the chance of the city switching the Scout network back on. The instant that happens, my Scout will automatically mail my evidence to every single address attached to the World Organic Council—along with everyone else in the city. The location of your bomb will go with it. So I can wait. It's up to you, Doctor."

Marks' expression twisted into the blackest glower Jerry had ever seen mangle a human face. On the already-mangled body it was still more horrific. Then it faded into a pacific smile and Marks stepped forward, accepting Jerry's challenge, perhaps only out of curiosity to see what trap Jerry had spread out with the full assurance that it could be safely sprung.

He approached the bomb and Jerry let him. The albatrosses hopped away, and Coyote gave a disappointed chirp, though Jerry still hoped they would come through when the real need came. Marks attempted to get back into the bomb's self-isolated network with his Scout long enough to convince himself he could not. At least not in any reasonable amount of time, and he was beginning to recognize time was, if not Jerry's ally, then his partner.

From his position kneeling by the bomb, Marks looked up at Jerry expectantly. "Shall I come over there, then, and take your Scout by force?"

"No need. I'll come to you."

He tucked Coyote into his belt and walked at the pace of an elderly man—or such a man without the benefit of Immerman's and Marks' biochemical boosterings, anyway—which was the fastest speed he could manage. But he no longer needed to run. All he needed, he hoped, was the strength in his one good arm and one good leg.

He stopped a few steps away from Marks.

"The Scout is yours, Doctor, if you can take it from me."

A Hole in Wednesday

Marks' glare mixed suspicion but again, insatiable curiosity. He started rising to his feet and the challenge.

When he was halfway up Jerry flung himself forward and wrapped his good arm and leg around the doctor and they tumbled back to the floor, both howling in pain. Marks was still stronger. Jerry could tell from Marks' preternaturally powerful wrestling that Marks would win any fight immediately.

But Jerry had no intention of fighting. He only needed to hold Marks in place, as he had the much stronger Mitrokhin back at Camp Natufian. This he could do.

"What are you playing at now?" Marks spat. "Another inane and transparent attempt to convince me you'll detonate the bomb with me next to it?"

"I didn't arm the bomb to blow it up," Jerry said, laughing in spite of himself. "Modern sensors are calibrated to regard stoner fields as non-threatening, but just for good measure I unshielded your bomb and then reactivated it so its radiation signature would mask the fact that I armed the stoners."

"Armed . . . ? But stoners can't be . . ."

"These are antiques, Doctor. Dangerous to use without the proper supervision. Didn't you see the sign on the way in? And it's much easier to circumvent their antiquated safety mechanisms. Thanks to your bomb, your Scout's sensors never detected the stoner fields spinning up. And I know for certain thanks to Sandra Von Hentzau, you bastard, without those safeties in place you can activate a stoner field while the chamber door is open."

"How . . . how many . . . ?"

"*All fifty.*"

"You're insane, Carson! With so many fields interacting they might be impossible to shut down! We could die if they try to do it, or be trapped in here forever!"

He struggled mightily, but Jerry locked him firmly in place.

"All true, Doctor. But 'you build the biggest cage for the biggest predator.' You walked into my cage."

And the albatrosses, as Coyote insisted they would, were flying out of the room, one of them carrying Coyote. In seconds

Coyote was out of the room, and would be readable by anyone who found it.

Before either man could speak again fifty stoner fields activated and flooded the exhibit room.

Time stopped.

Thirty-Four

On a day that was not Wednesday, a man who was not Jerry Caird Carson and a woman who was not Sandra Phoenix Von Hentzau stood side by side on West 14th Street watching the last stage of construction of Manhattan's first new tower to be built in a subgeneration. It rose from the site of the demolished Mayor Tower on West 14th Street where Marks and Galapagos had made their headquarters. It was thirteen stories, a twisting, bright, green-threaded corkscrew to represent the Thirteen Principles upon which the New Era had been founded.

Manhattan Dome planned a great museum within the new tower, a chronicle of life from the primordial seas so distant even modern genes no longer remembered them, to the New Era, the pinnacle as far as its denizens were concerned, as well as being at the apex of the tower. It would be called The Tower of Evolution, as named by the World Organic Council's newest member, Gilbert Ching Immerman.

It would also be, by Immerman's design, a subtle constant reminder of how evolution must be an ongoing process for humanity to survive. It would even include a display of extinct humans.

Several stories beneath the Tower of Evolution, buried but permanently stoned in one of Immerman's experimental self-isolated stoners, was Linda Carson. They could not save her life, but her body had been surgically restored where the rogue stoner field severed it, and the stoner and a vidcube Jerry recorded and placed in the cylinder with her could protect her memory. Possibly until the end of time, thanks to the fusion-powered battery built into the cylinder.

Northpath Marks had been right about Jerry Carson more times than Jerry had cared to remember, or admit at first. He revealed dark places in Jerry that Marks likely knew better than Jerry himself. He had been correct that Jerry had grieved more for Linda than the other three million of Lower Manhattan who died on a day that horrified people so thoroughly they refused to even name it.

But this time Jerry had not needed Marks to show him another deep-down truth. The only human survivors the man who was no longer Jerry cared about the most were his infant son, whom he held now, and the woman standing next to him, who as Ele'ele Venn had taken the unborn son into her womb and sheltered him. She had also taken Immerman's immortality elixir. It not only helped spur the healing of her wounds from the firefight she barely survived, but also aided the child's development better than any normal natal therapy.

The man who had been but was no longer Jerry Carson learned, to his secret gratitude and Immerman's open discontent, the elixir was not passed down from mother to child. The fetus required treatment directly. When the child was old enough he could make his own decision about the elixir, and whether to join the Family that the man who had been Jerry Carson started calling the Immers. Until he was older, the man and woman would keep the child sheltered from the truth.

The man understood Immerman better now that he had a family of his own. He would indeed do anything to protect them, just as Immerman had vowed for his own extended Family. Of course, if Immerman and the man who had been Jerry Carson ever met at cross-purposes, particularly where the Family was concerned, there was no doubt Immerman would do anything to neutralize the threat.

A Hole in Wednesday

The man who had been Jerry Carson had been rescued by teams of scientific organic agents who worked an obyear to dismantle the interlaced and interlocking fifty stoner fields in convex and complex geometric unweavings Jerry didn't pretend to understand. After, of course, they read Coyote's contents in order to figure out exactly why Carson and Marks were wrapped up together in such a bizarre circumstance. Both were freed; Marks was tried swiftly and publicly. What remained of Galapagos after Marks' purge and capture was quietly absorbed into the Family, where Immerman's reductionist tendencies took it apart and then pieced it back together to his liking.

Jerry's surviving family members assumed he had died in the stoner attack. Painful though it was, Jerry soon decided to stay dead. To protect both of his families, old and new, he had to become a new man. Perhaps more than one, depending on how many Days he existed in.

But daybreaker or not, Jerry Carson must disappear.

For now this new man was also the newest member of the Immers, but no less under Councilmember Immerman's protection for all that. How long he and the woman would stick around was a matter for a lot of private debate between them.

"Your Scout AI was right about the elixir," Immerman told him at their small funeral service for Linda Carson, which had been timed to take place at the start of the building of the Tower of Evolution. The stoner was placed in a cairn carved out of Manhattan's bedrock with Immerman's own slider, and once lowered, plasma polycrete was poured into the hole to provide burial and protection. It was the last time they would ever see Linda's face, and possibly the last time any human would for ten thousand years or more. Or, the man who had been Jerry thought as he looked at the rising scenes of evolution around him, whoever their descendants were in ten thousand years.

"Right in what way?" Ele'ele Venn had asked. She was still opposed to the elixir, but Immerman's patriarchal guardianship of its secret was becoming apparent by then.

"It isn't a forever fix. The age-slowing factor only extends life by a factor of seven."

Only! the man who had been Jerry thought bitterly. How quickly humanity could be spoiled. Give them an elixir allowing life a half-millennium beyond their allotted time, or thousands of obyears with the judicious use of stoners, and still it was not enough when the dream was ceaseless existence.

"What a fitting joke in a world of living through seven days!" Immerman said, oblivious to the ruminations of the man beside him.

Immerman came to the funeral wearing formal green robes looking exactly like the ones worn by the memorially stoned corpse of Sin Tzu, founder of the New Era and officially revered as the greatest human in history. Immerman was appearing and acting progressively less like the austere and sharp-cut Immerman from Camp Natufian.

The new World Councilor continued, "And more, what the Scout did not foresee, is how the bacteriophages stop reproducing for some reason after a year. So for a time the biological portion of the elixir will need to be an annual vaccination. But we will make this the focus of our next primary biological efforts."

The joke was that a man who always worked to see the glass as already broken would try so hard to create an immortality elixir. But then again, while it was a common mantra that pondering mortality made you appreciate life more, perhaps doing it so regularly would generate a fanatical obsession to extend his life as long as possible.

Immerman did not notice Venn's faint smile. The elixir's allowing slow-aging rather than bestowing immortality was at best a small victory for her, but a victory nonetheless in a world changed utterly since Jerry Carson's first daybreaking.

The results overall had been wholly satisfying for Immerman and the Reductionists, the Immers. Immerman gained a seat on the World Organic Council thanks to being the hero who stopped the terrorist Marks. With the probable help of baksheesh to the other Council members in the form of the immortality elixir crossing palms, Venn said with justifiable cynicism. Venn became the head of the hounds in NYC. Leonid Mitrokhin, as Piet Vanwoerden, officially controlled the archives for the eastern half of the North American Ministering Organ. Whosoever controlled the archives controlled history. Mitrokhin would make certain, as he was not able to do in late twenty-first-century Russia, the remnants of the world that existed before the Dayworld would be protected.

Whether or not they would have any attention paid to them, the man who had been Jerry thought, was another matter entirely. Few seemed to learn the lessons of history in any generation—in or out of the domes.

The man who had been Jerry Carson requested directly to Immerman to join the Nature Rehabilitation Corps. Immerman was still considering the request.

"And the elixir?" Venn had asked her grandson anxiously. "What do you plan to do with it, Gilbert? Will you reveal its existence to humanity at large? Share its secret with them?"

Immerman did not answer for some while. "Whether or not to share . . . will be a decision long in the making."

Another victory of sorts, as far as Venn was concerned. The man who had been Jerry wished Immerman's hesitation was altruistic, but suspected otherwise. *Protect the Family* was Immerman's mantra. This included reserving the secret of extended life to just Family and those among the government elites who could serve and preserve them.

It was a propitious time for Immerman to join the Council. The stoner attacks had shaken everything up from bottom to top, and Immerman was adaptive enough to take advantage of the disruption to slip himself into place while everything was so fluid.

"Eight billion people are simply too many to allow everyone access to the immortality elixir," Immerman continued. "But as a world councilor I can subtly use genetics to reduce fertility. And thanks to Northpath Marks, we have been handed the simplest solution to burgeoning overpopulation. He demonstrated fertility can somehow be controlled through the stoners, so once we determine his method we can begin the more subtle work of bringing down the world population to manageable levels. And perhaps one day, far enough so we can stop living only one day out of seven."

But among these victories, the New Era's elite, frightened by what they viewed as attacks on their control, took great pains to make the Dayworld further entrenched. The Tower of Evolution was only one small symbol. Next they scapegoated the police as responsible for allowing the terrorist attack and the Battle of Dallas to happen, along with the near-nuking of Brooklyn. Police departments everywhere were disbanded and the officers' temporal passports revoked. If the former officers wished to continue serving, then they would be interviewed for positions as agents under the blanket title of organics, which included the hounds, and ultimately answer and directly serve the World Organic Council.

More jarring, the Council eliminated the calendar.

No more would the world use a calendar of twelve months as many societies had for thousands of years. The Days would stay the same—Jerry Carson, had he not been officially deceased, would still be an official resident of Wednesday—but there were now thirteen months, named for the Thirteen Principles of the New Era: Unity, Variety, Joy, Hope, Comradeship, Love, Freedom, Plenty, Peace, Knowledge, Wisdom, Serenity, and Fulfillment.

The year, the Council continued, was no longer Anno Domini 2440. To celebrate the New Era, to make certain the calendar was properly aligned worldwide with the new influx of residents into Manhattan's depopulated Days, and to emphasize the government's disavowal of religion and the existence of divine beings in corporeal form or otherwise, the new style would count from the time the New Era began in June 2084, so henceforth the calendars read N.E. (New Era) 356.

Venn and Vanwoerden, bringing out the specters of Von Hentzau and Mitrokhin among themselves and with Jerry, resurrected the ideas of their twenty-first-century protest movements to try to slowly but steadily turn the government from within toward something better, more servant to the people than master.

But people at large would accept the changes because they were desperately hoping all of the Thirteen Principles would still become one with their lives and psyches, just as was always promised. They went back into the stoners every subnight with these assurances as their last thoughts.

A Hole in Wednesday

Northpath Marks would have predicted no differently, had he not been stuck away in a self-isolated stoner at the bottom of the Pacific Ocean.

Immerman might not have. But then he was a Reductionist, convinced that if you just rearranged the pieces you could change everything. Jerry remained more holistic, looking at the whole being greater than the sum of the parts, which themselves weren't as mechanical as Immerman believed. He could see the future pattern. The system would only finally break when someone stood up overtly to break it, though in a way less apocalyptic than what Marks had in mind.

Whether or not he was that someone, he wasn't sure. He wasn't so certain of his own identity anymore at all.

"Who are you?" the woman who had been Sondra Von Hentzau asked him after Linda's funeral deep below Manhattan's streets.

Jerry had given this question more consideration than when Councilor Immerman considered whether to release the immortality elixir to the world.

He had become a traveler of the most dangerous sort his era knew, a chrononaut sailing from obday to obday. So for a first name he took the name of another ancient traveler. *Jason*. Though if he brought back a Golden Fleece, the ancient pre-Classical Greek symbol of kingship, he was certain Immerman would have demanded he hand it over.

For the middle name, the author of a great tilter at windmills as he suspected he had been doing all along and was still doing when it came to fighting the Dayworld. *Cervantes*.

And the surname would honor his grandmother, along with their ancestor who was a nineteenth-century Scottish noble who had devoted his fortune to medical research. His original middle name moved to a more prominent position. *Caird*.

They left the shadow of the Tower of Evolution and strolled north toward East 30th Street up the newly teeming Kropotkin Canal. The day was pleasantly mild, back to comfortable parameters after Immerman and Caird purged Galapagos' experimental subroutines from the NYC computer network controlling the domes' microclimates.

They walked for another moment as if they were once again the only two people for miles. Then Venn told Caird, "Immerman plans to spread the word about how much of the world has recovered from the pre-New Era devastations. He wants to let people know they can leave many of the domes and cubes if they want. And he is considering trying to convince the World Organic Council to start deconstructing the NYC domes."

Caird shook his head. "Domes mean security for people in the New Era. Whether or not the land outside is toxic, many people, if not most, will want to cling to the dome like a security blanket. Maybe we can get New York's domes down, but the rest of the world . . ."

"How long will *we* stay here?"

This was a question which had been the heart of discussions so private they went to great lengths to hide them even from Immerman.

Venn did not want to take the immortality elixir in perpetuity. Caird, though fascinated by the process after taking his first annual dose to the point where he watched a microscan of his body repairing the telomeres in his DNA strands, realized he certainly was against the idea for himself too. He was still dubious at the prospect of how solidly sanity and empathy could truly last in an immortal body, or even one extended for thousands of years. He had stared into both Marks' and Immerman's serpents' eyes, and seen himself reflected too deeply for his comfort.

"We'll stay long enough to ensure our branch of the Family is well and truly intertwined with the Immer tree," Caird finally answered. "A generation at least. Maybe two. And then we disappear."

"Disappear where?" Venn asked, though Caird recognized the hope in her eyes.

"The spaces between the teeth!" He laughed. "The wilderness. The mountains. Where else? Where else would we want to be?"

When he laughed, his son laughed. Caird held the child aloft. By happenstance the boy was in Caird's line of sight to the statue

A Hole in Wednesday

just now being mounted atop the Tower of Evolution, above where Immerman's secret office would be when he wasn't sitting with the World Organic Council in Zurich, the world government capital.

The gold statue featured a man and woman with arms outstretched to the sky as they held an infant, who in turn was reaching skyward. It was meant to be symbolic of humanity constantly reaching out to better and improve itself.

It was no coincidence that the baby in the statue was the mirror image of the one in Caird's arms.

Immerman likely had deeper plans than even Caird and Venn suspected to protect the Family, while altering the government for the better and perhaps working toward the Dayworld's conclusion. If so, so be it. Maybe their child really would be the one to end the Dayworld someday. Maybe it would be their child's son, or grandson, or . . .

He remembered Immerman's koan of hanging from a cliff by his teeth, from what was now another life and yet only a breath away. From this vantage the cliff appeared to be Caird's old life. The branch was the last material, genetic or psychic or spiritual or whatever else, of Jerry Carson. So Caird would open his mouth to answer the question, the calling, instead of hanging forever over the cliff.

And when he fell he would either learn to fly, or somehow come back in another life.

ABOUT THE AUTHORS

Philip José Farmer was born on January 26, 1918 in North Terre Haute, Indiana. He grew up in Peoria, Illinois where he spent much of his childhood reading everything from the Bible and books on mythology to the classics by Baum, Carroll, Cervantes, Defoe, Dickens, Homer, London, Swift, and Twain to popular works by Burroughs, Doyle, Haggard, Verne, and Wells.

He sold his first story, a mainstream tale titled "O'Brien and Obrenov," to *Adventure* in 1946 before he decided to try his hand at science fiction. His next published story, "The Lovers," appeared in the August 1952 issue of *Startling Stories*, and is noted for breaking the taboo on sex in science fiction, as well as for earning Farmer a Hugo Award for "Most Promising New Talent."

Married and with two children, he soon quit his job to become a full-time writer, but after selling several more stories to the science fiction pulps, his career hit a stumbling block when he "won" the Shasta Prize Novel Contest. The grand prize was four thousand dollars (a lot of money in 1953), but he never received his winnings. Instead, the publisher asked Farmer for rewrites while the prize money was invested in another book, which bombed. By the time the truth came out, Farmer had lost his house and was forced to take up manual labor full time.

Farmer left Peoria with his family in 1956 and moved around the country working as a technical writer for the space-defense industry, eventually ending up in Beverly Hills, California in 1965.

All the while he continued to write and sell science fiction short stories and novels, launching his popular World of Tiers series and even winning a second Hugo Award for the novella "Riders of the Purple Wage." Then, just before the moon landing in 1969, he was laid off from his technical writing job, so he decided to write fiction full time once again. This time it stuck.

In 1970, Farmer moved back to Peoria with his family and again his career began to take off, this time with a third Hugo Award win, for *To Your Scattered Bodies Go*, the opening novel in his bestselling Riverworld series. For the next few years, Farmer sought inspiration from the popular literature he so loved, writing novels such as *The Mad Goblin* (a Doc Savage pastiche), *Lord of the Trees* and *Lord Tyger* (both Tarzan pastiches), *The Wind Whales of Ishmael* (a science fiction sequel to Moby Dick), *The Other Log of Phileas Fogg* (the "true" story behind Jules Verne's *Around the World in Eighty Days*), and *Venus on the Half-Shell* (written as if by Kilgore Trout, a character from the works of Kurt Vonnegut). He also wrote two "biographies" during this period: *Tarzan Alive: A Definitive Biography of Lord Greystoke* and *Doc Savage: His Apocalyptic Life*.

The next two decades saw the publication of the Dayworld trilogy, as well as the last installments in the Riverworld and World of Tiers series. Farmer also fulfilled his lifelong ambition to write authorized Oz, Doc Savage, and Tarzan novels with the publication of *A Barnstormer in Oz*, *Escape from Loki*, and *The Dark Heart of Time*. Late in his career, Farmer switched genres with *Nothing Burns in Hell*, a detective novel set in his hometown of Peoria.

After Farmer retired from writing in 1999, new collections such as *Pearls from Peoria* and *Up from the Bottomless Pit and Other Stories* continued to appear, as did new collaborative works such as *The Evil in Pemberley House* (with Win Scott Eckert) and *The Song of Kwasin* (with Christopher Paul Carey).

Farmer passed on February 25, 2009, but his fan base is as ardent as ever, ensuring that his works will continue to be reprinted and enjoyed by readers for generations to come.

Danny Adams is the author of the early medieval historical novel *Lest Camelot Fall* (Musa, 2014) and coauthor, again with Philip José Farmer, of the short science fiction novel *The City Beyond Play* (PS Publishing, 2007/2012). Adams has also been published in *Abyss & Apex*, *Appalachian Heritage*, *Asimov's Science Fiction*, *Ideomancer*, *Mythic Delirium*, *Not One of Us*, *Paradox*, *Space & Time*, *Star*Line*, *Strange Horizons*, and *The Worlds of Philip José Farmer*. He also reviews science fiction and fantasy books for *Publishers Weekly* and is an assistant reference librarian at Ferrum College in Virginia. He lives in the Blue Ridge Mountains with his wife Laurie, numerous cats and dogs, a Phil Farmer-inspired library, and the creatures and ghosts who wander seven Days an obweek through the wildland immediately behind his house.

Meteor House Titles

THE WORLDS OF PHILIP JOSÉ FARMER
Anthology Series edited by Michael Croteau

Volume 1: Protean Dimensions
Volume 2: Of Dust and Soul
Volume 3: Portraits of a Trickster
Volume 4: Voyages to Strange Days

WOLD NEWTON SERIES

Doc Savage: His Apocalyptic Life by Philip José Farmer

The Khokarsa Series
Exiles of Kho by Christopher Paul Carey
Flight to Opar (Restored Edition) by Philip José Farmer
The Song of Kwasin by Philip José Farmer and Christopher Paul Carey
Hadon, King of Opar by Christopher Paul Carey
Blood of Ancient Opar by Christopher Paul Carey

The Pat Wildman Series
The Evil in Pemberley House by Philip José Farmer and Win Scott Eckert
The Scarlet Jaguar by Win Scott Eckert

The Phileas Fogg Series
Phileas Fogg and the War of Shadows by Josh Reynolds
Phileas Fogg and the Heart of Osra by Josh Reynolds

SCIENCE FICTION ADVENTURE

The Abnormalities of Stringent Strange by Rhys Hughes
Airship Hunters by Jim Beard and Duane Spurlock
Dayworld: A Hole in Wednesday by Philip José Farmer and Danny Adams

NONFICTION

Crossovers Expanded, Volume 1 by Sean Lee Levin
Crossovers Expanded, Volume 2 by Sean Lee Levin

meteorhousepress.com

CPSIA information can be obtained
at www.ICGtesting.com
Printed in the USA
LVOW07s1605231116
514274LV00001B/95/P